THE STOLEN CHILD

By

I0634010

Jennifer Cook

Argus Enterprises International
North Carolina****New Jersey

The Stolen Child © 2010
All rights reserved by Jennifer Cook

~*~

A-Argus Better Book Publishers, LLC

For information:
A-Argus Better Book Publishers, LLC
Post Office Box 914
Kernersville, North Carolina 27285
www.a-argusbooks.com

ISBN: 978-0-9845142-1-2
ISBN: 0-9845142-1-X

Book Cover Artwork by Sue Law (Murray)

Printed in the United States of America

Dedication

This book is dedicated to Sue Murray, my sister and inspiration. And to Kevin, my beloved husband, for all his help!

jc

Prologue

At the end of Saint John wharf was a most unusual sight. A man carried a very small baby, wrapped in a dirty, yet beautifully embroidered blanket. He had long, blond, oily hair and roughened brown skin and a striking way about him. By his swagger he was most certainly a sailor. Perhaps a Captain, judging by his high quality, hard-wearing boots.

The baby screamed in a muffled, strangled sort of way. A few women on the docks turned in surprise at hearing the sound of the young baby crying.

One hardy fishwife squawked, "What is that there man doing with that poor bairn?" She bumped her fish basket down and placed a chubby fist on her hip.

The man himself had the face of thunder. He stopped and looked down uncomfortably at the screaming baby before continuing to walk down the board walk

Sally was sitting to one side, peering between people as they swarmed about the wharf. She could hear the man cursing, and saw him looking wildly about. A few more fishwives shook their heads and continued on their way. Obviously the babe was hungry, and there seemed to be no sign of its mother. Where was she, was she dead? Perhaps she was sick?

Rising to her feet, Sally turned and settled her baby Ben neatly on her hip. Her brown hair hung limp and lifeless on her shoulders. She had nothing to her name, but the clothes on her back and her kind Irish spirit. Since arriving in Canada, neither she nor her husband Sean had been able to make a decent life for themselves.

Subsequently she felt compassion toward other people going through tough times. Maybe she could help this man calm the wailing baby. Taking a deep breath, she strode toward the tall and fearsome male. Her bare feet padded across the worn boards.

She started to ask him, "Do you..."

He interrupted, "Have ya titty's milk?"

The shame of it. Sally felt like rushing away, but turning to go she caught sight of the red, almost purple face of the screaming infant and her heart wrenched for the poor little mite.

She scowled at this rude, useless man, "Of course I do! I have a young'n, don't I?"

He scanned her up and down. "Ya'll do," he said handing the baby over and sighing with relief. "Go ta that boat, Helen, and feed her there."

Sally pulled herself up and spoke in a stern voice, "I will not step onto a stranger's boat. My husband would not like it. I am not 'easy'."

The man was exasperated. He raked his hand through his hair. He looked at her with wild eyes that looked filled with pure evil. "Do it, or ya'll regret it," he shouted.

Sally was shaken. She looked down at the screaming child. Then, as evenly as she could manage, she said, "I will sit next to the boat on the dock and that is all." She raised an eyebrow and cunningly stated, "Here, you can have her back, or accept my terms!"

The Captain stepped back and cursed some more. "Just ba sure ta sit right next ta the ship," he commanded, he turned and headed back to the boat.

Quickly adjusting Ben on her hip, Sally scuttled after him. The infant's screams started to tremble. She looked at the babe with concern. Birthing blood still stuck in her hair and was smeared down her face. However, she no longer had the swollen-crushed look of hours old and her head was perfectly shaped. Her little hands flapped wildly in the air. Sally concluded the babe must be over a few weeks old. *Where is her mother? She hasn't even been washed and it smelt to high heaven. The poor wee thing.*

Glancing up to be sure she was still following the Captain, Sally noticed several bystanders watching the procession with interest. The Captain walked up the gangplank of what must be the ship Helen. Sally dropped her carpet bag down on the wharf and sat down.

He shouted, "Oy you, come and stand over me girl. Make sure sha's always watched like. I'll have ya head if sha's na safe. I have business to get ta." Turning, he strode back down the wharf.

"Yas, Captain Everett." A young sailor gave Sally an overly-familiar grin, showing a rotted teeth and few missing.

Sally swallowed away her sickness and averted her eyes. The stinking, rugged sailor came somewhat too close for comfort. She attempted to ignore him.

Holding the infant in one arm, she popped Ben down on the planks, then struggled to lay out her ratty shawl with one hand. The sailor didn't offer any help. Carefully she moved her four-month-old son on to it, as the other infant carried on screaming. Ben just lay there quietly, his huge eyes watching everything she did.

Sally laid out the beautiful quilt and placed the near-naked babe onto it. She flicked open her bag and grabbed out a rag. She ordered the sailor, "Go and wet this." She hesitated for a second, then yelled after him, "Clean water, mind. Seawater will do, but be quick about it."

At that, the sailor ran to do as he was bidden; he knew the bairn must not die or it would be the end of him. A second sailor came and watched over the babe while the first was gone. The other sailors of Helen glanced over in her direction every now and again.

This child must be very important to the Captain then. Sally gently pulled away the rags swaddled around the baby girl's rear end. The wee mite looked like she hadn't been changed in days and smelled even worse. Her buttocks bled with raw acid burns from the stale wraps. *There is no way a babe can feed peacefully in this condition.* Sally blinked back tears in empathy for the infant's struggles.

Glancing briefly at the finely stitched blanket, she noticed the creamy, soft material. Little roses had been lovingly and painstakingly sewn around the hem. Even smaller leaves and stems were around each rose. In the centre, a larger rose looked almost real. This was the most beautiful work Sally had ever seen. She grew suspicious as to the Captain's right to this child, but quickly this thought was squashed by fear of losing her chance. Sally would not voice her opinion to the Captain and raise alarm. He could take the little one away and the girl could meet a worse fate than in her arms.

Ben bumped his foot against the planks and stared at the little screaming stranger. The sailor returned with the dripping wet cloth. Sally couldn't stop her eyes filling with tears any more.

"Quickly, go get me a whole bucket of seawater," she gulped.

Seeing some fresh blood on the girl's blanket the sailor grew alarmed. "Is there anything else that could help, Miss. The first mate has plenty of coin on hand."

She hesitated, never had she seen a babe this bad before. "Not that I know. We'll see how she goes after the wash."

iv

Salt water had healing qualities and was cool against the soreness. As the little girl was bathed, she calmed and drew in quick deep breaths through her quivering lips. Her little body shook with trauma. Ben reached out to grab the bucket. Sally kept the bath very brief, for the main thing the babe needed was feeding.

When she was freshly swaddled and wrapped to protect her against the slight breeze, Sally settled to feeding her. But even though the infant was very hungry, she seemed to have no idea what to do. Sally wondered if she had ever been fed before, but she must have been somehow to survive all this time. Eventually, she established a firm latch and suckled for a few minutes until she fell into an exhausted sleep. Sally knew the babe needed more to fill her belly, but still at least she was now resting.

Sally became aware again of the people around her. The fishwives had stopped to watch. They all cooed in relief as the little girl settled. Ben had also thankfully dropped off to sleep. So, gently, she tucked the baby girl next to her own boy. They looked so peaceful together. Ben turned toward the little girl and placed a skinny little arm across her belly. In turn, the babe turned her head toward him. They drew comfort from each other in their safe, warm nest.

Sally saw the Captain approach her from along the wharf. At least now his expression had softened a little.

However, before Sally could think of anything else charitable toward the Captain, he boomed instructions at his sailors, "Get off ya arse, ya bloody idiots. The cargo is ta ba laid off on shore within the hour, or I'll lose the deal". After yelling more details at his first mate, he finally turned to her.

Sally stood, feeling disturbed at such foul

language. The children were still fast asleep at her feet.

Staring the giant in the eye as her heart thumped, she snapped, "Where is the child's mother? And what are you doing with a little babe?" The unbidden words tumbling out too fast to catch.

"Sha has na mother. Sha's mine," the Captain snarled. He leaned forward and growled, "Mine. Na one else's." An expression of frustration crossed his face. "Fa three weeks sha's refused ta swallow food, or drink fram tha goat teat. The cook struggled ta feed her wiv a rag soaked in milk. Sha hardly sleeps and when sha's awake all sha does is wail." He looked toward the sea. "Sha's got the will of her father, a will of iron. Yet, to look at her now, ya wouldn't know it. Sha knows what sha needs, but I can't provide it."

He paused cussing an arm in her direction as he went to walk away, "If ya insist, stay on the wharf. Send this sailor ta do ya bidding. He'll buy all ya need ta eat and the what not. Just make sure sha's safe and cared for." He turned swiftly. "An' send ya husband ta me when he returns."

Sally stood speechless. She watched the Captain directing his crew as he passed them. He was her saving angel and her nightmare. However, she was in no position to look a gift horse in the mouth. At least now she would get good meals and clean drinking water. To care for the two babes, she must first care for herself.

Ω

Before Captain Everett had handed the little girl to her, Sally had been trying to feed Ben, while sitting at the side of the dock. She had wistfully watched the tiny sprats swim in swarms through the clear water. With her stomach rumbling with hunger, she wished she could catch and cook them. With a deep sigh she put Ben up onto her shoulder and patted his back gently.

Sally was very worried. Ben's eyes had begun to darken and to sink into his head. He wasn't growing much. She was sure her milk was beginning to dry up, though she hadn't told Sean this for the worry it would cause him. Nor had she mentioned it to the Captain. A screaming new born baby was enough to distract any feeding Mother from rational thought. Her simple desire was to feed a motherless child.

Now with time to think more clearly, Sally hoped her milk would suffice for two babies. This tiny baby could be the key to unlock doors for her and Sean. Their luck was about to change she could feel it. Almost taste it.

For the rest of the day she sat, with a sailor attending to her needs. He fetched her good nourishing food, milk and water to help her regain her strength. Sally ended up giving the babies a side each, finding the more satisfied the babies were, the longer they slept in their make-shift bed. The sailor guarding them peeped at her while she breastfed, so she covered herself and the babes modestly with her shawl.

At her instruction the guard erected a bit of old sail to shade the babes through the mid-day sun. Most of the time he seemed bored and restless, but he never lay down to sleep, or left her completely unattended. There were plenty of crew available to guard her the few times he ran about to do her fetching and carrying. Neither did he speak to her. Sally thought he must be simple.

As she sat there, she started to think she could be a nursemaid for this Captain. Maybe her husband could become a sailor for a while, but that would mean sailing the endless seas and neither of them would like that.

Just as the sun was ebbing on the water, she heard Sean calling out to her. She stood and spoke to the sailor. "Look there, the man calling my name, he's my husband. Please, go, and fetch him."

Shortly, Sean approached, following behind the sailor with a concerned look upon his face. Seeing the bundles of food and drink next to her, he was confused. He rushed up to her agitated, assuming the worst. "What's happened! Did someone hurt you again?" He wildly looked around. "Where are they... Did they pay you with food?!"

Sally quickly reassured him. "No. Look at the bairns!"

His eyes alighted upon the two babies; his son sleeping blissfully and by his side an infant, admiring her hands.

His anger changed to confusion again. "Where did ..."

Sally interrupted, "I had to care for this baby girl. She has no mother. Here, sit and eat as much as you can, while I tell you about my interesting day."

Ω

Sean leaned down and stroked the baby girl's cheek and he would swear on the bible in that moment, at three weeks old, she smiled at him.

"I am not so sure but I will speak with him to see what he has to offer." Maybe the Captain would want her as nursemaid, but not him as a sailor.

Sean thought for Sally's sake he would have to let her take the job without him. How was he to provide even a little of what she needed? His despair and love were stronger than his selfish desire to keep her and his son by him. Their current existence wasn't 'thick and thin'; it was hell. For weeks he'd watched her wither away, her eyes beginning to dull with hopelessness. But just now he had saw light in her eyes. A little hope shone from her face. He would have to do right by her.

As Sean suspiciously entered the Captain's cabin, he looked around. Muck covered everything in sight. Salt and grime covered the windows, weakening the light. The stench was powerful. Grey dirt had ground into the bed linen. The sickly smell of the baby's vomit and secretions had permeated into every crack and crevasse. After checking himself so as not to add to the smell and mess by spewing on the floor, he attempted to breathe very shallowly.

A crass voice stated, "So ya must be the husband?"

Sean turned to find Captain Everett sitting behind a large messy desk.

The Captain continued, "Ya wife was clever enough not ta come on me deck for any amount of money." He grinned and cleared his throat in suggestive sounds. He stood, walked around his desk and leaned on its edge. Captain Everett conceded, "It actually was good sha didn't. It gave me time ta think of what I wanted ta do with the bairn."

Sean, who was as tall as Captain Everett, stared him in the eye. "What do you want?"

Captain Everett cocked his head and threw his fleece. "Well, I would like ta buy your wife."

Sean turned and walked toward the door.

Captain Everett grew alarmed. "Stop! I'll not buy her then."

Sean made to keep on walking.

Captain Everett tried to persuade him, "Think of the babe; sha needs a Ma an' a home. Otherwise sha'll die."

Sean stopped in his tracks. He did not want the baby's death on his head. He cocked his ear toward the Captain.

Captain Everett eyed him with more respect. Sean would not be bought at any cost, that seemed clear. He was obviously an honourable man. Just what Everett wanted.

Everett continued, "Since ya not cheap, I have a plan ta put to ya. Ya see, I want my daughter ta have a good and healthy home for as long as sha may need. Your wife says ya a farmer. So I'll buy ya a property, a house and pay for the babe's keep for up ta fifteen years. Maybe longer." Sean turned to face him and returned to the desk. Captain Everett emphasized, "But that's only if sha survives. I'll entrust the land and assets with me lawyer, ta be handed to ya if sha lives ta fifteen years in your care. But, sha must be cared for and have a happy life. If I see any sign of neglect, I'll remove her. Though sha's not to be spoilt, mind."

He warned, "Sha'll be watched over by others, including myself and I'll visit yearly."

Sean still looked warily and ready to walk out at any moment. Captain Everett paused and plastered a pleading look upon his face he hoped looked convincing, "Look, I had ta test ya honour. Please do this for me. Sha's all I have. Sha must live and have a good life."

Looking down at his hands, Sean thought through this proposition. He did not like to be given what he had not earned. Desperately he wanted a farm, but this wasn't the right way. He turned and looked up slowly. "I will agree to your proposal if you will set me up on a farm, where I can earn a decent living. I will save over the time and buy the whole property from you at the price you originally paid for it." He paused and gazed at the shoddy room. "We will do it through the lawyers on a yearly basis. The farm, the workers and all its needs will be chosen and inspected by me." He looked Captain Everett straight in the eye. "I like to work and pay my way. I will not just be given such a huge gift for simply caring for such an innocent child. I must earn it."

Captain Everett considered this, "I'll pay her way, though: her education, clothes, shoes and other needs. I will clearly instruct ya on how ta do this. Sha's ta be educated well above your station."

Everett looked out his grimy window. A small sly smile spread across his roughened face, "She'll be trained ta be a lady of the highest class." He tugged open a jammed draw and pulled out a large sack of coins. "This should keep ya over the next few months in town while the arrangements are made. This money's not part of the agreement. Just a starter ta see if she does all right. If she dies over the next month, I will not ask for it back, but then ya'll not get the farm."

Sean swallowed deeply. This amount would keep them modestly in town for a year. However, he would set them up in a nice home for a month with all the necessities. Then, if the bairn survived, he would put some of the money to find the perfect farm and put the rest into tools.

Captain Everett continued to detail what he wanted the Donaldsons to do and where to stay while in town.

Sean had to ask, "If she is to be trained as a lady, why do you want her to grow up on a farm?"

Captain Everett paused and considered his answer. "The very poor live a miserable life..."

Sean nodded in agreement.

Captain Everett added, "But what ya don't probably know is the very rich live just as miserable lives all ta often."

Sean was not sure what to say to this. Surely being disgustingly rich would bring joy?

The Captain stood as to end the meeting and added, "However, the middle man likely will have a happy home."

Sean thought this was true. He stood to go.

Captain Everett quickly acknowledged, "Ya wife didn't ask for even a penny to look after me girl. Sha has a kind heart so I expect sha'll run a good home."

Sean was about to leave, then thought to ask, "Tell me what's the bairn's name?"

Everett's brows shot up in surprise, "Oh...Oh." He paused and looked into the distance. "Well, I suppose it must be Hazel. Yes, Hazel."

Sean shook his head as he turned to leave. He had never heard of a person named after a nut. But, in fact, it was a rather mystical name and he supposed it would suit her better station in life.

As he was opening the door, Captain Everett's cool voice stated, "Remember, I'll 'ave people watching ya whole family and Hazel." He paused, "Always."

Ω

Sean did not immediately tell Sally of the arrangement. He wanted to wait and see if she could accept and love the child without the weight of the agreement sitting on her shoulders. Besides, the infant had been so badly treated on the boat it might not survive. Then Sally's high hopes would come down with a crash and he couldn't bear the thought of that.

Rather, he said to Sally, "Come, he wishes us to look after the babe for a bit and make her well." As he helped Sally up, he continued, "He has given us money and directed me where to stay." Sally smoothed her rumpled skirt and stared wide-eyed at the pouch of coins Sean held.

He slipped the large pouch in his pocket, but kept his hand holding onto it. *No way is anyone going to pickpocket this money.*

She stammered, "He doesn't ... Doesn't want me aboard?" She paused, her eyes widening, "We're just to look after her with all that money."

Sean gently stroked her cheek. "Yes, that is what Captain Everett wants. He never even mentioned you coming aboard and neither did I. The sailor guarding will watch over us for a bit... He's to stand outside our door. I suppose another guard will take his place when he's off duty. This is the arrangement for now." Tenderly he reached down and picked up his own son.

Nestled into one arm, Ben cooed and studied a button on Sean's shirt with avid interest. With his other arm, Sean carried the carpet bag with their few belongings. Sally trailed behind him carrying the tiny fragile babe wrapped in her beautiful blanket. The foul guard scratched his buttocks like he had fleas and followed at a distance.

For the next few days they lived the high life in a three-room house with a full kitchen!

However, between the two babies, life became a struggle. Sean usually expected Sally to take care of their Ben. Just as a man would. Women looked after the house and children. The man worked hard and long to earn a living for the family. That had been the way of it their whole lives.

So, it was a great surprise to Sally when Sean began to help her. He held his Ben mostly, but occasionally Hazel as well. He would carry Ben out on his trips to the market. But most surprising was the way he helped with setting the nappies to soak, and wringing them out for putting on the line.

After a few days of Sally eating good food and drinking fresh water, her milk came in abundance. Ben began to plump. His cheeks had a slight tinge of pink. He even discovered his toes and began to roll from his tummy onto his back.

Hazel, on the other hand, did not come to life. She looked so helplessly little. Her clothes were still way too big even though she was dressed in the smallest size. They were made from a soft white cotton, with a light pink ribbon sewn into the collar. Her feeds were often short and half hearted, like she was too tired to feed. She fed twice as often and woke many times in the night. Her cheeks were pale and lifeless. Many times Sally touched Hazel as she slept just to make sure she was still alive.

Her raw buttocks were covered with deep sores that were very slow to heal. Sean went to fetch the doctor twice, who as a male had very little knowledge of care for new babies. To the doctor, a baby birthed and lived, or died depending upon their luck. He just suggested the old wives tale of letting her own excrement dry on her bottom.

Sally thought this ridiculous. Never in all her life had she heard such a thing. After all, the poor mite had experienced that already, on that treacherous boat. Then a next door neighbour suggested putting butter on the sores and that seemed to make them even worse.

Finally, Sean took them to visit an old midwife of questionable origin who suggested the sores be coated with clean tallow mixed with a teaspoon of wild honey. This was to be applied at every change. They were to wash Hazel in warm seawater, making sure she did not drink it, followed by her tiny body being massaged with oil. Lastly, Hazel was to lie for a long while by the fire with no covering.

The midwife cackled, "To let the pure air of God touch her and make her well." The midwife lifted one wrinkled eye to Sean and warned, "It'll take weeks, mind. A babe's skin is weak. Like paper."

Sally was a bit dubious of these instructions. She had heard of tallow to protect the skin and seawater to heal, but honey and oil! Who had ever heard of such a thing! And the worst of this was leaving a bairn with no clothes on! That was a sin; the child could catch a chill, or the devil.

But after a few more days of despair, Sally was completely exhausted. And a thunderous visit from Captain James Everett had topped it all. He was not pleased with the weak state of his daughter. Sally's head spun as she walked. Sean did not look much better. So she'd relented and tried the old midwife's remedies. Within a day Hazel was sleeping a little better. After two, she was feeding in more earnest. Yet, it was a full three weeks before Hazel was healthy enough for Sally to even consider she may survive. Then finally Hazel's belly became full and round like a pumpkin and her cheeks turned rosy red.

After spending a few more weeks in town, Sean and Sally were trundling down the road in a good farm cart, pulled by two middle-aged work horses at a brisk trot. They were heading toward their new home, a village called Sussex only a few days' drive from Saint John. Sean had scouted for a few weeks before settling on the large Sussex dairy farm for its gentle hills, lush grass and friendly village. The cart was filled with supplies, tools and two carpetbags that held the few clothes and belongings they still had left from their home in Ireland. The two babies were tucked behind the main seat, wrapped tightly in a box.

Ω

Sean had grown up on a poor farm in Ireland. Many landlords surrounding their Irish home had succeeded, but his family farm had failed due to his Dadai's mismatched marriage. Mamai had been Protestant and Dadai Catholic. The Irish were an unforgiving lot when it came to religion and subsequently nobody would buy their produce.

Then the worst of it happened, all in the same year. Both Sean's parents died with fever. Still being young, as they were only in their forties, they left the worn farm and all its debt in their son's lap. Then the old milking cows died also in the harsh winter. Later that spring a huge frost took out the most of their crops. Still they had hoped they'd sell some of the good oats and potatoes.

Yet even after the old folks had passed away, Sean's produce was still rejected by the villagers.

Due to these unfortunate events, Sean and Sally struggled to make ends meet. It shook them hard. Eventually they had to do something, or they'd slowly die. So Sean took their meagre leftover stock to the town market and sold them well under their worth, for hardly even a week's wage. He then sold their land also well below its true value and ended up with just a little more than enough to sail to Canada. They both had high hopes of a better life having heard the promises of a new land with riches and opportunity for all.

After arriving in Canada from what had been a disastrously rough sea journey, they welcomed the successful and easy birth of their first born son, Benjamin. Taking this as a good omen, Sean started to look for work, but to no avail. Canada was as beautiful and exciting as they had been led to believe, but they were not welcome. The Irish were considered to be unruly, uncivil animals that would run wild through the city causing fear and havoc to the more civilized people about.

To add to the difficulties of finding a job, more new immigrants arrived every day. Casual workers were a dime a dozen and most of them had some experience in the docks and towns, so they understood the ways of business in the city. The Donaldson's only knew the ways of the land. Sean took any kind of respectable work he could find although he often came home either empty-handed, or with just a copper coin or two.

Often Sally could not make the rent of their small, single roomer. She soon resorted to searching through rubbish for food. Along with many others, they just looked with longing for someone to take pity on them and offer them a proper job. Inevitably, after missing their rent once too often, they were thrown out of their pungent, damp room and into the unsafe streets. Knowing no one from whom they could call on for help, at nights they hid and slept where they could. They even slept in an outhouse privy for one week.

Sally had kept her infant Ben strapped to her body. Like rats, they'd looked for any way to get food. Their poor baby Ben suffered. Inevitably despair set in.

Ω

Now the tides had turned and Sally could hardly believe God had now blessed them with such an extraordinary life. Sally peeked at the babies who were snuggled down in their box of straw. Both children's eyelids were drawing closed as they settled to sleep.

The life she had only dreamed of was finally beginning. To add to it, she now had two precious children to share it with. Sean had even arranged a maid to help her. She had never had to instruct a maid before. Her stomach twisted into bundles at the thought. Growing up, she had heard family talk of the big family farm, with its two maids! But then times became hard and each had to depend on themselves. Back in Ireland, the English had tormented her fore-fathers. Yet, this Englishman, Captain Everett, had saved them. This was uncharacteristic of the English. So it must be of God. Sally even thought the Pope would agree with that reasoning. Although, Sally decided it was best not to write and ask.

Sally raised her hand to her face at the horrible thought little Hazel would not survive the year; so much depended on it. So much depended on one little baby. Sally thought of it as almost a borrowed chance. Hazel was so little, with her skin still tender. She was not as strong as Ben. Ben had been twice her weight at his birth and she was already over two months old.

Sally leaned over to look at the two babies. Hazel curled inside with Ben around her as if to hold her warm. Her little fist suddenly stretched out and settled across Ben's side, then her little face turned to the sky and her lips puckered into a satisfied expression.

Sally smiled at the way Hazel looked like a kitten stretching in the sun. They always slept best together. She would swear they loved each other already, and it seemed they were destined to be the closest brother and sister.

Ω

Hazel's first real memory was of Ben swinging his new sword proudly in the air. She'd snatched the favoured wooden sword out of her brother's hands. This was followed by a screaming tug o' war match which the tiny Hazel won. Meanwhile, Ben, at the small age of three years, broke down and cried while little Hazel ran through the large rooms, welding the sword above her head.

Smiling to herself at Hazel's wicked sense of fun, Sally comforted little Ben, "She'll bring it back, Ben. She always does. Maybe Dadai will just have to relent and make her one too."

Even from an early age, Hazel was too quick and slipped through a grasping hand like silk. She did not have a mean nature, but she was rather cheeky. By the time she was eight years old, she would dash away the second her chores were completed. She would run through the long ripe grass intended for hay, up the hill, "Come on, Ben. Come with me, the day is simply beautiful." They would laugh as they rolled to the bottom and sat up, straw sticking out their hair.

Standing at the farmhouse door, Sally and the maid Mary would smile as they watched them run toward the stream to catch little fish. Sally's huge pregnant belly slowed her down and little Carrie held her hand, watching on. Mary commented kindly, "Thar two peas in different pods them two. Dun no if anyone will be able to tame that cheeky girl. She should be in the kitchen at her age... I was."

Sally laughed it off lightly. "I sure she will

settle when she's older." Shaking their heads, they would go back into the kitchen to have a cup of tea. Ben and Hazel would not be seen again till the evening milk. Hazel had a wild nature, full of adventure and Ben was quite content to just follow along. He often smiled sweetly down at his tiny peer with a look of pure contentment on his face.

Although Ben had always been bigger and stronger than Hazel, her sense of sheer determination and strong will often won the day. They were always the best of friends and did everything together. Climbing trees, playing mothers and fathers and school, they raised a calf and looked after the chickens. They smiled and laughed through most of their childhood. Those around them would often also be smiling with them. They stood together against all on comers. Ben was soft, caring and giving. Hazel was determined, feisty and honest. Not to mention she could chat the hind leg off a donkey.

Sally often wondered about their roles through their younger years. Ben seemed set to glide through the world trying to keep the peace, while being coerced by Hazel into mischief. Hazel, despite her beautiful dresses and little dolls from the Captain, seemed set on finding the nearest adventure and conquering the world. Yet, despite any of Sally's concerns, she knew there was no changing them, or who they were without destroying them. Anyway they were happy and healthy, what more could she ask for?

However, as the world usually sees it, the time of change affected them both. In his youth, Ben thankfully set his course on becoming a strong, gentle giant of a man and a hard worker on the farm. He had a good sense, direction and focus. Farming brought out the best in him and with his gentle manner he developed excellent horse training skills. Soon Sally considered her earlier concerns for him to be of no substance after all and Ben turned out to be a fine young man.

Hazel on the other hand was a little harder to tame. Just when she had started to naturally soften into a woman's role, all the ground Sally thought she had made up was whipped away after Captain Everett forced Hazel into strict ladies' training at only eleven years old. Hazel had to spend her days with an old widow at the local mansion learning the art of society to avoid being taken away by the mean Captain. Fear often drove Hazel and the Donaldson family to do everything he commanded. Hazel grew only knowing resentment for her father and those she loved the most feared him.

Ω

Despite a rough beginning, Hazel eventually accepted being a lady. This was much helped by her very patient teacher, Mademoiselle Bella Fleur, who, after a short time, grew to mean the world to Hazel.

With passion and flare, Bella taught Hazel the 'zest' of high society life. But what completely convinced Hazel to become a lady was when she discovered dancing. Everyone around Hazel had seen her nimbly climb the highest tree as though it was a lost art. She would run and spin through the long grass ripening for hay and skip from rock to rock over a swift stream and never slip. All of these skills developed through a farming life she poured into dance.

Youth was on her side, her body could bend like a reed and her balance was perfect. Fleur was drawn into playing the piano for long periods just so Hazel could dance. Eventually, Miss Hare was employed to play so Fleur and Hazel could to dance together. Fleur had loved the balls and at a young age she had taken to dancing as well. However, she did not possess the natural skill of Hazel who was a dream to simply watch. Over five years, Fleur worked with Hazel on speech, walking, sitting, eating, manners, tutoring and imparting appropriate behaviour.

But, by far and above, they spent most of their time in the ballroom. Perhaps too much time; it was the place Hazel grew to love. She would be a lady from the time she stepped in the mansion door to the time she left and ran home over the fields with her best shoes dangling over her shoulder. Occasionally she would jump upon a pony's bareback and gallop with her hair streaming, flicking freely behind her. But on those occasions Sally would despair, "Hazel! Look at your best dress, made from the finest the Captain has given you. I may not be able to wash it out this time. It smells like horse. A lady should not smell like horse in a day dress."

Through all of these years, changes and adjustments, Ben and Hazel always had each other. Never did they consider each other more than brother and sister, yet their bond was unbreakable.

Sally wondered whether someday they would fall in love, marry and live on the farm. They had been born only four months apart, so everyone knew they were not true blood kin. Never did Ben or Hazel think that way. Even when it was carefully suggested, they would laugh it off. In fact, Ben began to pay interest in other girls despite Hazel's childish disgust.

When Hazel was nearly sixteen years old, Ben began a steady relationship with Bessy from the village. Hazel had swallowed her envy and become friends with Bessy, who truly was a lovely young woman. Sally had expected Hazel to reject all of Ben's girls and was surprised to see her relent for sweet, young Bessy.

Perhaps it was because Ben was truly in love with Bessy and Hazel loved Ben more than her own selfish wish to keep him to herself. Besides, Hazel knew she didn't want to marry her own brother! Most importantly, Hazel wished to see him happy, so it was with a contrary heart she accepted Bessy.

Captain Everett allowed her to live with her family for so long she thought he would never take her away, but on one tense yearly visit Captain Everett simply stated, "Sha's ta come with me."

1.

Hazel's ears began to drum, her sight fuzzed. Had she heard right? She was to go with him? Hazel eyed the Captain across the room. He usually only stayed a few days. The shorter it was the better. Why couldn't he just go away as he usually did, leaving her behind?

The whole family stared at him. Mamai started keening, holding her hand out to Hazel. Hazel took her hand and stared in numb shock. Carrie grabbed baby Sean before Mamai dropped him. Dadai stood up stiffly, staring Captain Everett in the eye he took a step forward.

Ben hoped Dadai would grab the idiot and throw him out. However, Sean slowly nodded his head, and a tear slid down his face.

Sean confirmed, "I gave you my word and you gave yours. I will be true to my word, just as you have been." Sean now owned the farm completely, as the last transaction had been paid through the lawyers some time ago.

Before she knew it, Hazel had been shown to her seat on the cart and was sitting with her carpet bag at her feet and trunks in the back.

Captain Everett shook Sean's hand and delivered his threat. "I promise to destroy your farm and family if any of you try to take Hazel from me."

The family were huddled nearby listening and they all knew the Captain meant it too. His eyes were hard, dark and determined. He would have his girl with him.

Ω

Hazel knew she must go, but hate hardly described how she felt toward Captain Everett for causing her family this pain. Hazel shed only a few tears in front of her family. However, the first night away from them she'd cried so much her ribs and chest stung when she drew breath.

After three days of grief, Captain Everett called in a doctor to sedate her for a few days. Relentlessly, he carried on with his business. He barely spoke to her, or looked at her. His eyes remained narrow and his mouth tight. It was obvious there was to be no turning back.

Ω

Over next few years aboard Captain Everett's ship, Hazel state was, at best, morose. At her worst, she remained in her quarters for days. Slowly, very gradually Hazel had felt a pressure building around her. An uneasy feeling dwelt amongst the crew. Seemingly they'd become too used to her presence.

Gripping the side of the ship's rail, Hazel willed herself not to jump overboard into the deep waters to escape them. The wind blustered around her. She desperately wished she could fly away. Her family were a distant golden memory and it was likely she would never see any of them again. In every direction she looked there was nothing but the vast sea surging out to the distance horizon. She wished she was anywhere but aboard this large wooden ship.

As the next few days went by, her fears grew deeper. Hundreds of hungry eyes now observed her every move. Hazel drew a deep breath.

Turning, she saw the crew had set to work hoisting up the sails. Their hair hung in greasy tassels. They spoke in low tones. Intermittently, she heard vulgar comments, followed by sniggers. They did not seem to enthusiastic about the next anchorage in Scotland for a single delivery.

Delivering goods to only one man was unusual. Every six months, they returned to drop off to Lord Dirl and never was anything picked up. This was the only individual drop off Everett did in all the world. Under the cloak of nightfall, they would sail into the inlet, behind an island and, come morning, row the cargo to the shore, unseen by any village nearby. Hazel decided the Captain must be beholden to someone to perform this act of duty in such secrecy.

Almost as soon as she thought of him, she could hear him call out a command as he emerged out of some foul corner of the ship. She did not know where he had been over the last day and hated to meet with him.

In her haste to turn and go back to her cabin, she tripped over the ratty, grey cat and stumbled. The cat hissed, splaying his claws in her direction. Its ear had had a chunk ripped out of it and he had a bald patch on his back. One of his eyes was permanently shut. Hazel sighed as she straightened herself up. She took a few more deep breaths to find her inner determination.

Like usual, the crew pretended to take no notice of Hazel's presence as she slid by them. Yet they all watched when they thought she wasn't looking. Their stench overwhelmed her as she brushed past. To these men, women were just objects designed for their pleasure and comfort. Women provided for their needs and were to be owned. Very few of these men truly gave themselves in love to a woman. Here she was sailing with them, the only woman that she knew of aboard. Her position seemed dangerous at times. She was safe with none and rarely spoke to any of them.

They sailed from one country to the next. The only thing that comforted Hazel was the movement of the sea. The gentle rise and fall of the waves calmed her. The salty smell of the sea triggered a feeling of consolation. She assumed it came from when she had been only a babe travelling by sea with her Father.

Eventually, Hazel had noticed a pattern in sailing. Through the British summer season they would travel through Britain, strike out from Ireland to various places in America and Africa. Then through the dangerous British winter they would head to the mild climates of India, China and briefly down past Australia. In the eighteen months Hazel had sailed, they had only once been down to the vast and wild New Zealand. The usual circuit would be completed up the other side of America. Occasionally they stopped at a tropical island, or two.

Continually, goods would be picked up and dropped off. Most of these transactions were done through the light of day, under perfectly honest conditions.

Occasionally, in the thick of night, while the moon was black, especially when the mist travelled over the waters there was nothing that was seen. Nothing was done. Just the ship became mysteriously full of cargo. Packed away tight in boxes. The cost of these items was high, but the yield was by far higher. Money and riches flowed through the boat like Hazel had never seen before. From exotic feathers, to fine drinks to uncommon jewels, the best weaponry, to the finest materials of extremely rare value. Even a simpleton would know Captain Everett ran a thick and heavy trade through which he was exceedingly rich.

Yet, to Hazel, he remained a thug. Roughly dressed, he continued to live and breathe as a sailor. He seemed both a pirate and a merchant. To be related to such a weasel was degrading. To make matters worse, Hazel felt drawn into the comfortable routine at sea. Despite spending much of her time on board with guards 'to keep her safe', Hazel loved the sea. The smell of the salt sweeping off the shore. The warm tropical sun. Unusual sights, sounds and smells. Despite her interest she did not reveal her true feelings to Captain Everett, so that he would not have any kind of satisfaction.

Unfortunately, the sailors had peculiar habits. They did and said things way outside acceptable behaviour of anywhere Hazel knew. Outside of a village and high society.

Each strange country offered an alternative life which the sailors grabbed with both hands as the opportunities arose.

Nonetheless, Hazel noticed sailors tended to have short lives. Usually bought upon themselves. Sailors were killed by the savages, poisoned by the Asian's, eaten by African's, or from their own kind a straight forward British murder. However, by far the worst, but most common, was the slow agonizing death of a disease contracted from the whores found all over the world.

Hazel was sometimes allowed on shore in the safe ports. She saw worlds far beyond her own which opened her eyes to other societies. Their ways were ingrained. Black African's were split and divided among themselves and also conflicted with the Europeans who swarmed their land. War and slavery ran rife. Alternatively, she found in Asia hard working poor people, who quietly made their way, yet always the sailors watched their back. The Chinese would silently slit a throat for a small social offence. Australia and New Zealand were rough colonies struggling to create a European life out of a new land. A venture for which they had spent their whole life savings. Hazel had heard southern parts of Australia were full with criminals. She shuddered to think upon them. Thankfully Captain Everett did not often go to port in those areas.

Ω

Hazel stood staring at the ratty cat she had tripped over. He reminded her of a grey cat Carrie had treasured. Hazel glance back once more at the Captain and Mamai's most recent words echoed, "I am tellin' you this for your own good. Look at Ben, he is only a few months older than you. You were given to me by that pirate from the sea." Mamai's mouth had hardened at the mention of Captain Everett. She had stared into space. "It's 'cause of you we all live. So I could feed you and raise you as my own. Just let people think we're family. Like I got you from a sister, or something." Softly she whispered, "I wish you were mine. I love you like you're mine." Sally looked Hazel in the eye, "You have a way with you that people love, and, always remember, we love you so much."

Hazel found comfort in those wise, loving words. With sudden passion that she thought long gone, Hazel vowed quietly to herself, "They might not be able to come to me, but I will find a way to return."

Ω

Turning back to her Father, she watched as Everett raised his head over the top of the ladder and emitted a loud groan. He seemed to recoil from the purity of the wind. His jacket flapped in the breeze. His dirty blond hair hung like rats tails, sweat stuck to his brown skin and a light wash of salt had dried upon his forearms. He looked up as the sails rose smoothly.

Saliva rushed into Hazel's mouth. How could she be of the same blood to such a creature? She quickly turned away so as he looked at her he would not see the revulsion on her face. She had his unmistakable green almond-shaped eyes that curved round to a delicately straight nose. Captain Everett's nose was slightly sharper and crooked. Yet, even her left ear sharpened to a point, as his did. Though her hair and face were different and must be much like her unknown birth mother.

Hazel's face usually had a clear healthy peach tone. She had tried desperately to maintain her skin while sailing over the last year. Without much of a mirror she could not be sure, but she suspected her face was browned. Her straggly hair had seen better days as a shiny chestnut brown with soft, wide curls. Still, in comparison to her Father at this moment, she was as fresh as a daisy. He and the ship's crew smelt like an outhouse privy.

On reflection, Hazel decided her Father had organized her childhood like a game. A piece on the chessboard. Ready to be sacrificed in a single move.

Rounding the corner of Captain Everett's cabin, she found a few of the men stood in her way and did not look like they were going to move. Hazel scowled and pushed them slightly as she passed.

To her side a drunken sailor staggered, leaning toward Hazel. She quickly tried to sidestep, but he moved before her. Stepping the other way, she attempted to go round, but still he stood in her way. He looked toward the Captain, who happened to be walking away toward the mast yelling, "Hoist the sails, southern bearing. A little closer to the island. Then, Tag, you have the longboat ready for sea, we will row ashore."

The sailor holding Hazel sniggered, breathing warm, stale air into her face. "He's not lookin'." He gave her a shake to get her attention. "Look at me... We alls wan' ya," he tipped backward with the sway of the boat as it caught the wind and careered toward her as it righted the other way, "ya never know, ya mit strike it rich wif uld Jack'. He gave off a loud unnatural laugh punctuated by a hearty burp. The smell was putrid. The other few men nearby melted away, leaving Hazel under Jack's mercy.

He caught her arm and griped it tight enough for the pain to shoot up to her shoulder. Her heart started to race. They were getting braver. Father was getting slack. She wrenched on her arm, but was unable to free it. As her mouth opened, he clamped his thick, black hand over her face. A pugnacious finger blocked her view. Hazel eyed his jagged nail encrusted with black grime and dried blood. He pushed her back pinning her to the wall. She wildly strained her eyes to her Father. *'Oh, he is no use.'*

Jack grinned, showing his browned teeth. He whispered, "'e's had ya 'ere too long. Ya call 'im "Father", but ya must be gold for some uld man. Who are ya goin' ta?" He paused as if expecting Hazel to answer despite the hand clamped over her mouth. "It don't matta. I 'll 'ave ya."

Jack dragged his soiled hand over her breast and down her dress. Anger surged through Hazel's spine to the back of her skull. She started to struggle in earnest. Desperately she thought, *'Please, Father, turn around'*. Then, over her skirt, he grabbed her crotch. Shock pulsated. Hazel thought, *'What is he doing?'*

Suddenly, Jack let Hazel go and walked away steady, like he had never touched a drop of rum. At the same moment, her father turned and eye-balled her across the deck. Never once did he look in the direction of that vulgar man. Her discomfort and shock must have been apparent but he'd simply turned back to the mast and issued another instruction.

Hazel's hair bristled in white anger. Everett was the reason she lived like this. She barely existed any more, it was like he owned her. But not for much longer.

Ω

Captain Everett continued to order his crew to and fro, preparing their smallest cargo drop off for his old friend, Lord Dirl. He could hear the crew groaning as they went about their duty. The crew did not understand their Captain's arrangement with Lord Dirl, but they did not need to. They worked for Captain Everett and would do as they were told without difficult questions.

He rarely sailed the Scottish shores for any other reason, apart from the odd liquor smuggling here or there. Richer seas were waiting elsewhere. He would quietly sail in the Scottish inlet as the full moon rose, beyond the islands, past North Berwick and anchor behind Fidra Island. Most of the time, they would row in the dark to Black Boulder Beach and simply drop the boxes at the end of the small wharf. Other times they would wait for morning and signal the great house with a flag. Then Captain Everett would briefly meet with Lord Dirl to drop the goods and take a cargo order.

Everett glanced at Hazel who almost ran in the other direction when she saw him come up on deck. He had been checking the supplies down below all morning.

As he commanded his crew back into good order, Everett considered the way that Hazel had remained distant. He dare not watch her too closely as she ran from him. Instead, he kept his eyes on his crew. He wanted to find a way to connect with her somehow, but he did not know how.

Ω

All her life he had seen to it she had all she needed, but he could not change from the Donaldson's Master into their friend. He ruled over them, pushed them and instilled fear in their hearts. That was the way he knew, the way of a Captain. He needed to make sure they would do as he said; to care for Hazel in the manner he wished.

To begin with he wanted them to be too fearful to take advantage of their situation. Yet by the time Hazel was five years, Everett could tell he had gone too far, frightened them too much. They hated him and so did his daughter. If he was ever going to have a chance at having a relationship with her he had to take her away from the Donaldson's, but was resolute he would only take her when she was of age. They had provided her with the happy home he wanted for her and he might not be able to provide that for her anywhere else. After sailing with her as an infant, he knew he couldn't be a mother and a father to her. Yet he had always wanted her to see the world with him. But had he left her there too long?

Ω

Again Everett looked over in the direction Hazel had gone. To his surprise, she was still there. Their eyes locked. She looked at him with revulsion. Quickly, he looked away.

Ω

His plans were failing. Everett wanted Hazel to have everything he had wanted when he was growing up. A loving family, a happy comfortable life and to see the world. Then he would present her in the London ball season as his daughter. He knew that there would be some interesting, yet pleasing repercussions, at her presentation. Some people would be very upset. He smiled at that thought.

However, since Hazel was so distant, he had thought she would not handle a social presentation well. Even if he never presented her, he considered her childhood to have been a good one. Year after year he had seen her strive and grow into a strong, beautiful young woman. Just as he had wanted, her life had been very different from his own. For never would he wish his youth on anyone.

Far from a comfortable family life, Everett's childhood had been tough. Living on the streets and abandoned by his Mother at five years old in the gutters of London. He recalled his feelings of fear as all around him people rushed by, minding their own business.

Ω

As Little Jim Everett crouched down under a step and kept a look out, tears slid down his young cheeks, running rivulets on his dirty face. He wiped a hand across his nose, smearing the tears, snot and dirt. Where was his mother?

Tears rolled past the corners of his mouth. He absently scratched his scabby scalp.

He waited there, where she left him, for three whole days. Waiting. Wanting. Hoping. The only reason he left that spot was for the undying need to drink water. He saw women at the end of every day throw their washing water out onto the streets. He moved his stiff limbs to stand in the spot where the water would be thrown. He took off his hat which thankfully had no holes and waited.

Very shortly he heard the slightly jammed window open and the soapy, brown water was promptly thrown. He managed to catch a fair amount into his cap. He desperately drank all of the water. Lapping up every drop. This was his first step to survival.

Soon his hope changed to despair, his despair to anger and his anger to determination. He quickly learned sleuth, cunning and trickery from other children running wild. Thankfully, a boy called Wink took pity on him and taught little Jim all he knew.

Wink said he was eight years old and he hadn't taken to the streets until he was six. Five-year-old Jim was too young. He said he had run from cruel slavery, but he could be found by his owner at any time because he had black skin. Not that he looked much different to the other dirty children. Wink taught Little Jim to become a master pickpocket within a year and a professional at stealing food. In fact Jim became so good that he never starved. He thrived in a way that he never did with his mother.

However, his childhood was hard, dark and desolate. The cold of the streets on a damp winter night chilled his bones. Many other youngsters would die on the streets every year. At night they would vainly huddle together under a partly sheltered bridge, or whatever shelter they could find. It seemed every morning one came down sick, or had grown hard and blue in the night.

Wink went stiff, too. Jim awoke one morning to the deathly cold. Wink's body was curled around Jim's with his arms tight around Jim's waist. He struggled to release himself from Wink's death grip. Tears flowed as he pushed out. He knew before he turned to look that Wink was dead. All the same he shook Wink to check. Little Jim's teeth chatted and his tears were already starting to freeze on his face.

That had been the most difficult day living on the streets. His best friend was dead. Yet he had survived. Jim vowed that he would leave the streets somehow make a better life.

With fierce determination, he set his course to succeed in life. To come from the gutters into riches. His life was not to be one of misery and poverty, but excitement and success.

Carefully, at the young age of eight years, Jim began to save from half of his loot. No-one ever knew and no-one ever looked. After all, he was only a struggling street boy, or so they thought. He never became involved in any of the traps, like gambling on dogs or rats.

Then, when he was twelve years, he had looked for his chance. This was the time that most boys set out on their chosen way of life. Some aimed high in education, others embarked on an apprenticeship of trade, some started to take over rural duties, and by this time he had saved a tidy sum to begin a new life.

Little Jim had watched the comings and goings of people in their everyday life. Through simple observation he began to learn about money. The hustle and bustle of the markets. Men at business in their suits. He would scamper after them throughout their day's work, studying their trade. Over time he began to realize that the people who owned the ships and imported fine goods were the ones who bought the wealth into the town. Thus, at twelve years old, he decided he was going to be a Captain, or rather start as a cabin boy.

Ω

At the beginning of spring, he shed his old stinking rags for some fine serviceable clothes purchased from a reputable seconds shop. He bought his first pair of hardy lace-up boots. His first hurdle was to figure out how to tie them. The shop keeper took pity on him and showed him how to tie a decent bow. They pinched at his wide feet, but he didn't care. He felt rich. He walked with his head held high down to the dock. He went from ship to ship asking for a position.

On his second day, he was employed by Captain McCoy, who was Irish by descent but English born on this side of the water. He said, "Me 'eld Dadai died of the pox, Mamai returned to her English family. Middle class she was, so ere I am. Irish n' English. It gits the old ones swearn'. "

Being a cabin boy put Jim in the position of spending much time in the Captain McCoy's cabin. Carefully hidden by the desk, he learnt how to run a ship, manage cargo and control the crew. He stayed low and out of sight. Keeping himself out of the crew's minds, he watched everything carefully. Most nights he would sleep in a snug spot, at the hidden end of the Captain's desk. The Captain never really even noticed, just as long as Jimboy materialized to do his every bidding as required. He was supposed to sleep with the crew in the depths of the ship, but never once did he sleep in his allocated hammock

Jimboy meticulously saved the few pennies he earned. He added to his pouch of coins that he kept secured under his clothes.

Over time he learned of what items would sell at the best price. At the age of fourteen, he started to quietly buy his own supplies. His very first purchase was a fine, white china tea set from the heart of China. Painted with delicate blue flowers, touched with gold at the edges. It was so dainty that the pale rim was slightly translucent allowing light to filter through. This was extremely rare in England. Fine enough to be served to the Queen herself.

He wrapped each piece in many layers of paper. Carefully, he laid them on straggly wool in a wooden treasure box. Then he packed it down with old rags. Wisely, he attached a strong lock and hung the key by a plated cord around his neck. Finally, he strapped the box to the legs of the Captain's desk and laid his dirty blanket on top. The Captain did not even give his small corner a second glance. Nobody ever entered the Captain's cabin unless welcomed, so Jimboy's stash was hidden in the safest place.

Upon the ships return to England to unload its cargo, Jimboy took his chance to quietly leave the ship with his box. At the sight of the china, the upper class merchant couldn't help drawing in a sharp breath of amazement. Jimboy knew he had won the deal before they even started negotiating.

After considerable haggling, he walked away with ten times his original purchase price. To add, he had sold it for a much higher price than the normal china sold in the retail market. He had made an excellent deal. To the surprise and pleasure of the merchant, Jimboy returned to him many times. Enough, in fact, that the merchant became famed for selling the finest china in the land.

Promptly, Jimboy opened a bank account and deposited three quarters of the money. He spent a meagre amount on a thick wool blanket and lovely soft pillow that he smuggled aboard without anyone paying much attention. The money he had left over he carried in his pouch, ready for his next investment.

Thus, he began his mission in life. Within four years he was the proud owner of his first ship, but being only eighteen years, he wisely anonymously employed Captain Pentral through a lawyer.

Ω

Everett knew Pentral as a hard working sailor. The lawyer wrote to Pentral, using Everett's full name James Larent Everett rather than his widely used boyhood name of Jimboy. The letter claimed that Everett was travelling abroad. He wanted Captain Pentral to assume that he was employed by a rich upper class gentleman.

After a few more years, he found Captain Pentral was a sure bet, honest and an excellent Captain. He had tripled Everett's wealth. So Everett became a Captain himself of his third ship and purchased two modest properties in England. He begun to enjoy his success. Even though he could've lived a leisurely life if he chose, he did not. He loved the sea. The surging of the great powerful waves. The smell of the salty wind. On the sea he was alive. Yes, he had become exceedingly hard, ruthless and cut-throat, but satisfied with his iniquitous life.

Except he did not count on meeting the pure, virtuous and yet astoundingly beautiful Celia. She shattered his life. Changed his priorities. Ruined his happiness.

Ω

Captain Everett barely spoke to Hazel. Thus Hazel was confused as to the point of her being on board the ship. Besides loving the sea, she did not really fit the life of a sailor. After all, what was the point of giving her ladies training if she was to be sailing? Right from the beginning, Hazel thought Everett was going to sell her for an exceedingly high price. What other use was she?

However, as the years passed, Hazel had begun to realize that he was never going to sell her. She was a trapped circus bear that people looked at, but did not touch. They expected a performance. The twirling and whirling. Balancing a ball. The perfect daughter to the scabby Captain.

Yet, she was not a show pony. She needed a way out. What was unclear was how to make that happen. Several times she planned and plotted, but it felt like a dream far in the distance that she would never reach.

Hazel begrudgingly admitted that Captain Everett was quite intelligent. Somehow, he had skilfully built himself a strong empire. He had many properties scattered over the world. Unfortunately, she was rarely allowed to visit them, rather she was trapped on the ship.

Captain Everett seemed like a scoundrel of the dirtiest nature. He did not mind stinking, being covered in grime and eating slops for food. His speech was foul and he found perverse pleasure in using women. The whores always seemed enthused to see him. Hazel could only assume he paid them well.

At times she would spy, hidden behind the wooden cargo boxes on top of the ship. Everett would be beside himself if he caught her, which was all the more the reason why she spied.

Never in all her life had Hazel seen men who truly degraded women like these sailors. Never had she experienced true ugliness. Some of the experiences Hazel wished she never had and would never wish on anyone. It was most unfathomable to consider why these sailors ended up this way. In fact, it was quite sad, really. However, she had no time for pity. It wouldn't change anything.

To dwell on pity would break her heart. The poor young women, barely girls, traded to be a wife. Often more than not, they were brought onto the boat kicking and screaming. Begging for their Mama until someone, usually Jack, slapped them across the mouth. The first mate would push him away.

With cunning, she found ways to keep the disgusting, foul dog sniffers away from her scent since Jack had attacked her. Hidden away in her pocket, she had a sharp letter knife. She had used it a few times before the sailors became weary. The blade was made from the finest of steel. So fine that it sliced the skin as paper. Within the last few weeks all of the sailors had learned not to touch her.

On this night, the deck was a little quiet, but the stars twinkled and the moon was a large, yellowy cheese. They were anchored near a small English town to import liquor.

Hazel shivered, wrapped her cloak a little tighter against a sudden cool breeze. She heard the men rowing closer to the ship. Then she heard the light high sound of a female. A young one at that. No doubt it was another girl that would be sold to a desperate colonist who needed a wife.

To Captain Everett, the girls were just a bit of profit on the side. Yet he always insisted that they were to be untouched by the crew. They were not whores. There was no profit in whores.

Helplessly, she watched from behind the folded sails. She peeped over the edge to see what they would do with this girl. Usually the girls were kept under lock and key. Hazel wished she could intervene and set the girls free, but what could she do against a hundred men.

As they climbed up on the deck, Hazel could see, in the light of the moon, a young, slim girl, with long blond, braided plaits. Likely she had been snatched from her home.

The girl whimpered and cried. Tom grabbed the young girl's clothes and pulled them tight around her neck, "Shut up, Molly. Ya slut." Breathing heavily, he bought his face up to hers. Molly cringed at the smell of him.

Jack smiled in encouragement at Tom. "Unless ya want more." Molly started to wail in fear. Her poor white face crumpled and she began to panic under the pressure. Tom smacked her around the head. Others around him gave cheers of encouragement. Instead of bending into submission, as the other girls usually did, Molly, wild with fear, began to fight and scratch.

Hazel considered this to be unfortunate, since the sailors probably would not bother with a meek girl. Oh no, but a fiery one was cause for excitement. They all wanted a piece and no one was there to keep them in line.

Where was Captain Everett for goodness sake? Even the first mate would have subdued the mob by reminding them that the girls were a product that must be kept in good repair.

Hazel hurried past the boxes searching for Captain Everett. He would have a piece of her mind when she found him. She had barely asked him for anything. This time though she would threaten and coerce him into stopping this, otherwise help him! Never had she seen them this bad.

Desperately she knocked on his cabin door but to no avail. The door was locked.

Slowly sounds came from behind her. She realized the hitting had stopped. She could hear grunting from inside the crowd, married with small whimpers and occasional screams.

Oh God no! They were raping her. Hazel stepped forward as though to run and stop them, but standing stock still she realized she couldn't. They would turn on her. A small knife would not help her.

Hazel knew she was not supposed to be out on the deck. She should never have come out this night. Captain Everett had repeatedly warned her to never come out of her room at night. He claimed he feared for her safety. To be contrary, she would sneak out on a clear night.

He was right! If the sailors found her out here she would undoubtedly have the same fate as Molly.

Behind her Hazel heard a box banging down on the deck. A harsh laugh and a young sailor squeaked, "Quick, let's join in. It's free. Why waste our money on a whore?"

Sick with fear, Hazel moved in haste to the other side of the cabin and watched as the boys joined in the moaning and grinding of the sailors. This was unspeakable. Men getting perverted pleasure from watching. Each waiting a turn.

Hazel knew it was too late for Molly. Shaking, she tucked down behind a box. Leaning against the wall, she slid down to slump over her knees. Her frosty breath came in short heavy blows in the cold air. She covered her ears and slowly started to rock side to side. Tears streaming down her face.

In the terror Hazel felt a scream rising, but she could not make a sound. Molly was trapped. She was trapped.

Hazel stayed for many hours. Long after Molly was dragged down the trap for prolonged torment. Long after the men crawled to their hammocks. Then only the rhythmic slap of the water hit the side of the ship.

2.

Charlie found her after returning to the ship with Captain Everett late that night. He carried the lantern to light Captain Everett's path when he saw blood smeared across the deck. He almost pointed it out to the weary Captain. Yet he didn't. He stood staring at it, wondering, as the Captain used the ladder to board the ship.

The wind whistled past his ears and flapped the lowered sails. Blood wasn't so unusual aboard this ship, but it was fresh. Still liquid. Wet. Strangely, it was right by the entrance to the ship. Never would the cook make a kill here. Rarely would a sailor pick a fight in such an open spot. Quickly searching around as the Captain came to the top of the ladder, Charlie found the blood was pooled in a central spot rather than spread as it would be in a brawl. His suspicion grew.

A deep, foreboding fear crept along his spine as he held the lantern high to light the Captain's way. Deep from within his spirit he began muttering a prayer of old. His Granny use to teach him these on the comfort of her knee. For times of need. Times of fear.

Once Captain Everett was safely deposited in bed, a little worse for drink, Charlie began to mull it over. Did the crew finally get Hazel? She could be dead! No, no there wasn't that much blood. Just enough to draw a person short.

He decided to find her, if only to see that she was safe.

Waiting at the Captain's door for a few min-utes, he carefully opened the door a crack and

then entered the room. Captain Everett was a-
sleep on the floor curled around his treasure
chest. Charlie presumed he preferred the famil-
iarity of the floor from his cabin boy days. But
rather than contemplating this for long, he
quietly slid open the desk draw. He wrapped his
hands tightly around the master keys so they
wouldn't rattle. Slowly edging the drawer to a
close, he crept out of the room.

For stealing these keys, Charlie could pay
with his life. No one would believe he was only
checking Hazel. There were no exceptions in this
dark and dismal sailor's life. Death stamped out
the greater risks. Charlie knew the sea would not
be a merciful death. All one could hope is for
cold seas that make death come within half an
hour. The warm seas spread the inevitable
drowning out for hours. Although either end was
slow and painful.

None of this was as important to Charlie as
Hazel. His greatest desire was to get close to her,
but he was not enough. He was barely past a
cabin boy posting as a deck hand. Any money he
had was the few coins in his pocket. What lovely
woman in her right mind would bother with the
likes of him? All he had to offer was what the
Lord had blessed him with at his birth. Even that
wasn't much.

However, he could at least keep her safe.
Watch her. Be near her and hope. His whole life
had been centred around this one cause.

Ω

All the money his Dad had earned was from
watching her. Dad's provision for the whole family came from spying on Hazel for Captain
Everett. Not that it amounted to much. However, his Dad had done well at writing down his

observations at the Donaldson's farm. He had the job for over fifteen years.

Who would know what his Dad was doing to keep himself going these days? All Dad needed to do was worry about himself. He wasn't watching Hazel any more that was for certain.

Charlie had consoled himself that he had not left his siblings behind under his Dad's mercy. They were all away from home, working, or married. Even little Annie was laundering at the old mansion. Thank goodness, otherwise Charlie would still be there to protect them rather than following Hazel.

Ω

Charlie went below deck, down the steps that led down to the guest rooms, doctor's rooms, cellar and food storage. This was a completely separate area from the sailor's quarters and cargo. This area at least smelled clean and fresh, unlike his sleeping space. Being locked away in its own little section of the ship gave the rooms a little more security. Especially for the liquor. Men would bash a way through a liquor storage door if possible.

Slipping into the skinny hall, Charlie's anticipation began to build. Gently, he stepped. Slowly. No sudden movement. Nothing to cause alarm. He pressed his ear to Hazel's solid door. All he could hear was the rhythmic creak as the ship rocked. A deep moan came from deep below as the wood adjusted to the cooling night. The cold crept along the floor boards.

Wrapping his fingers around the various keys, he slowly edged a key in the lock. Barely the key scraped into place, but did not turn. After attempting several keys, one unlocked the door.

Charlie could hear steady rain patting on the deck above him. The door handle squeaked in protest. Charlie cringed. Thankfully the door hinges were well oiled and the door opened without any more creaking.

Picking up his lantern, he padded into the room. He was surrounded by a faint smell of dried roses. So sweet and rare. Holding up the lantern, he found he was in a relatively large cabin, like a sitting room. Well, large for a ship. Not a bunk at all. No other room on the ship was like this. Feminine. Simple touches of cushions, a rag-rug carpet in cheerful pinks, a small shelf with several books standing between two heavy stones and large roses embroidered upon the seats. Rich and comfortable. This room was better than the Captain's salon cabin.

Yet, the room was plain in comparison to her previous home. Only once had Charlie dared to go close enough to the window to look in at the farm house. He longed for all he saw. The family speaking kindly, smiling and sharing. The warm hearth and special mementos. This ship cabin was a fairly pale comparison, but spoke much of Hazel's home.

Charlie could see a second door that was hooked back. Slowly nearing this door, he peered in to find Hazel was not on the smooth, cream bed. Neither did it look used that night. With dread he skirted around the door to find the dresser behind it. The room was completely empty.

Charlie despaired. They had her. She could be hurt and suffering, or dead. He must find her. Hurrying now. Not bothering too much with quiet. He flew out the door. He stopped in his tracks to shut and lock the door. No need to raise suspicion too early. Running in full force, he exited the private quarters and ran to the centre of the boat.

He was completely oblivious to the sharp wind and drenching rain. Down into the centre of the boat and through into the cramped room of the sailors, he burst in only to find deep sleep. Snoring, a bit of coughing and a relatively little movement from the sailors themselves.

Charlie's blood pumped. He heard a low moan and gasp behind him. Turning in horror, he saw her. Bloodied face, ripped skirts, but long wet blond locks, not the honey brown of Hazel.

Quickly, he knelt by this strange girl. She cringed away from him, barely dragging up her blackened legs. The sorry sight grieved his heart. He let a tear slide as he wrapped his arms around her. She whimpered as Charlie gently picked up her. He felt a wave of relief that this was not Hazel. Followed by a rush of guilt. No one should suffer this way. Anger washed through him and down to the pit of his stomach. These filthy vermin, drunk and without care, inflicted this terrible trespass. Again, Charlie was drawn to his Grandmother's mutterings as he prayed for the health and healing of this young girl.

After laying her down in the doctor's rooms, Charlie found he was back to square one. Obviously the blood on the deck was the girls, but still Hazel was missing.

Charlie thought there was next to no possibility that she had run away due to the ship been anchored on a reasonably rough sea. To add to that, the only two small boats of the ship had been used that night. Still, he checked over the side to see them both bobbing in the water.

He began to slowly search the ship. This did not take long since that there were not many rooms unlocked. This was a cargo ship and not designed for passengers. He searched the vast deck. As he came down past the boxes, he saw a small scrap of material sticking out. He pushed back the boxes to find her there, white as a sheet and her eyes shut. Her hair was plastered against her face.

Charlie could barely breathe for fear. Gently, he placed his hand on her chest, he could feel movement. Ever so slight. For the second time that night, he picked up a broken girl. Hazel's hair fell off her face and Charlie was alarmed to see her blue, purple lips. Hurrying to the Captain's Cabin, he raised the alarm.

Captain Everett jumped up from the floor, wobbling slightly. Charlie saw a flick of silver. A knife ready to slit his throat. Ignoring the threat, Charlie clattered the lantern down. Without a word, he rushed to Everett's bed and lay Hazel down.

Captain Everett would probably be disgusted with himself if he knew that Charlie had already sneaked passed him as he slept, but he wouldn't be finding out. Those keys would be returned very shortly, at the first opportunity that Captain Everett was out of the way.

Ω

Captain Everett looked at the rough, young man who had bought in his daughter. Charlie's black hair was plastered, wet against his face and his dark blue eyes expressed deep concern. One glance at Hazel was all it took for Everett to realize she was in serious danger. Forgetting his concern over Charlie, his voice scratched into life. "Quickly, get those clothes off her. I'll get the cook next door ta fetch the doctor."

Everett hadn't run in many years. He had no need. Now he moved so quickly that he toppled and bashed everything in his wake. Never had he seen anyone survive the deep cold illness. Without a doubt, that is what she had. Even the lids of her eyes were an alarming dark shade of blue.

Everett admonished himself. Never, never should he have taken her from the safety of Canada. He pounded on the kitchen door.

He yelled, "Wake up. Wake damn ya. Open this door." Of course he should have bought his keys before he left his cabin. The bloody cook would no doubt be dead asleep.

Everett started to return for the keys, but then he hesitated. Perhaps he should get the doctor. With lightening speed, he fled across the ship. Jumping the sails. Crashing through the skinny hall and whipping open the doctor's door to find him wiping blood from a young girl's face. Everett stopped in his tracks. The girl's two red eyes stared at him. They were full of pain. Everett felt a rush of concern and confusion.

Doctor Murphy assumed Captain Everett had heard of the girl's assault. He let out a snort. "Her name is Molly. She seems to have been molested by the crew."

"Molly! I was ta pick her up tomorrow."

The Doctor eyed Captain Everett and he added, "I have no idea who did this. She was blessed enough to be laid in my hands, rather than left in theirs. She still has all her teeth, so she can be thankful for that."

Almost forgetting his purpose, Captain Everett struggled to pull himself together. "Leave her now. Ya must go ta Hazel in me cabin! Sha's wet n' cold. Near death." The doctor snatched up his bag and pushed his fat legs as fast as he could. Within seconds he began to puff from the strain. Captain Everett passed him with ease.

Captain Everett briefly considered Molly's assault. She must have been dropped off early.

The men got her from the docks. Everett had already paid for the girl to be delivered tomorrow. The crew had seen the opportunity to take her aboard for their pleasure. The poor girl.

No trustworthy men were aboard earlier this night. All of the senior sailors had been conducting business on land. Some were still there.

To add to the mystery, Hazel should have been safely locked away in her rooms. She had been told to lock herself in by night and not come out. But she had come out. *Damn her.*

Everett instantly relented. He should have gotten her a maid. A minder to report back to him her every move. He should have kept her safe. *Why on earth wasn't she in her room?*

Shame washed over him as he realized there may be a connection between Molly's degrading and Hazel's state of affairs. Oh, the dishonour. She should have never been exposed to such a thing.

As Everett threw open his cabin door, he promised himself that he would have to give her a better life. Her life on the ship certainly was not working. He had been selfish to keep her here. She barely spoke to him as it was. He had no idea what to say to her. Clearly she needed a more secure life than this. He should have settled her in his English house well before now. He promised himself he would at the next opportunity, when the waters calmed. *That is, if she recovers.*

Looking at her now, wrapped up in bundles of blankets, with only her face showing out of the layers, she looked like death. Her sopping wet clothes were in a bundle on the floor. Everett felt tears slide down his already wet face. They were unbidden, but unstoppable. Surely she was not lost.

He looked at Charlie whose face had gone a

deep shade of red in embarrassment. Captain Everett regretted the need for him to undress her, but there had been no one else at hand and certainly it was wrong for her father to see her exposed. Besides Charlie seemed a good sort, unlike most aboard this ship. He had only been left for a minute, so nothing disgraceful could have happened. Captain Everett croaked, "Thank-ya fa finding her."

The doctor came panting through the door. His hands shook as he checked her. The cold had even gotten to him.

He mumbled, "Heart is beating." He paused. "Her breathing's very shallow." The doctor glanced at Charlie who stood there muted. "Quickly, stoke up the fire very hot. Cover the windows with blankets. Heat the room to beyond a comfortable warmth."

The doctor raked the two men up and down. "And for goodness sake, get us some dry clothes, Captain Everett. We don't want to join her." Looking at Charlie sharply. "Especially, him. He looks like he has been in the rain all night. What person would do that?"

Captain Everett glanced at the young man at his side. He didn't care why he was out in the rain. The fact was Charlie had found her and possibly saved her life.

After the doctor was gone and Charlie was sent to wrap up warmly in the crews quarters, Everett stared into the blue face of his daughter. Memories flooded back of a time when she was a babe wrapped in blankets, in his cabin on the ship Helen. Though at that time, her face was never blue, rather an angry shade of hungry red. He had often held her as a babe until they both fell into an exhausted sleep.

Now he feared she would die in a completely different way. Carefully he lifted her and carried her to the black pot-belly stove. He arranged the woollen blankets snugly around her hair and face. Wrapped himself in another blanket and held her to his chest for many hours.

He did not dare close his eyes. Occasionally, he rocked and would lay his hand to her cold cheek. He did not move from that spot. Well after the sun rose, he finally felt her face begin to warm and he allowed himself to sleep for a little while.

Ω

At mid morning, the doctor entered the room with a great bustle, puffing and blowing, but even that didn't wake them. He was surprised to see a father so caring of his daughter. He had his arms wrapped around her, a great bundle of blankets. It wasn't seemingly for parents to be so affectionate to their children.

He sighed, never in all his years had he seen such a thing. Yet, he peered at her face and saw that it was surprisingly pink. Oh well, Captain Everett must have warmed her up. At least she was past that stage. She would not die of cold.

Now she would have to rest and drink plenty of nourishing broth. His mind ran rampant.

Vegetables. Meat. He would need to speak to the cook and send a few of the crew to fetch the goods needed. Chicken and a little salt would do nicely.

He rubbed his tummy in anticipation as he walked out of the cabin. He would have a bowl himself! Mm...mm...delicious. He needed a treat after the long night of dealing with these ninnies. Who knows how they got themselves into these situations. Women were trouble. A ship was always better off without them.

Grumbling he limped toward the gallery. This

was getting too much for him. He was too old. Maybe it was time to retire to his villa in England. Ah, lovely. However, he would do his job well with Hazel, because Captain Everett obviously loved her. What a waste of time on a woman.

Ω

As the doctor expected a fever rose in Hazel, as though to burn out the pain. She did not rise from her bed until weeks later. Neither did Molly, who suffered from broken bones to say the least.

Hazel felt like fire. The old doctor Murphy tended her almost constantly, except when he was briefly tending to Molly. The Captain had made it clear that Hazel's death would be on his head. So she must not die.

After her recovery he would retire peacefully with a little extra from the Captain. If Hazel lived, he would be bound to get a large sum! Molly, on the other hand, was not important. She was only something that was over used and needed a little repair. Just a woman. A whore, really.

Murphy wondered why the Captain even bothered with Molly. However, Everett insisted that she was cared for properly. He had called up the black woman, Riden, to care for her.

The hag, Riden, sang Molly strange songs. Patted her back as she slept. Putting her old wiry arms around Molly as the nightmares raged.

The doctor considered this interesting since Riden would hardly ever surface up onto the deck. Rather, she huddled down with the animals, caring for them. Even when it was time for them to be killed for the pot, she would lovingly stroke them while quietly slipping the knife into their throat.

Admittedly, the doctor found the meat tasty.

Riden's meat was better than hunted animals that ran in fear. *'At least she played a useful role on board,'* he thought, relenting a little with his uncharitable views on women.

Ω

After a few days, when the weather cleared, Everett carried Hazel back to her own rooms to be closer to the doctor's quarters. She spoke in delirious mutterings. Everett placed her on her luxurious double bed and patted her limp hair down. Rolling over, she curled into herself. He left her to the administrations of Dr. Murphy.

Her fever eventually broke and Everett was greatly relieved she was on the road to recovery. He turned his thoughts to that terrible night's happenings and was determined to come to the bottom of it all. The crew had been nursing hangovers for a few days. Most had been avoiding him, or at least not looking him in the eye. They all knew where he stood on the matter. A paid whore was one thing, but to abuse a woman and such a young one was something else. Disgraceful. They could all lose their jobs – or their heads - least they forget.

Captain Everett aimed to find out how Hazel was connected to all of this. The crew was a little confused about her involvement. However, the one thing they were sure about was that somebody was going to pay.

Captain Everett was almost white with rage as he interrogated the crew. Insistently, he dug up the dirt, finding that most men pointed to Tom as starting the mayhem. A few named Jack and no doubt Jack encouraged Tom, but even that was unreliable. Molly was enticed into talking to Riden and the doctor. Her descriptions were evident enough to point along the same lines. Thus, more than a week after the crime, it was Tom that he called out to pay for what had been done. Tom had originally come to him from the rat-infested streets and begged for mercy and kindness. He had proved a good sailor, but tough.

Not once did Everett ask Hazel what happened. Not one crew member named her as involved. No one even said they saw her. So it was fair to assume that Hazel was separate from the situation. Everett hated to ask. The shame of her being exposed to these men doing terrible acts. It was his fault. To make matters worse, he realized Hazel considered him to be like the other sailors. Rough and ill mannered.

The doctor confirmed that Hazel had not talked of anything happening to herself. Not in her fevered uttering and not when she was coherent. Actually, the doctor claimed that she referred to feeling faint and falling on the deck in the early evening. Not that Everett remembered any bumps, or bruises on her. However, she did tend to walk to the secluded areas of the ship.

He was a little suspicious of Charlie. Yet, it was Charlie who had rowed Everett's longboat back to the ship. He had lit the way to Everett's cabin and then said he found Molly in the crew's quarters. This all added up, but Charlie claimed to have taken a walk for fresh air and by chance come upon Hazel hidden behind boxes.

As Charlie told Captain Everett this, he did not make eye contact. Everett dwelt on the un-likelihood of Charlie walking in the pouring rain for the sake of fresh air. Charlie must have been searching for her. Yet, he claimed he was upset by Molly. Captain Everett thought it strange that a sailor would care about the two women, even being such a young sailor. He didn't really know Charlie. He was too new. Maybe he had a better childhood than the rest of the crew and cared for others.

Still, Captain Everett had not hesitated to tell Charlie he would be handsomely rewarded for his trouble in his next pay packet. Probably it would be used on beer and whores. Even so, it was Captain Everett's responsibility to give credit where it was due aboard his ship. Charlie may squander his fortune, but that was his choice and well deserved reward.

Ω

Charlie watched her. They all watched her, but he knew her every move.

At the distant end of the ship, Charlie paused to study Hazel. She leaned on the rail while staring over the ocean. He thought to himself, *She is not for the sea. This life was too limiting for a woman like her. Too rough and perverse. She has nothing suitable to occupy herself.*

Though neither was he suited to this life for that matter. Not after the shock of Molly's situation. Vainly he hoped she had not seen Molly's assault that dreadful night.

Nonetheless, Charlie could see that Hazel had changed ever so slightly. Her stance had stiffened. She walked with a quick clip. An amount of anger oozed from her inner being directly at Captain Everett. There was no denying it; she must have seen Molly ripped to shreds.

Yet, Hazel had seemed happy to be with Molly, as they recuperated slowly under the doctor's watchful eye. They often spent the mornings together chatting in a distant corner on the deck. Sometimes they shut themselves away in Hazel's rooms. Yes, Hazel was brighter until Captain Everett finally sold Molly on to some man in distant New Zealand. They hardly ever sailed there, so Hazel would not even have the chance to visit often.

From her attitude toward Captain Everett, Charlie was sure that Hazel thought all of it was his fault. Maybe it was. Nevertheless, Charlie had never seen Captain Everett buy a girl without a senior crew member in charge of her while aboard. Something must have gone wrong with Molly's case. Remembering back to earlier that fated day, Charlie had heard Captain Everett give instructions to his first mate to collect Molly the next day.

Captain Everett had kept Molly aboard for four months while she mended. By the time she had been sold on, the whole crew were ashamed of their actions. Even those not involved. Just to look at the angry red scar running across her temple on a daily basis. To see the puffy eyes slowly reduce until only one eye showed some permanent damage. Still, to look at her on her last day here you would barely know, with her pretty face peeping out from behind her loose hair.

It was obvious to all the real trauma was on the inside. The way Molly flinched at the merest touch. How she turned away if someone raised their arm too quickly. Charlie knew how she hurt on the inside very well, since he was chosen to guard her. He was considered safe; after all, it was he who had saved her in the first place.

Occasionally, Jack hissed at Molly when she was nearby, and Charlie would grip his long dagger in warning. Captain Everett had given him the best weapons on the ship. The others weren't allowed anything much more than a butter knife these days. Still, he chose to remain very close by her at all times.

Only when Molly visited Hazel did Charlie

keep a respectable distance. He did this to allow them some space to chat in private, but it was also to avoid close contact with Hazel. He had no idea what to say to Hazel. He had never actually met her properly, or been close enough to even greet her.

Ω

Hazel did not go to the local school like her siblings. She had private tutoring. The village children in school thought she was above them. They thought she was too different in her fancy clothes and posh airs. No one in their right mind would actually talk to her. Not those who were in rags, snot running down their face and bare feet. Yet, she only lived at the milk farm. Her life had always been a mystery to the villagers and the Donaldson family certainly didn't say anything.

For Charlie's whole life, his father had been watching her. Sometimes even spying on her family. He would go to the edge of the Heathburn Wood and stand in the darkest, thickest trees. Hardly anybody would go there. The wood was not good for hunting, or riding, but it gave a great view of the Donaldson's Farm. His Dad watched the comings and goings every week.

At the age of five, Charlie would go with his Dad and siblings to play in the forest. Even then Charlie knew he had to be silent. Dad used to growl under his breath at any noise and threaten to break their necks if they so much as squeaked a sound. They knew better than to test their Dad. The three boys and two girls were terror-stricken of their Dad's belt that he would whip around their head leaving welts and sometimes cuts across their cheek. So much so that Annie the youngest sister would run and cower in the corner whenever her Dad returned home.

Also it was no secret that Mum died on child bed while giving birth to Annie. Charlie's Dad made sure that she grew up knowing her mother's death was on her head. Annie barely survived as it was and then only because their kind old Gran's soft heart. Annie was supposed to be left to pass quickly and be buried with Mum. However, Gran had held her and could not bear to let her go. The old goat provided all she could for Annie. By the age of two, she had learned to hide by her Gran's rocker whenever Dad was around. Sometimes even under her skirts.

But Annie's good fortune ran out when Gran died. She'd cried and howled as Gran was buried. Dad turned to her and slapped her several times across the face. Blood dribbled down her chin as she had cuddled into Charlie. At the young age of six Charlie protected her.

Many years later, Charlie figured that something was not normal with their situation. Dad barely did any work, bar writing the town folk an odd letter for a penny. He was educated enough. In fact, when asked, he told others that he was a writer, but would never pinpoint for who, or what he wrote. He always alluded that he wrote for an important editor. However, he did send away letters at least once a week. And always after watching the Donaldson's house.

Ω

As the months had passed, Hazel and Molly had become almost inseparable. They drew from each other a companionable comfort, despite the fact that their traumas were so different.

For Molly, Hazel was a safe haven from the terrible, vicious men that surrounded her every day. Eventually, Molly shifted into Hazel's rooms.

Molly found she relived the multiple rapes nearly every night.

Hazel would often wake to Molly in the middle of the night. She would hug her till the screams stopped. Tears would run down both their faces until Molly calmed and slept peacefully for the rest of the night. However, Hazel would stay awake until she finally cried herself to sleep. The strain showed on each of the girls.

One night while they lay in bed, Molly told Hazel her story, "I'm only fourteen, Hazel." Gathering her thoughts, Molly seemed not sure where to start. "I lived in a large English village my whole life... My Mother loved me so much. I never thought much on my Dad. He was always... distant. We hardly ever saw him because he went away on business a lot."

Hazel asked, "What was your household like?"

"We had a maid and a stableman most of my life. We lived in a large villa, not too flash, but not bad either. I had two brothers and two sisters..." Molly's voice trailed off. "When I was twelve I had noticed something was wrong with Dad... when he started to hit Mama. The strain was showing. Money must have been tight. The stableman was let go, but never the maid. No... never the maid."

Hazel said nothing, waiting for Molly to say what she needed.

Molly thought for a moment. "Dad would not see our standards drop too low. Not in front of the nosey neighbours peaking out their windows... I think he had cheated a few too many tradesmen, so that they had stopped buying from him... he always attended the town clubs gambling and drinking." She paused to reflect.

Molly continued, "My sister, Daisy, disappeared first. Dad put on a sad front, but shortly after Daisy had gone I noticed his mood improving. He even hired another stable-boy." Molly laughed bitterly. "You know, Hazel, Mama never got over losing Daisy. She grieved every day. Never did we hear from her again."

Molly stared into the distance. "Dad did not even bother to be rid of the stable-boy before he trundled me off to a faraway auction to be sold at a high price. I was to be a virginal whore."

Hazel shut her eyes in horror. A tear slid down her face.

Molly added, "I cried and pleaded. Begged some more, but there was no swaying Dad. He looked past me like I didn't exist. We walked with this man who had purchased me. He was dressed as though he was rich. As though he was a gentleman, but he was only the owner of a high-end Madame's house."

Molly gave a cruel laugh. "An innocent young girl is in high demand..." Molly looked at her hands. "I thought my luck had turned, Hazel, when Captain Everett came and offered double the amount of money to buy me... But my Dad didn't want me overnight. Maybe I reminded him of his guilt. He... dropped me... off early." Molly and Hazel broke into fresh tears because they both knew what had happened after he had left her at the docks. She had been rowed out to the ship and climbed aboard where all of her worst fears came true.

When Molly left the ship Hazel was heart-broken. Her closest and dearest friend in this life upon the sea was taken away and for the second time in her life her heart tore in two. Molly had clung to her, begging Captain Everett not to take her ashore.

Captain Everett said, "Now, now. Come on. We'll only go on ta land fa a few days. There's a man I want ya ta meet. If ya are not happy, I will not make ya stay in New Zealand." He bent her fingers off Hazel's arms, forcing Molly away as another sailor held onto Hazel. Captain Everett shook Molly like a rag doll when she started to scream in hysterics.

Molly went mute at the shaking, he held her firmly by the shoulders. Captain Everett hissed, "Look, ya can't stay here. Think of what these scoundrels did ta ya." He glanced around, looking at the sailors nearby. "Ya cannot live aboard with them. It will eat ya up. It's just not right. Not for ya. It's time to give another life a go. This man is good. He wants to marry ya, if you're willing. Ya will not be a prostitute, that is not what I want for ya. Ya must believe me."

Captain Everett groaned as Molly started to wail uncontrollably at the thought of prostitution and men. "Stop ya cry'n," he insisted. Then he pushed her to the edge and hoisted her off the ship into Charlie's arms standing below in a longboat, ready to row them all ashore.

Hazel screamed after Molly. She wrenched herself away from the sailor and pounded her Father. Yelling and screaming. He looked at her with almost sadness in his eyes. He stated, "This is for the best for both of ya. Ya not recovering and neither is sha. Ya both worn at the edges." With that he pushed Hazel away and jumped over the edge landing in the longboat with a loud thump. He yelled at Charlie, "Go. Go now."

Both of the girls cried and reached for each other. The last thing Hazel yelled to Molly was, "I will come back for you. I promise! One day I will come for you. Don't let them get to you. I will come!"

She saw them get out of the longboat at the shore. The sand was golden and water clear blue. But Hazel did not notice the beauty of the wild Bay of Islands. The only thing she saw was the several dark-skinned savage men and a few women wearing some sort of grass skirt. To one side, an old European man stood next to the savages. Hazel soaked in the whole situation. Maybe the savages were the old man's slaves. Perhaps Molly was going to be fed to them; she wasn't sure what would happen to her.

Hazel remained inconsolable for weeks after. Captain Everett had come back after two days ashore and told her Molly had chosen to stay. Hazel had not believed him for one minute. She could not imagine Molly finding any comfort in such a strange and wild land as New Zealand. No doubt Molly had been thrown to some savage by now. Hazel was overcome with terror at the thought. *Oh, poor Molly!*

3.

Never once, in all Hazel's time on the sea, did they ever return to Canada. This was despite the fact that Captain Everett had a grand house in The Port of Saint John. She was sure that Captain Everett knew if he was to make a stop there, she would try to escape him without a moment's hesitation.

She longed to return to her beloved family home. To curl up in her Mamai's arms. To tell them she was all right and to see that her family were safe. They must be worried. The few times she had sent a letter to them it may, or may not have been delivered. All mail went through her father after all. Rarely did she receive anything from them. She was sure Captain Everett withheld most of the letters.

She could hear her father's voice yelling instructions to a slow and ungainly crew. They were drowned in drink and women from the previous night. The crew always seemed to heighten as they entered into Spanish waters for their final stop over before home. The combination of a warm sun, hot bathes and loose women all added to the anticipation. Hazel knew to steer well clear. At least they returned clean for their next stop over in England to see their families.

A chilly feeling climbed down Hazel's spine. Twisting and slithering to her feet. Her stomach tightened into tense nerves. The time was drawing near.

Soon they would cast off to England for their long stopover. Followed by slowly heading up to

Scotland to make that unusually small supply drop off to Lord Dirl. However, before they cast off from England she would take her chance to escape.

Very carefully, Hazel had developed her plan. All she needed was the right timing. This year alone they had circuited from Italy into England twice. Captain Everett never told her any destination, but she was sure he would follow his usual pattern.

Most of the crew had family in England that they liked to visit. Often she waited on the ship for their return. She normally had only the company of a few guards for ten days, or more. Anchorage in England was always long, providing the perfect circumstances.

As usual, on her first day in London, Captain Everett sent her for a dress fitting. Each time she was measured for clothes that father deemed suitable for her to wear. She would come away with a variety of clothing, mostly suitable for the sea. Thick oil coats, heavy, rough cotton dresses and shoes with a bit of grip. Her father ordered one very beautiful gown as well, more suited to be worn in front of the Queen. Also, a gown that would serve well at a garden party. Oddly, he included one riding outfit, and of course each dress had the accessories to match.

Who knows when and for whom she would wear these precious garments. Captain Everett barely let her off the ship. Besides, he surely did not attend balls, or ride horses on show. He was too sea roughened. These gifts reminded her strongly of the strict grooming and ladies education she received at Mademoiselle's. The education that Everett was so particular about. Strange it was, since he is as rough as guts and spoke in such a strong Cockney accent. Not to mention his disgraceful manner.

Hazel ascertained there was a reason, but maybe not as she had thought. Originally, she had assumed that he would sell her, but now she had been with him too long. Already she had seen several girls, besides Molly, bought and sold. Always for a good price to some greedy men in distant colonies where it was difficult to find a wife. Alternatively, she had heard the sailors say these colonial men would force themselves on a native woman, who would find a way to escape. However, these young white girls would not escape, for where would they go and anything could happen to them in the wilderness. When she heard these rumours Hazel thought of Molly in New Zealand, there were was no help for her, no option to escape, she was stuck there.

A feeling began to stir in Hazel. Everett had a plan for her as well. She could see it in his eyes. The way they calculated things when he looked at her. Flicking toward her with shifty indecision. Unfortunately for him though, she also had a plan.

Ω

Unloading on the London docks took at least two, if not three days. The wharf was readily accessible and the cargo was easily removed via a short ramp. The men worked long, hot hours while the last of the summer sun roasted their skin. After a few good days working, they were keen for time to roam the city. To drink and be merry. Visit family and friends. Conceive another child, or two. Captain Everett spent hours conducting business.

Essentially they were out of Hazel's way. The next day she would make her move. Her skin itched with anticipation.

Obsessively, Hazel had started to plot. To her

shock, she felt more like her true blood, Everett. Like him, she felt herself becoming hard. She felt cunning and malicious of mind.

Quietly, she stood on the deck watching the comings and goings of various other ships. Two deck hands watched over her. They were ruthless and sea wary. Like hawks they watched her for fear that something may happen to her. No doubt they remembered what happened to Tom after Captain Everett put him to trial for the harm he had done to Molly. Tom had a slow agonising death, to say the least.

Hazel searched for an excuse to get away from these guards. She needed to pin down some money. Glancing at her father's cabin, she hoped a situation would arise. All she needed was a few minutes to slip away.

With the sun heating up into a comfortable haze, she sat on deck in the shade of the lowered sails and mast. Most of the men had gone about their business

Slowly, one guard, who was lounging in the shade of the boxes, succumbed to sleep. Now all Hazel needed was the other to follow suit, or perhaps go. She racked her brain for ideas or excuses for him to leave her for just a minute.

She heard the sound of soft footsteps. Swinging quickly around, she put her hand on her letter knife. She drew in a deep breath, but seeing Father standing there staring at her, she relaxed. *Where did he spring from?*

His eyes looked up to the right, as if in deep thought or decision making.

Captain Everett stated, "The weather is warm." He used an unusually controlled, almost polite voice. "Would you care to ride on the green?"

You would think that his speech had miraculously been sweetened overnight. *What could he be playing at?* Hazel's brain reeled, nothing came to mind.

'The green', this would be the park that the English rode horses, open carriages, or simply strolled through the day. She had never been riding anywhere, but on the farm where she rode wild and free. Still, she knew what was expected from her on a formal ride in town.

Frowning in indecision, Hazel stalled him, "What horses do we have?" This venture was bound to ruin her well laid plans.

Everett answered quickly with perfectly refined tones, "I have a house here, with a groom and at least three good horses from which you can choose." He surprised her with a grin that was almost appealing.

Her hackles rose. Hazel was about to refuse, but then thought that it may be good to see a bit more of London before she stole away into it.

Hazel purposely raised her chin, "It will be my pleasure to ride with you." Daintily, she offered her hand to him. In kind, he gently held her finger tips and kissed her hand. Hazel had difficulty in not ripping her hand away. Her fingers shook slightly.

Captain Everett stared at her in an odd fashion. Almost as if to test her interest, he suggested, "Well, we will make a day of it. I am sure feeding the ducks and a picnic will be to your liking." He paused, "It is time that you learn of my life here in London. I will meet you ready at the gang plank in, let's say, two hours."

Hazel realised the opportunity that she had been given. She turned her face slightly away and took a step toward the sea so he would not be able to catch her lie. She glanced at the unusually clear blue sky. "How about I meet you in your cabin, so I would not spend even a minute more in this blistering heat." She said this despite the fact that her skin was already browned to a crisp. Hazel had been on board for so long, she could hardly avoid the sun's effects. She hoped he would assume that her proprieties lie in the direction of a proper English lady. However, he may sniff out that she was deceiving him. He was as keen as any mangy dog. Feeling resentful, Hazel thought the extensive lady's education should be put to good use. A true lady does not voluntarily expose herself to the sun.

Everett hesitated, "Jolly good. I'll meet you in my cabin and I will arrange a parasol, for the sun is way too hot for a lady to be exposed. You will find it inside my cabin door." He had taken the lie hook, line and sinker.

Hazel turned toward him and looked into his clear green eyes. She couldn't quiet force herself to smile. So instead she settled with a simple, "Thank you."

Hazel found Everett's high class speech peculiar. He spoke with perfectly modulated English. Playing along with this strange charade, she gave a nod and small curtsey. Now she would get what she needed most. Money. She must be early. He was not to catch her taking it.

Ω

Of course, this outing created a difficulty for Hazel. The posh dresses and the hair style would usually require a maid. She could do up the buttons to the middle of her back, but not to the three quarter. She racked her brain for someone she might trust to do this task. The cook, who was gruff, but always kind. The ship's surgeon who was every bit the professional after Molly was raped. Perhaps old Riden, but her fingers were gnarled and stiff.

A sharp knock, startled her from her

thoughts. No one could enter, since she had wisely locked the door.

Hazel called, "Who is it?"

A young voice replied, "It is me, Frankie. Capt n' sent me to help ya."

Yes, he was perfect from the few options. He was only ten and she could easily protect herself from him. She replied, "Good. I will let you in when I am ready for you. I might be a while." After a pause, she instructed, "First, organize hot water for the tub. Be quick. I will only need four buckets since I must be ready quite soon." She heard him running off.

Ω

Quickly, she washed. This was the added touch she needed to help her escape. Without doubt, she had been too long without a bath and that would not do. Unbeknown to Captain Everett, he had provided her with just the excuse she needed to have a hot bath in the short, cramped tub. After all, a lady must be clean, soft and sweet to smell. Unfortunately, she would not be able to achieve the perfect peach and cream complexion. Instead, she scrubbed her brown skin almost raw.

Hazel shone and pulsed from the heat as she dried with a towel. Hot droplets glistened over her well-formed body. She rubbed her arms vigorously. At least the tan was even along her slim arms and shoulders. The hot tropical sun had tanned her right through her light cotton shirt that hung loosely from her shoulders in true sailor fashion. Perhaps her face was a little browner, not that she had a mirror to see. Sighing, it would do no good to contemplate on the way she had allowed her standards to slip aboard this ship.

She relished the pleasure of feeling clean.
Oh, how she missed the simple pleasures of her
old life. Cleanliness, loving company, arguing
with Ben, a drink of fresh water and farm
animals.

Captain Everett had destroyed it all. Hazel's
eyes sharpened at the thought of him. He'd
stolen her away. Given her life and destroyed her
life. She felt a surge of loathing for him, she was
going to ensure he would regret what he had
done. Hazel was determined to take her life into
her own hands. Her life was her own.

Ω

Hazel quickly ran her hand down Captain
Ever-ett's smooth mahogany desk. Papers were
carefully stacked and weighed down. The whole
room was in perfect order. Very unlike the
description that Dadai gave when he was in
Captain Everett's office all those years ago. Never
could Hazel remember seeing Everett's office
anything but tidy and organised.

The desk had a large world atlas on the front
panel and carefully carved into each land mass
animals and vegetation represented each
country. The sea had various waves and sea
creatures. There were no names to indicate each
country. To Hazel it was a mystery. A scholar
interested in travel and the world would
understand the forms, but she had never learned
to understand an atlas. Certainly there was no
time to make sense of it now.

During the times she had entered this room,
Father had taken from his top drawer a small
sack of money. He instructed her escorts as to
the spending on her dresses and accessories.
Anything left was to be given back to him with an
account of the money spent. Of course he gave

an excuse of wanting to ensure no one took advantage of her.

Now she depended upon there being some money in the drawer. Not that she expected there to be much. After all, he kept the bulk of his money in the large, locked treasure box at the far end of his desk. He had it padlocked to his desk and bolted to the floor, so it must hold a lot of money. He always wore the key on a leather strap tied around his neck.

Carefully, she moved around the desk so as not to disturb the neat piles. Glancing around through the windows and at the closed door, she ensured that no-one watched. Quickly, she opened the drawer, removed three small bags heavy with coin and shut the drawer again. The bags fitted neatly into her rose purse. She tugged the purse shut with the pull strings.

Hearing a shuffling out on the deck, Hazel wildly flung up her skirt, looped the pull string through her garter and tied a double knot to ensure the purse did not move. She took two quick steps toward the front of the desk and as the cabin door opened she pretended to be studying the engraved map of the world.

Ω

Captain Everett strode into the room. "There you are. It is a beautifully embellished map." He paused. Hazel turned to look at him. He noticed she was working hard to remain calm and look innocent. However, Everett was distracted by her flushed face and slightly fast breathing. Assuming the worst, he said, "Are you all right. You look as though you might have a fever."

Hazel stood, "Oh." Her eyes flicked, "Ah, well. I walked smartly to get here. I thought I would be late. I may have been a bit hasty in this heat."

She proceeded to fan herself rapidly with her hand.

Everett's eyes sharpened. He knew a lie when he saw one. Hesitating, he contemplated what to do. This was his daughter. So his usual sailor methods for interrogation would be no good. Not forgetting, she was a lady.

He turned smartly and picked up the parasol that Hazel had not even touched. *People do tell white lies to protect their privacy. She will need to be trained to soften the truth. Many things must remain unsaid so as not to offend the sensibilities of society. Yes, yes that must be it. In time she will learn to portray a white lie without people knowing.* The silence between them was beginning to drag.

To Hazel's great relief, he turned to her and intoned in his best cultured voice, "Never mind, we must go."

Hazel flushed even more. His eyes would not meet hers. He knew she had hidden the truth. As they walked out the door he added, "We will probably have to keep the horses at a walking pace."

Ω

Charlie sat on an empty wooden crate. He leaned forward intently, whittling away at a fine piece of driftwood he had been saving in his pocket for some time. The wood curved half way around a hole where a wood knot would have been. From the curve it curled down into a neat bulb making it comfortable to hold. The sea had sanded the wood smooth. Just the right size to fit in the hand. When Charlie had found it on a distant shore, he thought it would surely be suited to something carved. He had been waiting a while for inspiration.

Yesterday, Charlie left the ship to follow Hazel and her guards at a distance. She had visited the dressmakers. On the way back, Hazel stopped to look at a beautiful pond. She particularly paid attention to the lovely swans. They were a sight to behold.

Charlie had never really looked at a bird unless it was for the pot. To be fair, Old Mr. Graham spent hours showing him how to whittle animals, but never a bird. Somehow, Old Mr Graham used to bring even simple pieces of wood alive. Many children of the village had two, or three of his beautiful whittled animals. Occasionally, even a cart, stable and fencing.

Mr. Graham was the oldest person that Charlie had ever known. He survived into his elder years by the charity of the village. On his porch, he had welcomed everyone, especially children. No matter what the weather, he would be there tinkering away. At times, the children would snuggle in his small house if only for the want of some warmth, for he had his fire going nearly all year round.

Charlie's old Granny very rarely complained about their home, but at times he saw her shaking with cold because of the lack of wood for the fire. Charlie would often go searching in the deadly cold rain just to collect in a little seasoned wood from the vast forest.

Often Charlie would take a few logs to Old Mr. Graham. In kind the village repaid him with food and other necessities for the fine toys he gave the children. The only food Charlie gave Old Mr. Graham were the berries he collected in the woods, or a few wild onions. Always Charlie's offerings were appreciated, but his Dad never gave anything extra.

Charlie didn't only play with the wooden toys, he learned the skill. From a young lad, he watched Mr. Graham. He spent hours on the porch, until one day Mr. Graham gave him a small hand-crafted knife. Charlie was overcome with gratitude. Never had anyone given Charlie anything so precious. He treasured the knife and kept it hidden in a small ratty leather pouch tied with a leather thong about his waist. From that day be began to whittle. More often than not, at Old Mr. Graham's side. Whenever Father was near, he hid the blade, or he would be sure to lose it.

Old Mr. Graham always said that Charlie had a feel for the wood. He had said it was a rare skill and should be used so it would grow. More recently, Charlie had put his skill to more mundane use by making knife handles, knobs for doors, cutlery and other various household items. Through the years, Charlie continued whittling at the old man's side until his very sad, yet peaceful death.

This time though, the wood was destined to be a swan. Upon the shores, after a storm, he found this piece of naturally sculpted drift wood that required very little work.

Before he had followed Captain Everett and Hazel, he had never been to the seaside. He was amazed by the various sands over the world; from soft to harsh. The sea life was amazing. Especially on the hot tropical islands. Once while swimming in New Caledonia, he had a huge snapper come right up to his face. Little stripy fish zipped by and large rainbow fish wallowed in the shallows. For the rest of his life he would remember these adventures. Yet, being a part of a rough crew, aboard a large ship, was not a home to him. Simply a necessity. So he could be close to Hazel.

As he carefully cut away at the swan's wings, he noticed a shimmer of cream in the corner of his eye. He looked up to behold the most exquisite beauty he had ever seen. Hazel had her chestnut hair piled up at the back, looped through pearls and bountiful ringlets cascading in front of her ears. Clinging to her figure as she moved was a fine cream cotton dress that was nipped just under the bosom. From there, rose budded material hung down creating a straight appearance. This was very unlike the woman of his Canadian village who wore the old tightly laced-up dresses. In fact, for the last few years Hazel had mostly worn the loose shirt and light skirt more suited to sailing.

Charlie supposed that this new dress was the fashion he had seen among the elite this season. Very daring. Hazel was stepping up in the world. She clutched a matching rose bud purse in her hand.

Hazel flashed one look in his direction. She frowned slightly and he quickly made himself look busy at his work. She confidently walked straight toward the Captain's cabin, where Charlie supposed she was meeting Captain Everett. How on earth could she go out looking so lovely with someone like the craggy, sea worn Captain. Never had Charlie seen the Captain look anything but crusted with salt and sweat.

Charlie waited for a moment to see if she would come out of the cabin. When she didn't, he quietly slipped down the side and peeked in the window. He saw Hazel sliding the drawer of the Captain's formidable desk closed. Hazel stashed a bundle into her draw string purse. Charlie eyes popped out in shock to see her slide her skirt up, exposing a fine-looking leg. Quickly looking away to the deck. He thought about how lovely and beautiful she was.

While settling his desire, he realised she was hiding money bags. Hazel had a scheme brewing. Charlie pondered on whether to tell Captain Everett, but no. The Captain was a harsh man. Cruel to some, but fair to most. Charlie could not take the chance to test if he would be cruel to Hazel.

After all, his last act of cruelty lead to the death of Tom. Who deserved a good punishment, but surely not the slow, agonising death he'd received. The Captain had used a hook-whip on Tom. Five strikes would have been plenty. However, fifteen had been fatal, resulting in shreds of skin peeling off the sailor's back. Within a day the wounds turned to a yellow, stinking mess. Following nights of excruciating pain, the sailor curled up into a foetal ball, and shaking from head to toe he took his last breath.

Charlie remembered how Captain Everett, as soon as he was finished with Tom, walked straight to Hazel who was hiding behind the boxes. He stood there and snarled at her. Charlie would have sent her away himself, if he had known she was there. The whipping was not a sight for women to see.

For a moment, he had thought Captain Everett was going to throttle Hazel for being there. Maybe even whip her too. Charlie knew he would've jumped in the way to prevent the lashes getting to her. The frustration of the situation had shown on Captain Everett's face.

Besides, Charlie owed Captain Everett nothing. He would not take the risk by telling Everett what he had seen. Hazel might not be safe with the Captain. Perhaps it would be better for her to escape; then he would help her. Somehow.

4.

A few days later, Hazel was ushered into a pristine parlour by a plump maid, who puffed slightly after exerting herself. Not once had she the chance to run, for she had never been completely alone. Rather, she had shifted from the ship to Captain Everett's handsome town house in central London. Her escape plans had changed from one idea to another.

Hazel had steadily walked into another world. She had become someone she didn't know, the mistress of a full house of maids overnight.

Turning to the maid, she stated, "Thank you, Bonny." After a slight pause, "That will be all." So this was the world for which she had been trained.

All Hazel had to do was give orders to run the household in the way that she preferred. Captain Everett had given her full charge. The household staff seemed very happy to follow her every whim.

However, it was not pleasant. This house was not a warm happy home, with her brothers and sisters. She could not laugh over a puppy playing, or run through the grass. Milk a cow, or help make butter. Actually, she didn't help at all here. From dawn to dusk people did everything for her. Dressed her, cleaned for her and even washed her. They were not family, or even friends.

Hazel stiffly sat on the edge of a plump cushion. She listened. There was no noise in the house and no life in the parlour. Only loneliness.

Outside roared with life. People milled

around the square shouting their wares. A horse and buggy clattered by. These things spoke to Hazel of having a purpose. She did not really have a purpose.

However, to her the noise of the town was a strange bellowing. Street life had continuity of noise she found invasive, almost an annoying bother; a very ugly sound. She could not hear one bird singing or the wind swishing through the trees. Slowly she closed her eyes wishing for home. A tear slid down her face. Everything she loved was so very far away.

Instead of sitting, she stood since she had little else to do. With steady control, she slipped across the room and stared out the window. She looked, but did not really see the many people. Instead, she contemplated Captain Everett. Her heart was clenched like a cold hard fist. How she hated him.

Oh yes, he was trying. Since stepping off the ship he had completely changed into the perfect gentleman. The correct clothes. The right manners. Smiling. Chatting with her in a first class manner about the weather and other useless topics.

He seemed to want to get to know her. Be a father to her, but it was too late. He had planned out and manipulated her whole life, but he couldn't make her accept him. No matter how hard he tried. He was not there for her when she grew up. He had not meshed his life with hers. Now he had no right. He was just using her. Reaching out to her, but destroying other people's lives. He stole girls, pirated goods and unmercifully killed people. She would never love such a man as him. Their blood was not thick. No heart pumped between them. Hazel slammed her palm on the windowsill. She would not have it.

Captain Everett had told her that he wished her to stay here in town with him for a time. She had been given an exquisite room, decorated mostly in a soft rose pink, with dark red roses sewn into a heavy quilt that covered a large, but lonely bed. Everett knew that she loved roses. Even the cream pitcher and bowl had large roses, painted beautifully. The room was truly lovely, with a soft relaxing feel. However, she was not going to be lured into this comfortable world.

To make it worse she would never be able to return to her home in Canada. The many letters that she had longed for waited here in this house. From her whole family. She had been given them after they had returned from the horse ride that day.

Captain Everett had given her the excuse that he thought she may become too upset reading all of the letters. So had only allowed her to read a few while on board the ship. Now time had passed, he thought she would better receive them.

Her family wrote of their daily activities and how much they missed her. Her Dadai had written explaining that Captain Everett would destroy their life if Hazel escaped and returned home. With each letter she read, her heart broke a little more.

Hazel wrote back to them of her adventures at sea. She did not tell them of the horrible, disgusting experiences. Like seeing young Molly stolen, raped and sold, or about the sailor whipped to death. She cringed at the thought of Jack, the stinking sailor who grabbed her. Those things would have disturbed her Mamai for the rest of her living days.

Instead, she mentioned that it was a hard life at sea, but an adventure seeing all the different worlds of the earth. Hazel told of the elephants in

India, tribes in Africa and the refinement of Japan. She described the London town house, the many maids and fine riding horses, but never mentioned her loneliness, or the great limitations Captain Everett made her live by. Hazel did not want to cause any more pain. Just to reassure them, she promised that she would not run from Captain Everett to them. If she was to return home it would be because Captain Everett had let her.

Hazel was careful not to imply that she would stay with Captain Everett. After all, that was not to be her future. She had been delayed, but in the next few days she would make her move. The timing was perfect.

Ω

Captain Everett had warned Hazel that as the summer was ending, the social season would start in several weeks. Invitations were already arriving. Those fine dresses were to be put to good use after all.

Everett had said, with a gleam in his eye, "You will be the most picturesque girl with those dresses I had made for you. Every single one was made from the unusual materials that I've collected over our last year of sailing." He eyed her with an overly satisfied expression, "Not one other person will compare to you. With what you'll be wearing, you'll be the belle of the ball."

She supposed that he expected her to be grateful and perhaps thankful. However, she was sure that to him this was like another move on a chessboard. He was beginning to execute his plans for her. Surely they had not travelled for two years upon a wretched ship just to get her the most extraordinary dresses. Playing his game, she carefully turned to him, smiled sweetly and said, "Thank-you. It will be a pleasant change from the sailor's life." At that Everett had the decency to look guilty.

Captain Everett informed her that he had arranged her presentation to be in a few weeks. Invitations were being prepared. The whole of his staff had been in an uproar preparing for their first ball. What with flowers, food, coloured ribbon, plates, glasses and so on. Hazel had been battered with dresses, jewellery, and shoes.

Over the week, Hazel had quietly spied on the mail. Her opportunity finally came while Everett was out one day. Instead of taking the mail directly to Captain Everett, the butler had placed the mail on the hallway stand, ready for Captain Everett to pick up when he arrived home.

Hazel waited for the butler to disappear back to his warm stool in the kitchen. He was unlikely to return. She glanced around searching for maids then quickly, she stepped forward and picked up the pile of mail. In the pile she found three invitations to balls over the next week. Of course Everett would have refused them all on her behalf, for he insisted her first presentation was to be at her own ball.

Hazel was relieved to find the Slately Ball was on the same day as maids planned to practice her hair arrangement. She hurried away back to the Library. In a firm handwriting, that she imagined looked very adult, she replied an acceptance to the invitation as 'Elizabeth Overland.' She hoped the organisers were not pedantic at checking the return cards against the invitation list. The return cards sent matched the invitations after all. They would have hundreds of names and many that were not well known in high society circles. So hopefully they would accept their card back and write her imposter name on the list.

Ω

On the day of the Slately Ball, she sat for hours while the maids perfected her hairstyle. Hazel insisted that they leave it in, "So I can show Father and get his approval," she said. Having hair styled made her plans a little easier.

Hazel quietly finished her dinner then folded her napkin and waited until her plate was removed by a maid. She stood, as she always did, to go to bed. This had been her usual routine while staying in the town house. Cautiously, she had planned to lull Captain Everett into a ritual so he wouldn't suspect her deception.

Placing down his fork, Captain Everett stood in correct politeness as Hazel rose to leave the table. This was her chance tonight. Hazel flicked a look at the maids that stood to attention to wait the table. So as to appear honest, she approached Captain Everett asking, "Do you approve of my hairstyle?" Of course as a typical man he had not even noticed her hair and had barely glanced down the large table at her. He'd only had eyes for his food.

Captain Everett immediately looked upon her hair. He instructed, "Turn." He paused, "Yes, that is lovely, just the way I described it to the maid."

Hazel almost openly expressed her annoyance at this interference with her hairstyle. Her face contorted slightly as she struggled to control herself.

Spotting her face, Captain Everett tried to reassure her, "I am sure that it will be very much the 'in thing'. It is very close to the modern hairstyles of young women attending balls and having those pearls running through your looped hair with the gold, emerald studded roses scattered like so, give you such an air of distinction. All the other girls will have their hair done like you at the subsequent balls."

Hazel forced a smile. He continued, "I wondered if you realised I chose the emeralds to match your green eyes."

Hazel could barely pretend to be happy any more. She feared that she was not making a good show of being the dutiful daughter.

Everett noticed her unhappy expression. He hitched a breath, "You will become accustomed to this place and life. You were trained to be here by one of the best." He grasped for the best thing to say, "Time will make it easier. This is your destiny."

At that Hazel's throat constricted. She supposed that to Everett those poor girls were destined to marry those foul colonials and have unthinkable things inflicted upon them. She turned and swept out of the room. Everett could think of nothing to say after Hazel's quelling look.

Ω

As usual, the maids were dismissed from her room after unbuttoning the back of her dining dress. She quickly slipped off the top dress and one petticoat. She pulled on a thin day sailing dress that was relatively new, but a plain cream and serviceable. Over this, she carefully pulled on the stunning emerald green dress sewn with tiny glass beads.

To do up the difficult buttons, she turned the dress backwards and after every button was perfect, she squeezed the dress back around. Bonny, her personal maid, had been very forthcoming with informing Hazel how to manage her own buttons without help. Although she had given Hazel a queer look for asking strange questions.

The dress sleeves were slightly puffed revealing Hazel's shoulders. Pearls were clustered on each sleeve to match the pearls beaded in a line directly above and below her bosom. The dress swept down creating the fashionable empire style. She clipped on two large emerald earrings and struggled to attach her necklace. She turned the encrusted emerald necklace and centred it on her chest. A large upside-down tear drop finished off at a sharp point almost between her breasts. She could feel her heart beating faster.

Just as she reached over for her shoes, she heard a clatter. She spun herself to face the door waiting to be caught. There was nowhere to hide. She would tell them a tale. Of longing, yes that was it, to see herself dressed for her ball. Yet, if they came in, her plan would be ruined. But, after a few nervous heartbeats, no one had entered the room.

Hazel slipped on her shoes, stopping again to listen to the house noises. Nothing was close. She pulled out her ditty bag she had brought from the ship. No maid bothered to go into this bag. There was no reason to. So in it she had hidden the three bags of gold. She attached these to her garter, under her petticoat again, so they would never leave her side. She was comforted to know that the straps pulled under the weight. After putting on a plain black coat she slipped over top her dark brown, fur evening coat. Then she practised taking both coats off at once so that the plain coat acted as lining for the fur coat. She hoped no one would notice. Her small emerald purse fitted perfectly in her hand. She was ready.

Just to check that she looked perfect, she stood before the long mirror. She caught her breath. Looking back at her was a stranger in the most stunning evening wear she had ever seen. She reached a hand up to touch her throat.

Typically there were no mirrors on the farm in Canada. Even the old mansion where she had learned to be a lady had no mirrors. The widow had been so desperate prior to teaching Hazel that she had sold what she could. Certainly the ship had no mirrors because they could break at the first sign of a rough sea. Mirrors were a luxury and very expensive. One look in the mirror the week before had shown her that her skin was too brown.

Captain Everett had been right; the emeralds matched her eyes to perfection. She had wondered at his choice of costume since most young debutantes wore pale colours to reflect their youth. However, anybody looking would soon understand this colour on her. Dark green accentuated her long brown hair that was piled into shiny curls at the back, with ringlets surrounding her face.

At a ball, it would be perfect for not attracting the wrong type of attention. While the beauty of her outfit would attract attention, she would not look like a young girl who was virginal. She still looked young but she hoped the dress would give her a seasoned appearance. After all, she was eighteen. A bit older than normal to be introduced newly into society.

She picked up her letter knife, wondering where to put it. Her dress had no sleeves to keep it close at hand. Perhaps between her breasts. She tried this, but found it difficult to move. She gave up that thought when she felt it prick her tender skin. It was a silly idea. Possibly she would slice her skin in the rush to protect herself. She placed her hand to her head. Was she up to this? Blinking the useless tears away, she felt she had no choice. All her life until now had been his and for it to become hers, she must run.

Before she dwelt much longer, she fitted the knife into her bejewelled purse and snuffed out the candles. As a further precautionary measure, she wrapped a large, dark grey blanket around her shoulders to hide her rich dress and jewels. The dark colours would help her blend into the streets.

Hazel approached her door and listened intently for noise. It would be unusual for any maid to be up here at this time. They had finished for the day. Dinner would be awaiting them on the kitchen table. Captain Everett would be in his study taking care of his business.

Still, her heart started to pound. Blood rushed to her head. A hot flush washed over her face. She turned the door knob and quietly slipped into the hall. She felt all her senses heighten. The night life had begun to slow down outside. All she could hear now was the bumping and clattering of the rag men in the streets.

Yet, it wasn't until she was downstairs passing the library and nearing the study that a sickening feeling began in her stomach. Saliva rushed to her mouth. She felt like her insides where about to turn. Then she heard Captain Everett's voice droning on the other side of the study. He was speaking as aboard his ship, with that horrible vile gutter accent. Another voice replied. He must be preparing the boats for their next sail. A cold wash of anger crept over her body. She stepped quicker now toward the front door. She certainly would not be on that boat, or at any ball he had arranged.

Quietly, oh so carefully, she opened the door.

Her heart lurched as the door began to screech. She had only opened it a few feet. *Damn the butler for not keeping the door well oiled.* She squeezed through the thin opening into the crisp night air. The weather was turning. Hot days and slightly cool nights. Autumn was coming. Slowly, she shut the door behind her.

Relief flooded her senses. She had escaped without a commotion. As she began down the steps a movement flashed in the corner of her eye.

A man shouted at her, "Oy, whot ya doin'?" Hazel jumped and her hackles raised. A guard. Hazel closed her eyes for a few seconds. Damn, she didn't know he had guards. Plastering a smile on her face to buy some time she turned. *Jack!* Her face dropped. *That disgusting vulture from the ship.* She had avoided him ever since that day he had cornered and groped her.

Jack grabbed her arm and shook her. Her thick blanket fell behind her. He raked over her body with his eyes and snarled, "Takin' a little trip, were ya?"

Hazel tightened her grip on her purse. How was she to get the knife out! "Let go of me. This minute!"

Jack leered toward her, "I dan't think so, Missy." He stunk of drink, stale sweat and the tang of old piss. He shifted his eyes considering her predicament. He slurred, "Well, well. We can finish whot we star'ed." With that he grabbed a fistful of her hair and slobbered over her lips.

Hazel didn't hesitate, she slammed her purse into the side of his neck. The knife sliced neatly through the purse. The thin steel blade hesitated on his tough skin only for a second before slicing his flesh. The blade seared through veins, neatly into his throat, blocking his airways. Hazel's breathing quickened. As he crumbled to the ground, she looked straight into his eyes as they opened in surprise. All she could hear was a light popping sound as blood dribbled from his mouth.

Wildly, she looked up and down the street for witnesses. The rag men were quite a ways up the street. A drunkard covered in an old blanket was shuffling through rubbish and barely seemed to be looking in her direction.

Hazel looked down at the heap before her. She felt no regret. Deep inside she felt a burning satisfaction. She started to shake. She was no better than Captain Everett.

Stepping to one side, she knelt by the body and used her fingers to close his still eyelids. Remembering the technique to kill home beef, she stepped behind his head to remove the knife so as not to be covered in blood. The knife would not come at the first tug. Swallowing hard, she gripped the purse and wrenched the knife away. Blood spurted a little, but not much. He was already dead after all. Surely not one drop had touched her. But at this dark hour it was hard to say. Otherwise the night would be an advantage. No one would see his blood on the step 'till morning. He would look and smell like a drunk rather than dead. For now.

Taking a wide step over the blood, she held the purse low so it did not look conspicuous, but slightly out to the side avoiding the drips. Snatching up the blanket, she rushed off down the street, trotting through three alleyways. She had memorised six streets heading in any direction. Those long walks with an escort had been put to good use. Not hesitating, she knew exactly where to go. The evidence must be destroyed.

Very shortly, she found the rag men. Their furnace to destroy street rubbish burned brightly. Hazel threw the purse and knife into it before the rag men saw her there, or saw what she held. The heat melted away all evidence.

One rag man, with dirt covering every bit of his exposed skin, glanced up at her without pausing in his work. Shovelling rubbish of no use into the fire.

Hazel stated, "Just a little waste I had."

He grunted. A certain sadness surrounded his face. In the way he hunched. Hazel thought he was wishing for the next drink to numb his pain.

A sharp drink sounded good right at this particular moment. This was overwhelming. Her plan had barely started. While she was by the bright fire, she quickly checked herself for blood splatter. Hazel only found a smear on the back of her hand. Using a rag, she rubbed vigorously. The blood disappeared, but she carried on rubbing. Hazel knew she must stop and not allow the horror to affect her. Screwing up the rag, she threw it into the fire. She turned, lifted her precious dress and disappeared into the night.

Ω

Charlie hankered in a quiet corner down the street a little way, hoping the police wouldn't come to clear him off. He wore only one layer and huddled under a thin dirty blanket. Despite the summer heat in the day, the cold night crept through and licked at his skin.

Charlie was not going to leave. Not 'til the light was out in Hazel's room. Then he would return to the empty ship.

All the other shipmates were out drinking away their pay. Charlie could still not believe the fat bag of gold coins that Captain Everett had placed in his hands. His pay and reward was the most money that he had ever seen, or touched. Frittering it away on drink or women was not his way. Only occasionally had he indulged himself with a pint, but he had better uses for his fortune. With this amount he could set up for life. Captain Everett had given him that look that meant 'don't waste this chance'. The chance to make something of himself.

Looking up to the first floor he could see that Hazel had snuffed out all her lights. Charlie stood and stamped his legs to stimulate them a bit. He stretched, feeling a few bones crack. He had been sitting for way too long.

A flash of light caught his eye. A person bundled in a blanket came out the front door. Perhaps a parlour maid on the hop. No, no it couldn't be Hazel. But then Charlie saw her face. She was making her move tonight. Charlie felt like groaning, as a light rain misted in the wind. Jack was bound to catch her anyway.

Hazel had carefully shut the front door. Charlie hoped that she would go back into the safety of her house. The night was a different creature. Any kind of danger could be lurking in the shadows. Everything happened before him within seconds. As soon as Jack grabbed her, Charlie started running down the street towards them. The next thing he saw Jack crumble to the ground. One, or two twitches and he gave up his ghost.

Charlie stood stunned. She had killed him. How? Hazel stood there in a gorgeous gown, with the blanket at her feet. He saw her look down the road away from him. Quickly Charlie turned, swayed slightly while he searched through a rubbish pile. When Hazel had looked his way she would've thought him to be a drunken beggar searching for food. Silently, he shuffled around to watch her. Hazel reflected her farming life in that kill. She stood away from the flow of blood. You would think that she murdered on a daily basis by her calm poise.

She was very clever, taking the blood-soaked purse away with her as she ran down the street. She was leaving no evidence. No connection. Soon her run changed to a stiff walk. Charlie followed her at a close distance as she weaved in and out of the roads and alleys. Many people mulled and loitered in the alleyways. Even one or two rose as though to go at her, but Charlie only had to pounce a few steps and angle his dagger. The street backed away. They knew she was his. He guarded her.

Hazel walked with a firm step, but did not even notice her surroundings. She did not look around, cower, or even startle as a dog barked viciously to one side. If he hadn't known her as he did, he would've thought she had lived here all her life. She must have thought through her escape to the last detail. Rapidly she walked right down to the furnace, where she burned the purse and knife. *Clever girl.*

Loitering at a distance, he watched her enter a coach. As the horses started off with a brisk trot, he softly tucked down on the back of the coach bumper. No one thought anything of it. Youngsters did this all the time. Often they were battered and scared away by a bothered coach driver. Just as long as he didn't get caught.

Charlie wondered what she was doing. Obviously she was running away, but in a ball gown? With nothing much else? He would help her somehow. Captain Everett was not for her. He was too far involved in the criminal world. Look at those poor girls he pawned off. Charlie wasn't sad to be moving on.

After watching as she entered the ball, he

swiftly climbed a large oak tree. He peeked through the window to see Hazel having the time of her life. The dancing was beautiful. Like nothing he had ever seen. She loved it. Perhaps she would return to Captain Everett. This could be simply a rebellious night gallivanting about, but he doubted it. However, all he could do was watch her plan unfold.

5.

As Hazel waited for the porter to open her door, she smoothed her hair. Surely it was not overly ruffled. Jack had only grabbed it once. Stretching her hand to the porter she exited the coach steadily, even with some grace.

The entrance to the grand affair had a few people milling around. They turned and stared at the beauty that had just arrived with no escort. This was unusual for someone so young, but they assumed she must be a widow. A very young widow at that, but still free of the expectations of a fresh debutante. Anyway, she was wearing a stunning deep green outfit, with jewels that could adorn royalty. She was a sight to behold of true beauty and style.

Continuing forward, Hazel's legs felt weak. The coach had been easy to arrange a few days prior to the event. To meet it, she had waited at the door of an empty house on Gran View Drive. On her travels she had noticed the house never had a window open, never a door open. They must not be here for the season yet.

The coach had arrived a full twenty minutes after she reached the deserted house on foot. So she had to hidden on the side of the house steps. As soon as she spotted the hired coach she shot up the steps, turned to the door as though to be shutting it as the coach pulled up. She hoped they would not ask why the lights were not on in the house, or wonder where the butler was.

Thankfully, the driver asked no questions, but rather stared at her in stunned silence. He was surprised by her beauty and riches. He looked at her delicate features. Her flushed face, set aglow. He had never seen anyone with such comely looks. Then, promptly disregarding all sensible things, he had helped her into the coach.

Now arriving at the ball very late, Hazel introduced herself to the doorman as 'Elizabeth Overland'. As she had planned, the hosts had already entered the ballroom well before her and begun the dancing. She did not want to face the hosts who were strangers and convince them they actually knew her.

Hazel left her coat with the butler and rechecked herself in the powder room mirror. There was no sign of blood so she fixed a few strands of her hair. Then taking a deep breath she went to her fate. She only prayed that it would somehow work in her favour.

As she entered the ballroom, many stopped their chatter to look at her. Hazel supposed the entrance that Captain Everett had wanted for her was being achieved. She put on an air of distinction. A few ladies whispered to each other. Almost at a loss for what to do, Hazel simple walked forward. How to merge was something that she had not planned closely. What was she to do now? This was the first ball that she had ever attended.

Mademoiselle had trained her to dance with style and grace. Over and over until blisters formed, cracked and hardened. Reform again over old blisters, burning her feet. Mademoiselle never relented until Hazel could dance without mistake. Her feet became used to the shoes.

Hazel knew the proper way was to be meeting with people. Ladies that she could approach and chat with ease. Inwardly shaking, Hazel knew she had to do something. So she raised her hand slightly and waved across to a someone that she imagined, thus giving the impression that she was going to join a group across the room. She was just buying some time. No one across the large crowded ballroom had seen her yet, but these people staring at her did not know that.

She headed off around the dancing party as though to meet her acquaintances. What on earth was she to do?

Quickly solving her problem however, two gentlemen pounced on her almost immediately. In widowhood, she was approachable. They almost banged into each other, the silly fools, as they offered to dance with her.

Without hesitation Hazel accepted the request of the older man who looked the most wealthy. He wore a perfect suit, in sharp black. A luxurious, thick cream shirt that had heavy gold buttons and matching cuff links at the sleeve. In his shoes she could see her reflection. He displayed every bit of wealth. A fine catch. Just what she needed. From what she had been taught, wealth was everything in high society.

They entered the dance floor and began the waltz. Hazel smiled at this man. She thought he had introduced himself as Henry Fletcher. Not that it really mattered. Nonetheless, she thought that she should treasure the moment. He was her first real partner in ballroom dancing. Until now she had only danced with Mademoiselle.

His experience on the dance floor showed. He turned her in beautiful time. Her body flowed. His lead was strong and keen in judgement. She closed her eyes to feel the movement enter her. The truth and beauty of music, of dance became entwined within her. Oh, how she loved to dance.

She realised that he had not spoken since his first introductions. Surely people talked. All around her Hazel looked at couples, most spoke, but some did not. Maybe she was supposed to speak first. No, no that was not right, she was sure. The gentleman always lead, in movement, attention and speech. A lady was never forward. This was the correct way in high society. A world that had always been far from her up to now. A tinge of homesickness prickled her conscious.

Now was not the time for nostalgia. No, this was a time for perfection, beauty, mystery and deception. This was her chance of escape from the putrid and manipulative weasel that called himself her father. To give herself courage, she focused on the face of Molly. The poor girl, the very picture of innocence and love forced into a world of sex and debauchery. There had been nothing Hazel could do to save Molly. In part, Hazel was escaping for Molly. Punishing Captain Everett in the worst way that she knew. By depriving him the satisfaction of controlling her life.

As the evening progressed, Fletcher had insistently remained at her side. Almost fussing over her as an Uncle. Protecting her from the untoward kind. Directing those around her and keeping the wolves at bay. Not a word had he said in that first dance. He seemed a man of steel. Very correct and unyielding.

Ω

Fletcher had seen her at the door entering. He had been shocked by her lack of a chaperone. Had she been presented already! What was he to say?

Many years had passed since he had last seen her. She must have been just a child. By now she must be eighteen, nineteen. Her name escaped him, but it wasn't Elizabeth. She must have stolen away from her family to attend this ball. He didn't blame her really. No one had ever presented her to society at the usual age of sixteen.

In fact, she never even came to London. Always she had been kept away. Her family had been so unfair to her. Life to her must seem dismal, boring and aged. Really, he had to support her for this night at least and damned be the consequences.

Woe be the day her family found out what she had done. He must protect her for no one else was here to care for her. Posing as an unknown widow was an excellent idea. As a widow she had no need for an escort. Once society caught on to this little secret it was going to spread like wild fire through dry grass. All would discuss it as nothing else.

Glancing at her sideways he lost hope that society would ever forget her. If they did, no one would notice if she was presented in a few months, or next year. Nevertheless, he doubted they would with the way she looked. So stunning. By far the most beautiful woman here, maybe that he had ever seen.

To add to the intrigue, she had a delicate air. So young. Almost as if she needed saving. Probably she thought she did. Oh, well. At least she had the fortitude to change her name. Maybe in a few years she might quietly enter into society in a drab dress. Fletcher thought it more likely though that people would never forget her beautiful face.

Ω

Hazel twirled around the dance floor. Laughing, smiling and chatting. Completely pretending to be something that she wasn't. No one knew her. She could be anyone she decided upon.

Right at this moment she was Elizabeth Overland. Widow of a year. Married in the Great Columbia of Canada many miles away. This explained her slightly strange accent and why they had never seen her, her family, or met her deceased husband. She had travelled to Britain on a whim to see her father's homeland. Maybe she'd stay for a time. Perhaps she would leave in a few days for Germany.

Flippantly, there was no telling; Elizabeth Overland would do as she pleased. Before long, all the men, young and old yearned for her to partner them.

Hazel's plan was succeeding. No doubt Fletcher would fit nicely into her plan. He was so attentive. Willing to shadow her. A tower of dependability. How fitting for her hero.

Her one starring moment very quickly came to an end. She imagined that it would be a long time before she attended a ball again. Wishing that her situation was different, she glanced down the dining table. Fletcher, of course, took her into the dinner and was sitting next to her. However, he was attentively speaking to those nearby, but never asked her history, or showed an interest. This was a little unsettling. Maybe he would not be convinced by what she was about to do. This must work. It was the only way out.

Quivering slightly, Hazel reached up to her throat, claiming to no one definite, "I feel a little faint. I think I will retire to the parlour for a moment and will return shortly." Several nearby had stopped talking and listened to every word. After all, it was rare for a woman to announce, or even quietly slip out to attend the parlour. Almost unacceptable. However, she was new to English high society, so perhaps could be granted some grace. After all, a woman would attend a parlour if she was absolutely desperate.

As she headed toward the door people watched her back, she carefully laid her hand to her chest and held the sharp tear drop emerald. Shutting her eyes for a few seconds, she focused on Molly, then her burning anger toward Everett. She carried on walking. She lifted the emerald slowly, as in a dream up to her hairline. Gritting her teeth, she pierced her head. Pushing and digging the emerald under the skin. She steeled herself against the searing pain. Her step faltered slightly. Her eyes began to blur. They must, absolutely must think she is truly hurt.

Laying the emerald back with complete self-control, she carefully wiped several shaking fingers down the emerald point to rid any fluid. The blood began to dribble around the sides of her left eye. Drip off her nose. Just about there, one more step and she fell very close to the corner of the door. Splaying her hand out before her, she gave the door a satisfyingly loud thunk, while her head hit only her arm against the floor.

Carefully Hazel kept her eyes shut, fluttering them now and again for good measure, she heard a crowd fussing around her. Her head began to pump with pain, a groan escaped her lips. Blood ran into her hair.

Hazel could hear one lady going into hysterics. Others spoke in low, strained tones. A doctor was sent for in the mad rush.

Fletcher leant over her saying, "No, no this can't be happening. What am I going to tell them?"

Hazel still had the sense to wonder what he meant. But there was no way of asking, she must continue with the ruse. This was not the time to be questioning her act, or Fletcher.

Ω

Fletcher commanded, "Back away. Give her some air." Hazel gave another convincing groan. At that, Fletcher picked her up and carried her through the ballroom, out the door and into what must have been the study. Fletcher was convinced that she was about to embarrass herself by vomiting in front of the mob.

Lack of control would pronounce certain disaster in society at large. Instead she would be whisked away and the whole situation would be spoken of as a drama, perhaps a great romance. With himself no doubt caught up within all of the rumours.

This would not be such a bad thing if she was just any girl. Anyone, but the family from which she came. Of course, to Fletcher's relief, she did not vomit, or do anything else amiss.

However, he became quite concerned when she became absolutely still. The only part of her that moved was her chest and the blood that continued to dribble. Taking note of this, he promptly pulled out a handkerchief to press against the cut, stemming the flow. Heads always bled a lot when cut.

After half-an-hour, she still had not wakened and the doctor was still to come. Fletcher leaned forward and put his hands to his head. He knew this was very serious. He began to pray desperately that it would come to nothing. Otherwise he would never be forgiven.

Ω

Charlie saw Hazel fumbling around her face. Her dark green ball dress swished as she walked. He could not view exactly what she was doing, but something was wrong. Very wrong. He could barely see her. His angle was all obscured up the tree. Bending around and changing branches, he bent down for a better view, only to see her falling to the floor between the doorways.

People ran. Some screamed. Charlie thought he was going to shake right off the tree in fright. He had to get to her.

Swinging down from the tree, he thumped on the ground, catching his foot on a raised root. He fell to the ground heavily on one knee. A pain shot up his leg, but it didn't matter. Only Hazel mattered. Struggling up, Charlie forced his legs to move. He managed a few steps, then his ankle gave way beneath him. Grunting in frustration, he forced himself up again. *'The damn foot',* he thought. He tried to convince himself it hardly hurt. A cold sweat began to trickle down his face as he dragged his leg to the entrance of the grand house.

The porter at the front entrance saw Charlie limping into sight. His face was slightly green. He raved, "Let me in. Let me. She's in trouble..." He tried to skirt round the large tubby porter with a red nose and a pompous air. But no one would let him in.

The porter huffed, "Most certainly not. Look at you. You're a disgrace to society, your kind."

Charlie begged, "Please. She's hurt. I saw her fall. I'm suppose to-"

Just in that moment Slately came rushing down the outside steps yelling, "Quick, man. We need to get the doctor. A young lady has fallen and hit her head. It's an emergency." Slately yelled after the footman who had run to get the nearest horse and carriage, "Quick."

The tubby porter flushed red in the face. He had been shown up. Looking Charlie's rags up and down he stated, "It's no matter. You're still not coming in. You look like a street beggar. Such a sorry state! I don't care who you know. Never will the likes of you set a foot in this beautiful house." He growled, "Guards, get rid of him."

Two young, solid men came heavy-footed toward Charlie. Defenceless, Charlie could not stop them. Pain had begun to sear up the side of his leg. His face burned across one cheek. They picked him up in one swoop and dragged him across the street, then down a side alley. Charlie thought he was going to spew at any moment. Dumping him, they gave him a hearty kick in the ribs. Moaning in pain, Charlie turned over to watch them walk away.

Still determined, Charlie dug his fingers into the slimy stone pavers and begun to pull himself back to the end of the alley. He must at least see if she leaves.

As Charlie scrambled forward and around the corner, he could see the carriage leaving to fetch a doctor. Using his arms and one foot, Charlie dragged himself to a dark shadow against the wall. Water dribbled down the wall into a crude drain. He hoisted himself around and lent up against the wall in a sitting position. A blinding pain shot up his leg. His eyesight fazed and tunnelled until he passed out.

Ω

Hazel wondered at Fletcher's concern. He seemed extremely upset. She did not even know the man. Maybe he had high hopes for her. Oh well, he'd fallen for the act hook-line and sinker. Just as she needed and now she longed for the doctor. How much more could she take? In a city there must be many doctors. All she needed was one.

Finally the door rattled as the host and doctor entered. Fletcher jumped up saying, "I thought you would have been here sooner." He turned to the host, who Hazel had not yet met, "Slately, did you go down to the corner, on Mayfair. I am sure the doctor would be home!"

Slately replied in a fluster, "Yes, yes, but Dr Nibblet was attending an emergency already. We had to fetch Dr Hatten from North Kensington"

Ω

The doctor quietly attended Hazel. Gently lifting her eyelids. Inspecting her head. Dr Hatten mumbled, "This seems to be a puncture wound."

Hazel at this point decided it was time to wake. She gave a throaty moan as Fletcher asked in an irate tone, "What did you say, Doctor?"

Rather than answer, Dr Hatten encouraged Hazel, "Just slowly now. You are safe." He made a gruff gurgle from the throat, "Do not try to sit up. Stay lying down."

She fluttered her eyelids, swirled her eyes to the back of the room and settled them on Fletcher. She croaked, "Where am I?" She gave several hard blinks. Gazing, she asked in her most faint voice "Who are you?"

Fletcher began to frown, "I'm Fletcher, my dear. Henry Fletcher friend of-"

He was smartly interrupted by the doctor who seemed to be in a world of his own, "Tell me your name?"

Hazel stared at him. John Slately started, "Well, I am told she is -"

The doctor sharply rose his hand, demanding, "Stop speaking. I have seen this before." Turning to Hazel he asked in a gentle tone, "Do you know who you are?"

She wished that at this moment she could draw a tear, but instead had to make do with a distraught expression. All she mumbled was "I don't kn..., I, I'm sure - I think. Where am I?"

The doctor pursed his lips and nodded, "It's all right. Just rest. Shut your eyes. We will sort this out." He stood and as he exited the room said, "Gentlemen, come." As she watched them go, she could not help a little smug smile. Perfect, everyone has played their part to perfection.

Resting her hand weakly across her stomach, then swapping it to her chest, she sighed. Playing the patient was actually quite tiring. Especially since her head was throbbing.

The three men talked in the hall where she could only just hear snatches. The doctor explained that she possibly had short term to long term memory loss; only time would tell. Things would come back over time. The bleeding was a bad sign. The host, Stately, was insisting that she stay until she recovered enough to return to the comfort of her lodging. Hazel did not care who took her as long as someone did until she could execute the rest of her plan. Stately would do nicely. She could hear them shuffle back toward the door.

Fletcher retorted, "No, I will take her to my mother's. We are family friends." He knew that was not completely true. Yet he must protect her from herself. He continued, "Mother would expect her to visit for a few days as it is."

Hazel's stomach twisted as she heard the doctor declare, "Well, she won't be going anywhere until I have stitched the cut."

Hazel thought the cut can't have been that bad, but it was, so she must face the needle. At least she wouldn't have to act any more through the pain of the stitches. Hazel sighed. Well, well she wasn't the only one telling stories. Fletcher must be very in love with her to lie. Now she thought of it, it was strange that he had hovered over her all evening. She must keep up his interest. She would carry on playing the damsel in distress and court his attention over the next few days.

Ω

A few minutes passed, or possibly an hour. Charlie could hear voices yelling instructions. Yet, his eyes would not open. His head swam while he struggled to make sense of the words. Desperately, he shook his head to clear his mind. He blinked a few times. Charlie's leg contorted in protest and heat raced from his toes up to his hip.

Charlie gasped, "God, help me." At that moment his eyes focused and his hearing sharpened for a minute.

He heard a man snap, "Careful does it. Don't be rough with Miss Overland. Place her next to the maid." A slight pause, "With care, man! With care!" Charlie saw a servant carrying Hazel down the steps with several men following

The servant replied, "Yes, Fletcher, sir."

Another man started, "Look. It might be a bit much for her. She should just stay here, Fletcher!"

Fletcher growled, "No. Mother is expecting her. She'd best be with people she knows."

The man sighed, "Well, I'll drop by in a day or two to see how she is then. Are you staying in your rooms? Or at Cornerstone house."

Fletcher replied, "Cornerstone..."

With some relief, Charlie slumped back into a deep sleep. His black hair matted across his eyes. It did not matter; he knew where she would be. Covering himself with his old rotted blanket, he seemed like a poor, harmless street walker. No one would bother him as he rested.

Ω

After being tucked up in a plump feather quilt, Hazel began to relax. For the first time in over two years she felt relaxed. Safe. A temporary reprieve. Still, she could float away and never wake. Remain in a trance like state from the tiny golden laudanum drops she had been given. All her cares were simple and easy. Fletcher started to question her, "Where are your family, Lizzy? Still in Lacey Green? Here in London? Or the Prince Risborough Castle?"

Hazel frowned wondering at him calling her Lizzy He was a little familiar. She answered, "Oh, far, far away. On the land. Brother, sister, ann-i-mals."

Her speech was slurring, Fletcher knew he must be quick, "So they are near the farms in Lacey Green, or Prince Risborough. Did someone bring you to London?"

Hazel struggled, "Father." Her face contorted, "He, I, the sailor was in the way. The knife was in the purse. He grabbed me. So wrong. Molly, poor girls. Oh weell, they will be...." Hazel gave him a desperate look, "He is evil. He has plans for me! The highest bidder. I will not have it!" she spat, "I will get away. Go somewhere safe. To Mademoissselle!" She closed her eyes, "shhhhhhh. Dooon't telll," she slurred. Wasn't the doctor such a sensible, kind man for giving her this sleeping drug. With that her mind wandered and she fell promptly to sleep.

Fletcher gazed at her. How did she get away from her family? This must have been well thought through. Fletcher's maids had even found she had a day dress hidden under her ball gown. Perhaps she had planned to wear that back on the long trip home to her Aunt in Prince

Risborough, or maybe to 'escape' as she had said.

Already Fletcher had searched in London for her parents. Their London house was completely empty. No one in sight, not a light, or even one servant. Perhaps her father was in town somewhere. He came a few times a year on jaunts. Fletcher did not want to dwell on her father's usual state of infidelity and drunkenness. Everyone in high society 'ignored' him, though at least one incident a year was gossiped. Her father had a colourful reputation. Still, he would surely bring at least three servants. He had never had a reputation of violence, or misconduct with his family. Yet, she was afraid. Fletcher would have supposed that she was dying of boredom stuck in that stuffy castle all these years with only her Aunt. Still you'd never really know why unless you were part of the family.

Surely her father wasn't out there now drinking up and leaving his daughter to her own devices. He was inappropriate at times, but never was his wife or her sister. They kept strict code of social conduct keeping him in line. If they were with him that is. Never in a million years would they allow him to be in London with his daughter and no other escort. He pulled the gold rope and heard a faint tinkle. To be sure that her family were not in London, he would send Halt out to scour the town.

Ann, the maid, entered the room within three heart beats. His conduct with this girl was most improper, but he had needed to get information out of her as the laudanum began to take effect. No other person was to hear what was being said. The servants had accepted with a little suspicion that Elizabeth Overland was here due to an accident and memory loss.

Ann was faithful to her master. She could be trusted, even if she was a little young and fawned over him occasionally. He had only been alone with this strange girl for a few minutes. It was obvious nothing inappropriate could have happened.

6.

After spending hours in his office organising the cargo and crew, Captain Everett saw William Clifton to the kitchen where Clifton wished to visit an old friend from childhood years. Everett had promoted Clifton to Captain, to take over his ship *Loretta* while he wasn't sailing. Clifton had been sailing with Captain Todd for years. He was quickly promoted from cabin boy. He thought Clifton may do well, perhaps a little young for Captaincy. However, Everett recalled he had been young when he took on his first command. Clifton showed promise despite his high-class background and had the loyalty of a dog. When the time came to sail again, Everett decided Clifton would be promoted permanently to another of his ships as long as Clifton turned a decent profit.

Picking up the paper, Everett settled in the library for a good read before heading to bed. First, he studied the stock market, of course Batten's were doing well as were several smaller companies, coal mines, silver and gold. Therefore, the bank owners like the Clance's were disgustingly rich. The Clance's finances were an avenue Everett knew he could never touch. The Clance's never sold more stock than their 51% share. A shame really since Captain Everett would have blown them out of the water several times over. No matter what way there was to look at it, Clance was safe financially.

So, instead, Everett planned to destroy their reputation. Perhaps after Clance was socially ruined, Everett could buy out their share in the banking firm. Everett could feel his excitement mounting. Soon they would be destroyed, because he had the one thing that would be a disgrace to them. He had Hazel.

Hazel looked the image of her birth mother, Celia Clance. Except for the startling green eyes that marked Hazel as his child. Otherwise, Hazel had Celia's luxurious brown hair that fell in glossy waves, the same distinct oval face, her lips were full kissed with a natural dark red and even her forehead rose in the same way. There was no denying it, he was Hazel's father and Celia, that conniving, vindictive bitch, was her mother. Celia Clance had been the love of his life, his biggest regret and greatest loss.

Everett had kept Hazel much to himself and had not introduced her to anyone as yet. Nonetheless, many invitations for this season had come his way, as usual.

People would assume Hazel to be his bastard daughter, but her wealth would be so large that high society would simply look the other way. They'd chosen to totally ignore the fact that he had no wife. Hazel would obviously be named as Captain Everett's and society would assume she was due to inherit all his wealth.

After all, Captain Everett was unlikely to marry. There was no son. Or so they all thought.

Hazel was so beautiful. Who would not be proud to have her as a wife? She would undoubtedly be the catch of the season. As long as Hazel followed his plan, no harm would be done. Her success would not be harmed by Celia's demise from society.

Everett wished he could have more of a friendship with Hazel, but over their time on the ship nothing had developed as he'd hoped. He loved her at least. She was his precious daughter. He would see that no real harm came to her and that she married well.

Everett sipped his port, remembering back to when Hazel was a small babe in his arms. He was only twenty-two years at the time. Yet old enough that he had lived a lifetime; hardened by destitution, softened by love.

Directly after her birth, Everett had wrapped her up in a fine baby blanket and secured her under his jersey and coat. Occasionally, he felt her wriggle.

Far up on the hill, he spotted a cleft of sharp rocks just right to leave a baby exposed to the air. This needed to be done quickly. Glancing behind him to make sure nobody followed, he gave the horses flanks a tight squeeze. Racing up the side, the cold wind wailed through the pine trees as though in mourning. Frosty air puffed out Everett's mouth. Bits of tree, branches, leaves and an icy rain whipped his face. His horse slowed as it climbed further up the steep ascent.

As he rounded the side of the cliff, he stopped. Reaching under the bottom of his oil coat, he pulled out the little thing wriggling beneath. He held her small, light waist with one hand. Her whole body slumped in response to the difficult grasp about her middle. As her beautiful blanket slipped from her body, her pink nakedness was exposed to the slicing wind and sharp rain. In that moment she began to scream, high pitched and angry, as though in this instant she had been birthed into the ugly world.

She begun to slip to one side. In an instant, Everett dropped his slimy reins and grabbed her head to prevent her from smashing to the ground. He hugged her to his body and he knew he couldn't do it. He knew. This small life was a being that he had created with love and should not have to pay for his sins. No, his child would not pay. Quickly, he tucked her back up his shirt.

Even the fine horse he rode heaved and blew by the time they made it to the docks. Time was of the essence. His legs felt like stiff frozen logs, and he couldn't even feel his feet. The wet had even started to penetrate his oilskin coat. Struggling to stand as the numbness in his feet turned to sharp pain, he climbed down and simply slapped the horse's rump. The dripping wet stallion walked away, saddle and all.

Everett watched the fine, highly-bred horse for a moment as it wandered up the hill, left to do as it will. The cold wind whistled up and the spent horse slowly crumbled to the ground. The stallion fell to one side and its feet kicked in the air. Struggling, it tried in vain to right itself, but it remained there blowing in and out, waiting to die. Everett knew that he had ridden a good horse to its death, but now he had a baby to worry over. Not to forget that someone maybe pursuing him for Celia's sake.

Once in his cabin, he unbuttoned his coat and peered in the top of his jersey, revealing a little face resting upon her crumpled arms, curled under her chubby cheek. Her little eyes were closed shut and her little lip pouted. Captain Everett frowned at the bloody scrap of life, he thought again he should have just left her. Let her drop as he rode, before he had time to think. Maybe he should still dangle the baby over the side of his ship and simply let go. Allow the babe to slip into the rough sea, out over the wide ocean. No one would ever know.

She scared him with her smallness and frailty. What was he to do with a baby? Yet, the little infant had softened his heart. She was his flesh and blood. Such a vulnerable little thing.

Ω

Occasionally, over the following three and a half weeks sailing, he thought it would have been kinder to have got rid of her. The first few days were fine. Occasionally he gave her water. Surely he would find someone in Ireland to care for her.

Despite trying to resist, he felt himself drawing close to her. The little scrapper. She calmed at his touch. Loved his cuddles. The unusual desperation he felt for her was frightening. He had only seldom been touched by the need of another human being.

In Ireland he found plenty of women ready to wet nurse, but they came with a whole brood of children. Where would he keep them all? They would drive him nuts. Captain Everett cringed at the thought of his ship turning into a children's nursery. The crew would probably quit.

He could only spare one day to sort out a wet nurse. The only alternative he could find was an old sailor who claimed to be a cook and knew how to feed anything, including a baby. Thankfully, Old Hank did seem to know what to do. He said he had experience from twelve younger siblings and four of his own children.

The old man insisted on bringing aboard a nanny goat and kid purchased from the market. From there, they cast off to their distant destination, Canada. Old Hank was left to his charge, only to find that mash of any kind would be spewed back. Only the milk dribbled into her mouth stayed down. However, the Nanny only yielded a small amount of milk. Much of which was spilled anyway by the naked wriggly little babe. The fire remained hot, warming the cabin against the mid-spring weather. At least she didn't freeze.

Time drifted on and Hank became desperate.

The ship sailed in the middle of the wide ocean, so his options were few and far between. Even the kid goat was slaughtered and stewed so that Old Hank could milk the nanny more. However, the nanny, now stationed in the cabin, still had not yielded. She seemed to bleat in desperation for her little one.

In the end, the only thing that calmed the baby was a rough sea. The rocking soothed her.

Ω

After a week of torture, Captain Everett had begun to avoid his cabin most days. At nights, he would enter the cabin filled with the stench of goat piss, crap and sour milk. All this mixed with a variety of foods, male sweat and the smell of fear. Quickly he'd look at her before retiring below deck. The babe often cried 'till her open mouth produced no sound. Hank thought she may die from crying too much. He dared not leave the room.

A week out from Canada, Old Hank began to question his desperation at taking up this job. Had Ireland really been that bad? Slowly starving to death sounded better at this moment in time.

The little infant's bum was raw. Hank was absolutely sure leaving crap on the bottom had healing qualities. He mustn't wash her.

Perhaps he was beginning to hate her. No wonder he heard tales of women killing their young. Yes, yes she could die. Then he wouldn't have to hear the screams, or see her.

Ω

Quietly, entering the cabin at midday to find his drinking cup, Captain Everett saw Old Hank hanging his baby over a pot of boiling water. Everett paused, he gave Hank the benefit of the doubt, because he had heard that steam helped sickness. No, he was lowering her head into it. In one swift movement, Captain Everett shot across the room and grabbed his babe. With the other hand he grasped around Old Hank's neck and jammed his foot on top of his. Stretching him up, the old bones gave way quite easily with a soft pop. Everett dropped him where he stood.

Looking at his child, he felt lost. He should have got a woman. A nurse maid, with all her children. This was way beyond him. What had he been thinking to take her? Why had he plotted and waited for her birth? Spying, till he saw Celia bending in pain. He knew. He took what was his. He was to kill this child so that Celia couldn't have her. He took her because he wanted no one else to have his babe and claim her for their own.

However, facing reality, Everett knew without a shadow of a doubt this baby needed a mother and that he was not enough. She must have a good mother and secure life. Maybe after a few years he would take her on the ship again. Then she would not need a mother. When she could eat and drink. Then he could have her. Care for her.

Ω

Captain Everett swirled the last of his port in his glass. Sally was truly a God send when Everett found her on the wharf that day in Saint John.

He had considered taking Hazel when she was three, but he returned to Canada, to the warm home of the Donaldson's only to find Hazel was petrified of him. She hid behind Sally's skirts. No one in the house was happy to see him.

They loved Hazel. Knowing her feelings, they held her close, in fear he would take her. The family were healthy and happy. Everett was not going to deprive his daughter of their family home.

Captain Everett cursed at himself for his softness. Staring at Hazel's face he saw Celia staring back.

To hide his tender heart, he started to threaten the Donaldson's. Their fear had been too easy to play with. He'd reminded himself that they worked for him. So he kept behaving like a devil. Just to add to their fear he promised to take her.

Time drifted and he was never sure what to do with her. However, as she came nearer to womanhood, Everett decided to keep his promise to educate her well beyond a farmer's station. Hazel completed her middle schooling by eleven and had ladies training with a local French mistress of his choice. The old French widow had nothing left, but a large empty house and death. Probably starvation. Without giving argument, Mademoiselle Fleur agreed to teach Hazel all she needed to know about society.

Mademoiselle Fleur had known the vibrant life of France. The beauty of England. She had been the belle of every ball and was free. Her well-planned marriage had been useless after the French Revolution. No children were born and as the years slipped by her husband had frittered away the little wealth they had in Canada. When he died, she discovered that she was left with nothing.

Captain Everett kept Mademoiselle Fleur on her toes by demanding results. Otherwise she would lose her very generous income. Hazel was pushed hard to be changed from her farming ways to upper class composure. Her training and education was relentless. Captain Everett was very pleased, but never showed it. After he was sure she had been educated like a lady he decided to take her into society. He thought by sixteen she was well old enough to leave the Donaldsons. Widow Fleur had done nicely out of it and had several more girls training by the time he left with Hazel.

The way Everett looked at it, Hazel's life had improved many situations. Right from the Donaldson's family to the few spies who had kept everyone in line over the years, and everyone in between. Never had they been grateful to him. Always afraid.

A little fear was good, but to show no thanks? So, after her sixteenth birthday, he'd taken great pleasure in whisking her away. The time was right anyway. Didn't they see that! She needed to be presented. Besides he wanted to show her the wonders of the world first.

Hoping that she would grow close to him over a few years at sea, his intention was to show her his life and how he built his empire. To show her how he helped has many people as he could. Occasionally, he smuggled in much needed goods to help the poor who could not afford it elsewhere. Then there were the young girls he saved from a life of prostitution.

Some of the girls he purchased had come from well-to-do homes. Their fathers had gambled away their inherited money. These men sold their daughters to pay their way through 'hard times'. These poor innocent girls knew nothing of prostitution. They ended up in high- end Madam houses for extremely rich gentle-men visitors. Those girls who were brought to Captain Everett's attention were the lucky ones. The saved ones. Of course, Captain Everett sold them to reputable men who wished for a British wife, but only if the girl chose that way. They could go back to prostitution if they wished, or find some other employment. None ever had.

However, Captain Everett found the real world pierced Hazel's heart. Slowly, over the year, she withdrew. Everett found himself withdrawing too. He saw her confusion over the young girls sold to him and he sold on. He didn't even make profit. In fact, none. He never used them for himself, or gave them to the sailors. Yet Hazel didn't understand that the girls' families had sold them as virgins into prostitution. She didn't see that he was offering them a better life.

He usually protected them while they were on board. Except for Molly's situation, which had angered him beyond belief. Molly's stupid father had dropped her off to the ship a day early and left her with the sailors. Nonetheless, a life forced into prostitution, barely in womanhood, would have been even worse for Molly. A child whore was truly cruel and bleak. A life in the New Zealand colonies was difficult, but better for the girl in the long run.

Gradually Hazel grew hard, cold even, and Everett angry. He almost wanted to give up helping these poor girls. Maybe he would. Anyway, now they were finally settled in London, he had a plan for her. She would never know the devastation she was about to cause at her presentation.

Ω

In the wee hours of the morning, an irate and nervous Rob came to wake Captain Everett. "Sir, sir, wake up. The watch man. He's dead."

Captain Everett jumped to his feet and shook his head so as to wake. He had been in a dead sleep. At this hour, the door guards would be changing night watch.

Rob continued, "It's Jack at the front. He was murdered." Rob sat on the nearby chair, uninvited. This showed he was really strained. For no one sat in Captain Everett's presence without an invite. Rob shook his head in despair, "I'll never forget the look on his face. So peaceful. Like asleep."

Everett hastily dressed. Eventually Rob followed him down to the bottom floor and out to the front steps.

Captain Everett stared down at Jack, one of his best sailors. He had never been anything more. Jack had been rough as guts. At times he had been associated with a bit of crime, but nothing had ever been substantiated. Still, Jack had done his job well and always showed up on time before they cast off.

Captain Everett stared down at the dead body. The person that killed him seemed to know what they were doing with only one clean wound to the neck. Nothing messy; quick and neat. Probably a thug stealing a few coins. Barely any blood had pooled, showing the death had been quick. Everett glanced down the street on both sides. No one, of course. This was a clean and quiet street after all. At two o'clock in the morning it was completely deserted.

Rob asked, "Capn', shall I go for the coppers?"

Captain Everett turn to Rob, "Why, yes. That is probably the best idea."

As Rob ran off, Captain Everett checked Jack's pockets. They still contained three shillings and a rotating knife. That was suspicious. Captain Everett wanted no trouble with the police, so he took the coins and knife. Better that they thought it a theft.

He turned things over in his mind. This murder must have been revenge, or a necessity to defend. Jack had plenty of enemies, but he knew how to hold his own. How on earth had someone actually done this? Jack had won most of his fights in the ring. Unless he was killed by someone he trusted. Everett decided it would remain a puzzle.

Rob returned after a short while with two policemen. They came to the conclusion that was simplest for Captain Everett, a basic murder and robbery. So it was tied up neatly and Jack's body was trundled away to the morgue. There was very little to inquire about, other than asking around for witnesses. Most likely none would come forward. Jack's murder was only another death of no one important.

Captain Everett paid Rob a few shillings and sent him packing. There was no point losing him over this and there is no way he would stay guard at this door again. Superstition was strong among the sailors. So Rob may as well go happy to bed with a little extra money for his troubles.

Everett pondered over the fact that Jack had been guarding his door. Maybe someone wanted to get in to do him harm and found Jack here at the front door. Perhaps someone wanted to get out quiet like. Suddenly Everett's mind clicked into place. *Hazel.* No, she was not a trained killer. She would not have been able to do this so efficiently. Even so, it would pay to check.

Quiet as a mouse, Everett crept up to Hazel's room. Opening her door, he poked his head round. He held a little candle for its soft light. He could see the blankets were bundled around her. He crept up to her to take a look at her face. Everett still dreaded that she might be gone. He had to keep her safe. He looked. No face. Pulling back the blankets he found the pillows stuffed in place of her body.

Ω

Suddenly the silence of the house was broken by his screams. All hell broke loose. The butler ran in, wearing his nightdress. Maids came with nightgowns. The cook slept right through and had to be fetched. Captain Everett was having a turn. His face changed to a deep shade of purple. No words came from his mouth. None were needed. His girl was gone. He had fussed over her like none of them had ever seen. He must love her. Cherish her. Over the years they heard her every milestone and accident. All he ever spoke about was Hazel all these years. Why would she run away? Why? Had he not gone nearly every year to see her! Did she have someone to run to? Had someone taken her?

The servants were confused. Their master had always been so good and proper in London that they could not imagine anything else. Captain Everett had never given them reason to complain. In fact, they were treated and paid so well that his employment was chased after. Finally he started to gasp. They must find her.

Ω

After a time, Captain Everett collected his thoughts. They all waited for his direction. Standing there, wringing their hands.

He managed, "I think Hazel is a little stressed from settling in London. Quickly Tinker, go look for her in the Northern streets, Riley, the South, Pamela and Judy, the Western and let's hope to God that she has not gone to the East near Whitechapel. Send two men in that direction. Send the footmen."

"Yes, sir." They all ran to change into some heavy clothes to guard against the chilly night air.

He yelled after them, "Make sure you are all armed. I am heading to the docks. That is where she is." As a last thought he commanded, "No police – not even a mention." They would connect Jack's murder to Hazel. "Say to people she has been missing for over twelve hours." *That should deter questions.*

His staff would be paid handsomely this year for their silence. However, on second thought, if the police did find out, all he would need was a statement from Hazel to say Jack attacked her and a witness was always easy to find. Alternatively, he could suggest to them that she was kidnapped, but he knew this was not true. She had been so unhappy. What had she done other than push him away!

Everett checked around the room. Her green dress, jewels, purse and two coats were missing. On closer inspection, he found a day dress gone. Looking at her desk, he couldn't find her mother of pearl letter knife. Shaking slightly, Everett realised his refined, well-breed daughter had murdered a man to escape him.

They spent all evening traipsing the streets. Even in the roughest parts a few dead women were examined. Nothing was found. Nothing for days. All the leads were dead ends. Then Everett had an idea, she may not have pawned off the dress and jewels for money. She may have used them.

Ω

Snuggling down into a soft armchair, Hazel sighed peacefully. A maid covered her in a soft blanket and another put a hot cup of tea at her side.

Hazel smiled at the maids and said, "That will be all."

The maids smiled back, curtsied and only drew the door to, in case she called out.

Hazel was expected to stay put in the chair at doctor's orders. Thus, she was not to take on the strain of pulling the bell rope. After all, she might faint. In fact she was sure the young maids secretly hoped Hazel did faint so they could serve her longer. They told her often enough that she was a joy to look after, unlike the crabby old mistress. To add, Fletcher was just a man. Even though he was kind, he was a bit unembellished. Besides his valet was his main man. Serving Elizabeth had created interest and excitement for the whole house.

Shortly after the maids had left, Hazel stood and wandered to the window. The street was quiet on a Sunday. She heard in the distance the church bells tolling. She leaned to the side of the window, curled her hands around her warm cup and sighed.

Toward the front of the house she heard a knock at the door. Nearly all day this house had visitors of some kind. The post, delivery, business, a stiff old friend of Lady Eleanor 's.

Thank goodness the state she was in allowed her solitude rather than outside company. Come to think of it, she had hardly had company of any kind in the last three days. Lady Eleanor enquired through the maids after her health, but correctly maintained a distance. Surprisingly, Fletcher had hardly dropped in more than a few minutes a day. He didn't even claim he was busy. He simply enquired after her health. Hazel supposed he was not so in love with her after all.

Anyhow, it made it much easier for her. She had plenty of time to plan and wait until her father had finished searching the docks for her. Surely he would assume she was running back to Canada. By now he would be sailing after a Canadian ship of some sort. A few of them left the docks every day. Surely the fact her plain sailing dress was missing would lead him to think she was abroad. Any number of girls would wear a similar one and she could have given any name to board the ship. She could have used a surname of another family sailing. No one would be able to say for sure.

Fletcher had already mentioned that she must return to her 'family' soon and face the music. She did not remember mentioning a family as such. He was only assuming. He knew nothing about her.

With alarm, she realised he expected her to send word to someone, but she hadn't. He might be suspicious. How could she send word to no one?

While thinking this problem through, Hazel's ears pricked up when she heard a far away thrum of raised voices. Fletcher's voice sounded strained. Another man replied.

Everett!

Hazel would recognise his voice anywhere.

She stiffened. Hairs on her neck rose. The blood drained from her face. Hazel quickly realised she was stuck. If she went into the hall they may see her. *The window!* She pushed and shoved it up only a hand width. A fingernail caught, ripping from her finger. Blood dripped, but she didn't stop. She must get away. He must not get her. Glancing at the top of the window she saw it was blocked to keep thieves out.

Her ear pumped. Tears started. Desperate and petrified. *Hide!* She quickly folded her blanket neatly behind the seat and placed the tea beneath it. Just in case they came in, she needed to conceal herself. Her eyes tore around the library. *The grandfather clock!* She opened the large door of the pendulum and squeezed inside. She had to stop the clock. Hopefully no one would notice. She barely breathed.

As her breathing settled she heard the yelling.

Ω

Everett insisted, "I know she is here. She came here after the ball!"

Fletcher snarled, "No one here is called Hazel, or even Elizabeth. You are confused. I only have the Clance girl here. Of Prince Risborough Esta-"

Everett went white, he interrupted, "Clance!" The shock showed. He walked toward the open door. Turning, he stated, "I thought you had not spoken to Beatrice Clance or her sister for years. How many daughters does Celia Clance have?"

Fletcher frowned, "Three, I think. Maybe more." Fletcher wanted to be rid of him, "The girl has come to us so she can attend the season. She is too young to be in the family house by herself." He hoped Everett would not question him further.

Everett's mind spun. So Fletcher must be talking of a younger Clance girl ready for society. Everett insisted, "But she wore a dark green dress. She had on the jewels and -."

Fletcher interrupted, "Yes, yes well. I hate to admit, she purchased them yesterday near the wharf from a pawn shop. We were desperate to find another dress at short notice. Her other dresses fell out of her travel bag. The stupid porter boy dropped it. Many of her dresses were ruined. Poor thing." He paused, "We were rushed into the decision of having her here. Her family will be able to come to London soon... when Mr Clance is well." Fletcher scrambled for more excuses, "They decided she must attend this season after all. Despite Otto Clance's health. So it was a bit of a rush. The clothes and jewel's were new though. I can get her down to meet you, if you want?"

Everett paled, "No, no.... No bother." The wind had been taken completely from his sails. To meet the other daughter might inadvertently let the cat out of the bag. Celia might find out that Everett had their daughter in London. "I'll... I'll be on my way."

Fletcher gave a sorry look, "You know yourself that people pawn goods off for various reasons." He paused, "Did she have a reason to run?" Again he waited on Everett who seemed to be daydreaming. Fletcher continued, "Look, man, I am sure you'll find her, but not in this house. You know I wouldn't have you on. Why would I? We have been friends for years. I watched you rise. I helped you get your ticket. You saved my life." Fletcher looked at Everett with such earnestness that Everett began to think he had been barking up the wrong tree.

Everett said slowly, "I don't know what to do. I have been looking for her for days. She has never been to London before. She is my only daughter." He looked off to the distance, "She must have sold those valuable things to make her way. She had no money." Everett considered things deeply, "I wonder where she is. I have no leads. Only the thought that she has returned to her home in Canada."

Fletcher watched as Everett's eye started twitching.

Everett admitted, "She didn't really want to come away. Maybe I made a mistake. I should have reared her myself from the first, but the sea life is too rough to make a lady. However, she is a lady and her years at sea with me were too much. She's a tough one though. Must get that from me."

Fletcher consoled him, "Look these things take time. Come back into the study and have a drink. We will devise a plan. You'll find her." The men went back into the study and closed the door.

Ω

Hazel barely breathed. She felt faint and slightly off. Climbing out of the grandfather clock, she called her maid. In that moment she noticed something flutter to the floor from the clock. Quickly, she snatched the note off the floor and hid it in her hand.

The maid came in. "Miss, you should be resting. You do not need to fold this." Referring to the blanket.

Hazel barely whispered since she did not want to risk being heard, "Leave it. I must lie down in my room. I don't want to be disturbed by anyone."

With that, Hazel went up to her room, locking her door behind her. The strain of the situation quivered through her body. She looked down at her stinging hands. In the heat of the moment, her fingernails had dug neat groves into her palm. Blood seeped across her palm. Her jagged finger nail throbbed and dripped blood.

She must get away. If she couldn't convince Fletcher to give her freedom as a widow to do as she willed, she would have to leave. Run away again. Who knows, maybe he had plans for her like Everett. He seemed rather keen to keep her and was telling plenty of lies. A sense of relief washed over Hazel. At least he had deterred the worst person she had ever known. Handling Fletcher should not be so hard.

Ω

In the evening, Hazel joined Fletcher at dinner, wanting to appear well. As the meal progressed, she approached her real objective by saying, "Thank-you so much for your help. I feel much more myself today. I even recall one or two things. I think tomorrow I will be on my way."
Fletcher just eye-balled her, so she continued, "I think it best to return to my mother's. Surely I will recover best there."

Fletcher replied stiffly, "Yes. It is time for you to return to your family. I do believe your Aunt is only 3-4 hours out. So perhaps that would be the best choice."

Hazel frowned and tilted her head in frustration. "I do not know this Aunt well. So I will not go there!"

At that Fletcher's eyebrows raised slightly. He snapped, "You can drop the act. I may not have seen you for a number of years and you were a child at the time, but I do know you. Tomorrow you will return to Lacey Green in case your parents are there, and if they are not, then on to Prince Risborough Castle." His face scowled, "You will just have to face the consequences for you actions. Running away like that! I have only just managed to deter anything untoward and now you will do as you're told!"

A shock ran through Hazel. She thought, 'He truly thinks I am someone else'. Maybe she would have to play her part to get away. "I am sorry to inconvenience you. I will be on my way tomorrow." With that she left her dinner and rushed out of the room, trying to give a devastated appearance. She decided that when she was in his carriage tomorrow, she would simply tell the driver to take her to the docks.

Hazel was to board the ship for France at the 3 o'clock high tide. On the other side, Mademoiselle Bella Fleur was expecting her in Trouville-sur-Mer. Everett would never find her there. He didn't even know Bella had shifted back there on the money he paid her for training Hazel.

Hazel had intercepted a letter from Mademoiselle before Everett had a chance to see it. In the letter Mademoiselle had sent her new address by the seaside in France where she was setting up a lady's training school for young girls. Mademoiselle Bella had worked Hazel hard, but she was never mean. She was old, with no relatives and would love to have Hazel. Especially, if Everett was so cruel.

Since leaving Canada Hazel had sent Mademoiselle notes now and again. Mademoiselle Bella had sent only one other letter, heavily coded, via the Donaldson's, who posted Mademoiselle's letter with Canadian post marks. Hazel hoped Everett assumed Mademoiselle had just written Hazel a simple letter from Canada. However, after decoding the letter, Hazel knew it was a letter welcoming her to come to Trouville-sur-Mer.

7.

The following day Hazel leaned back on Henry's plush carriage seats. The letter she held made a good fan. She had watched on as Fletcher had written it;

Dear Mistress Hadley,

I am sending her to you in good health. She was welcome with us for her short stay and was entirely safe and well cared for. I leave her in your most capable hands, safe in the knowledge you will make the wisest choice in regards to her future.

Kindest Regards,
Henry Fletcher

Fletcher seemed to be certain she was someone else. He claimed to have met her when she was a child with her Mother and Aunt. Hazel could not conceive how he would be so sure she was this other person. She was sure he had called her Lizzy a few times. What were the chances she looked like a child Fletcher had once met, called Lizzy? Hazel supposed he was more certain because she had by chance called herself 'Elizabeth'. Fletcher also seemed to believe she had pretended to be a widow to attend the ball without a chaperone, because he had growled, "Lizzy, your family would never allow you to wonder around London, attending balls at your own free will. You have not even had your coming out yet!" How very close he was to the truth. Yet, so very wrong.

Unfortunately, no amount of coaxing, bribery, or pleading had convinced the coachman to take her to the London docks. Oh no, he had been warned of her desperation to get away from 'the family'. In a way that was true, but only to get away from her cruel father. At least they weren't returning her to him. So she hoped. To do that would be twisted fate!

After looking out at the countryside for a long time, she became fatigued. After another half hour, Hazel began to watch out the window to get a glimpse at her supposed 'Aunt's country estate'.

When it came into view the sight of it astounded her. Huge, willowy birches lined the drive, with tiny silver leaves. They swept down around a large pond hosting a multiple of blooming lilies in pinks, golds and whites. Beyond this lay a large castle within a generous moat. The towering grey stone matching the silver dollar birches. Windows shone in the hot sun.

To one side of the castle, many buildings formed a village of sorts. On the other side were small outer houses where Hazel supposed some of the privileged servants lived. Those smaller houses were the size of what she had lived in all her life on the farm. They were tiny in comparison to the large towering castle. As far as the eye could see, paddocks spread across the landscape. Looking at the lay of the farm lands, a small feeling of longing stirred.

Instantly, Hazel wanted to stay. She needed a place to rest and recuperate for awhile. Her head still needed time to heal and Captain Everett might catch her if she went to the docks too soon. Everett would not suspect her to be here. Surely Fletcher would not have been so cunning as to devise this plan to push her straight back into Everett's arms in the country.

However, the two men were friends. Pleading with God, she willed Captain Everett away.

Well, there was nothing else she could do. There was no escaping the carriage. Hazel began to tick over her options in her mind. The letter Fletcher had written was by and large quite neutral. She could claim to be anyone, a maid, cook or maybe a distant relative. By the time they rattled over the moat bridge into the front court, she had thought of a way to deal with the strangers she was about to meet.

Standing beside the carriage, Hazel smoothed out her plain cream, rumpled dress. She had her hair tied up with a simple cream ribbon. Her plain black shoes matched her plain black coat. In the old musty carpet bag, borrowed from Lady Eleanor, she had put her beautiful jewels, dress, bags of coins and a few other extras. No one here would see them, so she would not need to explain them. By all appearances, she could be from nearly any station of life.

Entering the front door, she followed the old shuffling butler to the study. With slight amusement in his weak milky eyes, he stated, "Wait here".

Hazel entered the study and replied, "Ta." Sitting down on a stiff wooden seat, she waited for some time for the Mistress to finish her lunch.

Ω

Charlie hadn't seen Hazel for a few days. He simply stood in the street watching Henry Fletcher's town house. Cornerstone was a tall formidable building of stones layered with mortar. The windows were tall and shiny, making them difficult to see through by day. To add, the maids religiously closed the curtains just before dusk.

Charlie became more frustrated as the days marched by. He carefully watched all the comings, and goings. Mail carrier, milkman, maids, business, messages and Fletcher. Damn Fletcher. He took her and now she had disappeared.

As the days began to stretch, Charlie started to consider Hazel may not be there at all. After all the hours of watching and waiting, she had possibly gone from him for good. He'd even watched Captain Everett come and go without her. Surely she was not there any longer. A week had gone by and not one damn flicker. Not even a face in the window. A feeling of moroseness settled upon his heart.

Charlie knew he should have spoken to her on the ship. He had many opportunities, but never the courage. He was weak and now she had slipped between his fingers. Any amount of trouble could have come her way. Thoughts swung around his head. Many repeatedly, until he thought he might crack. Had Hazel left the house without him seeing?

He rarely left his post. His bad leg kept him where he was. People who passed by in the day sold food, fruit and drink, so there was little reason to move. Only the once, damn it. Only once. He had been removed for loitering on the street by a grumpy police man who just came upon him by chance. He had to limp away, far down a side alley.

Coming to the conclusion she must be gone, Charlie decided to question the servants. However, getting information out of Fletcher's servants was like trying to draw blood from a stone. They clearly had been paid for their silence and obviously respected their Master to keep such juicy gossip to themselves. If only they understood what Hazel meant to him. She was the love of his life. He breathed for her. His existence was all about keeping her safe.

Charlie knew it was strange to be compelled to watch someone you had never spoken with. Yet, it was his whole life. Spying was familiar and comforting, but he knew it must stop. He must step out and take the risk of speaking to her. To do so would be better in the long run, no matter how it ended.

Charlie was sure he would get to know Hazel if only he could speak with her. The timing needed to be right. Soon then he would speak with her. He could not spy on her for the rest of his life. Like a shadow stuck to a person's side. If he only did that he would truly become like his Dad, a bitter old man.

Ω

Desperate for information, Charlie decided to resort to bullying the Cornerstone servants. The next time he cornered someone, they would talk. He was done with being nice.

He waited at the back of the house for the young footman to come for his usual mid-day smoke. The back court yard was a quiet space, out of the way. The footman was small in stature and Charlie hoped, despite his bad leg, he would be able to hold on.

Charlie planted his back to the old stone wall. Balancing on his good leg, he stuck the other out to the side. Over the last year sailing, Charlie had truly lost the gangly arms and legs of his youth. His chest had broadened, arms had thickened with muscle and he towered over most men. He was a man to be reckoned with.

As the pimply youth rounded the corner,

Charlie grabbed him straight away. He wouldn't have another chance. He demanded, "Tell me where the girl is!"

The boy spat on the ground and glared into Charlie's face. He sneered, "I know nothin'." His nostrils flared, the boy breathed fast in fright.

Charlie shook the smart ass by the shirt. He growled, "Tell me, or you'll pay." Charlie spun him and slammed him against the wall. Nothing and no one was going to stop him finding Hazel.

The youth hesitated, almost as if he would cower and take his punishment, but instead he simply stated, "She's gone to Prince's Risborough Castle a few days ago. To family she has there." Charlie let him turn and the youth promptly hocked a gob of slimy green saliva into Charlie's face.

Despite this, Charlie remained composed. Even though it was tempting to teach the boy a lesson, Charlie did not want the strain. He gave the lad one good shake and let him go. Anyway, the boy had served his purpose. He used the edge of his rags to wipe way the dribbling mess.

Ω

By the time the day was out, Charlie knew the trip to Prince's Risborough Castle well. He had inquired about the castle and its history in many London pubs. People loved to talk. Ask a simple question and pub patrons talked endlessly, especially about such a juicy piece of gossip.

Scandal was everywhere, Charlie mused. The various stories were much the same, so he assumed there was truth in the Hadley and Fletcher scandal. Henry Fletcher was a sly bugger.

Charlie had by good fortune to happen upon

Fletcher's coachman who had taken Hazel to Prince's Risborough Castle in Fletcher's private coach. Without being too direct, Charlie inquired, "I'm off to the Hadley's at Risborough Castle to work. Have you ever been there?"

The coachman smacked his lips together in anticipation of a nice long, juicy chat. He told long drawn out tales of the area, the town and castle. Most importantly, he talked of his most recent trip to the Castle. "I drove a young miss out there for Fletcher. She went by the name of Elizabeth Overland." He paused, "Strange it was. Fletcher told me to accept no bribes from her. That I must ensure she got there safely. I was even to use force if necessary. I thought at the time it was mighty strange thing to say. He promised to double anything she offered. Anything. I made out good from it all, because she offered a lot, if you take my meaning." At this the coachman lifted his eyebrows suggestively. Many of the pub patrons laughed.

Charlie felt like smashing the coachman's face, but it would bring disaster down on his head with his weak leg. Someday the coachman would get what he deserved for talk like that. Maybe not from Charlie, but someday.

$$\Omega$$

Carrying his necessities in a single nap sack, Charlie caught a ride with a farmer who came to the markets to sell his produce. The farmer went to the outskirts of town, into the English countryside.

Prince's Risborough Castle was about three-quarters of the way to Oxford, North West of London. In a single afternoon, Charlie could have travelled by private coach, but it was a very expensive. Besides, arriving in a fancy coach would broadcast to the village he was in Prince's Risborough Village. A grand entrance would create gossip and he may need to slip away quietly with Hazel. Surely she was in trouble. He wouldn't be surprised if Captain Everett had a hand in this somehow.

Charlie caught a ride with anything moving in the right direction. Once he even travelled in a movable wooden house the gypsies called a wagon. Bumping along the road, the house tinkled and the various packs of wild children screamed. Yet, they were happy to provide a warm fire and a dry space to sleep underneath their wagon.

Catching rides to Princes Risborough Castle took a few days, but it was cheap. He had nothing else to his name beside the fortune Captain Everett had given him and most of it was at the bank. He'd kept a small portion of his fortune in his money bag and sacrificed a tiny amount toward supplies for the next few months. In town everything was at your finger tips for the right price. Out of town there were vast amounts of land with nothing else and no one for miles. Charlie would have to depend upon himself.

Besides, he would need his fortune in time to buy a decent farm with a reasonable house. His dream was to live comfortably with the woman he loved. Yet it seemed so farfetched. He hadn't even spoken to her in all these years. But that was going to change. For sure. It was going to change.

Ω

Charlie was pleased when he arrived in the Risborough village. The few people he met were relaxed and friendly. After a few cheery conversations, he found himself bumping down the road in the milkman's cart to a dairy farm situated near the Castle. Maggy, he had been told, would give him a place to stay. She was known as a cheeky, warm widow, taking in boarders to earn a bit of spare cash. The men at the pub said she still had two girls to look after. Her eldest son carried on the farm, but he was still young.

Maggy welcomed Charlie with open arms. He soon ended up helping with the morning milking rather than paying board. Working lowered his expenses to barely nothing.

Charlie wanted to quietly investigate the area. Fit in where he could, without being noticed. He spent afternoons roaming the fields and forests next to the castle, slowly walking the castle's grounds, using a stick to support his leg.

Maggy told Charlie all about the Black Prince, Prince Edward of Woodstock, who built the Castle with a generous moat surrounding the towering stone walls. People said the Prince repaired the Castle after a fierce storm that all but destroyed his original wooden manor. Reinforced with marvellous stone work, the Prince had rebuilt the inner walls. The turrets were sculpted and every so often a figurine rose up. Fierce warriors stared down from various directions. Tall circular towers rose high and each had a curved panelled roof.

The much-loved 14th Century Prince had built the Castle to breed horses. To honour his memory, horse shoes hung above every door. He had been mourned deeply by his people at his early death.

Charlie admired the fine quality horses still bred on Prince's Risborough land.

After gathering as much background as he could in his first day, Charlie strolled over to the castle gardens to meet the gardener. This was not unusual, many people walked from the village over the castle lands. The gardener thought nothing of him ambling by, especially now he was dressed in his new clothes. Charlie had refurbished his wardrobe for the first time in his life. All the rags were burned. He told himself he needed decent clothes to get a decent place to stay, for he could not expect reasonable accommodation as a beggar. However, in the back of his mind Charlie wanted to look half decent when he meet Hazel. Certainly he must present himself as respectable.

Walking up to the gardener, he was dressed in a thick cream flannel shirt, with chrome buttons, sturdy dark brown trousers and matching leather shoes. He certainly gave a good impression.

Charlie called casually, "Why, hello there."

The gardener replied, "Good morrow."

Charlie walked closer to the vegetable patch.

The gardener suggested, "Heading down toward the Hazel Grove? That's a beautiful sight, if I ever saw one."

Charlie replied, "I just may. I was going in that direction. How are the lettuce growing then? Not too cold this summer?"

The gardener smiled, "No not too bad. The summer had a few great downpours and it has been cold too early this year. At night there is a chill already. Yet, today is sunny." Charlie conversed with the gardener, Peter, for some time, as though to pass the time of day.

Then Charlie asked the potent question, "Who lives in this fine Castle? I know it's the Hadley's place, but who actually lives here. I have only been here a few days and haven't had the chance to ask."

Peter answered in full description, "Well, it was passed on to Lady Hadley from her father, who was extremely rich and had well enough for his eldest son. So much in fact that while the eldest son, Sir Winston, got the lion's share, he gave one estate each on the younger siblings. Lady Hadley got this old castle and the titles to the farms out yonder. She loved the famous Black Prince horses and would ride every day before the accident." He shook his head sadly, "She doesn't ride now." He rattled on without pause, "The younger lass, Miss Celia married Otto Clance, but she still got a great mansion in the South, and Simon, the younger son, I do believe, got this great estate of some such, on the shores of Scotland, he spent a few years abroad, but returned after his parents death abroad..."

Charlie smoothly interrupted before he heard the rest of the Hadley's life history, "So she rattles around the Castle all on her own? What a large place to live by herself."

"Ah, no. She has a young niece who has been with her for a bit. They hardly have visitors though."

"A niece. Has she been here long?"

"Well I only just arrived here myself a few weeks back. I was with the eldest son, Sir Winston Hadley, gardening for the last 15 years, but I fell for a lass here a few years back. He was a hard Master and at times a little unfair, but I can't complain. After all he let me come here with good grace. Lucky that Lady Hadley had a position open up with the old head gardener dying a while back. I didn't take his place though. I may yet. As it is I'm second in line. Already the young lads have to follow my direction if Jo is working the hot house."

Charlie persisted, "So her niece may not have been here long?"

Peter paused, "I don't really know. I have been here on a few visits over the last ten years, but not many. She wasn't here then. There's never much news in this castle. Nothing much in the way of excitement happens. So there's not much gossip. Otherwise I'd know for sure all about her. She's a quiet, lovely looking thing. Still, least it's a peaceful home."

Charlie commented, "Oh well, at least the Mistress has some company then. She'd be lonely without it." Charlie figured Hazel could be posing as a niece for some reason. Perhaps the Mistress and Hazel had an arrangement. After all, Hazel had been doing a fair amount of play acting lately. Time would tell.

Charlie stated, "Well I must be getting on. I need to exercise this bad leg a bit more."

Peter called after him, "You head down to that Hazel Grove. You may even see her. She loves it there too. Tallyho."

Charlie pondered. This was the chance he needed. He may be able to meet her there. A private coincidence. Yes, it would be perfect. She may even be there now.

However, when Charlie came under the hazel trees no one was there. Just the most pretty sight he had ever seen. The beautiful great nut trees were already changing to rich golden tones and large leaves occasionally floated to the ground. They towered above a small stream running over green mossy rocks. The water plunged down into small clear pools in several places. At a closer look, he could see fish swimming in the pools. Little snow-drop flowers danced at the edge. Lush grass covered the ground and golden buttercup flowers sprung up here and there The place was serene.

Ω

Charlie returned to Hazel Grove many times

over the weeks to come. At first he came by in the afternoon after lunch. Although never did he come across her. However, he had stopped to chat with Peter many times. He learned much of the gardener's life. Over time gardening would come in handy, as would the milking experience in exchange for boarding at the farmhouse.

Charlie's childhood had been limited to the byways of the town. Most of the time he had tried to stay out of trouble. Apart from a bit of schooling, his only skill was whittling and now the basic knowledge of running a boat. These skills were not too handy toward his dream of a farm life. Prince's Risborough was the perfect place to start learning. He hoped Hazel would be here for a while, now he had the chance to learn some of what he'd need to know about farming.

Eventually, as the weeks drew on, Charlie decided to come later in the afternoon, but to no avail, so he visited before midday. However, he still did not come across her. This was beginning to present a problem. Doubts start to creep in. Maybe it was not her. He must find out. Weeks had passed since he had seen her at the ball. Despairing, he changed his work to the evening milk. Leaning up against a cow, stripping the milk from her udder was appropriate work for him with his leg in a bad condition. The chore gave him time to think. Yet changing to the evening was not so good. His ankle and knee had a tendency to seize up in the evening. Still it was vital to open up every opportunity to find Hazel.

Finally while discussing with Peter the advantage of leaving earth fallow every seventh year, he saw her. Hazel stared out to the forest, looking amongst the high trees. Seemingly, she was watching the birds. True to her pleasure, she carried a large bunch of ruby red roses.

Peter commented, "Ha! Look. There is the young miss. Watchin' the birds, as usual."

Charlie couldn't help, but stare at Hazel's profile. "Why, yes," he said slowly. He remembered her interest in the swans swimming in the ponds of London.

Trying not to pay too much attention to her in front of Peter's watchful eyes, Charlie stated, "Look, there's one of those blasted cabbage butterflies. Quick, get it before it does damage."

Peter, much lighter on his feet than Charlie with his bad leg, sprung forward and caught the culprit in one quick swoop. He returned its remains to the earth where it would be more help rather than a hindrance. Peter prided himself on his beautiful vegetable crop. He used every trick to protect the harvest from insects, disease and the unpredictable weather.

Charlie watched Hazel out of the corner of one eye. Blood started to pump through his body. Yet, he hadn't even moved. His hands began to tense. Now was the moment. Peter was explaining something, he must pay attention. Charlie leaned his ear toward Peter. He continued to converse for a few minutes before making his move.

Charlie was sure Peter did not suspect anything. He even started in the other direction away from Hazel, taking the long route around through the trees to double back on himself.

Charlie entered Hazel Grove on the opposite side to Hazel. Instinctively he hid, watching her for a while. She was bending over the pools looking at the fish swimming lazily about.

When she stood, Charlie could see her more clearly. Hazel wore a dress he had never seen before of pale blue and cream. The dress tucked under her bosom, cascading straight down, creating the most fashionable Empire line.

Delicate blue embroidered flowers clustered around the hem. Her fashion had changed so much since her days in Canada, where she had worn snug fitting whale-boned corsets.

She headed toward a nut tree. Picking and choosing nuts from the ground here and there, she placed them in a hidden pocket at the side of her dress. As if deciding she'd had enough of the hazel nuts, she walked to a fallen tree with smooth branches sticking out. A bow in one particular branch created the perfect seat. Sitting down, she watched the finches flit about, twittering and diving.

Charlie had never seen her look so relaxed and peaceful. He wasn't sure how Hazel was connected to this place, or these people, but he hadn't seen her this contented since her Canadian days. A wave of pleasure took him unaware. This was what he had longed to see. She had been strained with Captain Everett and his overbearing nature. To see her like this was like looking at a different person.

Taking a deep breath to calm his nerves, Charlie attempted to collect himself. Without thinking on it a moment longer, for fear he would lose the courage to approach her, he got up and casually walked into the glade. Within ten steps, she had spotted him approaching her. Surely she noticed his slight limp. He swung his walking stick for extra support.

Despite his failings, he called, "Why, hello. It's a lovely day to be out, isn't it? I am new to these parts. I'm Charlie Letrete from Canada."

She seemed not to recognise him. He must look very different from when he crewed aboard the ship. He was clean shaven, dressed well and his dark hair was freshly cut.

Hazel replied in a soft cultured voice, "Oh, lovely. I am Lily Clance. I am staying with my

Aunt here at the Castle. It is a beautiful morning isn't it." She spoke with modulated English and with absolutely no hint of her village Canadian burr.

"Yes, it is. I have been out nearly every day over the last week. The walks do my leg the world of good. Do you come out here often?"

"I love walking the grounds, but mostly I enjoy riding. Do you ride?"

Charlie was stumped at this question. He had never learned to ride. When would he have had the chance to learn? Yet he didn't want to seem lesser of a person in front of Hazel because of this deficiency However, lying was not how he wished to start. "Well, I have spent time on the sea. Before that, I was in various other places, but never have I really had the chance ride."

"You really must learn... Especially with your leg." With pleasure, she looked into this man's kind, dark blue eyes trimmed with long black lashes. He had a deep and compelling appeal about him.

"Maybe I will, one day."

"May I ask what happened to your leg?"

"Oh, just a nasty fall. I turned the ankle and knee. My leg is still rather weak."

"Did you spend very long abroad?" She asked as though he had been a gentleman travelling the world.

"A few years. I... I was aboard the ship Loretta for over a year."

"Oh," was all she said. She sat contemplating for a time.

Charlie expected she might admit she had been on the same ship.

Instead she spoke as though she did not know of it, "I sailed for a short time, but I can't remember the name of the ship. It was a while ago."

Charlie thought it was little peculiar she did not specify her recent journey. Perhaps she wished to keep up her charade of being 'Lily'. Maybe she assumed they had travelled on the same ship at different times.

Charlie thought he would go further in explaining his connections to her. He began, "Hazel, I...," he took an impregnated pause.

However, she continued the conversation by looking at the few hazel nuts in her hands and saying, "Hazel nuts are my favourite. It's such a shame they cannot be opened more easily."

Charlie was distracted. Looking at the nuts, he said, "They open easily by fire." Deciding to take the chance to stay a little longer with her he said, "I'll open them for you."

"Oh, I couldn't ask you to go to all the bother of starting a fire. I get the staff to prepare them for my lunch. They'll taste divine"

"It is absolutely no bother." Charlie gallantly used this upper class term 'bother' as Hazel had. He wanted so much to impress her. He held his breath for a short time expecting her to refuse again, but this time she accepted his kind offer.

Quickly, he collected together some reasonably dry lichen from the tree branches and a few weathered sticks. While he scrubbed out a small area for a fire, Hazel started to collect more wood. By the time they had collected a significant amount of wood, they were puffing slightly in the cool air.

They chatted about the land and gardens. Charlie told her about his friendship with the gardener Peter. Charlie bent and expertly flicked his knife across his flint. He smiled warmly at Hazel and she smiled back. It seemed this was the start of a firm friendship and he was pleased.

Hazel commented, "This is an adventure. It is the most excitement I have had in a long time."

With a slightly coy expression, Charlie replied, "Glad to be of service, Hazel."

Hazel frowned slightly and laughed, "People around here usually call me Lily." Her lips puckered slightly and she frowned.

Did she think he would ruin her cover? Obviously no one here knew her true identity.

Charlie relented and tried another tack, "Well, I will call you Lily if you want, but I would like to call you Hazel when we are together." He would help keep her secret.

She blushed prettily at this comment, "That would be lovely."

"Hazel if you ever need anyone.... Any help of any kind, you can depend upon me."

She smiled and replied, "Of course you are just the person I would call on if I was ever in need."

"Good."

The hazel nuts cracked and popped open, Charlie fetched them out with a stick. After a bit more excitement dealing with the steaming hot nut shells, they sat with a collection of many nuts. In a companionable silence, they both finished cracking open the shells and began eating the rich nuts.

Despite the fact many nuts were slightly overcooked and even burned, Hazel enthused, "These are so tasty, but I like them better with a little salt." Bits of charcoal flicked and skittered down her dress, but she didn't seem to care one bit.

"I will bring some salt next time." Charlie offered, hopeful of another meeting.

"Yes, that would be lovely." She looked off into the distance with a sweet smile upon her face. Things were looking better and better.

8.

Captain Everett had called in many favours in his search for Hazel's whereabouts. He promised the punters a substantial amount of money if they could prove who had sold the emerald jewels and dress to Fletcher. At the docks, he showed people a rough-coloured sketch of Hazel's face. He pointed out her unusual green eyes, but no one recognised her. Finally he circulated pictures of her, the dress and emeralds at the docks, but nothing had turned up.

The only lead Everett had was connected to the Slately ball. Despite Henry Fletcher claiming he had chaperoned one of Lady Celia Clance's daughters, Everett had asked around. He had quietly uncovered gossip of the most beautiful young widow, Elizabeth Overland, in a stunning dark green dress, wearing large emerald jewels of rare quality, who just happened to be to the exact description of Hazel, wearing the same dress and jewels.

The gossips had all assumed a 'great romance' was about to eventuate between Elizabeth and Henry despite the fact she had recently 'returned to her home' due to her injures. The most enthusiastic tongues added she was to recuperate then return to the ball season in short order. Everyone who was anyone was expecting to witness the 'great romance'. They said this romance would be talked of for generations to come.

Everett considered this very humorous since he had hoped his friend Henry would take to Hazel during her first season. They would have formed a great marriage, being separated by only about fifteen to twenty years. Not a large gap compared to many, and Henry Fletcher was still very dashing in his mid thirty's.

Everett added up the facts once more. A girl had appeared from nowhere on the same night his Hazel went missing. She claimed she was a Canadian widow and called herself 'Elizabeth Overland'. No one had connected her as being a part of the Clance family as Fletcher had claimed. The girl had a terrible accident and disappeared into Henry Fletcher's care under the pretence of being a friend of the family. The gossip sounded so suspicious, he simply had to talk to Henry again.

Yet, Henry owed Everett his life. Surely he wouldn't lie to him. Many years ago Everett had found Henry Fletcher as a boy beaten near to death. His breathing had been ragged. The night was freezing cold and there was going to be a heavy frost by morning. Everett crept up to this boy, intending to take anything he could find. At the young age of thirteen, Everett was well established in his job on the ship, but he was always looking for an extra pound to invest. The boy had groaned and turned his head. Everett had felt pity for this youth only a little younger than himself. He searched all of Henry's pockets and found nothing.

Just as Everett had began to walk away, Henry managed to scratch out in a weak voice, "Help. Please, aaa." Jimboy could walk away, but James Everett had been trying to become a different man. So he hoisted Henry over his shoulder and returned with him to Captain McCoy. The few articles of clothing left on Henry showed he was a man of wealth and prestige. From there Captain McCoy had taken charge, finding the boy's family town house and returning him to his family.

Captain McCoy and Everett had been rewarded lavishly for returning their only son who had been foolhardy to sneak away for an adventure. Both were welcome to visit the Fletcher household at any time. Over the years to come, Fletcher and Everett had become fast friends. Everett had only intended to use the Fletcher family to meet with the right people, but their association had come to mean so much more.

Ω

For the second time, Everett confronted Fletcher in the Cornerstone town house's study, where as a lad Everett had been given his reward.

Everett insisted, "Look all the leads come back here, Henry. I know she said she was the Clance's daughter... but she didn't even go by her own name... she claimed to be a widow... I know about the ball. The facts are confusing. Are you sure you had the right girl? I do believe Hazel looks like Celia Clance's eldest daughter, Isabella. You may have been mistaken!" In one part Everett wished Fletcher was mistaken and on the other he desperately wanted him not to be mistaken. But if Henry had lied or deceived him it would mean the end between them.

"Well, James, she did look like Isabella, but I am sure she wasn't. Perhaps she was the other daughter. Maybe the younger one, Violet!" Henry looked at him, alarmed.

"Tell me why you were with her again."

Slowly Henry told the true story of the ball. He felt he had no choice.

Everett stared at the crackling fire in a stunned silence. Slowly closing his hand into a fist, he dealt Henry a harsh blow to the face, grabbed him by the throat and pushed him to the wall. How dare he send his Hazel to her... Beatrice Hadley of all people!

Growling as an enraged animal Everett felt saliva bubbling at his mouth. The insanity just about took him over. Staring into nothingness, he slowly clamped his hand tighter around Henry's throat. Everett's mind blanked. His eyes pumped as blood rushed to his head. His face grew hot and red. A rush of pure anger backed his actions.

Somewhere deep inside Everett knew he had to look Henry in the face. He had never killed in cold blood. Always the heat existed when Everett killed a well-deserving criminal of sorts aboard his ship. Always he looked them square in the eye knowing the punishment of death was justice as sanctioned by the Motherland England. The last glint of sanity made him draw his eyes to Henry. he saw his friend's eyes bulging and his face deepening into a dark blue. Everett let go. Crumbling to the floor, Henry fell into a sickening silence.

Blood still surged and pumped through Everett's veins. An unrelenting anger still remained. He leaned down and felt Henry's steady breath. He'd live. At that, Everett swept out of the room to follow his daughter, after many months searching, to Prince's Risborough Castle.

Ω

As the months passed by, Charlie wondered why he had ever hesitated to introduce himself to Hazel. She was kind and good hearted and he enjoyed every minute he spent with her.

They had walked over the whole property. Roasted many nuts. Looked at the horses.

Always they had plenty to talk about. From her interest in birds, her love of horses and other animals to Charlie's wooden toys, amusing adventures in other countries and his living circumstances with Maggy and family. Even though they loved each others company, they had to be a little careful. No good would come if anyone saw them together too often. Aunt Beatrice might try to prevent their meetings. After all, Charlie was a stranger and had no real means.

On one occasion when they were far away from anyone's eye, Hazel touched Charlie upon the sleeve as they walked. The warmth of her hand penetrated to the very core of his being. The very touch had set his heart afire. Another time, when Hazel slipped on a small muddy embankment, Charlie reached out to save her from falling. Their touch had lingered.

Sometimes, they would meet when Charlie was helping Peter with the gardening. They would behave as though they hardly knew each other. She would stroll past and stop to talk to the gardener and his friend about the garden and the weather.

Hazel promised to teach Charlie how to ride. Though she was a little unsure about how to get away from the stables with an extra horse without causing suspicion. Not mentioning the fact that the horse would need to be saddled and reined.

On one particular day, Charlie was to meet her by the old well, on the far east side of the estate. As he approached, he saw her upon a horse.

She called out, "I have an idea about teaching you to ride, Charlie."

He grinned up at her, "And what would that be. I don't see another horse."

Laughing she replied, "No, but look I have some reins under my jacket. I feel very daring."

Charlie paused, well he had seen her do far more daring things. Much worse. Yet she never spoke about her past with Captain Everett, or the time she murdered Jack. It was like it was a memory she wished to block out. Whenever Charlie touched on an issue, or even mentioned about Molly, she did not comment about herself, or her friendship. It seemed she did not want to discuss any of it.

Charlie thought it was for the best. No good could come from living in the past. He was glad Hazel had stolen away to live with this 'Aunt'. Somehow she had come across a family connection.

Hazel's new sense of contentment was what mattered. So Charlie didn't discuss the past any more. He would respect her wishes. History was history, now they were together. What more could he ask for? His dreams had come true.

With a cheeky glint in his eyes, he nodded at the reins and looked up at her, "And who may those be for."

She smiled, "You, if you're not careful." Turning, she gestured to the paddock up the hill. "I'll be back in a minute. I am going to fetch that old nana horse, up the way. You wouldn't be able to handle anything more." She gave him a saucy grin and galloped off.

Charlie laughed after her. Thus he was soon upon a huge old horse that knew the ropes, but still had a trick or two. Charlie found himself off her back a few times while Hazel watched in fits of laughter. Finally she commented, "She is playing around with you. She knows you will fall off, if she craftily goes under those trees. Prepare yourself. If she turns toward those branches, turn her away with the reins. Soon she'll give it up."

After that he took to riding like a duck to water. In no time they were riding far out to the distant edges of the estate. Hazel showed him all her favourite spots. They often spent lazy afternoons sheltering by haystacks in the warm sun with the horses munching at the golden hay.

Ω

A few days later, they had ridden to the far river in the west of the estate. They both sat in the damp grass on the bank. Charlie looked at Hazel in a bashful and awkward way. Carefully he took from his pocket the small swan he had whittled. He had used a small glowing stick from the fire and cleverly burned the black eyes and black beak. Its neck bent naturally into a swan and Charlie had carefully carved the body and formed the wings. The swan had turned out rather delicate. A perfect gift for a loved one.

Charlie saw tears spring to Hazel's eyes has he laid the gift in her hands.

"Charlie, I have never seen anything so lovely before. It is just like the swans on the ponds in the London parks. You are so clever to craft such a beautiful bird."

"I know how you like to look at birds. It is for you."

"Oh, I could not possibly...."

"I want you to keep it."

Her face flushed with joy, "Thank you. I will treasure it forever."

Ω

Mistress Beatrice Hadley stopped at the door before she entered the foyer to the large old castle. Father had been so kind as to leave such a wonderful place to her. Prince's Risborough Castle had always been her favourite because of her love for the horses that were bred here. If she hadn't been given this property, she would have been dependent upon her snobby older brother, Sir Winston II.

Grooves puckered over her forehead as a burning sensation shot through her neck and back. She resigned herself to the fact she would soon have to give up wearing full-boned corsets. At least the new empire style allowed for a woman to not wear any. This summer she resolved to update her clothes to this latest fashion and give away her old wardrobe.

Staring aimlessly back out the door, she thought over the puzzle of Beth's arrival. Drifting through the entrance down the hall to the nearby study, she contemplated what to do about her. She had already written to her sister, Celia, trying to get her to return. Surely Celia would arrive any day now. Beatrice had never asked Celia to return before now. Then, in her last letter, she had almost begged Celia to return to the Castle immediately.

Beatrice once again turned over the events of Beth's arrival in her mind. It had only been a few months ago. Mistress Beatrice had entered the study unaware and read the note from Henry Fletcher.

Without looking up she carefully considered its contents. The butler had only said a worker had arrived. She blinked once or twice to prevent tears from falling. Henry had always been her true love, a love best forgotten now. He had become a family rival to the Hadley's since that terrible day all those years ago. So much time had passed since she had heard from him and their ties were so complicated

Why would he go out of his way to send a

working girl to them? He had no favours to be called in. Maybe this maid was his bit on the side he wished to be rid of. Maybe the girl had connections here. Beatrice eyed the girl's bent head. She still had her eyes cast respectfully to the floor.

She asked, "What is your name?"

Hazel looked up and replied, "Beth, Ma'am."

Beatrice sat and stared at the girl in stunned silence, because of what she saw. At that precise moment, Lily entered through the door suggesting in beautiful linguistics, "I think I will go for a ride early this afternoon. The weather is getting nippy later in the day. I think it would be wise to keep the horse out of the chill."

Ω

Beatrice's eye's flicked from Lily and back to the strange new arrival, she managed, "All right, dear," turning her gaze back to the girl, indicating to Lily that she was dismissed.

Lily had frowned, usually her Aunt asked a hundred questions as to what direction she would take, which horse she was riding and always reminded her of the places she must not ride. Lily tentatively said, "I..., I will ride by myself today... to the old well." She quickly exited the room. She expected her Aunt to insist she take a groom. Very rarely was she allowed to ride without one. Her Aunt was distracted by the new maid's unexpected arrival. She was eighteen years old and well able to look after herself on a horse. From now on she would insist on riding by herself.

Ω

Back in the study, Beatrice said, "Why have

136

you come here, Beth?"

Hazel smiled broadly, "Am hopn' fa a job ma'am."

Beatrice collected her thoughts while shuffling a few papers. The girl sitting in front of her had the look of James Everett with her green eyes. However, she had a feminine beauty leaning toward her mother. Her mother Celia!

Celia must have given birth to twins. There was no mistaking it, Beatrice now knew the girls were not born to Otto's lineage, but Celia's old lover, James Everett. Those green eyes of Beth's had told it all. Celia had never said a word in all these years. Beatrice never knew Celia was pregnant to Everett, but the eyes of this maid were definitely Everett's. Lily however had the light blue eyes of her mother.

Beatrice thought back through the timing of Lily's birth. Celia had married Otto, then seven months later had given birth to a very tiny little girl. Everyone thought Lily had been born early at seven months. She had been so small. However, now Beatrice knew Lily had been a small twin born near term. Twins were usually quite small at birth. No wonder she didn't die from an early birth. Very rarely did a babe live when born at seven months, but it did happen occasionally. They had all thought it was a blessing, a miracle from God that little Lily had survived.

Beatrice began to stare at this stranger who was Lily's perfect match to look at, except for the fact this girl had unfortunately tanned skin and a terrible gutter Irish accent. Beatrice frowned, Everett had established his perfectly upper crust tone as he rose in the world. Yet his ancestors were Cockney not Irish. Henry was good friends with James Everett. They must have devised some evil plan to send this girl here to upset the

Hadley family.

Beatrice asked, "How old are you?"

Hazel comfortably replied, "Eighteen vera soon, Ma'am."

Again Beatrice was lulled into a meditative silence.

Twins. Everett had one and Celia the other. The crying when Celia meekly married Otto... At Lily's birth, Celia had been so sad. She must have been grieving. Beatrice had always thought her to be weak and overly emotional. After all she had a beautiful young baby born with the 'blue eyes' of her Mother and 'dark hair' of her Father. Slowly Beatrice realised what had really happened.

Celia had begged to marry Everett. Father would not allow it. He had a much better match. James Everett was a 'nothing'. Shortly after James had been refused by Father, he had left port to export goods on his ship. Then soon after Celia had agreed to marry Otto. No wonder Celia had a change of heart so quickly. Everett had gone and left her pregnant. Celia would've had no option. She had no notion of how to be ruthless, or wise. Just complying, weak and emotional. The easy way out. The acceptable way out was to quickly marry.

Did Henry Fletcher realise this? Did he know there were twins? Beatrice read the note again and found no indication whether Fletcher realised this girl was not Lily. He had only met Lily a few times many years ago, but it would be easy to mistake this girl for Lily.

Everett must know about the twins. Revenge was surely sweet to James Everett. No wonder Celia never had Lily presented to society. Was she trying to hide Lily? Or perhaps she was trying to avoid shame from Everett calling her out? Had the damage already travelled far in society? Were people gossiping already?

No one had even questioned the early birth of little Lily. Beatrice realised with a flush of anger, Celia had not even confessed any of this to her. Not even a hint of it. Then to top it all off, this girl, a maid really, did not even realise the connections.

Ω

The girl simply sat, waiting for an eternity. She was beginning to look anxious and afraid.

Thankfully, Beatrice thought of something to say, "This is a surprise. Fletcher was wise to send you to me."

Beatrice's mind reeled. What was she going to do with this girl? She faltered slightly, "I...I would like to know what you are good at?" Something had to be done with her while Beatrice figured out what to do. There was no need to scare the girl. She couldn't be sent away for fear someone might figure out what and who she really was. Not to forget something might happen to her. Celia no doubt would want to see her. Besides she was Celia's daughter and her problem.

Hazel began, "Well I've done a lot of farm work. Milked cows and tha like, cleaned tha big hou's." She pause and the silence stretched, so she mentioned, "Nofin' flash, mind."

Beatrice asked, "Well, what would you feel most comfortable doing?"

Hazel frowned, wriggled slightly and changed her expression to one of interest. This was an unusual question from a mistress to a maid, "I just wan' ta do a bit of cleanin' and milkin'."

Beatrice concluded, "Then that is what you will do. Please wait here while I look for the stable master."

As Beatrice firmly shut the study door behind her, she sent a brief prayer the twins would not find out about each other until Celia had decided what was best to do. Hopefully their completely different stations would prevent any meeting. Oh, but what about the servants? Maybe she could buy a little time if she behaved like nothing was different. Most people were slow when it came to making these connections. But if the girls were seen together it would be the end of the secret. Beatrice considered bribing the butler, but his eyes were terrible. He would have been lucky to notice anything.

Beatrice quickly decided that Beth would be sent away to a quiet corner until some decision could be made. The stable master would be bribed to take her to a farm. Maybe for several months. She needed time to contact Celia. Beatrice knew of some farmers in need of help beyond Lacey Green. They had a very small, isolated farm they leased at the edge of Prince's Risborough Estate. For keeping Beth they would earn a fortune. This difficult situation could be kept very quiet for a year at least. Beatrice planned to make sure of it.

Furthermore, Beatrice thought Lily could be sent away to London for a shopping trip. No, no that might not be wise. James might see her there. Beatrice's anger flared when she thought about the fact Lily was here just so Celia did not have to face the trouble she had created.

All Lily truly wanted was to have her year of dancing. No doubt Lily would've been married by the second season. She was very beautiful. A gem on the inside and out. If Lily had been presented a few years ago, she certainly would have been married by now. Then there would have been less of a problem. Her status and value would not be tainted. Possibly Everett would not have had the chance to pull off his little scheme. At least Lily would have had some happiness in a good marriage by now, but now her status might be marred.

Beatrice knew she needed to contact Celia as soon as possible. She decided to write immediately. Celia needed to sort her own mess out. Beatrice did not even know the whole story. Damn Celia for being away in Scotland for the next six months. It was just perfect for her that she was not on hand to take responsibility. Yet Beatrice could just see her sister hiding it all. Hiding this other girl, Lily's twin. Hiding the whole situation from poor Otto. Pompous, fussy Otto.

She was pretty sure Otto did not know about this situation. Surely he would have fought, contested, or something to save Beth if he knew. Even if Lily and Beth weren't really his, they both had been born into his marriage with Celia. Neither baby would have had the tell-tale green eyes at birth. Otto would not have known Beth was to grow up with eyes that exactly matched James Everett's. In fact, only those who knew Celia and Everett well would have ever made that connection. Maybe Otto never would have. He would have considered Beth his.

What could she write to Celia without letting onto Otto? There must be more to the twins being separated at birth than Beatrice could figure out. If they had both stayed together with their mother, none of this would be a problem. Everett would not have been able to make a scene at this later date, or prove anything for that matter. People may have whispered about Beth's eyes, but they would have only have been whispers that amounted to nothing. After all, Celia was married to Otto at their birth. No one would have argued with that. For Otto's sake, she must not write of it openly to Celia. Somehow Celia must be convinced to return from her travels.

Beatrice had always felt guilty over the obligation by Lily's parents for her to live here with her. However, now Beatrice realised she was being used by Celia. This was no way for Lily to live her life. Lily certainly did not want this life. Eventually, Lily would confront them and stop being so compliant. She had always been a biddable child to a point. She had a certain kind of inner strength. Lily knew what she wanted in life.

Beatrice had always thought Lily had been wrapped in cotton wool. Being protected by her mother so fiercely. She had never been allowed to journey far afield. Not even around England. Maybe only once by sea. She always had a protective nanny. Her life had always been fairly simple and easy. Occasionally, Lily created a little excitement to abate the boredom. Lily's patience would only last so long. Beatrice had always imagined one day, maybe in a few more years, Lily would do something troublesome. However, now another sort of trouble had walked in the door.

Ω

"Beth. Please do take care. The country life can be rough. You are going to help at an isolated farm." Beatrice Hadley paused, "Well, for a time at least, until I can find a better posting. I... I am sending you there because the farmer has a damaged arm and requires help. I warn you though they are strict." Beatrice sounded overly concerned for Hazel.

"I will ba fine, Ma'am," Hazel replied.

Before she knew it, Hazel was sent rattling

away in an old trap cart full of supplies for the farm in the outer region, where she was to be a maid. Mistress Beatrice claimed it was ideal timing for a new maid to come so that she could send her to the milk farm in their time of need.

Yet nothing in this whole situation seemed to piece together. Hazel could not figure out exactly what it was. She could not put her thumb on it. She knew what the letter from Fletcher said. She had played her part of a poor Irish maid and fooled Mistress Beatrice. Now here she was, feeling like her life was once again being arranged for her. She had already travelled a long way that day, but now she was to go another two hours. Yet what choice did she have? Her body ached from all the travel.

At least she had been served food by the butler. However, normally maids would be sent to the kitchen for a snack. To add to the strangeness of the situation, normally any traveller, even a maid, would rest a night before journeying onward. So struggling to make sense of it all, she jiggled around on the old trap cart until she reached the farm.

On arrival, Hazel saw warmth pouring out the windows of a medium-sized cottage. Dogs barked all around. Stepping inside the kitchen, she was greeted by confusion.

The man of the house stood stiffly. He had rough mousey brown hair, with a plain, shaven face. A scar showed from his jaw down to the base of his neck. The man looked rather tough and ugly.

His wife was short, with generous layers of fat. She seemed to be bursting from her tight clothes. With a pinched face, she bundled off to the stove. She didn't need a visitor at this time of night. Six children crammed together around a large table, eating their evening meal.

Hazel's stomach growled. Clearly the older children were able workers. Was there a need for a maid? On the man's arm she saw a few deep cuts, but nothing to write home about. Still infection could run deep, so perhaps help was necessary with another milking hand. Being down a milker could destroy their trade.

The man spoke, "What are you doing here, Keith? We were not expecting anyone for weeks. And what are you doing bringing the Miss here." He looked pointedly at the stable master, "The usual boy is all I need to deliver the goods."

Keith, the stable master soothed, "Nothing much, except a long overdue chat, Eddie, and to catch up. We have been friends for years, haven't we?" He gave the farmer a hard look. "I have some news from home about your sister. I thought it best to deliver this news in person."

The farmer looked a little bashful and apologized for his abruptness "Oh, don't mind me. Come in, we will talk in the study. We'll not be disturbed." Eddie gave his children a hard stare as if to say 'they better not put a foot out of place or they would pay'. Turning to Hazel he said gruffly, "Miss you are welcome to help your-self to a cuppa."

Keith did not introduce 'Beth' the maid. Rather he instructed her, "Give Eddie the letter." Hazel silently handed Eddie Hunter the sealed letter from Mistress Beatrice Hadley. She supposed it was a letter of introduction for herself as Beth the maid and well wishes to the family.

Ω

Before he hoped back on his cart to return to the castle, Keith gave Eddie a firm handshake. Eddie smiled at him, "Thank-you vera much for delivering such a good load! We will not let the Mistress down. Let her know everything will be taken care of to her satisfaction."

Eddie slipped his hand into his pocket and touched the bags of coin. Inside was more money than he usually made in a year. To add, he had been promised double for the safe delivery of Beth, at a time convenient to the Mistress over the next six to twelve months. They had to keep it a secret mind. Living in the middle of nowhere made that easier. They had very few visitors, no neighbours for miles and the children did not even attend a school. Their mother educated them a bit at home. Enough to write their name, add numbers and such.

With all the money that was coming, Eddie Hunter congratulated himself. He would be able to move to a better community. Buy a house, a farm. A step up would be better for the kids and his wife. He would even be able to attend a local bar! Daily if he should chose! Drink to his heart content and gamble a bit. A little here and there. He gave a quiet giggle in anticipation of the thought.

For now this lass was to know nothing. He must inform his family of their secret duties by her. The kids, heaven help them, would lose their life if they said a word to anyone. Especially if they spoke to Miss Lily. The older ones would be in on it, and Margaret of course. He must tell them straight away. Beth could go to her room to settle in.

The younger lot would surely not know any better. She would just be Beth the milk hand to them. Beth would always need watching and never be allowed to disappear. She meant too much to him. The roaming dogs would be useful to prevent her running at night. This girl Beth could be the making of him!

Ω

Being autumn, the weather had quickly turned icy cold and wet. During one heavy downpour, Charlie found himself with his love, galloping up to an old stone cottage. Jumping off their horses they ran through the broken down door way. Laughing, they stumbled into the small house.

Shutting the door as quickly as they could, Charlie said, "That rain poured down without warning. We are drenched, Hazel!"

Lily laughed, "You should really call me Lily!"

"No, you will always be Hazel to me." He smiled.

She smiled at him with pure pleasure. "We are so wet we will need to dry out. Let's get a nice fire going to warm up."

Soon they were busy investigating the cottage for supplies. An old rotted, broken table snapped apart and made excellent firewood. Charlie lit the fire with his flint and knife. Lily found a dented old pot. After washing it out in the water pouring off the roof, she filled it up and set it to boil. During their search, she had found one cracked mug and an old tin of tea.

Lily enthused, "We can share this cup. It's a little chipped, but I can make sure it's clean using the boiling water from the pot. Then I'll seep the tea."

Charlie promised, "I'll find something to replace the table we've used. Someone must own this place. It looks a little broken down, but there are still signs of life here, look an old blanket. Seems as if they've been gone awhile, though."

"Well, my Aunt really owns everything here, so you don't really need to worry. Who ever lived here would have rented it. By the size of this place they probably could only afford to pay a chicken, or two for my Aunt's pot. This place is terribly small. I cannot imagine how a person would survive here."

Charlie did not remark on this comment. Hazel's upbringing had been on a rich Canadian farm. She had been far more privileged than him. He had lived most of his life in a cottage only a little bigger than this one. He almost told her, but stopped himself; he didn't really want to relive his past. Have to explain the difficulties of his early life. They were just too raw. Too deep. His past poverty was best left in the past and it could stay there.

Instead he stated, "I would like a farm house much bigger than this one. With two stories and perhaps four bedrooms." He looked at her to see her reaction. Even his dream house was so much smaller than her family home in Canada. With his small fortune from Captain Everett he would be able to afford a reasonable house and one servant. He planned to build on in the future.

She looked at him intently, so he went on, "I would like the rooms to be big and spacious. To own a herd of cows, some to milk, others for meat and maybe some sheep. I'd love to build a great garden full of vegetables."

"I love the vegetable garden at the Castle," Lily commented.

Becoming a little bashful, he quietly stated, "I would like a few children too." She smiled. Smiled!

Burning with happiness he leaned down and kissed her. Pressed his lips against her soft, moist mouth. Savouring the moment. After a few seconds that felt like an eternity, she returned his kiss. Then, all of a sudden, she pulled away, gasping at the shock of what just happened.

Charlie's face fell. Kissing her was the wrong

thing to do. He had pushed her too far. Said too much. Assumed this and that. She was not his and she probably never would be. She was too far out of his reach. She was high 'quality' and he was low 'quality'. They had been raised in the same neighbourhood, but lived worlds apart. She didn't dream of dreary small farm, cows or vegetable gardens. She wouldn't want to live in the country with him.

Ω

Pausing for a moment, Lily rose and stepped back. Never had anyone kissed her. Her thoughts ran frantically wild. This was all new to her. So very new. Lily loved him, without a doubt, but he had said he wanted a farmer's life. He did not really want her. He would need a farmer's wife! His dream could not be her dream. Besides, he boarded. Boarded! With a poor family. People like him have no money. Nothing established, or anything. Not even a small cottage such as this.

Lily felt she had no right to fall in love with a poor man. He would always strive to provide for her. She could not burden him.

For marrying him, Lily would be disinherited. Nothing would be given to him as a marriage settlement. She couldn't put herself as a burden upon him. Marry him. It was unacceptable to even entertain such an idea. What would her Father say! Her Aunt! Her...

Charlie interrupted her thoughts, stammering, "I... I am so sorry!" He raked his hands through his hair. "I don't know where that came from! We must go." He blurted, "I thought maybe you would want to escape with me."

Looking at him, Lily knew. This was her chance for her one moment of happiness with Charlie. Never could anything come of it, but the opportunity would never come again. These secluded meetings would have to end, or she may not be able to stop herself from falling further in love with him. Deeply in love. Too deep.

Charlie watched her face change from dismay into sad and distressed. Then adding to his confusion, she turned and kissed him again. Passionately. Hot, wet and promising. He could not stop it, not for one minute. This was just the beginning. She pulled him down to the floor. Charlie's emotions swung from despair to ecstasy. They kissed and kissed again. He had not lost his Hazel. He had her and she wanted him.

He took command, moving his lips around over her neck. Down to her shoulder. Slowly, very slowly he lowered her jacket, undid each button down the back of her dress. Her face changed to a passionate rose bud pink around the mouth and nose. She was burning for him. He could feel it. The way her body pulsated under his hand. Leaning into his every touch. Wanting, yearning, needing.

Slowly lowering her dress down off her shoulders, Charlie kissed down her arms. She reached up, placing her hand in earnest across his back. Stripping off each layer, he revealed the purity of her body. Untouched innocence open to experimenting, tasting and bending to his every need.

Her milky white legs clung to Charlie's waist in high elation. Taken up in the heat and passion, she barely noticed the first penetration. Horse riding had softened her virginal resistance. Slipping and sliding, they took their fill of each other, mounting into ecstatic elation.

Charlie believed their destiny was with each other. They would marry. They would defy all the odds. But right now he did not care about anything else. He would make passionate love to Hazel, caress her, feel her, then he would prepare to marry her. Even by next week. He would take her home. To Canada. Back to her family, where she really belonged. He would buy a farm nearby. With the fortune he had for saving her, he would provide her with a better life. Even Captain Everett will not be able to stop them because Hazel would be married to him.

Ω

A quick sharp clipping sound jolted Jane the maid back to her laborious task. A pair of brown leather riding boots passed by without any hesitation. Mud spread in clumps, flicking off Miss Lily's back heel. At least now Jane had actual dirt to clean off the floor.

Kitty walked in and called, "Jane, I ..." She immediately stopped talking and bobbed down, averting her eyes to the ground as Miss Lily passed.

Miss Lily, in all correctness, barely acknowledged the maids.

Kitty glanced up in time to see the back of Miss Lily's chocolate brown dress. She looked at Miss Lily's clothes with a judgemental eye. They seemed wet. Miss Lily must have been caught in the rain. She was wearing a perfect riding outfit by Lerral's. Her boots just so, but her riding jacket was the completely wrong colour of stiff navy from three seasons past. Kitty thought she should be wearing her matt velvet brown, with perhaps those new leather boots from Hetel's. Glancing down at her own dress of serviceable grey and solid shoes, She thought, *This shouldn't be my lot in life. It is too boring. If I was to wear Lerral's, I would wear it perfectly'.*

Kitty looked at her lace-edged pinny. Her mother was obviously expecting better than a maid for her eldest daughter, though the likelihood of any better was slim. Kitty's mother strived every day to manage a large house with her younger brother and sister. With no husband to her name. Only Kitty. In Aylesbury they said Kitty's mother is 'widow', but it was said to save face. The frill on Kitty's apron was from the edge of her mother's old day dress. Not even new.

Kitty glanced back to Miss Lily, who was disappearing out the door. Miss Lily's step seemed smart and almost a run. Her deep chestnut curls ran loose and slightly wild. They were in a terrible mess really. Something was amiss. Well, it would not be much. Maybe her bed had a wrinkle, Jane made it up after all, or perhaps she was bothered by the wet.

Miss Lily seemed gilded into the society life. Matching expectations of a lady and poised to marry the moment her parents found her the perfect groom. Yet, to Kitty's surprise, Miss Lily had remained unmarried all this time. The rumours claimed Master Clance, hated his daughter, but it was only maids' talk. Her current living situation was a little mysterious. Mistress Beatrice certainly did not need a companion and Miss Lily's life surely would not be sacrificed forever in duty to her Aunt.

Jane was flustered and her skin blushed into a light pink. She murmured, "I heard Madame is doin' a look around."

Kitty instantly grabbed a wire brush. She would put on her best show for the Mistress. Her skirt puffed as she knelt in front of the dirty footprints. She flicked out the odd fold. Tucked her hair under her pretty white lace cap and began to scrub with such focus her eyes almost went inward.

Jane glanced at Kitty and sighed, Kitty was so young. Hope is usually slow to fall, but in a house such as this, it surely would.

9.

Charlie was so confident and full of life after their encounter in the old cottage. So much so the following day he went to meet with the pedlar who sold quality jewels. He found him in the pub having a quiet pint. Charlie asked to look at his rings. The pedlar raised his eyebrows in surprise. Usually his customers would've been high society in the country. A goldsmith was highly prized in these parts. Yet, occasionally he sold a thin band in the village. He opened his jewellery box for Charlie to inspect.

Looking in the box, Charlie picked up a few rings, but settled on one with a large, light blue sapphire with a cluster of diamonds encircling the edge. The light blue matched Hazel's eyes. The gold was thick, with a whimsical pattern engraved on the band. He asked, "How much?"

The goldsmith hesitated, this ring was too fancy. Yet it was one that he had made up from a second-hand ring. The gold had been melted down and the jewels reused. He had redesigned the ring to match more modern standards. Of course, high quality would not know the difference. Yet, he was always ready to make a quick pound, so lowered his price a little to entice his current buyer. "I'd be giving it to you for half a crown."

Charlie counted, "Two shillings."

"Sold." He could've got a crown and one shilling from the rich, but he was still making a good profit at two shillings.

Charlie easily handed over the two shillings, using up half his money on hand. Hazel would have the finest and nothing less.

Ω

At first, Charlie had chatted everyday with Peter while helping sow broccoli in the vegetable garden. Often he would glance longingly toward the large grey castle. As each day passed by, his heart grew a little sadder. He stopped talking and began to wallow in the Hazel Grove, deeply contemplating where things had gone wrong.

At first, he gave Hazel the benefit of a doubt. She could have caught a cold from having on wet clothes. Three weeks slipped by. Charlie dreaded she could be seriously ill. Finally, he built up enough excuses to ask Peter about Hazel's health.

Remembering Hazel's false name 'Lily', Charlie asked, "Peter, I have not seen Miss Lily walking the grounds lately. Have you? Is she well?"

Peter stood and stretched his back out. He had sensed there may have been something special between the two of them. Well, it is better Charlie learned his place. Still, no need to make it worse. Peter briefly replied, "Why, she is very well indeed I believe. If she had so much as a cough I would hear of it." Carefully Peter averted his eyes to the ground, allowing Charlie a little grace.

After that, Charlie had returned to help Peter less often. His hope changed to despair. Every day he returned to Hazel Grove for longer and more mournful hours. He had no idea what to do. Hazel had simply cut him off. Vanished from his life. It was like she had been a dream that disappeared before his very eyes. Their friendship had been the most wonderful experience of his life.

Ω

Deep on the inside, Lily quivered. She was now sure. Very sure. Months had passed, and her cycles had stopped.

At first the change had been confusing. *Why had the curse stopped?* She had this deep, quailing feeling. Something was wrong, very wrong. She had continual hunger, boarding on a queasy stomach. Despite her desire to eat, she could be sick at any moment.

Lily wished for her mother's presence. To be ten years old again, with a simple problem, like a scratch from her wild kitten. She never could tame that beast. He was such a little scrapper.

She had come across his wet and lifeless body one damp, dismal evening. He had a little cold nose and oversized ears. His citrus coloured fur was matted onto his body. She had smuggled him back to her nursery, hiding him away in her bed. Nanny would have never allowed her to have him. Inadvertently, she saved his life by cradling his little body all night in her cosy, gold gilded bed.

The kitten was discovered the next morning by Nanny. Lily bit her lip when she remembered Nanny's ear piercing shriek, the kitten's claws had raked across Lily's soft skin and sent her heart jumping into her throat. Crimson blood dribbled down her arm.

Mama had held a soft white cloth to the scratch and whispered, "It will be all right, darling". While Nanny ranted on that Lily never had any sense and what would Lily do next.

Mama bathed away the pain with a warm herbal wash. Lily's tears soon ceased and she watched the kitten playing out the window in the enclosed vegetable garden. Lily remembered it wasn't long before she was skipping through the garden with the kitten trailing her and the scratch was forgotten. Marmaduke was a cat much loved by all, for he always cleared out the mice.

Lily had not seen him for many years. She longed to see Marmaduke and hear Mama whisper it would be all right, have all her troubles disappear. Life would sparkle and all would be fine again. But things were not the same as back then, her mother treated her differently now. Sure she was an adult, but an unmarried one.

Lily closed her eyes and they twitched under the strain. The weight of the situation was falling on her. The burden was so heavy. How would she offer a child a safe, secure life, all the comfort and caring. Her child would need a Nanny, one who knew how to care for children, one who knew what she was doing. Someone to tuck the child in at night. Lily had nothing, no means of her own. Nothing but a few coins. Her education was about being a lady, nothing productive enough to earn a living from.

Lily felt like a wave of heat was about to overtake her. Yet cool air blustered outside the window from which she looked. Yesterday, the sticky rain had pounded the perfect windows. Today the wind blew and leaves stuck to the window panes. She must let the maid know to have them cleaned on the morrow.

She had been here four years now, to be a companion to Aunt Beatrice. They had promised it was just for the year. By then she would be ready for her coming out. Somehow time had slipped by. In the second year there had been so much sickness at home with her father, Lily had to carry on staying with her aunt. Now it seemed they had forgotten about her.

No matter how Lily thought through her attachment to Charlie, she had failed. Failed her mother, father and aunt. She had only recently been given free rein to ride by herself and all she did was make the worst mistake possible. She had met, fallen in love and behaved as a wanton with the wrong sort of man. At eighteen, she should be more responsible, but it had all been so sweet, so tempting and so very easy. Love had crept up on her so slow and sure it had caught her unaware.

Frowning, her thoughts drifted away from herself. Mother visited nearly every year. Yet when she was here she could barely meet Lily's eyes. She would look at the floor if she heard maids whispering, her eyes would flick from side to side. Something was very strange. Yet, Mama always said all was fine at home. Everyone was healthy, her eldest siblings were married to fine matches, and her youngest sister Violet was now doing well in ladies training.

Lily drifted away from the window. Across the soft carpet. Now this had happened. Charlie had been balm for her loneliness. She had wanted something from Charlie. A memory. But never in her wildest dreams had she considered they would conceive a baby. She closed her eyes remembering the day in the old cottage. The surprise of the heat of the moment. Admittedly, they had been getting very close over a short time. Oh, how she loved him. The love making had happened so quickly. The closeness she felt toward him!

Now her choices were gone. Who could she tell? No one. She would break her Mama's heart. There had to be a way. So no one would know about the baby. And Charlie could never know about it.

That precious day at the cottage was the last

she had seen of him. She had not ventured outside again. The rain had started to pour down anyway. Resigning herself to make the right choice, she had not gone to meet him as agreed. A sprinkling of a few fine days had been and gone. More rainy days, but there would be no mistake once winter ended. Charlie would know it was over. He was poor. She was determined not to give in to her undying love for him. Lily loved him so much, she could not destroy his life by burdening him. If she did, eventually they both would be destroyed. She was absolutely sure of it.

A baby made no difference to Lily. If anything, it made her situation worse. To lump Charlie with a pregnant wife. To watch him struggle. She would not do it, no matter what happened with the baby. She would never admit to him, or anyone, he was the father of this baby, even when Aunt Beatrice found out, or father, or even more terrible still, mother. Mother would never understand. This disgrace could potentially take down the whole family if society got word of this. Giving birth was worse than a bad marriage to a poor man. She could cripple Father and Mother for life. No, no-one could ever know. She must protect them all from her mistake. Never would anyone know.

Blinking back the tears, a bout of unusual emotions over took her. She ran and hid in the library. Away from the prying eyes of the maids. Away from her Aunt. She must pull herself together. This pregnancy was not really happening to her. People lost babies all the time. This baby would disappear. She was not having a baby.

Ω

Once the winter season had been and gone,

Charlie's tears started to fall. The numbing pain had gone, only to bring forth the reality Hazel really wanted nothing to do with him. The extreme weakness of his tears ate into his heart and played with his mind. His thoughts were consumed by her. He stopped milking, he stopped eating; to him the whole world had stopped, too.

It seemed Charlie had lived his whole life to meet and openly love Hazel. Now the door was firmly shut. Nothing else in his life really mattered. Eventually Charlie left the farm where he had boarded for many months. Maggy did her best to convince him to stay. She had become really worried about him, but he could not stay any longer.

Charlie went further into himself. Returning to the little run-down cottage where they had their final meeting, he set up his sleeping roll. The temperature was not so bad now the spring had come. The air was sweet and slowly warmed. Anyway, he didn't care anymore if he was cold, or hungry.

Charlie spent hours pondering inside the cottage. He thought over every detail of their final meeting. Again and again. Every time Charlie thought it through, he decided it had been the wrong choice to make love to her. The wrong choice. He had been too intense and gone too far. Way past the order of love, marriage and acceptable behaviour. He realised they had stepped into a bind which she had ultimately rejected. Hazel did not want him. She was offering no solution. Charlie had no options.

Charlie disappeared from anyone's view. His clothes turned back to well-worn rags. His face became covered in straggly roughage and seeping insect bites. His hair grew into shabby lengths. Now he had no one, therefore no reason for living. God as his witness, he had ruined his life.

Ω

Lily pulled herself together remarkably well. She successfully blocked it all from her mind. Regardless of the fact she was well over half way through a pregnancy, she was not having a baby. With a forever increasing stomach, she was not having a baby. The sickness had stopped, so she was not having a baby. She had almost blocked it from her body. In fact, had Charlie ever really existed? Was he a person?

Yet, Lily always had her maid leave before she would change her clothes. Penny undid the buttons and left. Every time Penny looked concerned as she left the room. Being of excellent training, Penny had soon begun to leave before being asked to go. She knew her place without question.

However, Lily suspected Penny thought something was wrong. Without thinking, Lily began to push Penny away. She must protect herself; finally convincing herself she needed a new maid. Convincing Aunt Beatrice would be a problem and choosing a replacement. Perhaps little Kitty would do. Kitty never had a knowing look, or prying eyes like Penny. Surely Kitty would not know enough about correct personal service to question Lily's changing routine.

To hide her increasing weight, Lily conveniently used the dress fitting for her winter wardrobe. She described to the seamstress in exact detail how to fill out her dress, with pleats just under the bust. The new empire style was so forgiving to the waist. The dresses were not at all fitting. Lily instructed thick materials, with several layers. She explained the needle work in detail. Placing the flowers and flourishing the hem.

Never did the seamstress seem to notice Lily was trying to cover something. All the dresses were very modern. Thick for the freezing winter months. Of course, Lily did not admit to anyone, especially to herself, that she filled out the dress because she was pregnant. Nothing was happening.

Ω

The day came that she sat quietly reading in the library, the rain showered outdoors and there was a firm kick inside her body. Undeniable, a strong thump under her skin. She stilled herself, lowered her eyes. Her lips turned down. The baby. There it was. In that kick. A tear swelled and trickled down her face.

Lily blamed herself, Charlie and even her mother. Yes, she should have been married years ago. Mother should have taken her to the balls. She could have worn a beautiful dress. Been courted by several dashing men and fallen in love. Then married and lived a happy, contented life. *Why? Why didn't the fairytale come true?* Why had her mother held her back? Perhaps her father held her back. Yet he was always wanting her married off. So no, not him. Her mother had let this happen. Lily had a moment of desperation.

Ω

"Lily," Aunt Beatrice called, "Lily, are you there!" Quickly, Lily wiped her eyes as she turned to greet Aunt Beatrice entering the library.

"Lily. Lily, have you been crying. What is wrong? Have you..." Beatrice could not dare to ask if Lily knew about Beth. Instead she searched for something more reasonable. Besides, Lily definitely wouldn't know about Beth. Surely not. No.

Beatrice consoled, "I am sure you will have your coming out soon. No doubt you will find a lovely young husband." She gently put an arm around Lily. So close, she was to Lily's wishes for a normal youth, yet she was so far off. "Look, I will do something about it. I will talk to your mother. I will command she let you attend London next year."

Lily whispered, "No, No I..." Understandably, this was the last thing she wanted.

Beatrice interrupted, "No, I insist." This was the excuse Beatrice needed. Celia had only responded to her veiled letters with promises to return early for the next social season. To cut their seaside visit short. In the next letter, she claimed Otto could not possibly consider travelling to Beatrice for Lily's womanly matters.

Celia naturally assumed Beatrice was concerned about Lily. Obviously she had not even thought of Beth for years. Beatrice didn't have the courage to write about the truth. Celia's marriage to Otto could be ruined if he read the letter first and it was likely he would. Then there would be no way of saving the situation.

Beatrice quickly continued, "In fact I am travelling to see your Uncle Simon on the shores of Scotland. I am to leave right away. I will be passing by your father and mother. They were on the other side of Scotland themselves, but now your mother writes they are staying at the seaside in Sheringham. It is on the way to Uncle Simon's. I will stop to talk to them." Beatrice took a deep breath and announced the blow to Lily, "You will not be able to come. I must tackle this by myself!"

Lily's thoughts raced. Penny could be sent away in Beatrice's absence, but it would have to be done quietly. With a good references. Lily did not wish Penny ill, she simply wished her gone.

Penny was too close to Aunt Beatrice. She would be spying and Lily may be put in a difficult situation. Penny would have to go before Aunt Beatrice returned.

Beatrice thought she could not bear to look Lily in the eye. She lamely added her other excuse, "Besides you know how Uncle Simon is! He's a recluse. Hardly has more than a few servants. Since he returned from Africa with those black slaves, he's never been the same." Keeping her eyes to the floor she hurried on, "He was such a sweet boy... and now he never allows me to come to visit, so I am just going to go. I know. I know it is the first exciting thing I have ever done, but you mustn't come. I really must approach these situations myself. You can be cheered by the fact that next season you will be coming out. Next season is not so far away. Winter is already more than half way through."

Beatrice looked at Lily, she was so silent. Too silent. Lily seemed very sad. She searched for something cheerful. "You can start on your ball gowns. You must. Send for any material you want. I will tell the butler to let you have your pick of seamstresses and materials. You will have to organise it yourself. However, I am sure you will manage. After all, you are eighteen. You have just organised all your other clothes for the winter and spring season. It will be a delight for you to instruct on ball gowns"

Finally Aunt Beatrice stopped babbling.

Lily forced a smile, "Of course. Thank you."

Lily's mind reeled. With her Aunt out of the way, she might be able to keep the baby a secret. "How long will you be away?"

"Oh, probably only four months. No more than five. I promise!"

Lily was relieved. "That will be fine, Aunt Beatrice." She added to be polite, "I hope you have a lovely time."

Lily considered the time line. She could give birth and still have plenty of time to give the baby away to a foster family. No one would be the wiser.

Ω

Beatrice watched the trunks and bags being lifted up to the carriage. She had decided to travel with only her personal maid and the stable master, rather than the usual six servants required on any other trip. Beatrice's excuse was her sister already had a full household of servants.

Many of her servants had been disappointed, some bitterly so, since she hardly ever travelled. Yet she had no time to worry about it now. The situation Beatrice was approaching would be dire. Celia no doubt would be strained to her very limits. Especially when Beatrice demanded the truth. And she certainly would be demanding every bit of the truth.

Sighing, Beatrice turned to look at Lily, her greatest regret in all of this. Lily certainly did not deserve to be left behind after all her years spent at the castle. Yet, a more difficult sort of trouble was to come Lily's way when she found out about her twin sister. She had only been a little baby, separated from her little sister. This was sad, very sad.

Beatrice noticed Lily's bland, pale face accentuated by deep purple smudges under each eye. She was staring at the ground. Beatrice knew she was terribly unhappy.

Lily's pain left a lingering intensity, as she kissed her Aunt on the cheek. Lily stared at Beatrice as though she was going to say something. However, she ducked her head and ran up the steps into the castle. As Beatrice climbed into the carriage, she considered Lily extremely well-behaved, without reproach to not complain. Not even the once. In fact, in the last week of packing Lily had not even mentioned Beatrice's trip away.

Still, there was no use dwelling on it all. What must be done must indeed be done. She descended the castle steps and climbed into the carriage. She shuffled over to allow her maid plenty of space on the seat.

With a tap on the roof, Beatrice had the driver begin the long journey to see her sister Celia. Even though she dearly would love to, Beatrice had no intention at all to visit Simon in Scotland on this trip. The twins had provided plenty of distraction and she would be in no mood to visit her brother with good grace.

She hated travelling, but she was determined to make the long trip to see Simon another time. She dearly wanted to find out why he had been so distant all these years. Her kind and loving brother had changed. Perhaps for the worst. His trip to the wild land of Africa had done something to him. At the end of his senior year, he had gone to visit with a school friend, Albert Terran. Albert's father ran a sugar plantation importing his goods through Simon's father for years. The Terran's Plantation had seemed a safe sort of journey into the unknown. Just enough to satisfy Simon's itchy feet, but not dangerous enough to cause too much worry.

He was supposed to return after one year and attend University, or possibly the military. However, the real mystery to Beatrice was how

Mother and Father had joined him just a month before he was due to return to England. The winds had turned on them in Africa and her parents had died a horrible death from marsh fever right before her brother's eyes. Why had they followed and why did Simon now live such a reclusive life tucked away from friends and family?

Simon had told her he had brought a little bit of Africa with him; two or three slaves. Beatrice was not sure of the details. In his letters he spoke of the Scottish weather, business and horses. He barely spoke of anything else. He had not visited any of his family in the nineteen years he had lived in Scotland since his return from Africa. To travel there by carriage would be a terribly long journey for Beatrice. Her broken back may not stand such a long trip, or even the length of this trip for that matter.

Sighing at the thought, Beatrice settled herself in for the rough, long, bumpy roads to the Sheringham seaside.

Ω

A smile hardly ever crossed Kitty's face. With her lips pursed together, she stood and stared down upon the scene of her Mistress getting into the carriage. There they were behaving like they were better. They had everything and she? What did she really have, but a demanding family? Only she, Kitty, had to work. Work here among these spoilt brats who had so much money it fell between their hands like water. Her mother had a horrible foul black heart. All Mother waited for was her money! Her money! This very moment her mother would be at home praying upon someone's misfortune. Tearing down another behind their back.

Life seemed so simple for the Hadley's. What troubles did they really have? They did not have to hand their money over to their evil mother, who would just spend every last penny on herself. Though to be fair, Mother did spend a little on the youngsters.

Kitty always watched her mother parade to church as though perfect and righteous, but really within her, Mother was greed and selfishness. To make matters worse, Mother bossed her, nagged at every spot or wrinkle, criticised her clothes, stance, speech, food, washing, low wage and, worst of all, Mother criticised her life-long love Doug. He lived a few streets over in the wrong direction. Though, Kitty knew her mother was right when it came to Doug. Kitty was going to have to drop him to get anywhere. Otherwise, he would surely drag her down into the poor life and she would only end up delivering a new brat every year.

Kitty heard a clatter. Turning quickly, she saw the head maid, Mary, puffing her way down the hall.

"You, Miss. Get back to work," she growled.

Seemingly to Mary, Kitty blushed prettily and bowed in shame. Really, within Kitty stirred a fierce anger from deep within the pit of her stomach that flushed to her face. Kitty considered Mary rude. How could she speak to her like that? She was made for better things than just being a maid who scrubbed the floor.

She started her work immediately to seem respectful. The head maid carried on walking. As soon as Mary had left, Kitty stood and went back to the hall window to watch the Mistress's carriage drive away for her long trip to the seaside. This was the first time Kitty had ever known Mistress Beatrice to go anywhere. She had left all the servants behind except for two, the selfish bitch. This did not seem right, or normal.

Miss Lily had seemed very upset as well. Strangely, Miss Lily did not travel with her Aunt. Something was not quite right. Kitty could feel it in the very marrow of her bones.

Certain tables had turned recently. One day Mistress and her niece seemed content and the next the house had become quiet and secretive. Something had happened. A change and Kitty was determined to find out what it was. It could be the key to her escape from this hell-hole of a life. Away from her self-serving, self-justified and self-righteous mother. Someone had a secret and she would find out just what it was.

10.

Within the Hadley Woods, just beyond Prince's Risborough Castle, Captain James Everett squatted on the ground. The trees grew thick over head, sheltering him from the worst of the rain. Thick fur throws were rolled up and stowed under a log. A small fire cracked and hissed on the rich damp ground. The smoke gradually curled up, around the branches and disappeared into the leaves. In the distance, a sturdy horse grazed in a large clearing, nibbling on blades of grass and small flowers.

Everett had not been so alone in years. Yet now he strived for solitude. To gather his thoughts and prepare himself to handle the sudden turn of events he now found himself in. His Hazel, his baby Hazel, who had been brought forth from the very Hazel Grove he now overlooked, hated him. With all her heart she hated him.

She had run from him, killing in cold blood, deceiving others with a false name, twisting his good friend, Henry Fletcher, into a fold of lies and then returned to her roots here at the castle. Had she known these lands were her very life and blood source? Searching carefully through his complex store of knowledge, he could not decide if she could have worked out her birth family was in Prince's Risborough. It was possible, Hazel now knew Beatrice Hadley was her aunt. Maybe even further that Celia was her mother.

Slowly rocking back and forward, Everett stared into the well-established fire as soft rain pattered all around. Just as he had done over eighteen years beforehand, he concealed himself, watching closely the coming and goings of the entire castle. Yet again he waited for his child to make an appearance. Though this time she was an adult, not some unknown babe. Through the maze of trees he had a perfect view of the front entrance of the castle and the worn road leading up to it.

Thinking over his predicament, Everett began to chuckle. Throwing another log on the fire, he smiled thinly. His friend, Henry, had concealed his Hazel. Henry had lied to him and sent her back here. To this place, of all places. Fletcher had made a stupid, almost fatal mistake. Everett doubted it would be possible for Hazel and Henry to marry now.

Not once in the last few weeks had he seen any sign of his daughter. Very occasionally, he had spotted Beatrice. Maybe it was time to ask around the village, or to speak to a servant. No one here would recognise him with his overgrown beard and shabby hunting clothes. Especially if he used his guttural accent. A rumble distracted him from his thoughts. The large carriage rattled around the castle, over the moat bridge and into the inner court front entrance.

Well, well this was different. Somebody must be taking a trip. Everett scrambled through the trees and down the slight rise. He hid behind a cleft of rocks, watching as best he could through the main gates.

In the distance, he saw the porters carry a trunk to the carriage and lift it up onto the carriage roof. Beatrice stepped over toward the carriage, followed by another woman in a dark dress. He couldn't quite see the woman's face. Everett's heart began to pound. Surely it was Hazel. They both entered the carriage for a long trip to somewhere. Maybe to Celia.

Not that they would be completing their trip. Everett was going to get Hazel back. To explain. To make amends. To fix the shambles of their relationship. He knew it all was his doing. He would even take her back to Canada if she wanted. One more chance was all he needed.

Hurrying back to his makeshift camp site, he quickly packed up his few belongings. After a good long whistle, his sturdy brown horse came running. Strapping on the saddle and reins, Everett leaped up on the horse's back and took off in a trot. He would not take long to catch up to the carriage and it would be easy to trail at a distance.

Ω

Sharp, cold rain pelted down as Everett finally dragged a stiff, frozen leg off his horse's back. Too many years had passed since he had ridden for hours on end. Being in his late thirty's didn't help. Living rough had worn him down. Everett definitely looked like an old man as he limped around the dribbling carriage. Sighing, he wished he was in full strength for this confrontation. He needed an edge.

Just tucked out of sight, he waited while the stableman dashed inside the inn. Then sliding around the edge of the carriage, he flicked open the door.

Beatrice stood at the door as though she was just about to open it herself. Seeing Everett, she gasped. Collecting herself together, she carefully stepped down to the ground. Under the strain of her back, she wobbled slightly. Standing straight was difficult. She shut the carriage door behind her so the maid would not hear the message Everett was clearly about to deliver. He scowled at her and struggled to find decent words.

He growled, "Let me see her. I know you have Hazel in there!"

Beatrice's quickly considered his words. Hazel? Not Beth, but Hazel. Interesting! Hazel had told a little white lie. This saga was more complex than Beatrice had thought. Clearly, Everett had not intended for Hazel to be sent to the castle to upset the family. It was not revenge, but a mistake. A mistake Hazel was using to pose as Beth for some reason. Hazel was hiding.

Beatrice said nothing, so Everett reverted to his old habit of threatening. It was clearly evident Beatrice knew something; her face was like a book. He grabbed her by the scruff of her neck. She squeaked in pain. Everett throttled her slightly. "Where is she?!"

Beatrice croaked into life, "I do not know who you are talking of!"

Everett shook her slightly, "Yes, you do." At that, Everett kicked open the carriage door. Craning his head in the door, while holding Beatrice firmly by the arm, he expected to see Hazel. Instead there was only a maid. A frightened maid, stuck to the far wall, with petrified eyes.

"Damn it." Turning to Beatrice, Everett yelled, "Where is she?! What have you done with her?! Tell me you have done nothing to harm her, you snivelling, self righteous prig!"

Sticking to her guns, she snapped, "Mr. Everett, I know nothing! Let me go!" The stableman came running out toward them. Everett let her go with a snarl. He didn't have the patience for this!

The faithful stableman caught Beatrice as she fell to the ground. Leaning her on the carriage step, he turned to have a go at Everett, despite the fact he was clearly much smaller and nowhere near as experienced in fighting. Everett had to admire him.

Mistress Beatrice intervened, "No, Keith! Leave it be. This man just mistook me for someone else."

Everett glanced toward the inn door where several men were coming out to join the fray. The type who always liked to join a good fight. Backing away, he glared at Beatrice. Refraining from giving a smart retort, he simply turned and disappeared into the night.

Ω

Heat rushed to Beatrice's head. Stepping toward the pub door, she began to sway slightly. Her eyes began to speckle. Pain burned up her back. Vaguely she could feel solid arms close around her waist. Keith was picking her up and carrying her to her room.

Was this suffering really worth it? Worth the trip to save her sister's face? All through the morning her back ached. After a short lunch break, Beatrice was doubled in pain as the carriage bumped past miles of farmland. All the careful maintaining of her back had not made an ounce of difference.

Knowing her sister, she knew there was no other way. She must confront her. She was sure Celia had been avoiding Lily all these years. Her visits were only yearly and very short. Celia had been using her to keep Lily out of the way.

Keith laid Beatrice on a well-used, but comfortable bed. Beatrice felt the blankets being pulled around her. Falling into an exhausted sleep, she admitted to herself she loved having Lily stay with her. That she needed Lily's companionship. How else could she have lasted these most recent years by herself?

Ω

Beatrice woke the next day with a stiff back and was barely able to move. Consequently she stayed in bed for the following three days. Her poor broken back was not able to stand the journey at the pace of that first day. Each jar of the carriage, each bump had banged through her spine. If Everett had not grabbed her by the scruff of her neck, she would have surely collapsed to the ground in front of him.

Beatrice decided to halve the hours travelled. She had taken the wrong approach. A full nine hours in the carriage had been way too much. Surely cutting it to four to five hours a day would reduce the strain.

So after a full three days in bed and many hot baths, her back eased and she continued on her way. However, each day they drove less hours. The trip of just over 120 miles should have been completed comfortably in a matter of three to four days by carriage. Yet Beatrice took nearly two weeks.

She had come a long way since the accident six years ago. Several doctors had said Beatrice would never walk again! That her back would hurt forever. One silly doctor had even given her a small bottle of laudanum to finish herself off. Defying all odds, Beatrice now could sit, walk and on a very good day she barely felt a twinge. The years of hard work to get her body moving, had paid off, but she still could not ride her beloved horses. Rather Lily now did plenty of riding for her. Certainly it seemed long distance travelling was way over taxing. Still, Beatrice knew she had to do this for her sister.

Ω

Finally arriving at the seaside of Sheringham, the carriage ambled its way to the seaside
villa. Otto loved to visit the seaside at least once
every two years for the fresh seafood and
excellent golfing greens. They usually stayed at
their large villa for at least five months with only
a few servants. Otto professed he enjoyed
lowering his high living while staying by the
seaside. Beatrice suspected he fantasized about
living a pirate's life as told in his childhood
stories. Maybe the seaside gave him a little taste.

Trying to distract herself from the
intensifying pain, Beatrice looked out the small
carriage window. She could see Sheringham was
indeed quite simple, but the buildings were
beautifully constructed. Down High Street, the
roof tops slanted sharply and were finished off
with swirling decorative wooden trims.

Continuing down the street, the buildings
changed to little quaint shops with Dutch
trimmings. In the town centre was the smallest
clock tower Beatrice had ever seen, and as they
headed out of the town, there was a little church
built in traditional English stone with the most
stunning stained glass windows.

Beatrice could see the attraction of such a
small township, especially with the beautiful
sweeping beaches. They must be lovely in
summer. Celia and Otto had travelled to Sheringham later than usual this year, arriving at the
end of summer. They had originally planned to
miss their usual holiday for this year, but Otto
couldn't stand to stay away. To add, they now
planned to stay through the winter, into the end
of the coming summer.

Beatrice had always thought Celia did not
like the seaside as much as Otto. Perhaps it
reminded her of her lost love, James Everett,
who usually travelled the high seas as Captain.

Thinking of him, Beatrice anxiously looked back out the small carriage windows to see if he was trailing. She had not seen him since that stormy night.

Still, Beatrice did not care why the Clance's holidayed here, she was just glad they were not overseas like many other rich people who loved to follow the sun. For if they had been abroad Beatrice would be dealing with the situation by herself. She would be tangled up with this strange girl Beth - no, wait; Everett had said her name was Hazel.

Everett's little visit had thrown another slant on the whole matter. Who and what was this girl Hazel, besides being Celia's lost child and Lily's twin? Was she really a milkmaid? Well it seemed she must be from the reports Eddie had sent over the last seven months.

Damn Celia for not coming straight to see her when she had sent those letters. The first letter had been sent to the Clance's Scottish manner where Beatrice had thought Celia would be. Many long months had passed before the letter had reached Celia in Sheringham. Even then Celia had delayed, sending her lame excuses for a further month.

Beatrice's second letter was filled with veiled pleas. Yet again Celia had delayed, and then sent more excuses of Otto's failing health. Beatrice had thought Otto more likely had some drunken illness. For he always dabbled in drinking too much alcohol.

Ω

Keith the stableman and Jane her maid had helped Mistress Beatrice to the villa door. Again a sharp pain almost doubled her over. They stayed by her side until a maid sent them to the kitchen.

Keith and Jane took their leave after receiving a small nod from Mistress Beatrice. No doubt they would soon be finding comfort from the bone-cold weather in the nice warm kitchen with a bowl of hearty stew.

Now sitting at the edge of a plush seat, Beatrice could barely keep herself still.

The maid stated, "The mistress will be along shortly, madam." She curtsied and left the room.

After Beatrice had waited an agonizing quarter of an hour, Celia finally entered the room. Beatrice stood too quickly due to her nerves and swooned.

Celia rushed toward her sister, "Oh, I am sorry to keep you waiting. I was having a bath before – Beatrice!"

Beatrice slowly and almost delicately fell to the ground with pain. Quickly she attempted to blink away the tears while omitting a very unladylike groan.

Celia yelled, "Maid, quick. Get Mr. Clance and send for the doctor. Run" Celia knelt at her sister's side. "Oh, why did you come all this way? It was too much!" Beatrice only groaned in reply.

Ω

Only a few days ago Celia had received word from Beatrice. Celia supposed Beatrice had come to finally put her foot down and insist Lily be presented in the next season. Celia knew she would have to give in. Her excuses were running thin. Yet, for Beatrice to bear such pain travelling simply to talk about Lily? Celia would've given in if Beatrice had simply sent a letter demanding Lily be presented.

Otto came rushing through the door. "What on earth is she doing here, Celia?! Did you not send a letter telling her not to come? She is not up to this sort of journey." Otto's face changed into a deep shade of red as his anger rose, "What are we to do with her now? I was enjoying my five o'clock glass. I do not need this sort of thing! She should have been married off years ago. Damn Winston."

Before Otto could begin to rant, Celia, who had always treated Otto with respect and calm through their whole marriage, snapped, "Otto, stop it this minute. She must get to her room and," her voice rose, "I do – not – want – hear – one – more - word!"

Otto stared at Celia in surprise, he had not seen Celia this upset. Flabbergasted, he finally turned and ordered the butler to fetch the strong stable lad, who at twenty years old, was still fairly young for this household but was at his peak strength. Otto had only recently stopped calling him 'boy' and referred to him as a 'lad'.

Celia watched as Otto quietly left the room. Thankfully, he had not continued his fuss. The tiresome, old drunken lout. Rather than the stable lad, Keith came rushing into the parlour. He carried Beatrice with great care and laid her in the spare bedroom.

Walking with Celia to the door, he said in quiet tones, "Mrs. Clance, I just want you to know she has been like this for the whole trip. We've been on the road for..." He scratched his head, "...about two weeks to get here."

Celia gasped, "Two weeks! I can do the trip at a very leisurely pace in five days!"

"Well, we had to take it real slow like. Resting. Travelling a day, or two. Then stopping for a few days." Keith's sad and worried eyes alarmed Celia.

"Why? Was it that bad?! I mean she rarely travelled to London, but when she did it only took half a day to get there." In contemplative tones she added, "Beatrice had always needed to rest for a few days afterwards, but not for weeks."

"It was that first day, miss. She pushed herself. We drove slowly for the whole day. Then she couldn't continue on, she had to rest till her back got a bit better."

"Do you know why she has come this far?"

Keith averted his eyes. He had a fair idea about their visit since he had dropped off Lily's twin to the milk farm all those months ago, but Mistress Beatrice had not said exactly why. He replied, "No, I'm not sure. She was so determined to come and she left Lily behind, which is strange."

Celia thought the whole situation a little odd, too, but saw no need to concern Keith, "Not to worry, Keith. I am sure she is here to convince me to present Lily next season. After all, it is long overdue and she must be presented with Violet, who is already over fifteen years old."

Keith gave a knowing sigh of relief, "Of course, Mrs. That surely would be Mistress Beatrice's concern. She probably wanted to convince you she would be fine without Lily." Keith gave a doubtful glance at Mistress Beatrice's still form on the bed.

Celia stated, "You may go, Keith and thank you for all your help."

Keith's face flushed with pleasure as he returned to his meal in the kitchen. Wouldn't the other servants enjoy a natter about Lily's presentation next year!

Celia sat close to Beatrice, whose face looked pinched. Every now and then Beatrice would groan in pain and try to say something. Celia hoped the doctor would not be long.

Ω

Beatrice stayed in bed for over a week and then another few days at Celia's insistence. Celia refused to talk with Beatrice about anything of importance. She only stayed by Beatrice's bedside for short visits, insisting they would have plenty of time to talk. Surely, Beatrice would stay another month in Sheringham. Maybe even two. Celia reassured Beatrice that Otto was more than happy to have her. Now she was here they may as well enjoy some time together.

By the time Beatrice had recovered enough to stay up for at least half a day, four weeks had slipped by since she had left Princes Risborough Castle. She sent Lily a note saying travel was very difficult so she would not travel on to Uncle Simon's. Not that Beatrice had planned to go there anyway. Rather than being away five months, Beatrice planned to return after three. She'd warned Lily it could take a very long time for her to travel with her back in such a bad condition.

Finally, after another week, Celia had run out of excuses to avoid hearing what Beatrice had to say. Beatrice steeled herself. At best Celia tended to be a twittering mess in difficult situations. At worst she would end up having a screaming fit like she did at the news of their parents' sudden death.

Dreading Celia's response, Beatrice started off slowly, "I think I will order tea, Celia."

Creating small talk for the next few minutes, Beatrice began to fidget. The tea arrived and was served. She stood and began to pace the floor.

Celia said, "Beatrice, are you all right? I haven't seen you this unsettled in a long time. Not since..." Her voice trailed as she regretted her hasty words. Beatrice and Celia looked at each other. Sending vivid communication without sharing a word.

To break the moment, Beatrice swivelled, her skirts twisting in her haste. Now was not the time to speak of those days with Henry. Not now, maybe not ever.

"Celia, I have some... delicate news of an extremely personal nature. I know you have assumed I am here to insist Lily be presented next year and of course it has been on my mind. I am pleased to hear she will be, but that is not the reason for my visit."

Turning, Beatrice felt she should face Celia as she delivered this shocking news.

Slowly Beatrice continued, "About eight months ago, I had a maid appear on my doorstep." Beatrice looked at Celia, who frowned. "She had been sent by Henry... Henry Fletcher." Beatrice's eyes flickered at the mentioned of his name. They stared at each other as they considered the significance of Henry contacting Beatrice. Celia did not know what to say, so remained quiet.

Taking a deep breath, Beatrice continued, "He sent a letter with the maid, saying he was returning this girl to us in good health. He indicated he had cared for her for a short time and had promptly sent her back to us." Searching for the right words, she continued, "This girl, she looked like Lily." Beatrice waited for the words to sink in.

Celia frowned, "Was Lily playing a joke? That is unlike her. She has always been such a good child. Occasionally, she would get into a scrap, but she doesn't usually play tricks and has never been mean."

Beatrice waited patiently, "No, it was not Lily. Actually, Lily walked in when the girl was there. She stood at the door and said she was going for a ride. No. No, this girl was not Lily, but she certainly looked exactly the same as Lily."

Celia began her twittering, "Well, Lily will be told not to play such tricks. Dressing somebody up to look like her. The gall of it! No she must not behave in that way. I will send her a note -."

"Celia! It was no trick. This other girl looked exactly the same as Lily, except for one thing."

Celia had cast her eyes to the ground and she sat very still. Finally she asked faintly, "What is this one thing?"

"The girl had emerald green eyes exactly matching James Everett's."

Hearing this statement Celia stood to her feet. Her mouth opened as if to omit a scream. Instead her body stiffened and she fell to the floor. Not a faint exactly, but rather her eyes were still open and rolling to the back of her head. In fright, Beatrice ran to Celia and picked her up from the floor.

Beatrice begged God not to let her dear sister die. She immediately regretted telling her. Celia had always been the weak one. Beatrice thought that with a turn like this Celia might never recover.

Celia's body felt as stiff as a board and a thin sheen of sweat had developed on her forehead.

"Quick, maid!" Beatrice yelled. The maid who had been cleaning the floor boards down the hall ran in the door. "Quickly, go get some help. She is having a turn." The maid ran out the door. "Fetch the doctor and the stableman!" she yelled after her.

Considering the current circumstances, Beatrice now thought she would have preferred a scream. Finally, Celia went limp in Beatrice's arms. She muttered and babbled what were almost incomprehensible words. The most Beatrice understood Celia crying out was, "No, my baby."

It was obvious Beatrice had bought back a terrible terror for Celia. Something horrible had happened with Everett; that much was clear. Thankfully however, it now seemed Everett must be searching for Hazel elsewhere.

Ω

Beatrice expected the doctor only to say that Celia must rest a while. However, he pronounced, "It seems Mrs. Clance has had some sort of shock. And a very large shock to put her into this state." Pausing he paced the floor of the study where Beatrice and Otto sat to talk with the doctor.

The doctor then continued, "I have only seen this sort of thing a few times before. She shows none of the signs of Sudden Paralysis. Besides she's a bit young for that sort of thing. Though I have heard it happened to a young man of twenty once. One minute he was shoeing a horse, the next he was flat on his back, dribbling and his face slack. They said..." Coming back to himself, he turned to face Otto who was beginning to look traumatised at the thought of Celia being paralysed like an elderly person on their death bed.

Quickly the doctor reassured them, "No. No it is not that, but it is a serious condition of the nerves. She must rest and be at ease for at least a month. Are you both sure she has had no bad news? A death?"

Both Otto and Beatrice sat numbly shaking their heads.

Under no circumstances was Beatrice going to admit to anything. Celia's secret was not her business to tell. She did not breathe a word.

Doctor continued, "Well, that is interesting."

Picking up his bag to leave, he handed Otto a small bottle. "Give her a couple of drops of laudanum every day for the next week. That should be enough to keep her settled and asleep most of the time. I will visit from time to time. Here is my bill." The doctor left without another word.

Otto handed the medicine bottle to Beatrice, "Could you take care of this for me. No doubt you will spend most of your time with her. Thank goodness Violet is at ladies training school and doesn't have to see her mother like this." With a distracted, haunted look Otto left the room to find a nice shot of whiskey to calm his own nerves.

Ω

Beatrice sat at Celia's bedside for hours through every day. At times, she left her side to rest, or to soak her aching back in a hot water bath. Into which she added a special mixture of gypsy bath salts that she purchased in large quantities at gypsy Clarissa's yearly visit.

As the second week drew to an end, Beatrice lessened the laudanum drops to only one drop a day, just as the doctor had instructed. For the next few days, Celia seemed to be drifting back from the dreamland in which she had been hiding.

On one particular morning Celia seemed particularly lucid, so Beatrice tried talking to Celia again. After thinking the situation through she had decided she could not in all good conscience keep Hazel a secret. Beatrice again became determined that Celia, who always seemed the perfect wife, mother and a model in society, would have to deal with this problem. She knew it could damage her, but she had to take the risk. After all, at any time Everett could approach Celia looking for Hazel and she could end up in an even worse state.

She began, "Celia, I need you to listen to me."

"Of course I will, Beatrice, I have all the time in the world for you. Is your back feeling better?"

Ignoring the question, Beatrice continued, "Listen. Lily clearly has a twin." Celia made to look out the window. "Don't turn away. You have to face this. She is your daughter. She looks exactly the same as Lily."

"I don't know what you are talking about, Beatrice."

"Yes, you do, Celia. You know. Look at me, damn you, and stop hiding. I am not going to allow this current deterioration of your health to stop me from confronting you. You had twins to Everett. Didn't you?"

Celia did not say anything.

"To Captain James Everett."

At the second mention of his name, Celia turned to look at Beatrice. Her eyes were dead. All emotion had gone.

Celia again stated, "I do not know what you are talking about. Leave me alone."

Beatrice grew highly concerned over Celia's plain expression. That was enough for today. Tomorrow she would try again. At least Celia did not have a turn this time.

11.

Deep within the dark shadows of the night, a deep thunder rumbled and growled. As the lightning flashed in the window, Lily woke. A warm, tightening began across her stomach. She had not been asleep for long. The clock in the hall started a slow gong announcing midnight. Pain slowly crept up her taunt belly and she knew the baby was coming.

Swinging her legs out of bed, Lily went to check the door was locked. No one would enter for any reason. Just to be absolutely certain, she took her only key and threw it into the moat below. The key landed with a plop. She could not get out of the room and no help would come. No one would hear her calling through the thick walls.

By her instruction, all the maids now slept downstairs. No one could know. She hoped no one would hear. In the worst moments there would be no option for help. She would rather die than face the world with an illegitimate child. No one would come until well into the morning. The butler would have the spare key.

Another wave of pain stopped her walking across the room. Bending over slightly, she straightened as it eased. Unsure about childbirth, Lily expected it to be over quickly like the horse she had seen one spring, the mare had birthed the foal in just a few hours.

Lily made ready her few supplies. She rolled out a large, clean birthing sheet. Tucked inside this sheet, she had smaller strips prepared, along with towels, a tiny pair of scissors and a ball of string. There was nothing else to do, but let nature take its course. Another wave of pain passed.

Trying to block out her own fears, she searched for something to do. Her book was sitting on her side table next to her bed. She picked it up along with her bedside lamp. The lamp still had a low flame flickering. She settled onto her rocking chair for a good read and another pain peaked. Turning the flame up, she read her book for a while. The pains gradually intensified, till she couldn't stand sitting any longer.

Lily wandered through the room to her bathroom. An old-fashioned bath was still filled with water. Dipping in her hand, she found the waters faintly warm. Nearly every evening she had the maid filled the bath. They must think her a little mad to have a bath every night, but it was the only ease she had from her aching body stretched to its limit.

As another wave of pain washed over her, she wished with great longing for a bath. She checked the coals under the bath for a little life. They were still slightly warm. Reaching for the flint set and some dry moss, she busied herself with starting a fire.

The pains came thick, slowly climbing and even slower to fall. Her hands shook as she continued to bang the metal and flint together, vainly trying to flick the spark to the moss. All she could get was a bit of smoke. Giving up, she placed the flint down. Surely there was an easier way. The maids managed to flick a fire within one stroke. Did she depend upon her maids for everything? Well as soon as she may, she would learn to strike a fire properly. Another pain subsided her thinking. Surely these pains would not drag on much longer.

Struggling Lily lifted herself up off the floor, she wandered back to the bedroom. In the distance the thunder continued to rumble and presently there was more flashes of lightening. As she was about to place her bedside lamp back on the small table by her reading chair the thought occurred to her. Maybe she could use it's flame to start the bath coals.

Between contractions, she took the lamp back to the bath. She gathered the moss into one place, removed the glass lamp cover and placed a small stick of twisted moss on it. It instantly burst into flames, the heat singed her fingers. In haste she dropped it into the pile of moss. Feeling pleased with herself, she began to heat the bath tub. The coal caught quickly and it was not long till the bath base was warming.

Using the lamp to peer at the water, she could see it was still relatively clean and clear. Her spine began a familiar ache. The pain moved around her stomach, building to a climax. The intensity of it permeated out to every part of her being. Gasping for breath, she thought her eyes might pop out if it did not stop.

An hour slipped by as the bath heated and she paced the room. Finally she eased herself onto the inner bath rack that kept a person's body from burning on the base. Instantly the weight of her belly lifted and relief flooded over her.

The night continued for a long, oh so long, long time. It seemed to her time drifted and like nothing was happening. Each pain increased and meant nothing. As the bath began to cool, Lily knew she would have to get out to put more coal on. With a groan, she stood. She winced and gave a loud groan as another contraction built to a humming pain. As it disappeared, she climbed from the bath. Immediately another pain began.

Crouching over, she stared at the bath coals.
The pain was too much. She couldn't do it. She
may not be able to get back in. Going back
through to her bedroom, she hobbled over the
fine white sheepskin rug onto the birthing sheet
she had laid on the bed.

Folding over, her groan turned to a scream.
"Please, please God let it be over. Please." She
begged. Lily did not know what she was doing.
Here she was naked. Alone. Standing there.
Surely this was not how it was done. Not
normally. Wasn't the labouring mother supposed
to be in bed? Oh, oh; she needed help and
damned herself for banishing the maids from
upstairs. Grabbing the side of her bed she bore
down onto her knees and rocked slightly as wave
after wave of increasing pain passed through her
body till her eyesight fudged and tunnelled.

Yelling, she begged, "Please, God. Make it
stop." A great gush of water fell from her and
splashed to the floor and it stopped. The pains
simply stopped.

Sweat ran down her face. She lay her head
on the side of her expensive quilt, not caring in
the least for the grimy marks she made. The
maids would wash it.

Minutes passed. They felt like hours and
nothing. As she caught her breath, she lay her
sheet on the floor before her. No way would she
be able to climb on the bed. Maybe the baby was
not coming.

Kneeling on her haunches, she stared toward
the window. Already the sun began to lighten the
night sky. Lily realised she had been labouring
for hours. So long. Was there something wrong?
The baby, was it ill? With a wave of fear she
thought it must be dead. The horse had been
only a few hours. Contorting with concern, she
looked down to her bare tummy.

While she wondered what to do, it started again. Much less intense, but still painful. Uncontrollably, she had to push. Nothing would stop it. She had to push. Over again, Lily pushed till she thought she would snap in two. Yet, it moved down. The baby was coming. Pushing. Pushing. Again and many more times. Burning and twitching in pain the babe came forth with a great gush at the final push.

Breathing in great huffs, Lily sat down on the sheet collecting herself. It had come out. Thank goodness, the birth was over. Putting her hand to her brow, she tried to steady the shaking. Then came a muffled cry. With surprise, Lily looked. She had thought it must be dead; this thing that slithered from her body, but it was something alive. And as she looked closer she saw it was a boy.

Ω

Peter became a little worried over Charlie's absence. Charlie had not returned to the gardens for months. Surely if he was travelling on, he would have bid goodbye. However, it wasn't until Peter spoke to Maggy, with whom Charlie had boarded, that he knew there was something terribly wrong. As he worked and sowed in the spring, he considered what to do.

After looking far and wide, day after day around the castle, he finally decided Charlie was not aimlessly wandering the lands. Peter asked all of the villagers he came across if they had seen Charlie. He even made a special trip to the pub on the other side of the village, to see if any of the patrons had heard from him. But still he turned up nothing. With no other options, Peter prayed to God hoping Charlie was well.

Slowly, the time clogs turned and as his attentions began to shift to other things. An angel smiled down upon Charlie, for by an unusual series of events in the early summer Peter ended up going further to the south searching for dry winter wood. He had the intention of splitting a large, fallen log and stacking it into his wood shed so that by winter the wood would be very dry and burn hot.

Peter could not find a suitable log anywhere on the east side. So he began walking south which lead him to a small run-down cottage. Spotting a large log over the other side of the clearing around the cottage, Peter began to whistle cheerfully. He began to walk around the cottage. This log would last him the whole winter, it looked seasoned already.

Hearing a clatter within the ram shackle cottage, Peter frowned and glanced through the windows. In the corner of his eye he saw a flurry of material. It certainly was not an animal then.

To be polite, he decided to ask whoever it was permission for the log. For someone must live here, the log could be theirs. Finding the door ajar, he peered in as he knocked. A weathered, weary man of indecipherable age sat hunched over in the middle of the floor.

"I..." Peter began. The man turned and looked at him straight in the eye. "Charlie!" Peter said, stepping into the room. Charlie averted his stare to the ground and coughed in a way that sounded throaty and painful.

"Praise God! I have been praying for you, Charlie. You don't look good. You're coming home with me." Peter said, very gently, "My wife Leah will care for you. She is a good woman and will look after you."

Charlie only sat and stared at the floor.

"Come now, Charlie. You must get up. Just walk." After Peter spent a few more minutes encouraging him to rise, Charlie suddenly stood. He limped slightly toward the door and then stumbled.

Charlie didn't think, because it was too painful. His mind was numb now. He did as instructed, he went home with Peter.

Ω

Beatrice sat in the Library staring at the book in her hands without really reading it. Rather than read she pondered on what to do about Celia.

No matter what way she tried to approach the issue, Celia always denied there ever was a twin. Looking back in hindsight, Beatrice thought it would have been best to bring the twins so Celia could not deny what was before her very eyes. Though, to have done so would have been very complicated for everyone. For Celia, Lily and Hazel. Least she forget about Otto as well. Besides, if she had bought them, Everett would probably have taken Hazel back and maybe Lily, too, when he had caught up with her at the inn. To lose them both may have killed Celia. Sighing deeply Beatrice considered sending for the twins now instead. Celia had outright refused to return with her to the castle.

Yet despite Celia's denial, Beatrice could see her face was drawn. Her forehead furrowed and her eyes red. The distress of the situation was eating at her. Never had Beatrice considered Celia would hide herself away. She expected a screaming tantrum followed by a long-winded confession, rather than the silence and refusal to acknowledge her long- lost daughter.

Beatrice's attention turned to a faint thud in some other part of the house. A maid must have dropped something. Celia hadn't even noticed.

Then there was a second louder thump, much closer this time. Like a door slamming. Celia looked up and Beatrice began to stand as suddenly the library door was ripped open with tremendous force.

Jumping up in fright, Beatrice saw Everett storm into the room. Rather than the full beard and scruffy clothes he wore when she last saw him, Everett now had a five o'clock shadow and a clean fisherman's shirt. At first his eye's glittered like emeralds in Beatrice's direction, before landing on Celia standing next to her.

With her heart jumping into her mouth, Beatrice ran to the bell pull by the door and tugged on it as hard as she could. Swishing around, she saw Celia stepping forward to face Everett with a cool, calm poise.

Coming up short before Celia, James Everett stared at the woman who had his heart, for truly it had gone to her all those years before. All the bravo and violence he had used to force his way through the house to her, dispelled in one single heartbeat.

The blood rushed through James' and Celia's ears and hammered around their eyes. Everything around them was suddenly closed out. Like they were standing with only each other in the room, they were oblivious to everything around them. Everett saw the softness in her eyes. Her undying love had sprung once more at the sight of him. Once again, like all those years ago, he was simply lost for words. Chaos began to spread through the whole house, while they just stood there completely still.

Celia lifted up a single, delicate hand to him and he held it like precious gold. Their histories seemed to disappear. They both knew their love for each other remained pure and true.

Celia whispered, "James, does she live?"

Everett looked into Celia's eyes and instinctively he knew she was not the one who had kept Hazel from him. Simply the fact she had asked about Hazel's existence confirmed that. He replied with a confusion of feelings, "Yes she lives. Her name is Hazel."

"Hazel!" Celia gave a small smile and a slight unbidden chuckle crept out. She stated, "Hazel; what an appropriate name." The memories of long ago came flooding back.

Ω

Six months into Celia's first marriage, her husband, Edward Tollin, had died a sudden and shocking death. Celia had only been barely seventeen when she married Edward. Not even in love; it was a marriage of convenience. Arranged between their parents to cement the merging of their two companies.

Celia was the dutiful daughter married to a dutiful son. They made the perfect match, one of high society heaven. Except it ended the day Edward sat with Celia sipping his tea. They had been making small talk, when his fine floral plate and saucer clattered to the floor. He had slumped and never moved again.

Celia had dealt with the situation nicely and after the lavish funeral returned to her parents five months pregnant with Edward's child. Isabella Tollin had been born when Celia was still seventeen. A nursemaid and nanny were taken into service. Celia had the status of a widow and mother. Being only seventeen, society in general believed she still came under the protection and guidance of her father's household. So she was obliged to live with them.

After a suitable amount of time, Celia had entered back into the ball season where she soon made dark mourning colours high fashion. She was the star of every ball and admired by all.

Beatrice had also been introduced to society that season and the two lovely sisters had a high time. As the season neared an end, Beatrice had made an excellent match, but Celia would not consider anyone. She was ripe for romance, but not interested in marriage. No one retained her interest.

Beatrice's fiancé, Joseph, being a military man, was sent to fight. So their engagement had been long, lasting years and had finally ended in his death. This saddened Beatrice, but not nearly as much as she thought it should. So Celia and Beatrice had returned with their parents and darling Isabella to The Black Prince's Castle in Prince's Risborough to spend the hot summer.

Very early that summer, James Everett arrived to make a special delivery of twenty hazel trees he had purchased from Southern Europe. He had personally selected them for Sir Winston Hadley Senior for their fine produce of a heavy Moorish hazel nut and tall strong tree properties.

At that time, Everett was still a nothing. He owned a few ships and imported fine goods, but he was not an honoured guest. Yet he was not quite a servant. So his stay was expected to be a month at the most to supervise the correct planting of each tree, as he had been instructed by master growers overseas. Celia's father had allowed him to stay in a large cottage with one of the servants. He had spent days searching the Prince's Risborough Castle property for the best spot. He needed it to be well drained and protected from the sharp winds.

Wandering through the garden's and outer fields, Celia and Isabella happened across James Everett, who had been digging up a little dirt to test the soil.

Celia looked into the daring eyes of this young man. He had a slightly rough appeal. Smiling at him, she suggested, "I think the land over out past the vegetable garden would be to your liking. Water is well drained through a pretty stream. The land moves in bumps and folds, so the trees would be well sheltered." She suggested hopefully, "I could show you?" A walk with him would be most pleasurable.

Slightly stunned by her appearance and beauty, James Everett stumbled over his words for the first time in his life. Yet, their meeting resulted in a beautiful afternoon together. James had carried little Isabella as they viewed the land, as Isabella had only just started crawling.

In the weeks to come they had planted each tree. They planned out a large hazel grove centred round the beautiful stream that meandered down toward a small valley into the forest trees. During these weeks they fell deeply and passionately in love. Things moved fast between them. Too fast. Celia began sneaking to James' cottage where they made wild passionate love, over and over again. James found excuses to stay on longer.

Their relationship continued over the months, 'till the end of summer when James finally convinced Celia to let him approach her father for her hand. Celia knew all along Father would say no. No advantage would be able to come from their marriage. Their match was not even socially acceptable.

For the first time in Celia's life she argued with Father, who continually presented her with what he thought were better offers. Being a very young widow, it was difficult to marry whom she really wanted. The huge potential scandal of her parents not attending the wedding stopped Celia from marrying without her father's permission.

The damage would be too hard to bear.

Finally the day came where James was due to sail again, before the changes in weather kept him from sailing to the other side of the world at all. He was determined to convince Sir Hadley to give him permission to marry Celia before he left. He wanted a respectable wife, but there had been no persuading Sir Hadley.

As James secretly bid Celia and Isabella goodbye in the vegetable garden, he asked Celia to come away with him, but she refused.

"No, James. You will be back in ten months and if Father will not agree, I will come with you then no matter what he says. He can't stop me. Please, James. I ... I want to continue as an acceptable guest in society. If I run with you now, I will never be accepted at large again." She felt her heart tear as she continued, "I promise I will wait for you." She declared, "I will marry no other. Only you! I will forgo it all if you try once more with Father on your return. I will work on him in the meantime."

James glumly stated, "You are right Celia. We need to have a respectable marriage, but I love you and do not want to let you go. Not for a second and certainly not for so many months, but look I agree with you. Why, I haven't even a house to leave you in when I sail."

Staring at the ground considering his options, he continued, "You would not be able to come with me on my ship, either. All three of my ships are crude and ill-prepared for a woman. They are cargo ships. I would not subject you to that." Giving her one last kiss, he promised, "However, I will have my lawyer purchase a large town house this winter. I will have it filled with servants. I know it would be nothing compared to your Father's many estates, but it will be a good start. Maybe it will prove to him I am worth something."

So they had parted ways, with their future planned. Unfortunately, it was not to be.

Ω

A month later Celia had stood before her father dressed in her finest. She had not breathed a word to anyone she was pregnant. She was determined no one was to know.

Father asked, "Are you ready?"

Celia felt slightly off colour. Almost as if she would faint from the heartbreak she felt. "Why, yes, Father."

"I am sure you have made the right choice to marry Otto Clance. He is a good man, with an excellent business. Yet again you have done well with your decision."

That said, Celia had walked down the aisle to be married for the second time to a man she barely knew, all for the sake of convenience. She did this to save her baby, James' baby, from the terrible life of being a bastard. Surely James would agree with her. This was a sacrifice that had to be made.

In just one week after James had left, Celia knew she was pregnant and she sent word in haste in the vain hope James had not left as planned, but he had. With a terrible feeling of aloneness and hopelessness Celia had to decide what to do. Her options were few. She could be disowned by her family. Disowned by the Tollins as well. Then she would have nothing and no-where to go. Isabella could lose her inheritance, or even worse she could lose Isabella to her late husband's family. So Celia had no other choice but to marry her father's pick. He seemed kind enough and she firmly believed it was the right thing for a woman with child to do.

As she had walked down the aisle, she plastered on a smile and married Otto. All the while she wished with all her heart she had run away with James.

Ω

James Everett returned to England with high hopes. He moved into his new town house situated in the best part of London. He searched out Sir Hadley and approached him with a marriage proposal for Celia. James put his best case forward showing how his business had doubled to six ships. Two of them were even high class passenger ships. Surely that would impress Sir Hadley.

James sat in a comfortable club chair, in a private room and explained his value to Sir Hadley. He finished off, "I almost have a fleet! I am willing to offer you a share. An offer I have given no other".

Sir Hadley puffed his cigar a few times. He shrewdly eyed James and asked, "I want to travel to Africa, Senegal as soon as possible. I have to help my son. My silly wife insisted he go with his friend. I should have never listened to her wining. He's in a little strife and he is young, nearly eighteen." He sighed, irritated by the inconvenience. "I have not been able to book a decent ship for this summer. I need to travel with style, as I have my wife coming with me. We want to stay as short a time as possible. Can I get tickets aboard one of your ships?"

James was a little thrown by Sir Hadley's sudden strange request instead of discussing his marriage proposal. He decided Sir Hadley must be testing him. "Why, of course. I will call my man. He will fetch the tickets immediately for you. However, I advise you do not take your wife.

The land is extremely rough and unfit. Women have only been allowed there since last decade."

"Oh, no. I am determined she should come and witness the God-forsaken country she allowed her son to visit for the last year."

"I will have you in our best suite designed for royalty. They will be leaving in just nine weeks. The passenger ship only passes that way once in a while. I only take passengers there twice a year and return and only because it is so easy to access on the way. Dakar has good supplies, but it is not the most suited destination for a man such as yourself." James' footman took down the details for the booking.

James spoke to his footman, "Go right away. Wesley is already selling the tickets. They will not last the day. You must get the best room for the Hadley's aboard the Le Marchee sailing for Africa, with a drop off at Dakar and a return ticket on the next ship back. Give the tickets directly to Sir Hadley and I will meet you at Wittel's Men's Club in a few hours."

He turned to Sir Hadley as the footman left the room. He said, "I am the Captain on Le Marchee for the next few seasons. I like to know the running of all my investments. I am sure Celia will enjoy sailing with me. This will be the first season I have sailed a passenger ship." James gave him a pleased smile. He thought his marriage proposal was going well.

However, in reply, with a smug smile, Sir Hadley stated, "She is married. So you are too late. She is already pregnant and very happy."

Everett left the room in shock numbed with pain. Deep inside he knew she was pregnant with his child. She had betrayed him. Betrayed their love and married someone else. Anger boiled deep inside. Now his love for her equalled his hate.

For the last seven months he had missed her terribly. In his longing of her, he had returned early. He thought of her like no other. Never had he felt this for anyone. Well, if he could not have her, she would not have his child. Their love and life together was dead. So would the fruit of it also.

As if to rub it in, Sir Hadley, the sly prig, had tricked him into selling him the best tickets on the boat. He should send a boy to cancel. Everett looked around the street. No boys were nearby. The tickets did not really matter anyway. Only the destruction of Celia and the death of his baby mattered now.

A determination had rooted deep inside Everett's heart and permeated through his very being. He had no trouble tracking her down. Just one or two questions sent in the right direction and within a day he had word back that she was at Prince's Risborough Castle, preparing to give birth to her expected child.

He'd hunted her down. Squatting in the nearby forest, he watched her wander through the gardens, as fat as a hippopotamus. Even her face had spread and puffed. Yes, it was certain to be his child she was about to birth for it was only seven months after her marriage. The babe was coming a little early for such a fresh union. Everett was interested to know how she would explain an early baby to the pompous, oh so correct Otto Clance. Still, there was nothing Otto could do about it. He was trapped into a marriage with another man's child whether he liked it, or not.

He remained there for two weeks watching her waddle through the spring gardens.

Instinctively he knew her time was near. By now she could not even manage the stairs and slept on the bottom floor in a specially prepared room.

He watched her by night, also. All he had to do was creep over the kitchen bridge, walk a few feet into the inner court and he was right there by her window. Despite the cool spring weather, she left her windows ajar, the silly fool. He slipped his hand in and moved aside the curtain. There was no escape for her. That baby was his.

By the second night of remaining close to the window, he heard her groan; it was deep and sounded painful. Yes, now was the time. Her midwife and maid attendant were soon in her attendance. The night ended and the day drew on. Everett hid behind a supplies cart and remained ready near her window. Dusk began to fall. Everett watched, appreciating the agony Celia felt, hoping it was as bad as or worse than his riled and tortured heart. Even the attending maid had to leave from the strain and fear of the whole situation.

Gently a cold rain began to fall. The wind began to swirl around the stone castle. Cutting into the air, finally he heard his child cry.

The midwife said, "A girl. You have a girl."

Everett's heart lurched; he sprung up and gently pulled aside the curtain. The midwife worked quickly cutting the cord and wrapping the child. With haste, she handed the child to Celia, who seemed very quiet and still. Everett noticed there was a lot of blood. The midwife ran from the room. Celia was left alone.

This was his chance. Flicking open the window latch, he silently slipped into the room. Celia was extremely pale, her eyes were closed. He stared into her face. Almost feeling like relenting, he leaned over to touch her. Icy droplets fell on her face and her eyes flickered open.

"James. I... I" Then silence hung between

them. Everett heard Otto's fine English voice calling to a maid.

Everett narrowed his eyes and Celia looked away from him. He thought, she cannot even say anything. There was no excuse. She had lied, cheated and deceived him. Everett grabbed his child whose tiny face peeped out of the beautiful handmade quilt. He noticed the tiny dark roses stitched into the hem. Pushing her to his chest, he stared at Celia with all the anger and hatred radiating from his face.

In that moment, Celia felt she had lost her James forever. She cried out softly as he and their child walked out of her life and disappeared out the window. For unbeknown to anyone else, she'd felt the tide of a fresh contraction.

Everett had left with one child, but crouching on her bed with the little strength she had left, she very quickly gave birth to another. The second birth was closely followed by a single placenta. Working quickly by herself, she snipped and tied the cord. Thank goodness the scissors had been still on the bed. Grabbing a small ripped-up sheet, she wrapped up this new babe. Thinking methodically, she wrapped up the placenta in the birthing blanket and sat it on the edge of the bed. Hopefully the midwife would not inspect it and see the two umbilical cords attached to the one placenta. Shortly after her doing so, the midwife returned with extra clean rags and a maid.

The midwife ordered Celia, "Lie down. You are bleeding far too much!" As the Midwife began her work, she stated to the maid, "Get the birthing blanket off the bed, it's in the way. Burn it in the kitchen oven fire. Oh, then get the small tub and have it ready for the babe's first bath. If the babe is to live, she needs to be cleaned straight away"

Much to the midwife's relief, she did not need to help Celia for long, because the bleeding and fluids had finally stopped.

Leaning over the bed, the midwife asked, "The bairn, does she still live? Ah yes, she is tiny, very tiny, but still some do pull through such an early birth. She looks a fighter." Puffing she sat on a side chair. Looking at Celia, she said, "I thought you a goner there, girl. I have helped only twenty babes into this world in these parts but I have never seen such bleeding. Still, stranger things have happened. A shame Gladis was caught up with the Mistress in Aylesbury. She has delivered hundreds. She would have known what to do with the bleeding. Though all's well that ends well. Aye."

Without her mentioning a word, Celia realised no one would even know about the other baby. No one would chase after James. This tiny baby was all anyone expected and was all Celia could concentrate on now, her one little darling. Her worry was that now little Lily would need protecting from James Everett.

As time ticked by, all was forgotten. Memories of her first daughter were buried deep within her. Blurred and smudged until recently, when Beatrice had confronted her about Lily's twin. All the pain from her past came forth when she laid eyes on James for the first time in all these years.

Ω

James continued to stare into Celia's eyes. He now realised he had made a mistake all those years ago taking Hazel. The noise of yelling servants and running feet bought him back to the real world. Glancing around, he looked Celia in the eye and stated, "Come away with me?"

Celia's pain washed over her afresh.

James insisted, "I will never ask you again, but come with me now. We were made for each other. Come away with me."

Reality started to prick Celia, "I stood before God and married Otto, James. I made my choice, to be honourable in society for my children's sake. I will not break my word. Not now. Not ever."

Flushing with shame, Everett nodded. He turned and left the room. People pulled at his arms, trying to detain him, but they could not. He pushed them off; he shoved someone and slammed his fist into somebody's face. Everett stared straight ahead. Not looking back, for fear he would run back and try to beg Celia. Once again, he walked away from the love of his life.

12.

Sometimes there are people who hide from their destiny. Others hide from their true self. Hazel hid from her roots. She remained elusive. Playing her part as milkmaid, she felt safe here on the Hunter's farm. By now she had lived the life of another for over eleven months. She was well rehearsed at being Beth now. A hardy milk maid from the depths of Ireland. She saw no need to rush off and expose herself to Captain Everett. He and many others would be searching for her far and wide.

Attentively, she scrubbed the floor. Hazel was sure the floor would scream in protest if it wasn't cleaned properly. Well, the farmer's wife, Margaret, certainly would. Hazel worked endless-ly, cleaning and milking.

She had times to herself. Snatched as they may be, she walked to the well, or fed the stinking porkers. She loved to walk the paddocks, taking deep breaths. The warm, sweet air would swish through her nostrils. She often helped fetch in the cows. The clear blue sky would penetrate her skin. The worn buckets clanked at her side. To her, this life was freedom. She did heavy work, paid her own way and chose it over living the grand life. Nothing on this earth would lead her willingly back to Captain Everett.

Hazel felt safe here, but she knew it was time. Time for her to move on in the world. She had sent Mademoiselle Fleur a few letters when the Hunter's eldest son Fred went to Prince's Risborough village for odd bits and pieces. He would often end up taking messages and letters along with his list of purchases. He never bought back a reply, though, from Mademoiselle.

She wore a serviceable grey dress, wadded together at the waist by a belt and covered by a thick apron. This whole life was unreal to Hazel, yet she found much comfort in it.

Margaret, the farmer's wife, was not kind to her like her Mamai, but she had a familiar way about her. Margaret was overly rude to her children and her husband; her hands were often dirty from some thing or another. However, for some reason she was often happy with Hazel and certainly made lovely food for the whole family. The kind that deserved to be put before a King.

Slowly, slowly Hazel had begun to feel concerned about her contentment on this farm. Summer had just begun. She should have left a few months ago to Mademoiselle Fleur's. The plan was to help Mademoiselle to train girls into ladies as she had been trained all those years ago. Yet it was so easy to remain here milking on the farm.

One day very soon she was going to have to force herself to leave. How she would miss the children, though; even young Freddy, who was a little smart and sassy at the fresh age of fourteen. She would especially miss young Edith, who at eleven had such a kind heart.

Still, it was time to make a move. Hazel was living a lie. She had lied to them about her name, her past and deceived them into thinking she was simple. All the deceiving left her with a feeling of unease and sadness that did not feel right to her. Hazel could not keep this up for the rest of her life.

Next week, she'd promised herself. Not at night though, those horrible dogs roamed free. But she would certainly find time to get away at some point. The old horse would do the trick. Of course she would leave money in payment for the horse. Stealing was not her way either. Her bags of money were still safely tucked away. Hazel sighed and continued to clean the floor.

"Beth... Beth!" Margaret Hunter called. Slightly alarmed, Hazel sat up and watched Margaret trot through the door.

"Nearla done, miss!"

"Oh, don't worry about the floors now. I have a letter from Mistress Hadley. The stable-man, Keith is here, you are to return directly." Margaret paused. turning a deep shade of red. Hazel supposed Margaret was sad to see her go. Looking at Margaret, she saw a mix of anxiety and happiness flush across her face. Hazel was a little puzzled by the strange mixed expression.

Margaret continued, "You will have to prepare to leave tonight." As she walked out the door, she turned back to add as if it were an afterthought, "The children will miss you very much, but I suppose it is only fair. Eddie's arm has been better for a long while now." She paused, "We have been very glad to have you. You have been a bigger blessing than you know. May God go with you." Margaret nearly ran out the door.

Could she have seen a smile on Margaret's face? Hazel thought she must be mistaken.

Getting up, she picked up the bucket. Lugging along, it slopped over the sides. Midday had already passed. If she wanted to make it there before dark, she must quickly pack the carpetbag.

Ω

It was late in the afternoon by the time Hazel found herself at Prince's Risborough Castle with very little to do. It was only after she had insisted that the cook sent her upstairs to shut the windows. After this task Hazel had been told to go to bed so she took her time looking at each room, wondering about the family.

A sweet smell of fresh jasmine and roses wafted through the windows. Hazel gazed out to the far fields where the farmers were packing up their tools of trade. Early summer was always a busy time of the year for a farmer. Calves and lambs were running around and late ones were still to be born. Everything was warmed, the sun shone and the flowers bloomed. The lush grass went mad in a haste to reach the sky. A light blue and golden yellow settled over England with puffed, plump clouds floating in the warm breeze.

Leaning to one side of the window to catch the last of the sun, Hazel considered her position in this large sweeping household. She had no definite place here and would be glad to be on her way. As the sky turned to an indigo blue, so came the reminder spring had only just passed. A slight chill blew through the windows. In a month the nights would be hot and the days unbearable.

Gazing around her, Hazel appreciated the comforts of Miss Lily's private sitting room. This room was already cool. Perhaps the windows needed shutting a little earlier. She would advise the Cook.

On the journey from the Hunters dairy farm, Keith the stable master had mentioned Miss Lily loved this room. He spoke like he personally knew Miss Lily and her living quarters, despite the fact it was unlikely he had ever been in here, let alone on this floor and he must hardly speak to Miss Lily.

Hazel had only seen Miss Lily once, riding in the distance as she walked the cows out to their field. On the little milk farm, no one ever visited and she had never travelled to the village next to the castle. The distance was too far.

Keith had rambled on about Miss Lily being cocooned in a separate world from the middle of winter. She had been this way the whole time Mistress Beatrice had been away. Miss Lily had hid herself in solitude. Everyone in the house had been highly concerned for her health. Hazel could tell the servants had been gossiping non-stop.

In fact, Miss Lily's behaviour had been unusual since last autumn. Well, so the stable master had said. Miss Lily had stopped riding her beloved horses. Even through a winter as cold as the last had been, they had expected Miss Lily to be riding on the days when the pale sun shone through. The stable master had stated that in past years 'when your very breath could crack', Miss Lily had been known to ride out for at least half an hour. Not this winter though. Not even once.

The wind had whistled through the cracks, rain pounded in every corner of the earth and turned into sleet, snow and slush. Keith said the maids spent much of their time chatting freely in the warm kitchen. Their duties had reduced to almost nothing with Mistress Beatrice away and Miss Lily so sickly. They had little else to do.

Miss Lily had remained in her bed late nearly every morning. She had often sent Kitty her new personal maid away, asking not to be disturbed. Even the fact that she had little Kitty as her personal maid was strange. Penny had been Miss Lily's faithful maid for many years and Kitty was just too green. She was only a young scrub hand. Even Letty the kitchen hand would have been a better choice.

Keith rabbited on to say the head maid had called in the doctor at the end of winter. But

Miss Lily had refused the doctor's visit. They could do nothing to change her mind. After all, they were just servants. Mistress Beatrice would be back soon; she would know what to do.

No one could understand why Mistress Beatrice did not take her long standing, faithful companion, Miss Lily, with her on her exciting journey. Nothing as exciting as that trip had happened in all their years together. One possible exciting event had arisen and Miss Lily did not even get to go. "She did not even put up a protest," said Penny, who had eavesdropped.

The only conclusion anyone could agree on was Miss Lily missed Mistress Beatrice so much she was lamenting from the loneliness she felt. It must have been hard for her to be left behind like that. Aunt and niece had always been close.

By the time Hazel had arrived at the castle, she had heard Miss Lily's life history. Obviously the servants loved her dearly and were very worried about her.

Hazel felt melancholic as she exited Miss Lily's sitting room. Well, at least Mistress Beatrice had returned a few days ago.

Tonight would be Hazel's last night. On the morrow, she would be well-rested, then she would leave. She would make her move come early morning. Escaping would not be hard as only a few servants remained at the castle.

Most of the usual servants were enjoying a nice holiday. Every year Mistress Beatrice gave her staff a week to return to their families. Usually it was during the hot summer, but they weren't complaining to be off early. The stable master, cook, butler and herself were the only remaining staff. The castle was extremely quiet.

Miss Lily joined Mistress Beatrice and Mrs. Clance for dinner. Cook had served them. Hazel thought this a little odd since she, as the only maid, should be serving them. Cook reported that Miss Lily was as white as a sheet and looked ready to faint at any moment.

Cook went on to explain to Hazel she had done her best to tempt Miss Lily with succulent meals to bolster her spirits. Cook was a firm believer in food being the answer to all ailments. Hazel considered this as she thought of Cook's plump folds draping over her small bones. She smirked, *Cook must have had much hardship in her life to carry so much weight.*

At times, Hazel had an uneasy feeling from the way Cook looked so intently at her. Up and down with a knowing eye. Getting away from here would be for the best. Sighing, she continued with closing the windows.

Ω

Down in the warm cosy kitchen, Cook and Keith were gossiping at length about this girl Beth and their Miss Lily. They had been paid well for their silence, but they could still chat freely to each other. Just as Keith was giving long explanations to Cook about Beth's green eyes and Miss Lily's blue eyes, Kitty opened the kitchen door. She clattered in along with a swirl of light summer rain.

Both Cook and Keith jumped in surprise. Cook flapped her mouth and Keith changed to a deep shade of red in a nervous fit. Kitty was taken by their reaction.

Cook spluttered, forgetting her usual commanding countenance, "What, how,... what are ye doin' here?"

This was not how Kitty expected her reception. Rather than Cook being grateful of her return, she seemed somehow upset by it. Kitty had never left the castle grounds, but they were not to know. She certainly was not going home for a week. Pay, or no pay. She was not living with that woman, her mother, again. Not for anything.

Kitty flattened back an odd strand of hair. "I couldn't make it home in this rain." By their blank stares, she could see this did not seem to mean much to Cook, or Keith. She added lamely, "You know my family is far away in Aylesbury. The weather..." Still she could see her excuse was not easily accepted. "I could help you for a while, till it passes and maybe go when the rains end. It might be a few days yet." Kitty knew she was getting nowhere. So she tried, "I will cook my special pie, or perhaps make you an extra strawberry rose jam for your wife, Keith."

Finding a few words, Keith stumbled, "Good. Ma Missus... ah... will like that." He slapped on his hat, oil coat and smartly left the kitchen. Cook would have to deal with this one.

Cook finally found her voice, "Well, ye shouldn't have come here!" She spluttered, "Ye are on holiday! Go ta a friend's house if ye can't make it home in the rain." Kitty stared at Cook. Kitty didn't have friends here or anywhere near here. Doug was the only one back home and he lived like a rodent. This was an awkward situation.

Finally Cook decided, "Just go ta ya room and stay there. Don't go pokin' about. Mind ya business. I will talk ta the Mistress and see what she says. I'm not gonna spoil their dinna, mind. When they're finished will ba soon enough ta tell them ye returned!" As an afterthought she added, "Spread jam on some bread and take it ta ya room wiv ya. Don't come out till morning!"

The kitchen, as usual, smelt of yummy stew, roast and sweet dessert. Yet Kitty obediently went to the plain bread and spread her jam.

Staying as quiet as a mouse and keeping her head down, she appeared timid. The only part revealing her fury was her steel eyes and slightly puffing nostrils. Secretly glaring around her, she noticed the Cook was now ignoring her while she busily stirred the stew.

Walking to her bedroom Kitty decided she would not stay there. Something was going on. Something to do with the secret and she would find out what it was. She would go to serve Miss Lily as a personal maid usually would. She would go up at the usual time. Maybe she could find out what the secret was, perhaps whatever it was would help her secure a better future for herself.

Ω

Hazel walked through the long wooden hall, her footsteps clipped slicing through the airy silence. In the distance came a disturbing cry. Hazel considered this unusual. She was sure no one other than herself was up here. She had just checked each of the rooms to close their windows after all.

Nonetheless, sound did not travel far in this solid castle. At least a hundred years before, many layers of clay had been slapped onto the thick stone walls in each room. Large wooden logs had been used for the extensive inner frames. Dense planks had been sliced out of huge trees. Construction of the frames and floorings had been followed by hot sticky tar being applied between each crack to minimise the drafts. To complete the complex masterpiece the builder had ensured each door was inches thick and heavy to open. This castle was a relic, but privacy and warmth was easily maintained throughout the whole building.

Thus, the wail she heard must be close. Clearly, something was distraught. Maybe a cat. Hazel decided to investigate. No one was here to stop her. She did not have to worry about the few occupants left in the house. They were safely tucking into a sumptuous roast chicken. If they hadn't been, Hazel would never have interfered for fear it was Miss Lily, or Mistress Beatrice crying in their room. A maid did not openly impose on their superiors.

Slowly Hazel wandered back up the hall detecting the sound as she went. She finally came to a stop outside Miss Lily's bedroom. My, this was strange. Curiosity was definitely getting the better of her. Hazel quietly opened the door and crept into the bedroom, expecting to find an animal.

The wailing had now ceased. She began to look around. The room was truly one of the most beautiful she had ever seen. A finely crocheted quilt on the bed spoke of many hours of work. A large natural wool rug sewn together from the skin of at least eight sheep, spread generously over the wooden floor before the large fire. Beyond this stood two comfortable reading chairs and a small personal bookshelf. The fire already glowed from the grate giving off a snug warm heat. There was nobody and no animal to be seen.

Hazel felt her skin prickle. She turned to flee. She had never experienced a real ghost haunting before. However, right now she was spooked beyond all reason. She was sure she had heard something. Just as she reached the door the cry started again.

This time, Hazel instantly recognised the cry for what it was. In amazement she stood stock still. *A baby?* Hazel's face furrowed into a frown. She cocked her head to the side in thought.

Definitely a distressed baby of a very young age. Her Mamai had four births and three living children. She had been at all the births besides Ben's. By now, Hazel was very familiar with the call of a young helpless babe.

Creeping over toward the bed, Hazel peeked around the side. Still no baby. Yet the wail continued and it definitely came from over here. Walking up the side of the large double bed, Hazel spotted a dresser drawer open a crack. Kneeling before the drawer with trembling hands, she carefully slid it open. And as she did she opened a deep secret. Inside the drawer lay a baby that had been bundled away in a corner of this large castle. Not one person in all her time living near, or in this castle had ever mentioned, or even suggested Miss Lily had a baby. How had this happened?

The tiny wrinkled face stared up past Hazel's head the way the very young do. How had Miss Lily managed to keep this from the staff? They would never have been able to help Miss Lily and then keep something that surreptitious to themselves. All the maids she knew thrived upon the misfortune and scandal of others. Their tongues spread a juicy piece of gossip like wildfire. The consequences of this scandal would have been raked over and the baby's whole future decided by now. Hazel could almost hear them in her head. The whole birth would have been scrutinised. All the pain of the child's birth would have been blamed upon Miss Lily because she had committed the worst sin.

No wonder Miss Lily had been cocooned away and sickly. She had obviously been keeping this little secret very much to herself. The consequences for such a sin were too large. Forever she would be labeled a scarlet woman. The baby would always be Lily Hadley's bastard. Miss Lily would never be accepted into society if they knew. Never. Society would have considered Miss Lily a girl of high quality and believe she should have risen above such a basic drive as sexual passion. Especially at such a young age.

Alternatively even rape sometimes would still be blamed upon the woman. After all, women possess the very spirit of temptation. Take Eve, for example. Look what happened there! High society never forgave. Only God did.

Hazel gazed upon the face of this entirely blameless, innocent child. She felt so very sorry for Miss Lily and for this poor child. Why, Miss Lily must be so afraid. Carefully, Hazel picked up the little bairn. Wrapping the blanket over his tiny arms, she snuggled him close. She gently pressed her face upon the baby's head. A sweet smell of milk wafted through the air. Rocking him gently Hazel walked over and shut Miss Lily's door. Then she padded over the luxurious sheep skin rug and sat upon a delicate rocking chair. Hazel hummed under her breath and felt the well-fed babe relax. The little mite gave a soft burp.

Ω

Lily's hand shook as she daintily placed the spoon into the soup bowl. She bit the edge of her lip to fend off the feeling of exhaustion and pain. Unobtrusively, she glanced toward her Aunt. Thankfully, Beatrice was not looking at Lily in that precise moment. Even her mother seemed to have stopped twittering nervously. Actually, they both seemed preoccupied. As though something else was of concern.

Lily drew in a sharp breath. God forbid they were going to suggest she make a coming out this season! Ball gowns were the least of her worries. She was not going to suggest, or mention anything for fear it might be true.

Come to think of it, her mother's continuous chatter had been a little strained. Almost as if to make up for Aunt Beatrice, who may as well be mute. Lily mulled this over in her mind. Leaving her own issues to one side, this was very strange and suspicious. Aunt Beatrice almost seemed stunned. Again glancing across the table, Lily took a proper look at Beatrice, while her mother desperately started to fill the silence with more nonsense about the Queen. Beatrice sat with a very stiff neck. Her back must be sore despite the extremely slow journey back. Lily saw Beatrice's left eye flutter. Something was terribly wrong. *Did they somehow know about my baby?*

Lily stood suddenly. She could not handle this, this unseen pressure. Her baby, she must return to her little boy. Nothing else really mattered right now. After standing so quickly, hot blood rushed to the nape of her neck and across her eyes. Suddenly the room spun slightly. *No, not now! They might try to help me to my room.* Lily grabbed the edge of the table to steady herself. They stared at her, waiting. Waiting for her to say something.

Lily quickly stumbled upon the words, "I, ... I am not really feeling myself." Thank goodness her head stopped spinning, "I think I will retire." Stretching the truth slightly, she added, "I have a headache."

Aunt Beatrice readily agreed, "Yes, my maid mentioned you have not been well since I have been gone. No gowns have been prepared, I hear."

Lily, not wanting to lie to her own family, agreed, "My stomach has not been right for some time."

Mother suggested, "Oh you must have eaten

something ghastly Those types of sicknesses can drag on. I remember your Father in 1805 suffering for months..."

Lily interrupted, "Yes, yes. I know he ate the ripe fish. Well, I will bid you goodnight. I'm sure I will be well soon. I already feel so much better than a month ago."

She left the room smartly to avoid further conversation.

Ω

Lily flew along the hall, not quite at an unseemly run. She had never left her son for so long. How was she going to tell them about her baby? What was she to do? There was no way of keeping this a secret any more. Even if she could bear to let the child go, she had no real idea how to have him adopted out. Besides, the very thought of him being taken turned her knees to jelly. Her heart pained to think of her dear tiny baby being whisked away. For if she was to tell, Mother would surely send him away and want to sweep it under the carpet. No one could ever find out about something like this.

Lily knew her mother had a driving need to be seen as socially correct. This was the way she trained her children. To keep secrets close to one's heart. Never to outwardly do a thing wrong. Nothing would be forgiven if the world found out about your dark secrets. Mother often went so far as to snub people who were a little unseemly at a luncheon social. In public, conversations were always to be kept within safe boundaries. Difficult topics were discussed in private and were never revealed publicly. Occasionally, Lily had even heard Mother tell white lies so she would seem perfect, correct and justified.

Unfortunately for Mother, Lily had noticed

some people could see through her facade. At
times, Mother was caught in her lies. Lily noticed
in those moments Mother would tangle herself
into a web of confusion while trying to point out
the other person as the liar. Considering all this,
there was no way Mother would be able to cope,
or support her daughter and her bastard child
without trying to cover it up.

As Lily reached the first floor, she broke into
a cold sweat from the effort. Running toward her
bedroom, she felt a slick warm trail of blood
crawling down her leg. Blast, when was this
bleeding going to stop, it had already been over
two weeks since she had given birth to her little
Harrison Charles. Maybe she would die from all
the blood loss. Tears began to well in her eyes as
she reached the door. There was no one she
could ask either. She had not revealed anything
about her baby to anyone, not to a soul. Not even
to Charlie, who she hadn't seen for months.
Especially not to Charlie.

Lily opened the door and flew into the room.
She turned to shut it tight. Out of her pocket she
pulled a large iron key. Like she had many times
before, she locked her room against prying maids
and now she locked it against her interfering
mother and complicated aunt.

Puffing, she leaned her face against the door.
Pressing her hot forehead against the cool wood.
Charlie was out there waiting. Wanting her, but
he wasn't an option. She reminded herself he
had nothing and would not be able to look after
her in any capacity. No money. No home. Only
the clothes on his back and a little tinkle in his
pouch. Not even a cottage. Lily felt she could not
lean on him. He would be destroyed by the
strain. Anyway, it was too late. They were not
married and Harry had been born illegitimately.

A single tear slid down Lily's face. Her only

thought was she would not be able to manage. Staring down at the wool rug, she began to walk towards the bathroom to clean up. Perhaps she would wash up those nappies in the bath water and hang them to dry overnight on her chairs. She was already low on nappy supplies.

Tomorrow she would smuggle some more old towels and tiny baby clothes down from the attic.

That was when Lily saw her. Lily stepped upon the white sheep skin, then stopped. At first, she saw a person just sitting there holding her baby. A flush of anger swept down her face. Her baby.

Lily hadn't locked the room through dinner. She took a step forward, flashing her eyes up to the maid's face and she saw herself holding her own baby. The blood ran fast down her leg. She froze in confusion. Was she losing a grip on reality? Strange.

Ω

Hazel watched her mirror image fall to the ground in a cold faint. Lily hit the floor with a very hard thump. Her face was ashy white and lips a tinge of blue despite the warm room. Shaking slightly, Hazel rose and gently placed the tiny babe on the large double bed.

As Lily had entered the room, Hazel had waited quietly for her to turn around. She wanted to offer Lily help. Perhaps Lily needed a friend. Then as Lily began to walk across the floor Hazel could see her face, her hair. Maybe Lily was slightly taller, but she was easily Hazel's other half. Shock coursed through Hazel's body. Thank goodness she had been sitting down. However, it was a bit unfortunate for Lily though.

Hazel knelt down close to Lily. She stroked golden brown locks away from her sickly face.

Despite the shock, Hazel had a clear enough mind to know Lily was not well. The strain on her face. The tiny shaking of her hands and the whiteness of her skin.

Hazel remembered back to how Mamai felt after giving birth. The first labour was long, but fruitful as Carrie was born. However, the next birth was early and too quick. Mamai's little boy had moved slightly in Hazel's arms, opening his mouth. Struggling. Never quite managing to take a breath, he died in silence. The whole family went into mourning. Most of all Mamai. That time she bled too much and suffered with terrible heartbreak. For weeks she was unwell with the same sickly white face and cold sweat that Lily had right now.

Mamai had forced herself up and back to the household chores, claiming it would help. Her other children were still living and she had plenty to do. After a week of Dadai fretting over her, she finally collapsed into bed for three days. The strain and bleeding leached all of the life from her. The midwife returned and gave Mamai a deep painful massage in her lower stomach. She claimed it would slow the bleeding. The technique seemed to work for, slowly, Mamai had recovered.

Hazel saw that look in Lily. Despite all the confusing questions barking at her door, now was not the time. In confirmation, Hazel turned Lily to look under her. Hazel saw a slow seep of blood on her skirts and touching the fur.

Biting her bottom lip in dismay, Hazel lay Lily flat on her back. Shutting her eyes for a second, she recalled the midwife at Mamai's side pressing sharply into Mamai's tummy, wiggling her hand slightly to stench the blood flow on the inside. Fervently hoping Lily did not wake through this painful procedure, Hazel placed her hands low on Lily's belly.

Hazel jumped when there was a sharp rap at the door. A maid called, "Miss Lily, it's Kitty to help you undress for the night. I know you're not expecting me, but I couldn't make it home all the way in the rain."

Hazel searched for excuses. Clearing her throat, she called out in a smooth cultured tone, "I'm fine. I have already managed my dress." Hazel finished with a slightly annoyed tone, "Please do not come back again."

Kitty was flustered, "Of course, Miss Lily. Sorry for disturbing you."

The penny dropped for Hazel. Kitty had called out for 'Miss Lily'. Hazel realised now that Henry Fletcher had not been calling her Lizzy, but Lily. He had seen her at the ball and thought she was Lily, pretending to be Elizabeth Overland. Hazel flushed with shame to think she had acted as Elizabeth right to the end of staying with the Fetchers. He must think she was an idiot or, rather, that Lily was an idiot. He had sent her back here thinking Lily had shamed her family. Girls did not go to a ball under a false name just because they were sick of waiting to be presented to society.

A small groan from Lily brought Hazel's thoughts back to the problem at hand. For five minutes, Hazel continued the home care administration on Lily. Hazel could not know for sure, but every little bit helped, according to Mamai's midwife. Lily's eyes fluttered slightly, but she remained unconscious.

After a while, Hazel estimated she had continued as long as Mamai's midwife. She wondered what to do now. If Lily did not wake soon, a doctor would have to be fetched, then the secret would be revealed. Any doctor worth an ounce would know Lily ailed from birthing problems. Lily had the tell-tale signs of being gutted from the inside out. The constant pain; deep and unyielding. A doctor would know straight away. Then all would know.

Sighing, Hazel considered a doctor might be a necessary evil. Yet the baby would be taken from Lily. Hazel had the feeling this was Lily's biggest fear. Lily had obviously held this secret close. Nurturing it up to this point. The consequences of telling now seemed too great to face.

Hazel squeezed her eyes shut to block out feelings of anguish and desperation not even hers. They were the anxious feelings of this stranger. *My sister?* A door had now been opened between them. One that would never be closed, no matter what happened. From now onwards, they would always know of each other.

13.

In a fuzzy, confused swirl, Lily slowly swam back into her surroundings. Her eyes fluttered. Several thoughts conflicted in her head. Something was strange. A person was bent over her with their hand on her forehead. This calmed her a little. Her situation could not be very bad.

Then she heard a little cry. Lily's nerves heightened. Her baby. She clawed forward to reach reality. She must focus, her baby needed her. The wailing continued. Lily jerked awake. No, he mustn't cry, someone might hear him.

Hazel watched as Lily stirred and struggled to sit up. She held the little babe securely in her arms.

"Don't try to sit up. Not yet," Hazel advised.

Lily stared at her in fright.

Hazel soothed, "It's all right. Don't think about me right now. We will discuss our situation later. Lie back down."

Hazel did not want her to faint again. Especially now the babe needed to feed. They needed to keep him quiet. She continued, "Look at your baby. He needs to feed. He mustn't cry any more, someone might hear." She carefully bent down to lay the babe next to Lily. He started to grunt and fuss at her side.

Lily agreed, "You're right, he must be quiet." She hesitated still in a state of confusion, "I must sit on the rocker. I..." She struggled up onto her elbow.

Hazel interrupted, "No, no. That would not be good. It's perfectly fine to feed lying down." Hazel added, "Just like lying in bed."

Lily said, "Oh? I can do that?"

Realising Lily had not thought of this, Hazel replied, "Why, yes, of course, and in your condition walking to the chair may only cause you to faint again."

Lily's son had once again started to wail.

Hazel encouraged Lily, "I will help you loosen the back of your dress. An evening dress is by far the worst thing for you to wear because it is so tight. You'll ruin the milk, if you wear a tight top too often. Next time, you must keep it loose." She undid the strings and hooks. "There. Now I will get you a blanket." Hazel fetched a warm knitted blanket from the rocker, while Lily busied herself with the distraught baby. As the blanket was laid over them, Harry settled to feed. Finally, he was quiet. Lily sighed in relief.

Hazel sat in an armchair, surveying the scene and considering the situation.

After Lily had spent a few minutes organizing the blanket over herself, she stared at Hazel. Finally Lily asked, "Who are you?"

Hazel simply stated, "Hazel. I have been calling myself 'Beth', but my real name is Hazel."

Lily instantly thought of Charlie. He always called her Hazel. Lily had considered it a charming pet name connected to their meeting under the hazel nut trees. Sometimes, he suggested her hair was the colour of hazel nuts. Yet, here sat Hazel. Charlie had thought she was Hazel. Lily's heart missed a beat. Flicking her eyes back to Hazel, Lily decided she did not have the strength to consider this too closely at this particular moment.

Looking at Hazel's maid uniform, she stated, "You are a maid here! But you talk so beautifully and ... and I have never seen you before."

Hazel explained, "I am a new maid and I have never seen you close up before. Only once in the distance riding on the edge of the Hunter's dairy farm... I arrived at the very end of last summer and Mistress Beatrice sent me straight to the Hunter's farm to be milkmaid. It's on the outskirts of the Hadley's estate." Collecting her thoughts, she continued, "I only returned today. I was sent for by the Mistress. She claimed she needed a maid here while the others were on holiday. She has told me I am to talk with her and your mother tomorrow. I am supposed to be getting my duties. Your mother... Mother!" Hazel rushed on, "Is she actually your mother?"

Lily snapped the obvious, "Of course. I look just like her." Amazement spread across Hazel's face and Lily realized for the first time Hazel would be able to see her own birth mother. They must be sisters. Lily swirled with confusion.

"Oh, Oh," Hazel flustered, not knowing what else to say.

Lily softened, "I am sorry. I didn't think. You... you must be my sister. Maybe a twin. We look exactly the same."

After conferring for a short while, they quickly found both their births had been in spring of 1802. Then, for the first time, Hazel found out her real birth date was actually April 20th rather than May 11th that she had always celebrated with her family in Canada, as that was the date Sally first held Hazel on the Saint John wharf.

Hazel then chatted freely about her life with the Donaldson's on their large beef and dairy farm. She decided not mention Captain Everett. To involve him in the conversation at this point could tip the scales for Lily, whose voice already wavered as she spoke.

Lily was close to tears. The recent birth of her boy caused her emotions to sway wildly. Hazel thought talking about Captain Everett would open a whole new can of worms, not just another chapter of her life.

Lily contemplated, "Why on earth were we separated?"

Hazel replied, "I wondered that, too. We might ask your mother, perhaps."

Slowly sitting up, Lily patted Harry's back. He released a fine burp, suited to a fat old man who had eaten too much. Both of the women laughed at hearing such a thing from such a tiny wee body.

With her eyes cast to the ground, Lily carefully considered what her mother's reaction might be to such a question. She said, "Mother is not the type to talk about difficult topics. She is ... stiff. We could ask, but may never get the real answer, especially if there are more secrets." Lily paused, "She was unusually skittish and chatty tonight at dinner. Now I know why. It's not me and my baby, but the existence of you."

Hazel agreed, "Yes.... Yes, I see now. I was quietly packed off to the Hunter's farm... I had great difficulty getting away by myself there. Someone was always at my side... I wanted to travel to France..." Hazel's thoughts raced, "But the Hunters were stopping me. They must have had orders to never let me out of their sight." Hazel smarted as she recalled their occasional rudeness by imposing on her privacy. "Mistress Beatrice must have sent for me because your mother is here... Oh, your aunt must have had a turn the day I arrived. I do remember her being unusually stunted for words."

Hazel then considered the events at the ball with Fletcher. She stood and walked to the side. "Mr. Fletcher thought I was you and he sent me back to your aunt."

Lily frowned, "Henry Fletcher?"

Hazel confirmed, "Yes, that is he."

Lily replied, "Oh the shock of it. He is a family enemy. He broke off an engagement with my aunt. The scandal... He didn't turn up to the church on their wedding day. Aunt Beatrice ran out of the church and had ended up having a terrible accident. It was so bad she was not supposed to walk again." Lily pondered over this turn in the conversation, "They say Aunt Beatrice never recovered. She has never married and has lived in mourning since. I have never asked. I dare not, either."

Hazel considered this, "Well, it seems he has never married either."

Lily agreed, "No he hasn't. My aunt must have been shocked to find you on the doorstep, sent by him, of all people."

Hazel asked, "Her name is Beatrice, did you say?"

"Yes."

Hazel continued, "I have a letter. I found it while I was in the old clock at Fletcher's house." Lily raised an eyebrow and opened her mouth to speak, but Hazel continued, "Oh don't even ask what I was doing in there. It's a long story. I still have it in the pocket of my old black coat. It said something along the lines of:

B

If you still want to marry me, meet me by the old clock at midnight. It's urgent. Otherwise I will respect your wishes and I will not come.

H

Hazel added, "The letter is very old and faded. It must have been from Henry to Beatrice"

Lily was startled by this finding, "We must tell her," she paused. "Eventually, at least. We have several other pressing matters to work out first. This is not going to be easy."

They conferred for a long while about their options. One idea was to confront their mother, or Aunt Beatrice tonight. To add little Harry was on the forefront of their minds. They could tell Mother and Aunt Beatrice about Lily's baby. However, both agreed Harry would complicate their situation too much. One shock at a time would be plenty to deal with especially where their mother was concerned.

Ultimately they decided to do nothing for the moment. They would wait and see how things panned out.

Ω

The next day Hazel was called to meet with Mistress Beatrice in the study. She continued to wear her serviceable grey uniform to keep up the appearance of a maid. She wanted to see what they would say without letting on her true identity.

Hazel sat on a seat staring out the open window, while she waited for Beatrice to enter. Her stomach tingled in anticipation. This meeting would mean many things to everyone involved. She would be meeting her birth mother. Would they accept her? They might send her away. Maybe they would try to send her back to Captain Everett.

When she heard the door open, Hazel stood as a maid should, to show manners. Beatrice walked in, followed by Celia. The moment had come and there they stood, each looking at the other, wrapped up in their own thoughts.

Hazel studied Celia with a steady eye. This was her birth mother without a doubt. Her hair was the same golden brown, the shape of her eyes, her delicate nose, even her lips. Hazel could see, despite her own vivid green eyes, she and

Lily were the splitting image of Celia. Maybe Lily more so because Lily's blue eyes matched Celia's.

Besides all of this, Hazel looked into eyes full of emotion. Celia's eyelids flickered. She blinked more rapidly. She bought her hand straight up to her chest and took one tiny step back turning slightly green around the gills. She quickly sat down on the nearest seat with an unladylike thump.

Beatrice ran to her side. Grasping her hand, she murmured encouragements. Craning her head she instructed, "Please sit down. I'll only be a moment."

Hazel was lost for words. She sat and watched as Beatrice stroked Celia's hand to calm her. Hazel thought Celia must have had a fright seeing her. Time ticked by as Beatrice crouched and comforted Celia.

Finally Beatrice stated, "I think you better go, Hazel. I will call you back soon."

She had called her 'Hazel'. They knew her real name then. *How?* Hazel jumped up. She did not want to go. Not one bit. She would not be bossed. Not now, not ever. Anger swelled. They would not treat her like a maid any longer

Hazel replied, "No! I will not!"

Both sisters were surprised. They stared at Hazel.

Hazel stated flatly, "I know." Still they continued to stare. "I know you are my mother, Celia, and I want to know what happened? What happened with James Everett?"

Celia looked at the floor. She started, "I... I" Then she stopped, trying to gather her thoughts. She desperately did not want to say what happened.

Beatrice gasped with amazement, "What happened to your voice? You are speaking so well!"

She snapped, "That was just a rouse. I am running away from Captain James Everett and I didn't want him following my tracks. How did you know my name was Hazel?!"

Biting her lip for her own foolishness, Beatrice slowly stood and replied, "James Everett told me."

A certain queasy fear flooded Hazel. Quickly, she asked, "Is he here?" Hazel took a few quick steps backward. Beatrice thought she was ready to run.

"No he is not here." Beatrice stated. Hazel relaxed a bit. Beatrice read a few things into Hazel's reaction that she did not like to ponder on at this moment. Thankfully they hadn't admitted to Everett they had Hazel.

Hazel asked, "Why did you meet him?"

Beatrice said, "Your father caught up with me on my travels and asked after you, but I did not tell him a thing!"

Celia faintly fluttered her eyes. She whispered, "I will go."

Hazel stepped forward and insisted, "No, I have a right to know what happened! Do not leave before you tell me about Captain Everett!"

Celia flared, "No, you do not! It's not a matter that is spoken out loud. I will not have it!"

Beatrice could see Celia's hand begin to shake. An intensity of feelings overflowed. Fearing another breakdown, Beatrice intervened, "Now, now, Hazel. Do not be like that. Just give us a moment to collect ourselves. This is upsetting for everyone." Beatrice wondered how Hazel knew Celia was her mother so quickly. She supposed they did look alike, or perhaps Everett could have told her.

Celia had begun to twist her handkerchief around her fingers. She stared at her hands.

Both Beatrice and Hazel stared at her.

Finally Beatrice took the situation in hand, "Please sit down, Hazel. I will tell you. First I'll ring for the cook to take Celia back to her room." Celia had no response to this announcement.

The cook quietly led Celia out for a lie down.

Hazel carefully walked over to the window and stared out across the land. After waiting a few minutes, she asked, "Why did you send me to the Hunter's and why for so long?"

"I was not sure what to do about you." Beatrice explained. "I wrote to your mother a few times, but the first letter went to the wrong place. She had shifted from their estate in Scotland to their seaside villa in Sheringham. I had not marked the letter as urgent so the Scottish servants waited for a pile of mail to send on to Sheringham. I had to keep you away from Lily."

"Lily?"

"Ah, yes. Well..." Beatrice turned to a beet red. This was not easy. "You have a sister. Actually you have three sisters and a step-brother, but one sister is staying here. Her name is Lily and she is your twin."

"Twin?"

"Yes, your twin. The letter I had wrote to your mother pleaded for her to return for the sake of her daughter, but of course she assumed I was speaking of Lily. I felt I could not write down direct references to you. I did not know if Mr. Clance would read the letter. I was not sure what he knew about you. So I sent a second, more desperate letter several months after the first letter. It took your mother at least a month to send a refusal. It was not as though Lily was sick and Mr. Clance refused to travel from the seaside. By then my only option was to travel to her. That took me a very long time because of my broken back."

"Your broken back?"

"That is a long story. One day I will tell you, but for now we need to talk about James Everett and Celia Clance."

Beatrice considered carefully what she would say to Hazel. She decided Hazel deserved the truth. For over an hour they sat talking. They spoke of James and Celia's relationship, Celia's marriage to Otto Clance and the birth of the twins. Beatrice concluded by telling Hazel how Everett had stolen her away before Lily was born. Celia had thought Hazel was dead.

Hazel considered this complicated history. Celia had conformed to the expectations of others. She had moulded herself into society. Yet Hazel felt so sorry for her struggling with a forced marriage and the terribleness of having a baby stolen.

Over the hour, Hazel felt a comfortable bond forming with her aunt. However, despite the easy conversation, Hazel did not mention she had met Lily. Nor did she tell much of her own history with Captain Everett. She felt there was no need to detail his exploits. She only explained how she escaped from Captain Everett. Tactfully, Hazel did not mention murdering Jack. Revealing all her secrets might be a bit much.

Hazel spoke more about how she had been trained as a lady for five years by Mademoiselle Fleur and her beloved family in Canada. By the end of the discussion the only question jumping out was what to do now.

Beatrice stated, "After long thought and discussion with your mother, we have decided we would like you to become a part of our family... I must say it is so much easier for us that you can talk and behave beautifully. We were not sure how to handle your lack of education as a milk maid. Still, we need not think of that now." She paused, watching Hazel's reaction. "Would you like that?"

Hazel hesitated, trying to think of all the issues arising from this request. Her head swirled with thought. Thinking through the ramifications was too complicated. So she gave an answer from her heart. "I would like that very much. I would like to try, for a time at least." Hazel gave Beatrice a sincere, level look, hoping to communicate her honesty.

Beatrice blinked rapidly to prevent tears. She was not one for emotions. "Good. I am pleased and your mother will be also." Getting straight to the issue, she asked, "What do you think we should do? There is Mr. Clance to think of, Captain Everett and the wider society." Beatrice was relieved Hazel seemed level headed and strong. At least now she had someone sensible to help sort out the situation, Celia was a useless mess. A way must be found to explain this uncomfortable situation of a long-lost twin turning up.

Hazel stood. She frowned, again as she considered the difficult ramifications of the situation. After a few minutes, she replied, "I am not sure, but the truth might be a good place to start. Lily and Mr. Clance need to know the truth. As does Captain Everett. The fact we are identical twins prevents this remaining a secret. Several servants already know. Soon the world will know Lily and I are twins."

Beatrice insisted, "Well, society does not need to know the details. Gossips will stretch everything, anyway. Perhaps Everett will agree to refrain from mentioning you are his daughter."

Hazel gave her aunt a quailing look, staring intently.

Seeing her look, Beatrice agreed, "No, no.

Don't bother saying it. I know that is very unlikely. I might be able to twist his arm, though. If he agreed, we could simply say you were stolen at birth and he helped you to return to England. We could say Henry Fletcher met you at the ball and sent you on to the Prince's Risborough Castle. I mean it would be a scandal and there would be plenty of confusion but we could have an air of mystery. Also, these implications would not ruin Mr. Clance or Celia and it's all true." Beatrice predicted, "People could assume Captain Everett was the hero who sailed you home and Mr. Fletcher the one who helped you return to your family. People wouldn't make the connection between you and Everett despite your green eyes. Other people have green eyes. I think there may have been green eyes on my mother's side. God rest her soul." Beatrice sighed, "Well, it's a shame we cannot guarantee Everett would play along. Still he might."

Hazel suddenly screeched, "I will not have anything, anything to do with that man ever again!"

Beatrice did not know what to say. She opened her mouth in amazement. It was clear Hazel had been traumatized by Everett.

Hazel stared at Beatrice, surprised in herself. The words had just blurted out. This was something she had never said out loud before. With her hands shaking slightly, Hazel walked over to a chair and sat down.

Beatrice consoled, "Well, you won't have to. I will do all the negotiating myself. I have known Everett for a long time and he owes me a few favours. This is just the time to call them in." Thinking she had settled the matter, she stated, "We will have to introduce you to Lily. Perhaps at dinner tonight. I will explain everything to her this afternoon. Celia will come round to this plan. After all, it is a problem she would have to sort out somehow anyway and now we will get you dressed into something more suitable.

Perhaps the cream dress you wore on the first day would be good. I will have the Cook press it for you. From now on you can be a lady."

Hazel simply said nothing. She simply looked distractedly at the floor. How could she formulate in to words the way Captain Everett had been suffocating her whole life? The way he destroyed her, for his own selfish desire? How he was obsessed with her? Had controlled her? Aunt Beatrice seemed so confident Captain Everett would cooperate.

Yet, Hazel doubted there was any favour so great Aunt Beatrice could prevent him from coming for her.

And come he would, if she stayed here.

Ω

After a long ride on a borrowed nag, Kitty had arrived at her home town of Aylesbury. Cook would not let her stay at the castle. Damn her, and there was nowhere else for her to go accept home

Kitty sat with a stiff back, on the edge of a blush armchair, stuffed as hard as a rock. She was to deliver her wages to Mother and stay for the remainder of the holiday.

Her mother sat listening to the woes of Muriel. She barely acknowledged Kitty's arrival. All Mother had said to Muriel was, "Here's Kitty, home for a visit. You'll remember her fine position at Prince's Risborough Castle as maid in waiting." A twist of the truth as usual.

Muriel whined on about her son's indiscretions.

Patting Muriel on the hand, Mother consoled

her, "I'm sure Mark will be fine. He has probably been waylaid at Loosley Row."

Kitty glared at her underhanded mother. Muriel did not even seem to notice the slight dig implied. Everybody knew there was only one reason for a man to be delayed at Loosley Row, where the beautiful pastures rolled.

Loosley Row was a small grove with a few houses, situated next to a small village in Lacey Green where the esteemed Clance's owned a Villa and a small estate. The estate was edged by a few scattered houses down in Loosley Row. One of which had a very captivating, wild and beautiful witch, known to hunt every man who passed by her. People said men went willingly to her bed and always came back from it spent. With a burnt soul owned by the witch. The Clance's rarely stayed there, but when they did, Otto Clance even visited her.

This conversation implied poor Mark was being lured into the witch's trap. Kitty cast an evil eye toward her mother. Everybody who was anybody in the village would know this tasty piece of gossip by sundown.

Cleverly, Kitty never passed anything to her mother, unless it was suited for her own purpose. Occasionally, Mother would exchange a penny for news from Beatrice Hadley's household. Wicked in her own ways, Kitty had sometimes spun a few good yarns based on a slight twisting of the truth.

Mother continued talking to Muriel, "Now, now don't cry. Every boy needs to grow and make his way. Just be grateful you still have him. Unlike my Edward, God rest his soul..."

At this Kitty stood and asked to leave the meticulously clean parlour. Her mother's voice droned on. She could not stand it any longer. Here was her Mother starting again on the story of her dead husband. The same lie she had told over and over. Kitty had been only eight at the time, but certainly old enough to remember that night. She'd huddled up to the passage wall, listening to her parents yell and scream at each other. Then the yelling had finished, as it always did, with a loud slap.

Kitty's body flinched at the memory, for that night it had not stopped at one slap. She had heard another muffled thump, then a loud clatter as Father had thrown Mother into something. With that final blow, Kitty then heard her father quickly running up the steps. Too quickly, for Kitty had no time to move from where she sat huddled in the passage. She thought she would be punished for not being in bed. Maybe she would even be whipped this time.

Her father's hand had always been too heavy. He often would do other nasty little tricks as well. Stick his finger into her side, pinch her arm till it bruised and pull the tender locks of hair at the back of her neck. His nastiness spread into Kitty's heart and turned it to stone. But luckily this time he had taken no notice of Kitty, he ran right past her. That night, he left. He packed a bag with his clothes, all the money they had and left on their only horse.

Mother recovered from her bruises. She told anyone who asked that Mr. Caper had gone on a business trip. Six months later, at a suitable time, Mother spread the lie that Father had died a terrible death in a foreign country.

Kitty had never breathed a word of the truth for fear it would mean he returned. Somehow in her childish mind she twisted the reality into a fear of her cruel father returning. Her mother spread more lies to maintain good face within society. Mother had the house, with no debt, but no income, therefore less and less food. Being very proud, Mother would never admit to anyone their hardship. Even to the point if people were watching her in the butcher's shop, she would buy expensive meats so fellow shoppers would not suspect her to be poor.

For three years Mother, Kitty, her brother and sister continued to live on a pittance. They stayed in their large house with two floors, its six upper bedrooms, kitchen, library, study, and most important of all, the beautifully kept parlour. Slowly household items went missing. The silverware, mirrors, cabinets, but never was any item sold from the parlour. Oh no, not one thing. All mother's guests would come to visit in the parlour. The village pastor would call and take tea. The neighbours would call. All would sit and sip the expensive tea and nibble on fat biscuits, or club sandwiches saved especially for such occasions. While Kitty and her siblings starved and longed for some decent food, visitors remained comfortable and cared for in the meticulously clean parlour with everything in just the right place. All this just so Mother could keep up appearances.

Liquid hate toward her mother steeled inside Kitty's heart. In stony silences, Kitty controlled her own outer appearance while her inner being spun with jealousy, contempt and vindictiveness. The world had delivered only hatred to her so she gave it back. Kitty had not figured out the secret back in the Castle yet, but she would and with it she would have her way out of this situation with her horrible, conniving mother.

14.

Hazel felt in no hurry to leave Prince's Risborough. As the afternoon wore on, she found herself meandering through the kitchen vegetable garden. She could see the gardeners tended it well, for each box was richly abundant with vegetables. The sounds of nature surrounded her, not the sound of people. The whole castle felt completely empty with only the two servants remaining.

Aunt Beatrice had said she would travel to London in a month, or so. She needed enough time to heal from the pain her broken back was giving her after the trip to Sheringham. Hazel still wondered how Beatrice broke her back. But it would be rude to ask again right now.

At this particular moment Lily was meeting with Aunt Beatrice. The twins had agreed to pretend they had never met, to keep Harry safe. For, if Aunt Beatrice knew, questions would surely be asked. Hazel hoped Lily was holding up to the strain and wouldn't collapse on the study floor in front of Aunt Beatrice.

Hazel would have to leave when Beatrice went to London to talk with Captain Everett, but she thought Lily and Harry would be lost without her. However it couldn't be helped. If she stayed Everett would surely come for her and then Lily would end up alone anyway.

A cool wind started to blow in from the East and Hazel could feel another summer thunder storm rising. Putting an end to her walk, she quickly trotted toward the small moat bridge at the back entrance. Just before she dashed under cover, a few large drops splashed upon her cream dress.

Whipping open the back door, she entered inside the kitchen to find Cook stoking up the fire. Warm and delicious smells wafted through the air. Hazel had a sudden pang of home sickness. This room was very much like Mamai's kitchen, cosy and welcoming.

"Are there ya are then, Duck. Made it in befa it poured, did ya."

"Why, yes. I'm lucky."

"Well it seems ye are in mar ways than one."

Hazel was a little unsure how much the cook knew. She thought it safer not to comment.

"I know ya history. I was here the night ya war born. A dismal night it was then too, with a great thunder shower." She tutted, "A shame really that Mrs. Clance was left alone. If I had caught the man stealing ya, I would have squeezed the life out of him." Cook lifted up her huge flabby arms as if in demonstration.

Hazel thought it would be rather unpleasant to be squashed by such a huge woman. She was very solid and tall. Cook continued, "Or maybe I'd ave hit him with the rollin' pin. It's something terrible when a man steals off with a baby. I suppose maybe his wife couldn't have no baby herself. Still, all's well that ends well, in'it. Ya back here safe in our arms now."

Cook did not seem to know it was Captain Everett who took her. Just as Aunt Beatrice thought, people would add on their own assumptions.

Cook encouraged Hazel to wait in the parlour and have a cup of tea, but Hazel insisted on remaining in the kitchen. She settled down to drink the nice hot cup of tea Cook placed before her. Hazel soon decided she would like to spend many hours in this kitchen before she left. Often the kitchen was the hub of the house. All of the servants would come here and the ones she had met were very much like the farmers and neighbours she knew from Canada.

Hazel decided she would write a long letter to the Donaldson family telling them of her escape. She was sure the letters she had sent from Eddie's milk farm to the Donaldsons and Mademoiselle Fleur would not have been delivered.

Maybe she should have given the letters to the boy who picked up the milk at the gate herself. Frowning, Hazel realised she had never meet the boy personally because the Hunter family had always prevented her. The boy always picked up the milk from the far gate. Freddy Hunter had taken the milk to him every morning.

Hazel thought about her time with the Hunters and became more certain the whole family - bar perhaps the very little ones - had known she was to be watched. They must have been paid off well. Hazel was mildly frustrated. She had thought herself safe and free at the Hunters. But all the while she had been held captive without even knowing they were watching over her. Though Hazel could easily understand why Aunt Beatrice had gone to such lengths to ensure her safety over the past months.

On further reflection, Hazel decided it was better she hadn't known. Otherwise she would have tried to escape, for sure. She may even have attempted to pass those vicious dogs patrolling at night. They were dangerously under fed and would certainly have attacked her.

Besides, Hazel was glad now she hadn't left. Questions she had pondered all her life had been answered by meeting her birth mother, her Aunt Beatrice, Lily, and least she forget, little Harry. These people were her blood family. They loved her instantly. Like she had just been born.

She stared thoughtfully into her tea and carefully took another sip.

Cook laid a yummy warm scone with cream and jam before her and said, "'ere we are then, Miss. I will take the rest ta the Mistress and Miss Lily with their tea."

Hazel wished whole heartedly her life could remain like this. Family, kind servants and new friendships on the horizon. Aunt Beatrice had a wholesome, comfortable life in this castle. A life anyone would desire. Sighing, Hazel's thoughts returned to the complicated secrets of this household. Life, no matter how beautiful, would not be like this for long, of that she could be sure.

Cook returned from delivering the tea and scones puffing from exertion of walking all that way, she stated. "Mistress Beatrice has asked you to join them now. Lily wishes to meet you straight away."

Ω

Lily rose as Hazel entered the study. They ran to each other as if overcome by a first meeting and hugged.

Beatrice observed and thought this was a little over enthusiastic. Still these sorts of situations were difficult to predict. They were not the least bit wary of each other, as she thought they may be. Rather they seemed comfortable with each other. Their connection must run deep, as it often does with twins.

Lily whispered in Hazel's ear, "I must go up stairs to Harry. Follow my lead, please."

With that, they separated and smiled at each other. Chatting excitedly, they bonded as sisters. Each was so grateful to have the other in more ways than they could express in front of their Aunt. Both were relieved now they could live openly as sisters.

Lily enthused, "I am so glad we have a solution that allows us not to tell one lie and live as sisters. Although I am a little worried for Father. He is going to be very angry he was not told you were stolen from Mother at our birth. Still, Father is not such a bad person. In fact, he is quite jolly at times. I am sure you will come to like him."

Hazel realised Lily had not been told about Captain Everett being her real father. Looking at Aunt Beatrice for direction, she saw her shake her head. Hazel was not to say anything. Lily would be told in time, no doubt.

Lily turned to Aunt Beatrice with a smile. "We are going to write to him straight away, aren't we?"

Beatrice smiled at Lily's easy acceptance of her new sister. "I think we may need to give it a week. We must wait until your mother is strong enough to cope with any more strain."

Lily continued to smile, "Of course. For now, how about I give Hazel one or two of my dresses, like you suggested." Lily turned to Hazel, "You have only got one and a tailor will come in a week or so, but in the mean time, you can use one of my day gowns and one dinner gown. I am sure we would be the same size." Linking arms, Lily started to guide Hazel out the door.

Hazel agreed, "That would be lovely. We will try them on straight away."

Beatrice watched them walk off to Lily's room. She felt a great sense of relief. Lily had accepted the strange situation so well. Still, she hadn't been told everything as yet. Beatrice felt Lily was still a bit tender. Perhaps because of the terrible sickness she had while Beatrice had been away. The poor thing had lost her aunt in her time of need.

Briefly, Beatrice thought over Lily's strange actions of late. She had sent away Penny, her much loved personal maid and had taken on Kitty instead. Also, Cook had told her Lily had been locking her door. Most disturbing was the fact that Lily had stopped riding. However, Lily had been given full reins while Beatrice was away, so she couldn't interfere in Lily's decisions. She would discuss the matter with Lily at a better time, but not this week.

Ω

The girls twittered and talked of fashion until they reached Lily's room. After they had entered, Lily locked her bedroom door behind them. Both girls were forever aware that, down the hall, their mother was resting in the blue, forget-me-not room. They were very relieved to find Harry silently sleeping. They could see his peaceful little sleeping face through the open crack in the drawer.

Lily whispered, "I was quite worried about him. I've been gone an hour. Still, we will get the dresses for you while we wait for him to wake." They walked through to Lily's wardrobe and selected out some dresses.

Before long, they were sitting on the rocking chairs, with shoes off and their feet snuggled on top of the warm white fur rug. With the thunder storm stirring outside, the day had turned rather cool for summer.

Hazel commented, "I am so glad the blood came out of the rug so well. No one would notice unless they stood on the wet patch and it will be completely dry in a few days. Do you think it's cold enough to start the fire?"

"Probably not" replied Lily "We are still wearing dresses with short sleeves."

"That is true. Maybe later tonight we will need to. Summer has barely started and it's still cold in the mornings. You must make sure you put extra blankets on Harry from early evening to mid-morning, but you must only put a few on in the heat of the day. Later in summer when it's truly hot, he may need nothing extra during the day time."

Lily agreed, "Well, it would not be good to over-heat him." Sighing and looking at her fingers, Lily admitted, "I feel like I have ruined everything for us. We could have been sisters living together here, or with Mother for a long time, but I have ruined it now. I should never have..."

Hazel interrupted, "Please don't, Lily. Harry is a lovely little baby. You know you wouldn't give him back."

"No of course I wouldn't, but I wish it had been the right way. If I was married, we could be openly enjoying a new baby in the house. Mother would dote so much. She hardly sees Isabella's children. I suppose Father does not like to travel to the other side of England too often. There is no business for him to worry about there and nothing else to hold his interest."

Lily added, "Isabella seems happy enough with their large estate in the country. I was surprised she didn't hate to be so far away from London." She added, "Although now, having Harry, I understand a little more. There is no time to worry about London society if your time is taken up with having children. She has three, you know. A boy and two girls. They are very close in age. I haven't even met the youngest, Penelope; she is seven months old already!"

Hazel hesitated, but had to ask, "Lily, is there any way you could marry Harry's father? At least tell me who he is. I might be able to help." Hazel found it intriguing Lily had not said who little Harry's father was. It made her think he must be a married man.

Lily considered the complicated situation between Charlie, herself and Hazel. How could she say Charlie was in love with Hazel, but had spent his time with her all those months? How could she explain that Charlie was so poor he could hardly make his own way, let alone worry over her? She couldn't even help him farm. Hazel might understand, though. That could be part of the reason why Charlie loved Hazel. She shook her head as again tears began to slowly fall. With her voice shaking, she stated, "He is not an option. It's, it's too complicated to explain."

Hazel carefully handed Harry back to Lily. She took her hand and patted it. Hazel whispered, "Oh, I am so sorry. I will not ask again." Surely Lily's man was already married. Hazel dared not to ask that question right now. The pain cut too deep inside Lily. Over time, she might open up. Hazel would wait until she was ready.

Ω

Very rarely did Kitty find pleasure in others. Only in herself. When her appearance was perfect, her clothes washed in the correct manner and ironed to perfection, her hair flat and smooth, with not a lock out of place, she was satisfied. Everything in her appearance was perfect, her pretty face remained stony and closed. Others who looked upon her had only an inkling of what lay beneath, lurking in the shadows. Occasionally some people had an uneasy feeling in her company without knowing why.

However, Kitty had a cunning way of using kind words to smooth out concerns. It helped also that no one could fault her work. She always served to the very best of her ability, giving perfection. Never a spot, or wrinkle. The other maids were delighted to discover she was so good at her job. Even the cook had discovered her exquisite ability to make sweetmeats. Kitty surprised everyone, but never offered too much.

Keeping herself to herself, Kitty never boasted. She never complained out loud, only in her thoughts. Subsequently, spite and resentment were buried deep inside her heart. The fact was that she thought no one was good enough for her. They were not perfect like her. From the footman to Mistress Beatrice, Kitty cleaned up after them all. Week in, week out. Never was it good enough.

Worst of all was Jane the maid, who often had messy hair and spots of mud gathering at her hem. Kitty hated her unruly, disgusting habits. Like dripping gravy on her piny.

Yet Jane always laughed and bought joy to all around her. They all loved her. With her gossipy chatting and lively help, Jane was like an open book. The rare times Jane cried, the household seemed to cry with her. Jane was Kitty's complete opposite. Everything Kitty hated and yet wished to be. She couldn't stand to tolerate such insolence from Jane any longer. Kitty knew she must work to live, but only for now. She would not be a slave for much longer.

Miss Lily's secret was her way out. Over the months, the story of the long-lost twin had spread about and past the local village. Many excuses could be made for a long-lost twin. Kitty had been paid well for her short silence in the first week, but she did not have enough to make a completely fresh start.

Miss Lily's secret was bigger and would surely pay well. Kitty found out after she had helped Miss Lily and Miss Hazel undress one night. After undoing their buttons she would leave, but often, rather than return straight to the kitchen, she would stand at the door and listen. Most of the time she heard Miss Lily and Miss Hazel talking of normal matters relevant to their station. They now shared a bedroom and were becoming very close.

Kitty would listen for at least half an hour. One night she had listened long enough to hear a tiny wee scrap of life cry out and the girls fussing over him. This vulnerable baby was Kitty's way out. After connecting a few facts together, Kitty soon worked out the baby was Lily's and not Hazel's.

Soon she would have the right sort of opportunity and she would see to it. Yes, very soon she would finally escape her mother's grasp.

Ω

All four women sat at dinner one evening. Conversation flowed between them. After only a few days, they were feeling much more comfortable with each other. Everyone had much to talk about, for there were years to reminisce. Hazel and Lily had marked differences in their life stories. Hazel told of her wild and free farm years. She had been taught to work in most areas on a farm. Her only true love in high society was ballroom dancing. Beatrice noticed not once did Hazel mention her years at sea and no one dared to ask.

Lily spoke of a gentle, safe childhood, surrounded by adults, her mother, nanny and governess. She admitted to a softness for animals. Particularly she loved horses. Celia described Lily as a dreamy and sensitive child, very rarely kicking up a fuss.

Finally Celia opened up by telling them of the twin's birth and the following events. It was obvious to all present that Celia did not find it easy to tell.

Beatrice thought Celia handled the situation quiet well. They all readily agreed there was to be no more lies. Instead, they would tell others the truth without naming anyone, or revealing any details. They even discussed what to do about Otto. Agreeing that dealing with him was bound to be difficult.

The only part of the story no one mentioned was Celia's relationship with Everett. Her affair was by far too disgraceful for Celia to put into words. Out of respect, neither Beatrice nor Hazel mentioned the fact. Lily still did not know about Everett being her real father, but both Hazel and Beatrice had agreed she would need to be told in the coming months after a few things had settled down. Lily might find the love story between Celia and James overwhelming right now. After all, her Mother had always been so correct and righteous. Beatrice considered it best to tell Lily after Everett had agreed to his part of the story. Lily had been protected all her life and Beatrice thought the revelation of a different father would be a huge shock.

Celia announced, "I will write to Otto tomorrow. I should be able to get a letter away by the day after, so we must prepare for him by next week. I expect he will come directly."

And so he did. A week after the letter was

sent, Otto arrived in a great huff. Instantly he took command of the house. Maids trotted down the halls to fill his orders and they would quicken their step, scrub harder and become silent when he was near. An unseen pressure was created by his arrival in more ways than one. The twin sisters stayed in their rooms under instruction from Beatrice.

On the first night, he simply refused to talk with Celia, "I am sure it can wait, Celia. I have come all this way. I need a drink and a cigar. Then I will be going directly to bed. Whatever it is can wait until later!"

Celia and Beatrice gave each other a knowing look.

Celia said calmly, "Of course, dear. When you are ready, I will share the news with you."

The following day Otto slept late. Finally, late in the afternoon, Otto stated, "Well, let us go into the study, then." Turning to his manservant, he ordered, "Bring my whiskey into the study."

Walking smartly from the room, he only expected Celia to follow. However, Beatrice went with Celia and they both sat in the reception seats, while Otto sat behind her desk. The manservant quietly delivered the whiskey and left the room. The women waited while Otto took a few long sips. Beatrice thought it wise to allow him to drink. She hoped, it would calm his nerves.

Beatrice felt on edge. She wanted to grate her teeth. A few times she had to bite her tongue. She hoped Otto would not stay long. Surely the news about the twins would send him to London for one of his jaunts, or somewhere else at least.

"Well, what is it? Why did you send an urgent message for me to come here? You are both well, you said Lily is well enough and has recovered from her food poisoning. So, what is it?" He gave the sternest stare his watery, red, pickled eyes could manage.

Celia looked down at her fingers. Beatrice hoped she would not have another turn, or work up to screaming. Otto was a person Beatrice definitely did not want to deal with by herself and Celia did need to take some responsibility.

Beatrice was very surprised when Celia lifted her head, stared Otto in the eye and delivered her message clearly. Even with a little force. "Otto, Lily has a twin. Her name is Hazel. She was stolen away from me at birth and now she has returned."

The look on Otto's face was priceless. The shocking news had been delivered so swiftly. His face turned to stone for quite a while. The two women sat there waiting on the build up and explosion that was sure to come. Soon Otto was full of steam, boiling ferociously.

The kettle finally screamed, "What? Are you telling me Lily has a twin? A twin! And you are only telling me now! Of all the stupid, idiotic womanly ways this must be the worst." He jumped up from the chair. His voice raised higher and louder, "You did not think to tell me at the birth? How could you, Celia? And you, Beatrice, you know how your sister is, an emotional woman. But, you? I would have thought better from you! Did you not think to tell me at the time?" Otto's face changed to a vivid shade of red.

Celia calmly stood, facing Otto, "It happened, Beatrice did not know and now Hazel is back. I thought she was dead. Thank goodness she is not and we are blessed to have her. However, there is something else you need to know as well." Beatrice was impressed by Celia's cool composure. For once she is taking the wrath of the situation face on.

"What other disastrous secrets have you now got to tell me!?"

"Even though I have always thought you were a loving father to Lily, you are not blood related to them. Their father is someone else!"

Otto stared into Celia's eyes. His face renewed to a higher shade of red, turning to a purple hue. Beatrice hoped he would take a breath soon. He opened his mouth and closed it several times. He grasped the back of the chair as his breathing became fast and ragged. Beatrice feared he may have a turn, but finally Otto sat and managed to recover his wits.

"Lily is not mine? Have you lost your mind, woman?"

Beatrice stood and stated, "She is not your blood, Mr. Clance."

Otto stared at Beatrice. She could see he was calculating out the marriage and birth. His eyes flicked to the desk and he knew it was true, Lily was not his.

In a quiet voice, he said, "This could ruin me. If this comes out, I'm over. My business, my investments...." He growled, "Damn, you woman! It was a marriage of convenience. Yes, but I didn't know how convenient it was for you. You should have told me from the start. We could have come to some arrangement."

Celia said, "And we still can. Beatrice and I have a plan. The world need never find out the twins are not yours. Children are stolen often enough. Older children more often for... for the Madame's houses, but still a baby has been stolen now and again. We need only say what must be said to people. They will make their own assumptions, but that is their business. There is no reason our lives, the girls lives, or anyone else's should be ruined. We would not even tell a lie."

Taking another long draw from his glass, a stony Otto listened. Both Celia and Beatrice explained their plan. Society would be told the bare facts, the name of the perpetrator would not be mentioned and they would say Hazel was sent back to them by highly respected men. They had recognised her as being Lily's identical twin. People would assume Everett and Fletcher were heroes. The twins being identical made the facts speak for themselves.

Beatrice stated, "All we need is the two men involved to agree. They only need to keep their mouths closed, or say what we are saying."

Otto asked, "So these two men, how exactly are they connected to this ordeal?"

Beatrice turned to Celia.

Celia simply said, "James Everett bought Hazel back from Canada to London. Henry Fletcher sent Hazel to us because it seems he thought she was Lily. What we will not say is James Everett stole Hazel from me because he is her father and that he didn't know Lily was born shortly after."

Otto glared at them in anger. Standing, he picked up his chair and threw it against the wall. He then stomped to the door, flung it open and slammed it behind him.

Celia mildly said, "Well, that went reasonably well. He took it much better than I expected. No doubt he will want to talk again tomorrow."

Beatrice nodded in agreement. Otto was not about to run off and ruin their plan by gossiping to spite Celia because he would be shooting himself in the foot. He would bring himself down.

Beatrice suggested, "I think we should dine and get our rest while we can. I will go to tell the girls Mr. Clance is thinking the situation through."

Celia hesitated, "Beatrice I do not really want

to go to bed. There is something bothering me. I think it's only the strain of losing Hazel as a baby." She bit the side of her lip, "I have had vivid dreams of a baby. Often crying. The dreams are never long, but they are disturbing my sleep. I wake for the baby with an urgent feeling to tend to it. It's like a mother's instinct where she must attend to the baby. Once or twice I have been awake and I swear I have heard a baby cry." Celia frowned, "I simply want the confusing dreams to stop. I... I don't sleep well."

"Oh, it must be such a strain, Celia. But there is no need to be so concerned. Hazel was cared for properly by Mrs. Donaldson in Canada. You can be reassured that James at least gave her a good home. She is very much loved by them." Beatrice patted Celia's arm, "Come now. Have a lie down. We will be off to London before you know it and then surely you will be distracted from your dreary thoughts. Everything will be fine."

Both women went to bed dreaming of London.

Ω

Otto sent for Celia directly after sunrise, asking to meet him in the library. Her maid woke her apologetically for Celia was used to sleeping late.

Once Celia managed to get to the library, Otto stated, "I have some questions for you." He walked over to the window and stood staring out at the blooming rose garden. Yet he did not really notice any of the beauty before him. It was simply an excuse not to have to look at his wife of just under twenty years. For a moment he wished for his first wife, Annabelle; she had been such a sweet thing. The perfect wife and his true love. At her death, Herbert had been only a week old. Her labour had been complicated and the doctor had said her body just couldn't recover from the trauma it had been through.

Before him now, sat the wife he had married to be a mother to Herbert. Herbert had been four years old and Isabella nearly two when they had married. Until now, Otto had always thought the arrangement had been mutual for the sake of the children. He had been pleased to sire more, though he had wished for another son.

Begrudgingly, he admitted Celia had done her duty by Herbert. She had guided him with a loving, yet firm hand while he was young, and now he was a successful businessman in his own right. He and Isabella had both married well. Herbert had two boys. Isabella already had three, no, was it four children? Otto frowned as he tried to remember.

No one had been more surprised when Celia fell pregnant immediately after their marriage. Even more surprising was how Lily had lived through such an extremely early birth being so tiny and all. Otto smirked to think what a fool he had been to believe she was born too early. Little Violet had been born at healthy term a few years later. She had always been bonny. He thought it was a pity she wasn't a boy. Still, Violet would be married off soon, but Lily hadn't even been presented. Now Otto knew why. The reasons were not due to poor, lonely Aunt Beatrice. No, it was Celia fearing James Everett would realise Lily was his daughter. He had already stolen the first girl.

Thankfully they were not boys. Otherwise Otto would be obliged to do more than just marry them off.

Without turning around Otto finally spoke, "What will you do if Captain Everett does not accept to fulfil his part?"

"I do not know. Beatrice seems to think he owes her. She won't tell me what it is... Maybe he does."

Turning to face Celia he watched her closely as he spoke, "I want you to be completely honest with me now. Is Violet mine?"

Celia drew a sharp breath, "Of course! Despite what you may think, I have always been faithful to-"

"Yes, yes. I would have said you had been a faithful wife, but I suppose your sins are coming back to haunt you now." He gave a hateful cackle. "Well, I have decided you may go ahead with your little plan, but I am leaving you today."

"Are you going to do business in London?"

"I will be, but I mean is that I am leaving you in all ways. I will be a man to myself."

Celia quickly lowered her head and shut her eyes. She placed her hand to her mouth in attempt to stifle the smile on her lips. No good would come from irritating Otto unnecessarily. *Oh, what a relief.* Otto was truly a tyrant and very difficult to live with. More so in recent years. Despite Otto's ways, Celia had worked very hard to be a good and model wife in society. She always thought the cracks had never shown. Now she longed for a rest from the continual pressure Otto so readily placed upon her.

"I expect you to stay here with your sister. I will not be wanting to see Lily, or the other girl. Oh, don't get me wrong. They were both born in our marriage so I will see them rightly married and with suitable money. I will return to see you now and again if I have to. I will bank a generous yearly allowance, but don't waste it because you'll get no more."

With malice tones, he continued, "I imagine it will grieve you, but I will not continue in our marriage as we have until now. Rather, I fancy, I will take a mistress. However, I expect you to remain faithful to me. If I hear of anything inappropriate, even a suggestion, then you will be cut off, as will all of your children."

Otto stepped back to the window as he continued, "To add, if this plan to protect the family does not work and if Everett, or Fletcher will not agree and it subsequently leads to my ruin, I will divorce you and cut off all of your children. I may even marry some other tart and leave my various small estates to the children she has for me. Of course Herbert would inherit the lion's share. You would miss out and so would your whole family."

Celia went a pasty white. Her life would be ruined.

Otto stated, "I will be leaving everything in your hands. I will be going directly to London by 8 o'clock and do not wish to speak to anyone else. Goodbye." Otto stiffly left the room.

15.

Lily was surprised, "You mean to say Father left?" She paused, "Without even coming to see me or meeting Hazel? That is unusual. He has always poked..." She paused trying to find kinder words, "Always stayed for at least a week. He often would enquire about my education and riding. He's never gone without seeing me before."

Celia carefully said, "Yes, he has gone. To London, I believe." Somehow she would have to find the words to say Otto Clance was not actually Lily's father. Her eyes flicked in indecision as she tried to decide what to say next.

Lily said, "Well I suppose the news of Hazel was a bit of a shock. Maybe it was too much."

Beatrice and Hazel waited for Celia to say more. Neither of them were wanting to tell Lily this part of Celia's difficult history. Celia should be the one to tell. Besides it was more believable if Celia told her.

The minutes seemed to tick by, as no one said anything. Lily contemplated that, in the light of Harry being hidden in her room, it was better if her father were not here. He would've placed an extra demand upon her time.

At a loss of what to say, Beatrice turned the conversation elsewhere, "Are you going to be horse riding this week Lily? You may want to take Hazel out to show her the grounds?"

Lily avoided answering her Aunt directly, "Well, I am not overly sure if Hazel can ride."

Hazel smiled, "I can ride, but I might be a bit rough around the edges for a lady's standards. I was trained to ride as a farm hack. after all"

Lily teased, "Oh, I am sure that a lady would out ride you, though."

"Maybe, but I am sure this little old farm hack would be able to out jump a lady."

Everyone smiled as Lily replied, "Well, my tummy is still a little unsettled, but give me a few weeks and I shall take you up on that challenge."

To which Hazel replied in her most snobbish tone, "Why, that would be simply lovely." The whole table laughed as they contemplated the ironic situation of Hazel being a lady who could ride as a farm hack. Such ladies were simply unheard of in high society.

Ω

All the while Celia watched Hazel closely as she talked. This daughter whom she hardly knew. She had a lovely, vibrant nature about her; commended to her other family in Canada, no doubt. Celia thought she must write to thank the Donaldsons for the wonderful upbringing they had obviously given Hazel.

Perhaps she would travel with the girls. Now she was free from Otto, the choice was hers after all. Canada was said to be exceptionally beautiful. The trip would have to be soon, though, otherwise the twins would be old maids before she could present them to society. Celia's thoughts drifted off into a dream of ball dresses and dashing men dancing with her girls. Many things would need to be done, beautiful dresses crafted, garden parties planned, invitations sent out along with so many other intricate details. She sighed, and a small smile played across her lips.

Looking at her sister, Beatrice was pleased to see her happy, "What are you smiling about, Celia?"

"Oh, we simply must go to London next season. You must come with me Beatrice to help with the girls. Of course there are the twins and Violet. We will have such a lovely time."

Beatrice's smile sparkled, "Why, yes, I would love to join you. We could stay in Father's town house. I am sure Winston will not be using it. He hardly goes there, now that he has his own house on Kingston."

The older women continued to chat, reliving their times past and dreaming about the coming season.

Hazel and Lily gave each other potent looks filled with sorrow as they listened to the lively conversation while considering their own situations. Both began to realise the impact their issues would have upon their mother and aunt. Lily with a new born and Hazel ready to run.

Furthermore, Lily considered how much she would miss not attending the ball season. Hazel regretted she did not have the time to spend months, or years with her new family. Dancing and laughing her way through life was not an option, all because of Captain James Everett.

Hazel found the pain particularly difficult to withhold, when Celia suggested, "We must take a trip to Canada to meet Hazel's adopted family. Really I must, Beatrice. Besides it would be best for all involved in our difficult situation if we went on a trip." Hazel longed with all her heart to return to Canada and introduce them all to Mamai, Dadai and the family. How wonderful it would be to see Ben, the girls and the village. Home sickness suddenly swamped her. Captain Everett would ruin it all. He would certainly ruin the Donaldsons' life if he found out. A tear fell down her face.

Beatrice noticed as she tried to wipe it away, "Oh, are you all right dear?"

Hazel quickly finished wiping the tear away and blinked fast to prevent more. "Yes, I am fine. It's talking about home. It really is very hard being away so long and I would so love to return, but -."

Celia quickly interrupted trying to reassure her. "Well, you will dear." She continued in hoping to distract Hazel from her melancholy, "Then by the time we return, before the bad winter weather, all of the gossip and wonderment about Hazel, the long-lost twin, would have subsided. Everyone will be so busy with the season."

Noticing Hazel had recomposed herself nicely, she continued on, "I know a little attention would still be shown to the girls after a trip away. A few will ask questions, but they will not have the time to ponder long. You remember how it is in the ball season, Beatrice. So much time and energy is used in the dance, walks and little private parties. People will have little time to talk about old news. There is bound to be some new scandal in the wind. Oh, Hazel dear, how perfect it is that you love to dance."

"I absolutely love to dance. Why, Mademoiselle Fleur spent hours dancing with me so I know all the usual dance steps and a few with French flare." Hazel said, giving a saucy grin despite her mixed feelings.

Lily was a little shocked, but laughed anyway. She would have never have said anything so bold, especially in front of Mother.

Celia growled in fun, "Don't be so naughty."

Amongst all the laughter and merriment continuing through the day, the twins wished in vain these dreams could become true, but they both knew without a doubt they would not.

Ω

Over the following month, a pattern developed between the four women. The elder two
began planning for the twin's upcoming season
and sent for passage to Canada. Usually passage
needed to be booked months in advance. They
were worried they may be a little late.

The younger two shared the care of Harry in
secret. Harry fell into a set sleeping routine more
or less forced upon him out of necessity.
Through the girls' meal times he slept, then Lily
would always return to feed him by saying she
was going to change into her riding clothes, or
fetch her coat. While Lily was gone, Hazel
entertained Mother and Aunt Beatrice. Lily
always enthused how she loved the outdoors. So
she would go with her mother or aunt on
outings, though Aunt Beatrice never went riding.

Hazel admitted she did not love riding, so it
was easy to avoid most outings. She would
excuse herself to the private upstairs parlour, or
for a rest, through which time she would play
with Harry, change him and put him back to
sleep in the drawer. He was so tiny and had little
energy to spare. He easily fell to sleep after he
was wrapped and placed in the drawer. Usually
he would wake for an hour and then sleep for at
least two hours. This made it easy for the girls to
keep up an appearance throughout the whole
day. Naturally all four women respected each
person's personal space and routines. They all
had times of solitude and others as companions.

The twins therefore were never questioned
for their time away. However Hazel knew this
routine would not last forever. By the month's
end little Harry was already staying awake
longer. The unbearable summer heat was
making sleep more difficult for him. He developed
heat rash and was generally quite irritable.

This current lifestyle was like a dreamland

for Hazel. She relaxed, enjoying the peace and tranquillity of Prince's Risborough Castle. Yet for Lily, it was a time of deep foreboding. The future for her was by far harder to face than for Hazel. Then the time finally came.

One morning Aunt Beatrice announced, "Girls, your mother and I have decided we will leave for London tomorrow morning. As you know I will go to sort out James Everett and Henry Fletcher. Your mother will organize the trip. After all, we must leave for Canada in a few weeks, before the Summer's end, so we can have at least a month to spend in Canada. That will leave plenty of time to travel and return for the main social season through the winter months. We will need to return well before the weather stops us. In due course, we will send for you and also for Violet to travel to London. Probably by the week's end. We must get you measured for your ball dresses before we travel. That way they will be ready for you when you get back from Canada."

Celia asked again, "Do you think the girls should stay here? Maybe they should come with us?" Lily held her breath waiting for her aunts reply.

Beatrice hesitated, "No, Celia. It's safer to leave the girls here. You know how James can be... He is volatile at the best of times. I have a good hold over him, but with his temper he could have a huge outburst before he calms. The girls will be much safer here."

Hazel and Lily breathed a quiet sigh of relief. Hazel thought running would be much harder in London with Mother and Aunt Beatrice. Running away would create a huge scandal in town.

Beatrice concluded by saying, "We will need to spend the morning packing. So have a lovely day without us."

Rather, Hazel and Lily spent the day together in a sombre repose.

Ω

Aunt Beatrice scolded, "Lily, I have never known you to cry when I have left before. You never cried when your Mother left either. You will be fine. It's only a week. Hazel is with you. I am sure you will not get sick this time." Aunt Beatrice patted her back, "Just avoid eating fish."

Lily felt rather wretched. "It wasn't fish. I haven't eaten fish at all this year." In the weakness of the moment, she almost admitted the truth about her pregnancy except Hazel quickly intervened, giving her aunt a warm hug.

Hazel slipped the letter she had found in the old clock into Aunt Beatrice's hand. She said, "I found this in a grandfather clock, when I stayed in Henry Fletcher's house. I have been wanting to give it to you for a while, but I didn't want to upset you. However, you need to read it before you see Mr. Fletcher." Hazel said sincerely, "I am so sorry you did not get this letter all those years ago."

Beatrice was surprised. She took the letter and tucked it in her coat. "I will read it later." She had a sickening feeling about what it would say.

Hazel agreed, "Yes, I think that would be best. Have a good journey." She hugged her mother, while Beatrice advised Lily to eat fresh foods. Lily was a little numb and only nodded her head.

Lily wiped away a few tears. She felt like bawling, but forced herself to restrain the tears. Hazel put her arms around Lily as their mother and aunt rattled away in their carriage. The moment the carriage was far away, Lily began to cry on Hazels shoulder. A few servants gave her some strange looks, not knowing understanding in the least what was about to happen.

Ω

Later that evening while eating dinner, Hazel sent the servants away and turned the conversation to their future. "Lily, I will not be able to go to London."

"Well, I know I will not be able to. I am trying to think of a decent reason not to go, but I suspect that fate will turn on me soon. I suppose that when they find out, I will be sent away in shame." Lily sadly paused. "But, why would you not go to London? There is no reason why you can't."

"It's because of... There are circumstances, ... situations that I have not told you about. There is a man..."

Lily moved forward in surprise, thinking of Charlie, looking at Hazel with concern. "Do you have a lover, Hazel?" Lily hoped Hazel had no connection with Charlie.

"No, no, never. None, except Ben have come close in that regard. He is my brother, you will remember, from Canada, but he has only and forever will only be my brother. He is in love with Bessy."

Lily inwardly sighed with relief. She said, "Well then, what man? Why would you have to leave?"

Hazel looked at Lily. She was so gentle and lovely to be with. How could she explain Captain Everett and what he'd done to her? Hazel was still surprised Lily had the strength to keep Harry a secret. Lily had endurance and determination, but she was so fragile. She wore her heart on her sleeve. Casting her eyes to one side,

Hazel decided the full truth would have to wait. "The man that stole me at birth is not going to give me up easily."

"Oh." Lily waited for Hazel to say more.

Hazel struggled to find the right words, "I was running from him when I was recognised by Henry Fletcher as you. As you know, Mr. Fletcher sent me here, but Captain Everett is the reason why I am running." She paused to consider what to reveal next. "He was overbearing and obsessive. He is a dangerous man. He mostly lives a rough life upon the sea, but plays the gentleman in London. He was the one who had me trained as a lady. Yet, if what I have heard is correct, he dragged himself up from being poor." Hazel's thoughts raced, "He now is a powerful man in London and would do anything to have me under his power again. I know he had plans to use me in some way. Maybe to embarrass your family by showing me off to his high society friends. It would have been so easy since I look like Mother and you so much. I even stole three bags of gold from him, too!"

Lily nodded and slowly said, "Yes, now I understand. He may come to take you back and refuse to play the kind saviour who delivered you back to our arms." A tight knot of fear began to eat Lily's stomach at the thought of Hazel leaving.

"Aunt Beatrice thinks he owes her a big enough favour to have him play along, but I cannot take that risk. I must leave and hide, somehow." Hazel paused to allow the words to sink in.

Lily nodded in glum agreement.

"I have to leave here in the next few days, Lily. I must be well on my way before Mother sends for us."

Lily's eyelids flickered. She lowered her gaze

to the table. "Please don't go, Hazel." Her voice wavered. "I can't... I don't know..." Slowly tears began to fall onto the table cloth.

Hazel shut her eyes in turmoil. "I have to, Lily. If I don't run, he will come for me and take me away from you. He is a man of pure evil... You would not understand." Her voice lowered to a whisper, I don't know what else to do."

Hazel had her bags of money, more than enough to hire a suitable wet nurse. She could take Harry with her to France, Trouville-sur-Mer. Though, somehow she doubted Lily would be separated from Harry now. Still Hazel suggested, "Lily, maybe it would be best if I take him with me. I could get a nurse -"

Lily whipped her head away as though she had been slapped. Standing, she quickly spun out of her seat and walked to the other end of the table.

Hazel stood, but said nothing. There were no comforting words that could be said.

Whispering, Lily began, "No, no." Then turning, she ran back a little toward Hazel. Her eyes pleaded as she said. "Please, Hazel, take me with you." Imploring further she insisted, "I cannot let Harry go. I would rather forsake my life than be apart from him." Tears flowed down her face. Her eyes went red and her skin became clammy.

Hazel was speechless as she thought through the idea. Various issues clashed in her head. Running with Lily could be slow, difficult or traumatic. Lily knew nothing but her safe upper class world. She would not be able to slip quietly past in the night. Little Harry could be concealed easily enough. If anything was to go wrong, or become difficult Lily would likely crumble like a delicate flower.

However, Lily was her sister and in great need. If she was to come to France, she could stay with Harry and be his mother. Even further, she was a part of her soul that had been distant for so long. With Lily she would have a close friend. But Everett could still catch her one day, and then what would happen to Lily? She could end up caught up with Everett, too. Slowly Hazel started, "I am not sure..." But Hazel couldn't bring herself to refuse and quickly said, "How could we get away without resistance from the servants? If it was just me, I would slip away with one bag, take a horse and ride in the light of the moon. The staff would never know until it was much too late, but with Harry being so very young..."

Lily's voice shook with the trauma, "We will think of something." She sat back in her seat and lifted her glass of wine to her trembling lips. Desperately trying to come up with a decent plan.

Now resolved to taking Lily with her, Hazel continued, "Surely we can find a dignified way to leave so the servants do not suspect. Then when Aunt Beatrice and Mother do discover we are gone, they can save face by saying to others we are travelling. That would cause them no shame. We could leave them a note telling them what to say and then they would not need to know of baby Harry. Well, not yet, anyway. Maybe never."

Lily agreed, "Yes, that is what we must do." Her voice wavered and she whispered, "I ... I do not want to bring any shame on my family, Hazel."

"I know, Lily."

"I am so, so very glad to have you here. I do not know what I would do without your help. I always knew I would have to leave. I thought if Mother found out she would send me to a distant convent to care for Harry until he was at least three. That's when they take the babies off you and send you home to your parents, you know. I have heard whispers about it. It's still an option. There are plenty of willing convents in France at the right price, of course."

"Well, it need not come to that. We will go to France..." Hazel thought for a moment. "We can both go to my teacher's school. To Mademoiselle Fleur in Trouville-sur-Mer." Hazel reminded Lily about her ladies training with Mademoiselle Fleur in the old Mansion in Canada. She emphasized, "She is very kind. The Captain wanted me to fit in his posh English world. However, the Captain does not know Mademoiselle Fleur is now in France running a training school. We would be safe and cared for there. I can work for Mademoiselle Fleur and maybe you could, too, when Harry is older."

Lily pondered upon this plan. With more confidence she said, "I think it will work. I would be happy to help train the girls, if Mademoiselle Fleur accepts me."

"Well she is French and more liberal with her thinking. She may growl a little about Harry, but I am sure she would be fine. She mentioned once, or twice her illegitimate friend born to the French King by his mistress. Apparently, the King openly accepted his bastard children. So I am sure she would accept Harry in the end."

Lily blushed in shame over the whole situation.

They hashed over several plans before settling on one. Neither of them could think of any other way than running. They must run from complete disaster. Run for everyone's sake.

Ω

Kitty stood up from leaning on the door. She had a knowing look on her face. This was her

271

chance. She would watch the twins closely. Very closely. They would not be leaving without her. Pursing her lips together and jutting her jaw, Kitty set her course with the twins.

Ω

After only one night from Beatrice and Celia's leaving, a letter arrived for Hazel and Lily. This letter had been sent by Hazel through the village messenger, who gave Hazel a sharp look after reading the address. Quietly Hazel slipped him an extra gold coin. The messenger simply nodded his agreement. Hazel had painstakingly copied Aunt Beatrice's style of writing to compose a letter requesting the twins to join their Mother and Aunt in London after all.

Hazel sent for a hired private carriage since her aunt had taken her large one. The castle did have a few older, smaller carriages, but Hazel insisted they were too small to carry them and their belongings to London. In truth, Hazel needed a private carriage so she could direct the journey. They would not go to the Hadley's town house. Rather they would be dropped off at an inn right by the wharf.

The servants of Prince's Risborough Castle did not even think to question the girls as they asked Kitty to pack their belongings. Through this time, Lily quietly took Harry into her private sitting room and locked the door. Hazel instructed Kitty on the packing.

Hazel said, "Could you please have a few extra carpet bags sent for me, Kitty. I would like to pack one or two things in small bags." Hazel had thought a few carpet bags could be used later in their escape. They would be lighter and more manageable for the three of them than the cumbersome heavy wooden trunks.

Kitty whispered, "Why yes, Miss." Quietly heading for the door, she stopped, then turned and took her chance, "Miss Hazel, there is something I need to tell you." Hazel stopped folding and looked at Kitty.

"Yes."

"I ... I." Then it all tumbled out, "I know about the baby, Miss. I haven't told anyone."

Hazel's mind swirled with thoughts.

"I promise I haven't said a word. I won't either... I won't. You could take me with you. I would help. I could be your servant. Carry on as I am. I mean ladies do not travel without a maid and certainly not without a nanny to look after the little one." Kitty stopped talking and an impregnated silence stretched between them. She wanted money. All she needed was the girls' to trust her.

Hazel considered this confession quickly. If they left Kitty, people would likely know of Harry within the hour, or even less. Surely they would be chased and held against their will by the gardeners, or the footmen. They were forever faithful to Mistress Beatrice. If they even suspected foul play, they would not hesitate to act. Hazel had Lily and the baby to think of now. They would not be able to melt into the forest or a distant village.

Kitty was a quiet, timid girl and she was right. They had planned to hire a servant for at least part of the journey. She would need to be paid well for her silence and they would not be able to take her to France. Kitty would have too much power over them to travel far. To buy some time Kitty could come to London, at least. Then they would have to let her go the day they boarded the ship. That shouldn't be too difficult.

In a style she had often seen Captain Everett's use, Hazel walked up to Kitty and grabbed her arm. She hissed, "You may be useful. You can come, but if you so much as breathe a word, you will pay. Mark my words." Hazel paused, eye-balling Kitty.

For a fleeting second, Kitty's eyes narrowed slightly and her face remained like stone. Then with a blink of her eyes the true Kitty disappeared and in its place she became totally submissive. The picture of innocence. "Of course! I will be the soul of discretion." She added, "I want to get away from my family. It's complicated at home." Kitty looked at Hazel with eyes as round as dishes. She insisted, "It's for the best that I go with you."

Hazel paused before responding. She would not forget Kitty's look of stone. Maybe she could not be trusted, but she must come with them so they could escape away without intervention. Hazel said, "I will talk with Miss Lily."

Ω

The two huge trunks were hoisted onto the hired private carriage. Lily very carefully carried one particular carpet bag into the carriage. She was directly followed by Kitty and Hazel. Once they were tucked in with overly hot travel blankets, they waved to the Cook who was crying at seeing them go. Cook was not expecting to see them for more than half a year, until the end of the coming ball season.

Lily's face was drawn and pale. A few tears escaped. The driver did not even notice how carefully she cradled the carpet bag in her arms. He shut the carriage door and started the journey.

As they rattled over the moat bridge, Lily opened the carpet bag to reveal the plump face of sleeping Harry. The slow gentle rocking of the carriage lulled him into a deeper sleep. All of the women looked at his soft, innocent face and smiled.

A well of love overflowed Lily for this beautiful boy. Today she was leaving her family home she had known for so long. A strange pain stabbed her heart. She continued to look at Harry, knowing in her heart he was worth leaving all of this behind.

Gazing out across the passing fields, Lily saw her beautiful horse bred just for her on these very lands. Calmly the horse took another mouthful of grass. She was dark grey up her long legs, matching her tail and mane. Across her glossy back her colourings changed to subtle light grey. On her rump she had many dapple spots that had lead to her name Dapple. Lily blinked back a few more tears. Only a year ago, Dapple had been the most exciting passion she had.

Now her life had completely changed. First with Charlie, the love of her life. Then Harry's birth and finally with Hazel, her twin. Each of these new people had led her on a path with sharp twists and turns. Never before had she dealt with such extremities. These people were meshed together in an obscure way that only she knew about. Her life had become a painfully tangled web she did not like to ponder on for too long. Maybe one day when she was settled in Trouville-sur-Mer she would explain everything to Hazel. That was if they accepted them all there. Lily hoped she would soon have a secure and settled life in France.

Carefully, she hugged her sleeping baby to her chest. Kissing his head softly, she lay her cheek on his head. Surely a free and open life, living as mother and son in France, would be better than living one of dark secrets in England.

Ω

As the carriage slowly ambled its way through the London gates, Kitty put her hand in her pocket to feel the letter she had carefully composed for Mistress Beatrice.

Nothing Kitty did would be less than perfect. She had written the letter perfectly in carbon copy handwriting, hoping it would give a clear message; she was made for much better than being a simple maid.

Kitty thought herself rather clever. With the tidy sum of money from Mistress Beatrice in return for the letter, she hoped to be able to prepare herself for the next social season. Hopefully Mistress Beatrice would take too long to respond and the twins would travel on. Then, Kitty would be able to make her pay for more information.

A little deeper, in the same pocket, sat a purse with several gold coins Miss Hazel had already given her for her silence. A small, wicked smile played on Kitty's lips while she stared out at the town as the carriage headed toward the London wharf.

16.

Dust rose as the carriage rolled its way into London. Children ran to the wheels hoping to catch a coin thrown from its window. Their bare feet were covered in dirt and insect bites. Their heels were as cracked as old worn shoes; and of much the same colour. Their clothes hung on their skinny frames and their eyes held a desperate pleading.

Lily searched through her purse and generously chose a shilling. She pushed open the small window and threw the coin to one of the lucky children. They cheered as the carriage moved on and scampered off, their dry feet taking them to the next traveller. Pickings would be slim at this time of the year. Lily felt sorry to see little children live in such demise. However, this was the way of it all throughout London. The privileged were trained to ignore the needy. Many did, but not all were so hard-hearted.

The London waste and sewer heated in the sun, emitting thick waves of stench, powerful enough to make eyes water. Lily quickly put a handkerchief to her nose. Summer was by far the worst time to travel to London. The city waited for the first large downpour of the coming autumn to clear away the muck.

They had come to town a bit early, as the weather was still too warm. Mother and Aunt had arrived a day earlier, keen to organise seamstresses and invitations. Nothing was ready for the social season and they had a trip planned to Canada before the main season started. They hoped to miss most of the pre-season balls and garden parties while away. Also to skilfully avoid most of the gossip circles speculating upon Hazel their long lost daughter. By the time they returned their news would be old.

However, this was not to be. No matter how much they wished these dreams to be true, there was nothing the twin sisters could do. They each knew for their own reasons they must run. Hazel from Captain Everett and Lily for the sake of her precious secret. Little Harry had already been hidden away for long enough. At nearly three months old, he was ready to start exploring the world. Yet, Lily was not willing for him to be discovered and taken from her. So it was to the docks of London they set their course.

Lily had not been in London for many years. Not since Aunt Beatrice had gone to the church to marry Henry Fletcher, but as it turned out, Beatrice had returned as a spinster. Her sister, Isabella had been bridesmaid, but Lily's mother had refused to let her be one. At the time she had not thought twice about it. Isabella was older and a kind sister. Lily had been pleased for her. She always thought there was bound to be another chance for her to be a maid for someone... One day, but there never had been.

Lily now knew why her mother had refused. She had been protecting her from Hazel's captor. Someone had stolen Hazel and obviously Mother had feared if he saw Lily, he might take her, too. Throughout her childhood, Lily had rarely traveled and had never been exhibited before society. She played the piano beautifully, but never played before a crowd. Yet, her siblings had played and sung like many children did before a group of adults.

All her life she had been kept out of the way. If she was honest, there were times when she felt unloved. However, it was far from the truth. Lily knew she had much more to be thankful for than those poor children on the streets.

Ω

Hazel sat opposite Lily, staring out the window. She was carefully thinking through their plan of escape. They would head down Thames Street to the East of London. The docks had plenty of inns to choose from and they would purchase tickets on the morrow for a ship to France. There they would be safe in Trouville-sur-Mer. Mademoiselle Fleur would surely welcome them with open arms.

As they neared the great Thames River, Hazel heard familiar sounds coming from the docks. She sat up a little straighter. Fish mongers called out. Rough men jostled. Cargo was carried to the storage buildings. The water slapped on the sides of the boats. Children skittered in and out collecting what they could. People called and shouted to one another. However, by far the most familiar was the strong smell of the salt wafting in from the ocean.

Even though she felt at home with the sights and smells, there was no excitement, only nervousness churned in her belly. She was now close to Captain Everett's lair. Their natural father. The one she'd ran from. Lily would have to be told he was their father. The words did not come easily for Hazel. Their situation was difficult enough as it was, with Lily's illegitimate baby, Harry, to worry about. Hazel promised herself to tell her once they were safe in France.

Shortly, the carriage came to a stop outside an inn. Hazel said, "Wait here, Lily. I won't be long." She stepped down onto the dusty street. Searching the crowds she saw no one she knew. Not a familiar face in sight. Good.

As she went in a little bell tinkled, announcing her arrival. Since it was only midday the bar was near empty. A crass female voice called out, "I'll be with ya in a moment, love."

Taking off her gloves, she waited. Finally, the bar maid popped out of the back room. Her dirty hair was piled high. Her lips were too bright a shade. However, one would expect to find gaudy fashion on the docks of London. "The owner's out right now, love. What can I do you for?"

"I would like a room. With a double bed. For one night and a single bed for my maid."

"Righty ho, then." The maid searched for the keys. Speaking quickly, she informed, "That'll be a shilling for the room, a half shilling for blankets and pillows and a shilling for anything else you require."

"Two shillings, then." Hazel bought out the second of her three bags of money. She opened it and reached in. Out came a stone. She stared at her hand and began to frown. *A stone? Where had that come from?* She reached in again and pulled out half a crown. "There you are. That should cover the night, bed linen and a meal for my sister, myself and our maid."

"Right ya are, then. I'll show ya up the stairs, then ya kin get ya things." The maid puffed as she trotted up the steps. "Were are ya goin then?"

Hazel hesitated, not wanting to tell. "Just on a short trip, here and there."

Wisely, the bar maid asked no more. She had learned the hard way to keep her mouth shut.

Hazel looked briefly at the lame, small poky room with a small double bed and skinny single. The beds looked lumpy, but at least they did not seem damp. No better would be found near the docks anyway.

The maid said, "I leave ya to yourself then."

Hazel called, "Could you please send dinner up at 6 o'clock."

"There abouts. 6 o'clock is our busiest time. We'll do our best."

"That will be fine, thank you."

The carriage driver hauled the trunks into the storage room. Kitty bought the carpet bags up to their poky little room.

Lily began to fuss over baby Harry who had decided he was desperate for a feed. After their trip, he was reasonably difficult to settle. Lily sighed in frustration. At this moment she could see the value in having a nurse maid, or at least a nanny.

Hazel said, "Babies get upset if you move them from their home. They don't like new smells and noises. They're better when they've grown a bit more. He is only coming up three months old." Hazel added, "I am glad we stayed most of summer at the Castle with Mother and Aunt Beatrice. Travelling would have been a nightmare with Harry in the heat of mid- summer."

Lily pursed her lips and tried to settle him again, determined that Harry would not to be a problem for them all.

Ω

Kitty went about organising their bags. Once she had finished, it was barely mid-afternoon. She sat on the stiff single bed, with her hands meekly in her lap.

All Kitty needed now was an excuse, then she could go to the bank. As she tried to think of one, Hazel solved the problem for her by saying, "Kitty, I would like you to fetch a few things while we are still in London. I need four woollen blankets for the trip, ginger for sea sickness and would also like the book, Robinson Crusoe. He will be a good read as we sail." Hazel was pleased to see Lily smile at her pun.

With the money in her hand, Kitty was off, like lightening. She went to the bank first. She looked at the tall wide concrete doorway before she entered. A smile played upon her lips. This was the start of her plan. How good it felt to think she would soon be rich. She hugged herself in glee at the thought. Trotting up the steps, she paused half way, patted down her hair and straightened her dark grey travel dress.

$$\Omega$$

Beatrice forced herself to sit still as she waited for Henry Fletcher. All these years she had not seen him. Not even once. She fluttered her eyes in an attempt to avoid the tears. They should have been married long ago. The letter she held in her hands testified their love was true. But it was a mystery that she had not found the note all those years ago. Instead her niece, Hazel had ended up placing it in her hands just a few days ago.

Six years had gone since Beatrice had looked behind the stone for a note from Henry. The last time was the day before their wedding. She checked behind the stone while passing it late in the afternoon on her way from the shoe shop. Celia had been waiting impatiently, so Beatrice had not gone into the house to see Henry right then. They had been busy all day and needed their rest.

Henry and Beatrice left each other notes behind the stone because Beatrice feared grumpy Otto would interfere with their mail. He was pompous and viewed it as his right to oversee her every move after her parents' death. However, after the accident, he had let her go by herself out to Prince's Risborough Castle. She had stayed there ever since. Partly for the sake of her back, partly to avoid Otto, but mostly it was to cut Henry Fletcher from her life.

Beatrice remembered back to two days before their wedding day when they had the silly argument over their place of residence. Henry had wanted to live in town. Beatrice wanted to live at Prince's Risborough Castle, with her beloved horses. After several outbursts between them she finally yelled, "Better we not marry then if we can't even agree on this," then flounced out of the house in a childish huff. Within the hour she regretted her words. But she had been caught up in preparing for their wedding. This had been their first and, as it turned out, their only argument.

To take back her words she only needed to send one message, but she had been too proud. Henry could write to her.

Now all these years later, Beatrice sat in Henry's office waiting for him. She almost couldn't believe she was actually here. Before she came in, Beatrice had gone to the far end of the Cornerstone house to see if the loose stone was still there. Now on Henry's desk she saw the missing stone was being used as a paper weight. She couldn't understand why he would do something so sentimental. He might still care for her after all.

Beatrice looked at the old letter in her hand, the one that should have been behind the stone that day. She opened it and read it once more.

B

If you still want to marry me, meet me by the old clock at midnight. It's urgent. Otherwise I will respect your wishes and I will not come.

H

Beatrice had dressed in white with her bridesmaid Isabella in pink on the day of their wedding. Despite her being a spinster for so long, Beatrice was told she made a beautiful bride. After having been engaged to Joseph for so long and then for him to have died at war. Beatrice had grieved for so long, but when she met Henry Fletcher he had taken her breath away.

They had all waited patiently in the church for Henry. Eventually, the Minister walked to the lobby. He shook his head. Beatrice had bit her lip till blood drew. Tears welled. Turning she began to run as fast as she could trying to escape the overwhelming grief she felt.

Her dress was long and it scraped the floor. She should have known better than to run in it. Everything had happened so quickly, the material tangled around her feet, then she fell down the hard stone steps. They said she twisted around and landed on a strange angle. Not that it mattered how it happened, what mattered was that her back had broken.

She blacked out and could remember nothing of the coming weeks. The doctors originally said she was going to die of broken bones. Celia said Beatrice would die of a broken heart. But she hadn't died of either. One doctor had even offered her a large bottle of laudanum to "take away the pain forever". He had given her an easy way out. All she needed to do was drift off in a drugged sleep and leave all the pain behind.

Death had been tempting. No one would have ever known, but she had resisted. Eventually, she became determined to get better. She would not be in bed for the rest of her life. There were plenty of good things in the world still for her to enjoy. God would help heal her.

She had struggled to start, but after a year she progressed in leaps and bounds. Her maid,

Jane, had assisted her in every way she could. The result was that now she could walk and make most movements. Although she still could not ride horses. Not yet.

So here she sat, in Henry's study.

Her heart broke again at the thought of the letter in her hand. There had been no need for any of this misery.

Henry swung the door open, Beatrice jumped-ed. He stood at the door and stared at her with a look of disbelief on his face.

Always one for sensible words, Beatrice said, "Aren't you going to come in and sit down?"

Henry's eyes looked like they were about to pop from his head. He quickly walked to the other reception chair and sat down. "You are here."

"So I am." Beatrice was interested to see he didn't sit behind his desk, but instead took the seat next to her.

Henry was clearly struggling with what to say. "I thought you would never speak to me again. It has been years... Miss Hadley."

Beatrice blushed slightly at hearing him call her "Miss Hadley". She thought by now enough water had gone under the bridge for them to forego correct formality. "I have great need, Mr. Fletcher."

Henry's heart sank. He had hoped she was here to make amends. Even if just to be a friend. However it seemed all she wanted was something from him. He leaned back in his chair. Thinking this would be interesting to say the least.

Beatrice continued, "You helped with... Lily. I am in need of something else."

Henry snapped, "I know. I sent you Everett's Hazel. It seems I mixed them up. I mistook her for Celia's daughter..." Raking his hands through his hair, he continued although slightly on edge now, "Trust me. Everett made it very clear. You should give the girl back. I do not know what types of games she is playing with Everett but they are dangerous, very dangerous."

Beatrice was surprised to hear Henry speak with such venom. Henry and James had been good friends for years. This was unexpected. She proceeded again carefully. "There is something else, something he wouldn't have told you. You see, Lily is Hazel's twin. That is why you made the mistake of sending her to us... She is her identical twin."

Henry stood and began to pace the floor. Damn Everett. He couldn't believe he had made such a mistake despite Everett's violence. Well, it was not a mistake in one way, but he had been mistaken in another. "Does Everett know of the twin?"

Beatrice drew a deep breath. This was harder than expected. Henry would not maintain eye contact and he was upset. She had hoped for better. Maybe even a reconciliation, but it seemed that wasn't going to happen.

Seeming she would have to ask for a favour from the kindness of his heart, rather than from his love for her. What had she been thinking? He could not still love her after all these years.

She said, 'It's... a delicate situation. He took one daughter and the other was born after he had gone. Celia never spoke a word of her to James for fear of losing Lily, too. James was extremely upset she had married Mr. Clance and not waited for him."

Still avoiding eye contact, Henry walked over to the window. "I see. He definitely was a little unfair on her then. What woman would wait for a man when she is with child? It's just simply not done."

"It has now put us in an unusual... predicament. I am sure Captain Everett had hoped to make life difficult for Celia by introducing Hazel as his daughter to society." She paused to allow this to sink in. "She does look strikingly like Celia, except for the eyes. He just didn't know how bad it would be for everyone if he had presented Hazel... because of Lily being her twin. Celia and I are about to tell him. We want the girls to come to the London season as sisters and be presented as Celia's."

"How on earth would you manage that? Hazel has already exposed herself to society as Elizabeth Overland... Interestingly, no one connected her to Celia, but they would have if Celia had come for the season." Henry forced himself to continue to look out the window. He did not want to look at Beatrice from fear of talking about the past. She had great injuries due to him. How could anyone forgive such terribleness? "I was surprised when she didn't come."

Beatrice told him, "Mr. Clance wished to remain in Sheringham for the winter."

"I see."

"There will be no lies to society." Beatrice spoke to Henry's cold back. "We want to say Hazel was stolen at birth and managed to return because Everett knew she was Celia's child. He would be the hero. We would say you met Hazel under a secret name at the ball to send her on to Prince's Risborough Castle. It would tie in and no one need know the whole story. The hope is no one will connect Everett's green eyes to Hazel's."

Henry was silent for a long while.

Time continued to tick, so Beatrice stood. "I will leave you then."

"No!" said Henry suddenly

Beatrice froze in her tracks.

Henry stated, "I will play along." There was

nothing else he could think to say. Any other words he might have said had simply vanished from his head.

Beatrice whispered back, "Thank you."

Silently she placed the old letter from under the stone on his desk. Then she walked smartly from the house as the tears fell.

It had been too long.

Ω

On returning to the town house Beatrice sent Captain Everett a brief note.

We have her. Come to the Hadley's town house.

After sending the note Beatrice and Celia did nothing, but wait in the library. Through word of mouth they knew he was in town. A few pennies would tell you a lot. He had been in town for a while. His crew had been going from pub to pub showing a sketched picture of Hazel with a written description below. Hazel's green eyes had been emphasised. They even offered a substantial reward for her safe delivery to Captain James Everett.

Thank goodness he had not written in the description that she was his daughter. Celia liked to think he held her virtue in high esteem. Fortunately also the note had only been circulated among the lower classes near the docks. The chances of high society getting hold of the sketch was slim. The lower class would forget as the months passed. If someone in high society had suspicions, they would likely mind their business. Discretion was sought after by many and valued higher than gold. Gossip was often whispered, but huge scandal could destroy wealth. In the extreme scenario, Everett could say he was confused if he was confronted about the sketch. Confused about Hazel's decision to leave with Henry Fletcher and go on to Prince Risborough Castle. He could say he feared he had lost her.

Celia fiddled with her handkerchief. Beatrice gazed out the window, thinking of her meeting with Henry a few days beforehand. He had cooperated so easily. She had not even coerced him with the sordid events of their past. Though she would of, if she had to, for the sake of the girls.

They heard Everett well before he entered the room. He yelled at the butler to move and shoved his way in the door. The butler was expecting him and was affronted to be spoken to in such a manner. Yet, he knew his place and he stepped aside.

Everett stomped down the hall.

The women gave each other potent looks. This was not going to be good.

Even though she knew he was coming, Celia jumped out of her skin when he banged the door open, nearly off its hinges. With great force, he slammed it behind him. His eyes were wild and crazed.

How dare Celia keep this from me!

He looked at Celia and boomed, "Where is she then? I know she is not here. My informant tells me no one has arrived. SO WHERE IS SHE?"

Beatrice began to say, "Calm..."

"Don't even speak, Miss Hadley!" Everett did not bother to look at her.

He repeated to Celia, "Where, Celia?"

Celia voice shook, "She is at Prince's..."

"Prince's Risborough Castle? Why on earth would you leave her there? She is on the run, she's irrational!" Everett closed his eyes at the stupidity of it all. She should have written to him straight away, then he would have had a chance with Hazel.

Beatrice accused, "Well, we know where she gets her irrational behaviour from, then."

Everett whipped his head in Beatrice's direction. "Don't you start! I assumed you had Hazel at the castle when I confronted you at the Inn and in Sheringham and you never said a word! Celia did not know if Hazel was dead or alive, when I confronted her BUT you did! I knew you were lying when I spoke to you at the Inn."

Celia tried to intervene. "James, I was not myself..."

Everett turned his wild eyes back to Celia. "Don't you talk. You didn't know then, but you must have known for months now and never wrote. You never even sent a message! I have been desperately looking for Hazel all year. I have been beside myself with worry. I have not sailed even once."

Celia said, "I..."

Beatrice interrupted, "We have a proposition!" She didn't think it wise for Celia to tell Everett the truth about Lily while he was in this sort of state.

Everett scoffed, "A proposition! What would you know about a proposition?"

Beatrice cast her die, "You owe me a few favours, Everett! I backed you financially with those new passenger ships. I helped you so Father would accept your match with Celia and you... you sold the ships from beneath me. I didn't get all the money back."

Celia frowned, "Beatrice where did you get the money from in the first place?"

Beatrice sighed, "In a round about way from my fiancée, Joseph. Kind of an inheritance he had willed to me. As you know he was heir and his parents had passed away six months before his own death at war. He had willed me a portion as his fiancée, stating in his will that we had been engaged for so long he wished me to have something. His brother honoured Joseph's wishes even though I was only a fiancée and he could have taken all of the inheritance. The amount was only a small portion of their wealth, but very substantial. Have you not wondered how I kept up Prince's Risborough Castle and the Estate all these years?"

Celia said, "No, I never thought..."

Everett interrupted in a hard voice, "You got most of your money back. From what I hear you have reinvested it wisely." Everett considered what to tell the sisters about his investments. Feeling rather malicious, he stated, "I sent your father and mother to Africa on one of those passenger ships. I sent them to their death."

Beatrice said, "They caught Swamp Fever. You didn't kill them."

Everett agreed, "No I didn't kill them. They would not listen when I told them not to go to land, but I didn't try too hard to stop them. There were swamps near a stop-over port. I suppose they couldn't understand why others could live there and still be well. I think some African's are used to Swamp Fever."

Celia said, "I never knew you were their Captain on that trip."

Everett told her, "I hadn't planned to be. I thought they had gone a few weeks before, but it seems your father changed his dates for the sake of a business meeting he had to attend. We had already left port by the time I laid eyes on them. It was too late for me to leave the ship." He looked off into the distance.

Ruthlessly he continued, not caring they were ladies. "Beatrice, I had difficulties... in Africa, I mean. I could not get caught up in the black slave trade. You know it's illegal these days. I was being bribed. There are matters I will not explain... It was for the best I sold the ships and stepped away from running passengers. I never trade in West Africa now." He looked away. He had said too much. Still, he was furious with Beatrice. She may as well face the hard facts.

Since Everett seemed to be listening better, Beatrice started to explain their idea, "We want to tell society Hazel was stolen at birth..."

Everett shouted, "You will not!" The passenger ships were forgotten and his temper rose. He began to pace the floor.

Celia raised her voice. She had never yelled at James before. "It's for Hazel's own sake, James." Then raising it louder, "If you love her so. You must want the best for her..." In desperation she added, "She will not see you otherwise!"

At that, Everett stopped in his tracks.

Beatrice continued, "We would not say you stole her. Just listen! We could say she returned to us through you. You would be the hero..."

Everett went a deep red in the face. He said, "I will not be anything, BUT HER FATHER. How dare you suggest otherwise. I have cared for her all these years. She is my daughter, not yours, Celia!"

Celia blinked away hot tears. His words hurt.

Beatrice wondered if Celia would tell Everett about Lily. She might not, considering he was hitting the roof.

After a brief, tense silence, Everett finally turned and stormed out the door.

Beatrice sighed. It appeared this would be more difficult than she thought. They would try again in a few days.

Ω

Explosive frustration mounted in Everett. He spurred his horse to run faster across the green fields of North Dean as he raced toward Lacey Green. He would ride directly onto Prince's Risborough. It was the second castle the old Black Prince had built, finishing just before his untimely death. It had been passed through lineage to Beatrice Hadley. For she loved the horses the prince had become famous for breeding upon the land.

Everett felt his anger rising at the thought of Beatrice and her secretive ways. He released a yell which tore from his gut, releasing with it some of his vexation. He had struggled so much to find Hazel. Only to find his love Celia and her damn sister Beatrice had been keeping her from him. Celia knew he wanted to find her. But she wasn't loyal to him, that much was clear. Damn Beatrice and Celia, they were as thick as thieves

At least now he had the answer to one of his nagging questions. Hazel had been safe all this time and that was what mattered the most. The thought of her being in harm's way had put him into frantic searching. To be so close to finding her rattled his cage. Yet it appeared she was made with tough skin. She certainly had been rather cunning.

By now she would be gone from Prince's Risborough Castle, he was sure of it. So the turmoil would continue. She could be under threat right at this moment and Everett would not be able to help her. Somehow he wanted to make her world safe. He would take her back to the Donaldsons in Canada if he had to. Anything, just as long as he could care for her welfare once again.

As he galloped through Lacey Green, adrenaline pumped through his veins. Despite the hard ride, he was energised by his passion. The tiniest possibility she was at the castle kept him going. He would have to be quick for the night would be dark without a moon and the light was already fading.

Several children watched him from the trees as he drove his way through Loosey Row. Clarissa had a mixed lot. The orphans he had given her were various shades and ages. They were like monkies climbing in the trees. Everett wished he had time to stop and greet her. But he dare not. He promised himself he would visit on the way back.

When he came into sight of Prince's Risborough Village, he pulled his horse up short, and twisted around in a few circles as the mare pranced. She was trained for long endurance, so was keen to go further. Snorting, her breathing heaved steam into the crisp cool air. Quietly, as the evening drew on, Everett walked her around the village to the back of the Castle. He did not want to startle, or alert anyone of his arrival. He didn't want any undue attention.

With the sun slowly setting as he made his way past the vegetable gardens, he saw a gardener starting off home. Everett called casually and nudged his horse to trot over. "So I hear Miss Hazel has left Castle. Tell me the news."

Peter smiled at the stranger and cheerfully replied, "Yes. She went with her sister and maid to London, I believe. I bid them goodbye this morning and watched the carriage roll away. They should have met up with the Mistress and their mother in London by now."

Everett's could barely turn away as he knew he must. The turmoil on his face would be too apparent. He couldn't turn his face back to the gardener. Instead he looked off into the sunset and called out, "Thank you. I will be on my way."

Flicking his reins slightly, he took off in a steady trot toward the village. He would not be able to go any further in the coming inky black night. Pursuit would be useless. His Hazel had disappeared yet again. All the trouble he had gone to was pointless. Frustration mounted, this whole situation was destroying his life. He would be on his way when he went back to London. The sea would calm his soul.

17.

The bank was huge and full with people. Some were working and others were making transactions of different sorts. Kitty appreciated the orderly, clean and structured environment. This was just her sort of place. Everyone was dressed smartly in suits, or sombre dark dresses. They walked quickly and spoke in low whispering tones. Every hair was combed and clipped. Every curl was pinned perfectly. Shoes were shiny. Papers rustled as they were sorted. The noise was kept to a low hum.

Much to her distress, Kitty was at loss of what to do. This place was new to her. She jumped when the guard came up behind her.

He had a deep commanding voice. "Can I help you, Miss?"

Kitty felt on edge. "Yes... Yes, I would like to make a deposit, if I may."

"This way." He guided her to a line of customers and explained she must wait for a cashier's desk to become available.

Kitty waited for a short time, captivated by her modern surroundings. People came and went. Large ledgers were used to record all sorts of transactions. Pencils scratched, shoes padded on the soft carpet, secretaries pens scraped and money shifted from desks to the safe. The light tinkle of coins knocking together always grabbed Kitty's attention. Everywhere she looked money moved.

The cashier called to Kitty, "Next... excuse me, Miss; this way, please."

Kitty started in fright. She had not been watching for the cashier. Shaken by her own silliness, she wobbled as she walked to the cashier's desk. She stated, "I wish to deposit some money."

In a strict voice, he asked, "How much?"

Flustered, Kitty blushed and said, "Well, I am not sure. Let me see..." Kitty tipped the money on the cashier's desk.

He gave her a hard stare as though she had done something terribly wrong and snapped, "Sit down." The cashier was a knowledgeable, yet pompous man with little time for the stupid. "Next time count the money before you come!"

Kitty's hackles rose. She lifted her face up sharply. With annoyance she stated, "I have counted, now! Three shillings." She may have been over-awed at first, but she would not allow a cashier to speak to her like that and get away with it.

The cashier gave her a glare and said nothing. He filled out the forms, asking her formalities. Her name, place of residence, date of birth and so on. She lied her way through most of it, except for her name and date of birth. She didn't want to be too traceable. She was no fool.

When the cashier had finished, she asked, "How do I purchase a safe box?"

The cashier raised his eyebrows. In a sarcastic tone, he told her, "You go over there." He pointed to the sign saying 'Safe Boxes Here'.

Again, Kitty flushed in embarrassment while her spite grew. She did not like being shown up by anyone. He must think her a fool. Only perfection was good enough. Her voice shook with frustration, "Thank you."

She organised her safe box and placed the letter to Mistress Beatrice Hadley inside. Kitty marvelled to think she was going to string the Hadley family along. She would squeeze as much money as she could before giving up the twin's whereabouts. This letter alone would cost them 500 crowns. The bank manager knew his duty.

Glancing at the large clock as she made to leave, Kitty realised time had ticked by very quickly. She left the bank in a rush. The afternoon was nearly over already.

Rushing up to a young boy on the side of the street, she said, "I'll give you a penny if you quickly show me the nearest market."

"Follow me," he said as he ran off down the road.

They ran in and out of streets and alleys. Within ten minutes, Kitty found herself in the middle of the markets. They still teemed with life. Hawkers still wanted to make another penny. Yet, she only had half an hour to pick up the supplies. The tradesmen would pack up on the dot of five and go straight to the pub. All over England it was the same.

Kitty gasped to catch her breath. "Boy, show me where the good quality blankets, spices and books are and I'll give you another penny. Quick."

Just in time the boy managed to lead her to everything she needed. In a rare moment of generosity, she gave him two pennies instead of one. There were not many times Kitty was happy, but this was one of those special occasions. The eve before the fall.

Ω

Kitty came flying through the door to find Lily alone, burping Harry. Kitty's cheeks were brilliant red and a lock had escaped from her bun. Not in many years had she been so disarrayed.

Lily had never seen her look so excited. Something was amiss. She asked, "Are you all right, Kitty? You have been so long."

"I am fine, Miss..." Kitty inwardly quailed. She had made a spectacle of herself by being so late. This day was not her best for maintaining control. What would she say? The truth, there was nothing wrong with it. "I went to the bank for the first time. I banked all that money Miss Hazel gave me. I have never been so blessed." Tentatively she added, 'I got all those things we need. Here they are." She held out her packages.

Lily said, "You went to the bank?" Suddenly, she remembered Hazel had paid Kitty for her silence.

Kitty went on, "I never had so much money. It was three... three shillings I banked, Miss. What else would I do with three shillings?" She smiled sweetly. Kitty hoped she had said enough to keep Lily, the nosey cow, from prying more.

Lily smiled to see such happiness over such a small amount of money. Kitty did not often grin. She looked much prettier when she did. She always seemed so solemn "You change so much when you smile, Kitty. You're very pretty. You should smile more often."

Kitty would keep a golden smile in mind for future use. A little happiness may get her where she wanted to go. She said, "Thank you, Miss," and smiled again.

Lily continued, "I am sure you did the right thing. Banking keeps your money safe." Lily thought Kitty was wise for such a young wee thing. She wished the best for Kitty after she was abandoned by them on the morrow. They would not be taking her to France that was for sure. Later tonight she would have to write Kitty a good reference letter. A maid would be able to find an excellent position in London with a letter from a Hadley.

Hazel quietly came through the door. Her

face was pinched and worried. "Kitty, leave us at once." she commanded. "Come back in an hour."

Kitty quickly stood, looked demurely at the ground and bobbed. She was annoyed by such a rude dismissal. The bliss of her afternoon was now ruined. How dare Miss Hazel should talk to her with such an attitude. She now felt a certain smug amount of joy in hatching her plan. Soon, oh so soon, Kitty would have the pleasure of ruining their plans. The sooner the better... Well, maybe not too soon. Kitty wanted as much money as she could get. Tomorrow she would send a boy with a letter to the Hadley House. She thought she would have better luck with Mistress Beatrice reading it. Celia Clance could be such a drip in a time of need.

At this thought, Kitty smirked and went down to the bar to have a little fun. Men were such fools. Yet, on reflection some women seemed to be bigger fools.

Ω

Hazel stared at the floor for a moment, listening to Kitty's footsteps going down the stairs. Her eyes flicked from side to side.

Lily asked, "What is wrong, Hazel?"

Hazel spoke almost to herself, in a vague unattached manner. "I went to the shop to get those buttons..."

"Yes... Yes I know. Did something happen?" Lily gently rubbed little Harry's back. She looked at Hazel with deep concern.

Still in deep thought, Hazel replied, "Yes..."

"Do you wish to tell me?" Lily grew agitated. Hazel's behaviour was unusually distant.

"Wait... Let me see." Hazel went to the single bed, sat down and tipped out the second sack of money she had stolen from Everett all those months ago. On the bed were pebbles with only a few coins scattered in between. Hazel gasped. Where was all the money? Even though she had suspected, she hadn't dared to look up till now.

She had opened each money bag only once before, when she stayed at Henry Fletcher's a year ago. Hazel had not bothered to tip them out before to check if the bags were actually full with coins, she had assumed they would be. Two had been packed deep within the old carpet bag. The first bag was kept out and now had been used up. Hazel had only just started using the second. Except from the second bag she would pull out stones rather than coins.

Leaping from the bed she grabbed her carpet bag. Rummaging through she pulled out the third and final bag.

Lily squeaked, "Hazel, what is wrong?"

Hazel did not say. The missing money was too terrible. She tipped out the third bag to find more stones and only a little money. Closing her eyes, she willed away the tears.

This was all the money they had. They did not even have enough to buy little Harry a ticket to France. Hazel felt her shoulders tighten, her head began to hurt. This was too much. She was responsible for their flight. Dragging them all this way to London to sail to France, without any money. Laying her hand to her forehead she rubbed her brow in an ill attempt to soothe herself.

Lily watched Hazel closely. Something was very wrong. Standing, she walked over to Hazel. Holding Harry with one arm, she rubbed Hazel's back. She said, 'What is... " She did not bother to finish her sentence, because she could see all of the stones, bags and few coins on the bed. "Oh, Hazel, where is all the money?"

"It isn't here."

"Was it stolen?" Lily's complexion changed to a milky shade of white.

Hazel whispered, "I... I don't know."

"Have you never looked in the money bags?"

Hazel explained, "Yes, I looked at the top, but I never tipped them out. The first bag was full of money, but it's all gone."

Feelings of anxiety overwhelmed Lily. Her hands began to shake. She felt a wave of dread. Before she even asked the question, she knew the answer, but she had to ask. "Do we have enough to get to Trouville?"

Hazel whispered, "No. Far from it."

The silence could've been cut with a knife. Hazel admonished herself for her stupidity. Lily refused to believe they would have to return to their Mother and Aunt. They could not continue to hide Harry while living under their roof. She asked, "Has anything else been taken?"

Hazel searched through the carpet bag again. She had not bothered to empty it before they left Prince's Risborough Castle. Only a few extra items had been thrown in on the top and loaded into the carriage. Hazel looked for her emeralds and green dress. "The jewels are gone too, Lily! Someone has stolen them and the money from me."

Lily asked, "When did you see them last?"

Hazel replied, "When I first arrived at the Hunter's farm, I looked. I didn't look inside the money bags, but saw the dress at the bottom of the carpet bag with the jewels and the bags of money were next to them..."

Hazel's thoughts raced. "It was them. The Hunters. I was told at the last minute Keith was there to pick me up. I had to pack my bags quickly. I never looked in the money bags, but the dress was there. I am not sure about the jewels. The 1st bag of money was tucked away on my body. I kept it in case I ever had to run suddenly." Hazel explained, "No matter where you are you need money. Someone must have put stones in the other two bags and placed a few coins on top." Hazel thought this through. "The Hunters could have stolen the money and jewels. I never even looked in my carpet bag at the Castle. I just took it when we left." Hazel glumly concluded, "I suppose we will never really know."

The twins sat in silence for awhile.

Hazel eventually said, "We will have to go to the London family town house and confess." Her voice was dull and lifeless. "What else can we do?"

Fear flashed through Lily and with venom she said, "No, we will not!"

Hazel admonished her, "Don't be foolish, Lily. Where will we get more money?"

"We will find a way to earn it. I will not risk losing you, or Harry." Tears sparkled in her eyes. "I know, without a shadow of a doubt, I would lose him, Hazel." She paused, "It's the proper way to take care of my sort of problem. Mother would not consider anything else. Father would be worse. You would run and sidestep the Captain somehow, but I would not be able to keep Harry safe. By law, my parents have the right and they will think they are doing the right thing by me... But in my heart I could not stand it. We will have to find a way to save some money then we will go."

"I know you are right. We might lose Harry straight away, or you may get a year at a nunnery, then he will be sent to an orphanage" Melancholy over took Hazel's feelings. "But there is no hope, Lily. We could write to Mademoiselle Fleur and she would send money, but it would take weeks. We cannot survive that long. There is no way to overcome this."

"Yes there is." Lily insisted.

"How?"

"Give me the night. We will think of something, surely?" Desperately she hoped she would think of something. She had not bought any jewels of importance. Every fine piece she had was a family heirloom. Mother would have not wanted her to take them, but now she wished she had brought even one necklace.

Hazel agreed, "All right, tonight we will try to think of an idea. We have paid for our stay. By morning we will have to have an idea. A very good idea indeed."

"Agreed."

Ω

Kitty noticed the sisters remained very quiet after her return. Something was wrong. Of course they would not be telling her. She stayed as quiet as a mouse, tending to the brat, Master Harry. At one point, Miss Lily put her nerves on edge by pacing the room. Being worn from their long day of travel, they all went to bed early.

Kitty pretended to drop off to sleep. She let her hand go slack off the bed. Her mouth was parted and relaxed. Every now and then she gave a light snore. She hoped to be convincing. Maybe she'd hear them talk.

Eventually they did. Whispering. Kitty was only able to make out a few words, but she heard enough to know they had no money.

Kitty's heart began to race. Her well-laid plans would be ruined if they returned to their family. How could she convince them to keep on running?

For a long time after the twins had dropped off to sleep, Kitty racked her brain for ideas. She lay awake tossing thoughts around in her head. Thinking of a solution was hard, considering she did not fully know the problem, or all their plans. They were planning going abroad. Otherwise they would not be staying at an Inn at the docks.

If Kitty had the money from Mistress Beatrice already, she would've found a way to give the twins enough to travel. But the money may not come for weeks. Eventually, she thought of a viable idea she would suggest to the twins at the right time.

$$\Omega$$

As dawn broke, Harry woke gurgling happily to himself. Hazel could not help but smile as she woke to his cheerful voice. "He is going to be a real chatter box, Lily."

Lily gave a half-hearted smile in reply and then continued to frown.

A flood of memories washed over Hazel. They had no money and very few ideas. She sighed deeply.

Hazel said, "I think we should tell Kitty."

"Yes, that would be best." Lily looked so down.

Sitting up from her bed, Lily looked at wee Kitty. She was sitting on the edge of the single bed. Already Kitty's clothes were perfect, her hair smooth and shiny. She must have been up well before them. The weight was even heavier because Kitty tried so hard. She waited attentively for the least instruction to help.

Hazel said in a monotone, "Kitty, we have no money, we think it was stolen. We have no real options; we think we will have to return to the Hadley's household."

Kitty put on the best face of shock she could manage. "But, Miss. Master Harry?"

Hazel grieved, "We know."

Kitty stated the obvious, "You cannot return with him. You will lose him."

"What else can we do?"

Kitty lowered her head as though to think. Slowly she started, "Well... you could sell most of your clothes. They would bring a fair price."

Lily agreed, "Yes, we have already thought of that."

Hazel was not so keen. "It would bring in a little, but not nearly enough for our plans." Hazel privately thought they may be able to survive long enough to hear from Mademoiselle Fleur, but she wasn't going to say this out loud for Kitty to hear.

Kitty continued with her suggestions. "You could work, Miss Hazel. Miss Lily needs to stay with Master Harry, but you could work."

Lily started to look brighter.

Hazel nodded, "But doing what?"

Kitty lied, "When I was at the market yesterday, I heard talk that a seamstress was needed at the little shop near High Street. I paid no mind, but can you sew?"

Hazel warmed to the idea. "Yes, very well in fact." She could work to ensure they had enough money to live, while they waited for help from Mademoiselle Fleur.

Kitty continued on, hoping to appeal to Miss Lily, since Miss Hazel seemed a little cold, "You could set up in a little quaint flat. Pay next to no rent and save... for your plans."

The twins considered her suggestions. Kitty thought they may not be completely convinced, so she added, "I could work, too."

Lily said, "We could not ask that of you." Kitty was supposed to be in their employment as a maid.

Kitty slyly put on an act to convince them of

her sincerity. She opened her eyes in an innocent look, glanced at Master Harry and replied, "I would do it for the sake of the bairn."

Lily said, "You are such a lovely girl, Kitty. I will give you the highest recommendations one day."

Kitty gushed, "I won't need them, Miss. I will be with you." So they had planned to let her go. Kitty needed to travel where ever the twins went. She would leave a crumb trail for the Hadleys to follow. For every letter she sent to the Hadleys, she would be paid more.

Lily gave Kitty a warm smile. She turned to Hazel, "What do you think, Hazel? With Kitty and you working and me keeping house? Would that do?"

Hazel was weary of Kitty. She was seemingly innocent and kind. But was it real? Yet, she was swayed by Lily's enthusiasm. There was Captain Everett to think of. Hazel had news from the bar patrons that he had sailed this very morning, with no supplies ready. This was unlike Everett. They said he was rushed. Helen was greatly relieved he had not caught her. There was a risk he would return any day, but she had no money. She had few options. Hazel said, "I think it may work." She would send a letter to Mademoiselle Fleur today. Mail would take at least three weeks. She would leave her forwarding address with the Inn owner. "Kitty, I need you to fetch some ink." Lily opened her mouth as if to say something, but said nothing. Hazel counted out the coins and sent Kitty on her way. Hazel explained to Lily her intention to send a letter.

With a little more spring in their step, the women made ready to leave. Hazel wrote a letter and gave it to Thomas, the bar owner, to deliver to the mail boat. Thomas had given her a funny look. Hazel's skin tingled. Had he recognised her?

Hesitantly, Thomas said, "It will be another penny to be delivered, Miss." Hazel felt relieved, so the strange look was because she hadn't offered the penny.

He promised to send it on the next mail round to France.

Sending a letter overseas cost a fair bit. Hazel hoped Mademoiselle would send plenty of money after receiving this first letter. It would take a while to save for a second letter.

Ω

Kitty fetched a cheap cart and driver from the docks. With help from a few big lads, the driver piled their trunks and bags on.

The driver asked, "Where ya goin'?"

Hazel was about to speak, when Kitty butted in. Kitty said, "Listen, careful like. We have no money to speak of and need to go cheap." Hazel allowed Kitty to carry on the conversation. Kitty knew the English way better, whereas Hazel was not sure.

The driver raised his eyebrows. The twins looked too 'well to do' to take them anywhere cheap.

At the astonished look on the drivers face, Kitty emphasised, "Really, really cheap... in East End, even Whitechapel. We need a small, cheap flat, but dry."

The driver was scandalised. "I can't take ya thar!" He stressed, "It's not fit." He eyed the two rich women, with the beautifully dressed baby.

Kitty huddled a little closer to the stupid man, so the women wouldn't hear. She hissed, "Take us there, or I'll call the coppers on you. I'll tell them you were stealing from us. Don't..." she growled, "underestimate me!"

The driver ran a hand through his hair. He couldn't get away quick, their trunks were on his cart. This young girl made his blood run cold, with her evil eye and threats. A witch, that's what she was. She should be burned. Pity the death sentence for witches went out fifty years ago.

Looking off into the distance, he mentally detached himself from the three women. He would do his job quick, be paid and to hell with them all. A witch and a double sister act. The two ladies looked familiar, although he couldn't quite put a finger on it. To Kitty's satisfaction, he hopped up on the cart and clicked to the old horse to start her walking.

Purposely he drove to a distant spot in Whitechapel very far from his own poor home. He wanted nothing to do with them and his family would be safe a distance away.

Lily held Harry, sitting next to the driver, while Kitty and Hazel walked alongside. In the busy traffic it was easy for them to keep up behind the cart.

As they entered the poor area, Lily's hold on Harry grew tighter, but she was determined not to baulk. Many dirty, scabby children played in the ditches. The odd battered ball flew past. Half-starved women carried heavy loads of washing. Men argued and spat on the ground. Everything became dark, grey and greasy.

Worst of all was the way they stared. Two well-dressed women, clearly of high quality in a poor cart was an unusual sight in this area. Strangers looked at their huge trunks, fine dresses and glossy hair. These people did not belong here. All who saw them wondered at the strange sight.

The further they went, the more the driver noticed Lily tensing. Glancing at her in concern, he could see she was quite scared. He didn't know their reasons for wanting to live over this side, but they must be bad. Really desperate. Despite Kitty's abruptness, he started to feel a little sorry for Lily. A reasonable street was only a few blocks away. He decided to take them there.

The driver pulled up to a tall building with a little bit of cheer compared to the sights they had just seen. To say the least, many windows were clean, bright and washing hung from lines up above. Even a few potted plants flowered on some sills. Yet, it still had a poor feeling of being overcrowded. Rough people scurried through the streets.

Lily swallowed deeply, trying to convince herself they had made the right choice. This street was not so bad. Well, not as bad as others she witnessed along the way. Unsure of what to do next, she looked back at Hazel who nodded. This was it then. They would stay.

The driver jumped down and hastily pulled off a trunk. It hit the path with a thump.

Hazel snapped, "Mind yourself."

Kitty glared at the nitwit.

The driver put down the second a little better. Took the money offered, doffed his cap and made to leave.

Kitty had been quietly waiting on the side. She stepped forward to stop the driver, she said, "Keep our whereabouts to yourself." Hazel and Lily were not watching, so she did a few waves in the air with her index finger and clicked her fingers.

The man turned pasty.

Kitty said in low tones, "Don't cross me, or you'll pay." The poor were a suspicious lot. Casting a spell would go a long way to keep a tongue still.

The man shook his head, hastened toward

the cart and drove off smartly. That young girl
was no good and he was glad to get away from
her.

18.

Beatrice finished her breakfast and patted her lips with her napkin. She decided she would go out for the morning. She put on her coat as a precaution. The day seemed to be clear and bright, though a nippy breeze usually blew in from the east even in early autumn.

Beatrice left a message with Celia's maid and left the house. The square would be lovely at this time in the morning. Not too busy and it wasn't far.

As usual Celia slept late. She was always ready for the ball season hours. Staying up late and waking up late was the way it went. She had always been like that. She enjoyed the excitement. The anticipation of presenting the twins and Violet was almost too much. Celia had already organised their dressmakers for the week and the following week they would leave for Canada.

Sometime after Beatrice had left for her walk, Celia came down for an early lunch. She noticed on the stand, in the hall, there was an envelope waiting. They had only been in London three days and the word was already out to the few who came to town early. Celia picked up the envelop and saw it was addressed to the 'Hadley Household'. Beatrice was suppose to be Mistress in this household because she wasn't married into another household like Celia, but she would not mind if Celia opened it. They did not stick to formalities in private. Picking up the envelope, she went into the dining room and laid it next to her spoon.

As she finished breakfast, she cast an eye to

the envelope. By the looks, it was the first invitation of many. The paper was thick and creamy. High quality, oozing of money. Hopefully it would be to a pre-season, early autumn ball. They were usually small but exclusive. Not that they would be attending, but this invitation was just the beginning of the season. Carefully she slipped her finger under the tab and opened the seal.

Confused, she merely found a letter inside. Not an invitation after all. Maybe it was from James Everett. In haste, she unfolded the beautiful paper.

Dear Mistress Beatrice Hadley,
Unbeknown to you, your nieces Miss Lily and Miss Hazel, have run away. You may consider it a blessing to know I am travelling with them and are willing to keep you informed of their movements for a price.
By the time you have this letter, I would have opened an account with London Bank under my full name, Katherine Mary Caper. I will instruct them to hold a second letter for you in a safe box and only allow you to have it if you bank 500 crowns into my account.
With this in mind, I will no longer remain in your service. I believe it's time for me to explore my options.

Yours Faithfully,
Kitty

Celia's hand shook and the page fluttered like a leaf. Standing with a start, she banged her thighs on the table and sat back down with a thump. Flushing red with indignation, she carefully stood again, moving her chair back.

The maid stepped forward, asking, "Are you all right, Madam."

"Yes, I am perfectly fine."

But she almost ran from the room. In fluid movement, she sped through the kitchen. The Cook almost dropped the spoon in the pot at seeing her in the kitchen. Never in all her life had she seen such a thing. With open mouth the Cook watched Mrs. Clance rush out the back door.

Celia ripped open the stable door. "Keith. Keith! Keith!" She was in a state.

Keith the stable master craned his neck out of a stall. "Is that you, Mistress Beatrice? Oh Madame. Were you looking for me?"

Celia ran to him, flushed and shaking. "How fast can you ride to Prince's Risborough Castle?" She puffed slightly from the unusual exertion of running all that way.

Slightly startled, he answered. "The better part of an afternoon, on the stallion. What is wrong?" He checked behind her to see if anyone followed. She was in great distress.

In desperation, she lowered her shaking voice. "You must promise to keep this absolute secret, Keith."

He glanced around for the stable lads. They were all still out exercising the horses. "Of course, except for the Mistress, I will."

"That is fine. Your Mistress is not here to consult. She would agree with me anyhow." Trying to maintain her poise, she continued, "Hurry, saddle. Go to Prince's Risborough Castle and see if Hazel and Lily are still there. But be sure you don't alarm anyone." It was obvious Celia was greatly concerned about discretion for she added "Can you do that? You will get double pay if you can do that and keep it a secret."

Keith's face went a little pink with pleasure from the thought of at such a large reward and to be trusted with yet another secret. But he had to say, "You don't need to, Madam. If the girls are in trouble, I am only too willing to help."

"No matter. You have been highly valued by Mistress Beatrice all these years. You deserve a raise."

Keith thought double pay was much more than a raise, but he wasn't going to argue more. He turned, grabbed the tack and began to saddle up the stallion. An extra bonus in the situation was the opportunity to be riding him.

Celia stood watching, anxiously rubbing her hands together. Keith informed, "I won't be able to get back tonight. There's no moon so it will be too dark and there is not enough sunlight left."

Celia said, "Go as quick as you can. Check for a letter from them in the house. Go about it quietly, without anyone seeing you. I'll expect you back before lunch tomorrow."

"Right." Keith offered the bit to the horse, who sidestepped a little, sensing the excitement. The stallion's ears pricked forward almost in anticipation. He finally took the bit and the reins were on. Keith jumped up and said, "Tell the stable boys here I have gone off to Risborough for the family's sake. I will enjoy seeing my own for the night anyway."

Celia hadn't thought of what she would tell the other servants. "I will," she called, as Keith rode off.

Ω

Hazel took the lead. She went into the building and spoke with the landlady. Thankfully, the landlady wasn't picky where her money came from. Anyway, she was nearly blind and couldn't tell if they were rich or poor, All money was good once it got in her hand. She didn't ask questions.

After looking at a few rooms, Hazel came back to tell Lily they had a two roomer: one living and one bedroom. The rent would be six pennies a week, with one week up front. Their money was being eaten up quickly.

Two large burly lads were each given a precious penny each to carry up the trunks. They had to go up six flights of stairs.

The women's progression was watched from nearly everyone around. When the lads came down from delivering the trunks, the noisy neighbourhood heard all there was to tell. By the end of the night, the whole street and several streets either way had heard of the classy women with the baby, maid and two large toff trunks. They all knew what floor they were on and the room. Old Mrs Cater's one, who died last week. Wouldn't she of been surprised to that think now the rich took her place of residence.

In the living room the trunks took up nearly all the remaining available space. The rickety old table had to be shifted to make room. Lily stood in the doorway in near shock.

Hazel glanced at her now and again. This was going to be very hard on her. The tiny flat barely had enough room to swing a cat. It was old and run down. Yet it was dry and had all the necessities. This flat was not the worst of the worst, but Hazel realised Lily did not know any worse. Hazel had the advantage of being exposed to the poor in the little Canadian village during her growing years. The farmhouse where she grew up had been quite large and comfortable, but not anywhere near the luxury that Lily had known all her living years.

Hazel was sure the hovels three streets down

would have ruined Lily. The shock would have been too great. Those houses were damp and rotten. Mildew crept in a mosaic up every wall. The rooms were cold, so cold and would never seem to warm. Their kitchens did not really exist, bar a simple fire grate. The single outhouse was shared by the whole building, not just your level. Children were sick and it seemed like someone died every day.

Hazel bit her lip. She was glad the driver didn't take them to the very worse after all. If they ever had to go lower, she would make Lily return to her mother.

Hazel said to Lily, "It's all right, Lily. We will make it nice..." Lily looked at Hazel with vacant eyes. "Think of Harry. It's only for a short time. Maybe a month." She glanced at Kitty who was nearby, so she didn't say Mademoiselle would send them money soon. Instead, she added, "Three months at the most." Hazel was sure Kitty was listening.

Lily nodded. She would endure this for Harry. Never in her life had she been exposed to such low standards. If she had known of such depravity, she would have given more to the poor. She had always assumed they lived in decent little houses, like the cute cottages on Prince's Risborough Castle Estate, or thatched ones in the village.

Lily suddenly realised she had become one of them. One of the poor. She would be trapped in these tiny rooms with Harry. By herself. The floor was dull and surroundings grey. Every-thing looked used and very old. Not on her life would she place Harry down on anything. She hugged him too tight; he gave a squeak in protest.

Hazel saw Lily's look of horror as she looked around the rooms. She tried to distract Lily. "We will need to be rid of these trunks as soon as we can. Otherwise we'll not be able to move around the room. We can go through everything tonight and decide what to keep and what to sell. Anything you can spare will go a long way, Lily. Make sure Harry has enough clothes and nappies though. I think I will cut down to three plain dresses myself. I will be able to fit them in my carpet bag. One coat, of course. One pair of solid boots. My apron for work... "

Lily was looking overwhelmed. Hazel tried another tack. "Come and sit on this chair, I'll make you a cup of tea. Kitty, would you please go to the shops and fetch a few basics. Tea, small amount of sugar, milk, bread, mutton and the cheapest vegetables. That should keep us for a few days. Oh, and some porridge for the morning. I'll get the water boiling."

Lily sat and asked in a small voice, "What is porridge?"

Hazel was relieved to hear her talk. For a minute there, Hazel thought it was all over. She had really started to believe this plan would work. "It's a type of breakfast. Cheap and fills you up very well. It will take me through a day of work. Besides, in a few months when Harry eats, he will love it. It's smooth and with milk added it goes down a baby like a treat."

"That's good." Lily sat stiffly on a wobbly, wooden chair.

Hazel busied herself, sorting her trunk. By the time Kitty returned she had a huge pile of clothes to sell and Lily had made a start on hers.

Lily had reluctantly placed Harry on several clean blankets to sleep. Hope was the only thing that kept them going. They all had hope of some type.

Lily could barely stand the cheap tea and could only manage some of the juices from the simple stew Kitty made. Her tastes were not able to cope with the unusual flavour. She was used to fine dining at the best tables. Not boiled meat. However, it would have to do. They only had a little money left and one more week's rent. First light, Kitty and Hazel would be out to find jobs.

Ω

Celia didn't tell Beatrice about the letter from Kitty. Celia thought she might stop her from putting the money in the bank. She knew what Beatrice was like, all their childhood there had never been a way to bribe Beatrice. If Beatrice thought it was right to tattle on her siblings, she would, and if not she wouldn't say a thing. No amount of promises, offerings, or words would change Beatrice's mind. Celia thought it was too likely that Beatrice at the threat of being bullied by Kitty would not pay the bribes, but Celia would. Anything to find the girls safely.

Celia was a bundle of nerves. So much so, Beatrice snapped at her to sit still.

Beatrice said, "You're putting me on edge, Celia. You can't change the fact that Everett rode to Prince's Risborough, returned today without Hazel and ran off in his ship... It's about time he was distracted with something else besides tracking down poor Hazel. He has developed an unhealthy attachment." Beatrice paused to think. "Hazel must have sent him away from the Castle, that is all I can think. Maybe he will come back and agree to our idea. We must carry on like he has. He could be away for a year, or perhaps never come back."

Celia hastily agreed. "Yes, yes." James was a concern for Celia, but not the most pressing. He must have gone to the castle and found Hazel missing. Never had he expected anything else. James knew Hazel by far better than she did.

They should not have left behind Hazel; or Lily for that matter. Hazel was running from him for her own reasons. Now Celia pondered on it, Hazel seemed petrified of James. Yet it was a mystery to Celia. Why would Hazel run from him? A father owned his daughter. Hazel had a responsibility to be obedient to him. Celia wondered what could have gone so terribly wrong between the two of them.

All summer, Celia had done so much of the talking, she didn't remember listening to Hazel tell much about her experiences with James. Apart from their first meeting, Hazel did not once speak of James. Not to her, at least. Certain matters were too difficult to discuss. Celia was disturbed to think what might have been said if she had asked Hazel.

Lily though, she was another matter. Why would she run? To be with her long-lost sister? No, she was not the wild type. Lily would not run, knowing the upset it would cause. Celia had raised her too well. She would not do such a wicked thing to her family... Unless she had a very good reason. Maybe she felt she had to protect Hazel somehow. Celia didn't think Lily would be able to help Hazel much. If anything Hazel would know better how to protect Lily because of her worldly experiences. In comparison, Lily was a good girl. She would have left a note explaining her part. Keith would find it.

Beatrice continued to speak, "No doubt Everett found out about Lily when he was confronting Hazel. It's a relief, really. I can't imagine having to deal with him when he found out about her." Celia's twitching distracted her. "You're still fidgeting Celia. I am sure he will come to speak to us on his return." She paused but Celia said nothing; that was unlike her. She must be really upset by Everett's latest tantrum

Beatrice continued "So many issues will be settled by the time he bothers to come back. You'll see. The girls will do nicely this season, don't you think?"

This pulled Celia out of her repose as Beatrice thought it would. Any mention of balls and the social season and Celia would respond.

Celia said, "I am sure they would."

Beatrice corrected her. "They will, you'll see. Did you arrange the tickets?"

"Tickets?"

"For Canada."

"I completely forgot."

Beatrice frowned. She couldn't distract Celia properly. "That is unlike you. The ship Lydia will be leaving by the middle of next week. They will be needing confirmation." Again Celia didn't pick up the bait.

In an attempt to get more response, Beatrice tried another tack. "I was thinking the best way to tell society about Hazel would be by newspaper. As soon as the paper gets wind of the story about the twins, they will write it up anyway. We may as well make sure they get it right. Then we can leave for Canada when the birds start chirping their gossip. As usual talk will be rife all over London this season. I can organise the newspaper article tomorrow."

Celia was not really listening any more. She hummed a reply and said, 'I am going to bed."

"But it's so early."

"I am tired..." She gave a lame excuse. "I will need my strength."

Beatrice was a little concerned. "All right, then. I won't be long myself." She didn't think to ask what Celia would need strength for.

Ω

Peter had been worried for Charlie since the beginning of winter and it seemed he had good reason. At the end of spring, Peter had bought him home to Leah. Charlie had literally dropped at her feet, falling into terrible illness from the combination of starvation, chest infection and neglect. Charlie had been staying in the ramshackle cottage for months, through the wet spring.

Leah had thought Charlie had simply gone on his way, but Peter had been right, his friend was in trouble. Leah decided her husband was obviously quite a discerning man.

Peter would sit with Charlie through the worst nights. His fevers reached extreme highs. He coughed by far too much. Peter prayed late into the night.

In the deep, dark hours, Peter would listen to Charlie talk. Sometimes he would cry out. Other times he would say 'Lily'. Most surprising was when he spoke of Hazel. To Peter's knowledge, Miss Hazel and Charlie had not met on these lands. Miss Hazel had only arrived this spring.

Eventually it became clear Charlie had known Miss Hazel for many years. Once or twice in his worst moments, Charlie would yell about Miss Hazel killing a man, stealing or falling. He seemed to think she fell and hit her head. Always there was a desperation about Charlie's cries. He expressed a longing to save her from her troubles.

From the burbled talk, Peter concluded somehow Charlie knew Miss Hazel was coming to Prince's Risborough Castle and had come to meet her here. While he had been waiting for her, he had met Miss Lily and fallen in love with her. The few times Charlie called for Miss Lily, he was at his most peaceful. Yet he was sad, so sad. Peter could not connect anything else together.

After a month, Charlie was barely any better. He was not neglected any more, but wasn't gaining weight very well. Every day he struggled out of bed, coughing worse than ever. Leah worried when he was up. Yet, she didn't say anything for fear he would never rise again

The village doctor had been and gone several times, but he was no help. His tonics did no good. The wheezing had settled into Charlie's chest.

In desperation, Peter had even fetched the witch from Loosley Row in Lacey Green. She came in and Leah had eyed her speculatively. So it was true what they said, the witch was beautiful and wild. Her clothes were those of a gypsy, long, layered and flowing. She wore a loose shirt, but it did nothing to hide her young, supple body beneath. Her uncontrolled autumn, copper hair grew long. Her locks were soft and luscious.

No wonder she was said to be a witch who captivated every man who passed her. Some went a bit far claiming she burnt their souls.

Lucky for this woman the execution of witches was long gone. Otherwise it would be for sure many women would have hunted her down and burnt her on the stake. Good looks were enough to stir some village women into a frenzy.

After staring for some time Leah remembered her manners. "Come, sit down. Charlie is sitting in the sun out the back, by the garden, he will come in soon. I... I like to leave him to himself for as long as I can when he is out there. He seems to be soaking in the sunshine the good Lord gave us, so it must be for the best."

The witch stepped widely as she walked to the chair. Her walk was unusual. Leah decided she did appear mystical.

To Leah's great surprise the witch agreed,

"The Son of God will heal."

Leah hesitated, realising the very clever way she had constructed the sentence referring to the sun and the son of God. Did she believe in God? This woman was a mystery.

People said she had several children and no husband, so there must be something substantiated about the gossip. She must be loose, rather than God-fearing. However, Leah knew how gossip burned like fire through dry grass. Talk started small, but became an enormous blaze. The rumours could mean nothing.

The strange woman continued, "I am Clarissa, from Loosley Row. I am pleased to be called by Peter, in Charlie's time of need."

Leah glanced at Peter. He didn't look captivated by Clarissa. Not that Leah had for one minute thought he would be unfaithful. They had a happy marriage and their first child was on the way despite their advanced years.

Leah was already over thirty. She had been delighted to fall in love with Peter despite her age. They had difficulty seeing each other over the last few years because they lived a distance apart. Peter had been a gardener with Sir Winston's household and Leah a kitchen hand with Mistress Beatrice's household. Their courtship had been long, but every time the households had met, they fell more in love. Short letters had been laboured over and sent to each other. Their attachment grew. Finally Peter had taken the position as gardener when Mistress Beatrice had offered it to him, after the death of one of her elderly gardeners.

Leah grinned at Peter as he doffed his cap and went on his way back to the castle gardens. She asked Clarissa, "Would you like a cup of tea?"

Clarissa smiled in appreciation and she

looked all the more stunning. Like a woodland fairy. She replied, "Yes, I would. I see you have a little one on the way."

Leah laid a hand across her belly. "It will only be another three months, or so."

They chatted amicably about the coming baby obviously protruding from Leah's belly. Leah came to think Clarissa would be good to have with her when her time came. She seemed to be so knowledgeable about babies and birth.

By the time Charlie came in, Leah had nearly forgotten Clarissa's reason for calling. Though, as soon as she laid eyes on Charlie her concern returned.

He kept his eyes on the ground. His beard was trimmed by Leah, but his hair still hung long and limp. The clothes he had borrowed from Peter hung off his frame. He had barely eaten a thing since Peter had brought him to their home. Walking toward his bedroom, he glanced at the two women sitting at the table. His eyes twitched and flickered.

Not a word was said as he left the room. Clarissa gave Leah a potent look. Her work was a medicine woman. She tended to the body, soul and mind. One glance told her Charlie ailed from his heart and he suffered from self-torture. The most difficult illness was one deep in the spirit. Only God could heal spiritual wounds.

However, Clarissa knew it was good to start with a person's body. Progress could be made if the body became well. She followed Charlie to his sick bed. He lay on the blankets, staring at the wall. Without saying a word she felt his forehead. Low grade temperature. She laid a hand on his chest and then on his back near his breathing sacks. They rattled with each breath. The wheeze was easy to hear. When he coughed, he curled inward and cringed at the pain.

Clarissa concluded his throat was swollen and raw to the worst degree. The infection had travelled into his chest and would be hard to shake. He had wasted away and had little strength left. Even as she sat looking at him, he began drifting off to sleep.

Ω

Back at the dining table, Leah waited patiently for Clarissa to talk. She seemed to be thinking through the best path of treatment. Out of her leather bag she had pulled several tiny pouches and an earthen corked bottle. The pouches each had a small painting of plants and flowers. Some had dots and others lines. Leah concluded Clarissa knew what each bag was and how it was prepared by the markings.

Clarissa took out two bags. She put in several teaspoons of dried willow bark into both, with a little Thyme and a few other herbs. They would be good for the pain, cough and to clear his breathing. Into the darker bag she also added Chamomile and a little Clary Sage for relaxing and sleeping. Alternatively, into the lighter bag she added Wood Betony to stimulate his blood and mind.

She stated, "He needs willow bark tea for the pain and to help him sleep. In the evening he can have this mixture for his cup of tea." She handed Leah the dark bag. "It will help him sleep well and cough less. However, this light bag is for tea in the morning. It will help him feel sprightly and cough more..."

Leah gave her a surprised look. The cough needed to reduce not increase.

Seeing the look on Leah's face Clarissa explained further. "This tea will give him a more satisfying cough. The gunk in his lungs will come out. Then there's the silver water. You've heard of rubbing silver on your hand if you get sick?"

Leah replied frankly, "Yes. I never thought anything was in it."

"Well there is, but the technique I am going to tell you is by far stronger than just rubbing on the skin. You have to have pure silver banged through a bowl of water. Tepid water will do. I use a hammer and hit the silver rod under the water for a long while. As long as I can stand. I like to leave the silver soaking for the night. Then the next day I take it out and the silver water is ready."

Leah hesitated.

Clarissa pushed her point. "The water will taste slightly of metal. The silver will be in the water. If you drink it, it makes you well so much quicker and it wards off sickness." She could see she was not convincing Leah, so she added, "It dulls the pain of sores in the mouth and if you place it on a cut it reduces the sting. Try it next time you have need. It's very effective. He will only need a few teaspoons a day."

Leah replied, "I have heard silver is effective, but I've never tried it. It's scarce around here... I will do as you say."

"Good. It will be worth your time. Be warned though, the silver won't last in the water if it's exposed to the sun. It needs to be kept in this sealed bottle in the dark of the kitchen and it will keep for many years. You may come to use it often for your own family. It's good for children."

"I will have to keep that in mind." Leah was intrigued, yet speculative. She would try it for herself the moment the opportunity arose.

Clarissa concluded, "I will be off now. I have been here long enough. I will see you tomorrow."

Ω

Leah did all Clarissa said and after only three days she noticed a turn in Charlie's health. He slept less in the day and the heavy raspy breath disappeared. Yet the sadness still followed him.

On Clarissa's third visit, Leah spoke to her their concerns, "Charlie is so sad, Clarissa. There seems to be no pulling him out of it. He barely talks. I had thought if he started to get better, the sadness would go."

Sipping her tea, Clarissa said, "Getting well is a good start, but these sorts of things take time. I think he has a broken heart and it takes a long time to heal. Sometimes it never will."

"Yes, I have seen that before. My father died when I was much younger. My mother's heart was broken and she never mended. Five years later, she died." Leah stared off into the past.

Clarissa nodded, "That often happens... Sometimes quicker, but Charlie is young enough to cope a little better. He may pull through."

Leah felt so sorry for him. "Is there anything that can be done?"

"I know of a few herbs that dull the brain. Sometimes they seem to help some. The time passes in a different way after you drink that kind of tea, but it can be difficult to recover once you stop drinking it."

Leah sighed, "That would be no good then."

"I would only use those herbs in dire circumstances and Charlie is grieving, but thanks to you and Peter he seems to be coping. He needs more time, Leah." She patted Leah's hand.

They both sipped their Chamomile tea, contemplating Charlie's future.

Ω

Peter had watched Charlie carefully as he improved from one day to the next. He was pleased the day Charlie picked up a fork and started to help weed the little vegetable garden out the back of their cottage.

From then on Charlie tended to the cottage garden with diligence. Peter took care of the castle gardens and was pleased to not have to care for his own. Especially if it meant Charlie was improving in health and doing something useful. The cottage garden was cared for the best it ever had been. There was never a weed in sight and each plant grew nicely. Charlie's work almost put Peter's gardening to shame.

Peter and Leah were always very careful never to mention either of the girls in front of Charlie. Considering his possible connections to them, they thought he may not handle news of them well. The day the twins left for London, Peter told Leah quietly in their bed that they had gone.

All of the servants had been very worried for Miss Lily. Her behaviour lately had been strange. The last winter she had barely left her room. She had never shut herself away before. Then they noticed in spring she did not walk through the gardens, or even ride her favourite horse Dapple. In summer she only rode occasionally. Never in all the years she had been in the Castle had she behaved this way. Rumours said she had food poisoning, but no one dared mentioned it to the Cook.

Of course Peter was new to the Castle so he heard all of these things from Leah and the other servants. No other servant was aware of the connections between Charlie and Miss Lily, except for Leah. He told her everything he knew and she did not tell a soul, for Charlie's sake.

They concluded Charlie and Miss Lily must have fallen in love and for some reason they had ended it. Most likely, Miss Lily had separated herself from Charlie due to his low social standing. She had stopped coming for walks and things to avoid Charlie. Ending an inappropriate relationship was a difficult situation to face. Leah did worry about Miss Lily, but Miss Lily had plenty of other servants to care for her. She had her hands full with Charlie.

Leah thought it must have been true love for the two of them to be so sickly. Peter agreed, but thought it best they separated. Classes did not mix. Matters would be too complicated.

After Miss Hazel's arrival, Miss Lily seemed to get better. Leah thought the distraction was just what Miss Lily needed in her time of heartbreak.

Ω

Peter had bumped into a stranger the day the girls had left. The man had asked after their whereabouts. Peter had not thought it unusual to be asked, but the man was dressed in fine clothes almost unsuitable for riding. However, it wasn't until the next day when Peter bumped into Keith, the stable master, that he became concerned for Miss Lily and Miss Hazel.

Peter knew Keith had gone to London with Mrs. Clance and Mistress Beatrice only a few days before. Yet here he was riding into the stables at full tilt. No one else was nearby to see him, except for Peter. At first he thought Keith bought terrible news, but he came straight from the stables and passing Peter he puffed a little to catch his breath. He had ridden the horse very hard. Yet he told Peter no ill news.

Instead, Keith stopped and asked, "Have you

seen Miss Lily and Miss Hazel, Peter?"

Peter replied, "No they have gone to London, Hadley House."

Keith had forced a smile and pushed out a laugh. "Pay me no mind. I had a slip of the mind. Of course they have gone to London."

Peter stared at Keith as he walked quickly to the kitchen. He did not even go to greet his beloved wife and children first, as he usually did on returning from travels.

Peter's suspicions were doubled when at first light he went into the stables, to fetch a hoe, to find Keith's horse, saddle and reins gone. There was definitely something wrong. Miss Lily and Miss Hazel were missing. Peter was sure. Keith had rushed in, asked strange questions and had left before first light. There was nothing wrong with Keith's family. For some reason Keith was not telling the household his real reason for returning.

This issue preyed on Peter's mind and he couldn't help but think Charlie was somehow a part of the puzzle. Miss Lily and Charlie fall in love, they separate, then Miss Lily is running away with her sister. Peter had another disturbing thought. The girls could be kidnapped.

He felt he must tell Charlie, but he didn't know how to explain. Instead he told Leah. She thought it best to let sleeping dogs lie, so another few days went by and Peter never said a word.

Charlie's words kept returning to him. The words he said in his dreams. Miss Hazel had done some terrible things if what Charlie said was true. What if Miss Hazel had done something to Miss Lily?`

He couldn't keep quiet any longer.

Peter approached Charlie in the garden late in the afternoon. "Charlie, there is something important I need to say to you about Miss Lily..."

Charlie interrupted, "Don't speak of her to me."

Peter backed away at first. After a decent pause he blurted, "She is in trouble."

Charlie quickly looked up from the garden.

Peter did not want to say too much for fear of upsetting Charlie. "They went to London, but seem to have not turned up at Hadley House."

Charlie supposed by saying 'they' Peter meant Hazel and a maid. He did not know of the twins. Lily and Hazel were the same person to him. 'Lily' was Hazel's fake name.

Charlie looked at Peter for a long while then turned and continued in the garden. He needed time to think. Hazel was on the run again. His thoughts twisted and turned. He could not shake the thought she could actually be in trouble. No way he could rest unless he found out.

19.

Keith had expected the twins to be at the castle, but they weren't. He had asked the gardener and looked for confirmation. The moment he stepped foot into the kitchen, the Cook was talking about how she missed everyone and how dull the last few days had been. Matching a few conversations together, Keith worked out the twins left for London two days ago. They were supposed to be going to the Hadley's town house, with Kitty the maid, but they hadn't. Keith now knew why Mrs. Clance was so concerned.

The stable master crept quietly around the empty house looking for a note. When he looked by Miss Lily's bedside, he found an envelope. Very slowly he sounded out each letter. The first word was definitely "Mother". He assumed the rest referred to Mistress Beatrice. Sweat beaded across his forehead. Nervousness bothered him too much to read the rest. Someone could catch him. From a young age he had been working in the stables. With horses there had been no need for reading.

Before first light, he started back. He was deeply troubled. Even more so when he arrived at the Hadley town house at midmorning to find Mrs. Clance in the library attempting to entertain herself with a complicated looking book. For one thing, she was never up before eleven and another, she didn't like reading anything important. The whole household knew her every whim.

Celia's clear blue eyes did not waver as Keith told her the news and handed over the note. She had known in her heart it would be true. The girls had run with Kitty. Slipping the note in her pocket, she excused Keith with thanks.

Keith would not be dismissed so easily. "I know they have run away, Madame."

Celia considered his boldness. "I will call on you if I need to, Keith. I may be able to get them back in a few days according to my informant. Please it is best if you can keep it to yourself... Don't tell anyone."

Keith was relieved. "I will leave this in your hands then, but do send for me if you need me." He left rather morose; he supposed the girls had been kidnapped. After all, what would two young ladies be able to run to, or do with no money?

Celia read the note as soon as he was gone. Lily and Hazel gave their many apologies, but mentioned nothing about their plans, or their reasons for running.

After quiet contemplation, Celia rang for the maid. She sent for her coat and to order Keith to drive the carriage to the front. Before Beatrice returned from the study, Celia planned to be gone. She was not going to speak with her. Not yet. The second letter from Kitty waited at the bank.

The carriage was shortly bought around the front and for the first time any servant could remember, Celia stood outside waiting for it. They all assumed she must be attending to something important. No maid had heard any whispers and Keith wasn't saying a word.

Ω

On arriving to the bank, Celia went to find out how much money her estranged husband, Otto Clance, had put for her in her account. She was relieved to find just over $5000 crowns were ready and waiting. This would be her allowance for the year.

Never in all her life had she actually been to the bank. Someone had always cared for her. Controlled her spending in one form, or another. However, Otto had left her in all ways except public declaration. Being responsible for herself pleased her, in a funny sort of way. After she had found the girls, she would contact her lawyer about investments and sorting out a monthly allowance.

Celia instructed a cashier, who ran to her every bidding. She withdrew 500 crowns and had them banked into Katherine Mary Caper's account.

Asking to meet with the bank manager, she found he was already with someone. The cashier had nearly tripped over himself to reassure her that the manager would not be long. She sat and waited on a plush leather seat designated for the wealthy customers. Observing the busy bank was rather fascinating. For the first time in her life she could see why some people enjoyed working.

The bank manager strode towards Celia. He ushered her into his office with many apologies for keeping her waiting. It had been 'unavoidable'.

Celia said, "No need to apologise, Mr. Clen. I enjoyed watching your staff. They are very efficient."

Mr. Clen stated, "I would have met you at your house. All you need to do is send a message."

Celia soothed, "I have never had to speak to a bank manager before, or been to a bank for that matter. It's of no regard anyhow. I am here on urgent business."

Mr Clen blustered, "Yes, yes... I have been expecting... a Hadley... well you're a Clance now, but you will be here to pick up the letter from that little madame!"

"Yes. Yes I am here for it. I have already banked the money through..."

Mr. Clen interrupted, "You banked 500 crowns into her account?"

Celia agreed, "Yes. As per my instructions. Here is the docket. Now I would like the letter, please."

He looked her in the eye. He said in a stern voice, "This is a very expensive letter, Madam. Are you sure it's right to buy it in this manner?"

Celia replied sweetly, "Yes. It's as expected." She held out her hand and he passed her the letter. As she turned to go, she saw him shaking his head.

He didn't understand how important this letter was. Even though she was itching to open it, she placed it in her pocket and went to her carriage waiting outside. Once inside, she flicked it open. Again, Kitty had used the beautiful cream paper. Each letter was scribed perfectly. Celia wondered if someone else had written it for Kitty. Someone else could be involved. Alarmed at this thought, she quickly read the short note.

Dear Mistress Beatrice Hadley,
Your nieces are staying at Thomas Inn, on the docks.
Yours Faithfully
Kitty

The letter was dated for two days beforehand. By now the twins may have left the Inn! She rapped on the roof of the carriage.

The driver stopped and opened the door to talk with Celia. She said, "Quickly, take me to Thomas Inn at the docks. As fast as you can."

The driver hopped up on to his seat and

raced the horses to the docks. They puffed and steamed as he pulled up before the Inn.

Celia did not wait for the door to be opened. She jumped down before the driver and ran inside. Pausing in the doorway, a few heads turned to look at the lady rushing in haste. This was bound to be interesting.

A man behind the counter said, "Can I help you?" He expected her to ask directions to a better establishment.

Surprisingly, she asked, "Have you had twin ladies staying here? With brown hair?"

Thomas considered his options. Captain Everett wanted to know about these girls. He was desperate for the one with green eyes. The barman assumed she must be his lover, or the some such. The reward from Captain Everett was too great to tell just anyone. He trusted Captain Everett, but this lady he did not know. Besides, he owed Everett a favour, or two. Playing it smart, he said, "No, sorry." He stared at her hard and stony

Celia blinked a few tears back. She turned and left.

In the back corner an old hag followed her out. As Celia was stepping up into her carriage, the hag croaked, "I can tell ye."

Celia turned. A few tears had fallen. Looking at the woman, she felt sick. One of the hag's eyes slightly protruded from the socket. Her hair was limp, grey and tangled. She had disgusting brown rags for clothes. Yet, Celia did not have the luxury of being picky. "How will I know you are telling the truth?"

"I know the colour of their eyes, the girls and they had a maid and babe."

Celia's heart began to fly. She would be able to find them. *Oh, thank God.* Celia breathed, "What do you know?"

The hag turned her head and stared at Celia with her good eye. She didn't say a word.

After a moment, Celia understood. She fished a crown from her purse.

The hag's good eye widened to see such money. Whipping it away, she buried it beneath her clothes. "One twin had blue eyes, the other green, green as the sea. They stayed here one night. Not last night, but the night before," she cackled.

Desperately Celia asked, "Do you know where they have gone?"

"No, but Thomas does. He won't tell ye, so don't bother tryn' to even bribe him. You will not offer enough 'cause his loyalties lay elsewhere." She laughed cruel and long as she walked back for her next drink. The toff had coughed up nice and easy.

Celia felt deflated. Her girls, her precious girls. Many tears fell. She should have gone straight to the bank yesterday afternoon. Maybe she would have made it to the docks in time to find them.

Celia had the carriage take her back home. Beatrice would be furious when she found out.

Ω

To Hazel's great relief, Lily liked the porridge. Kitty had made the best she could, to entice Lily's tastes. If Lily's breast milk dried up, she would return to her mother for the sake of the Harry's well-being. He would need a wet nurse.

However, Lily liked the porridge. A cup full was boiled in milk and sweetened with sugar. A teaspoon of salt would have been even better if they could afford any. But there was no need, Lily ate two full bowls. Hazel hoped Lily would become used to the cheap food over the coming weeks.

Hazel went job hunting for the first half of the day. However, she came home disappointed. "People laugh at me, Lily. I wore my plainest dress and they still think I am posh. I wish I had kept my maid's outfit now. I threw it away weeks ago. I only kept my apron because it's useful for cooking."

Lily asked out of interest, "Why would you have wanted to cook?"

Hazel replied, "I like to cook... I was reluctant to throw it away in case I felt like making a cake at Mademoiselle's. She would have growled at me for debasing myself, but I would like to cook as Mamai did now and again."

Lily suggested, "Buy a maid's dress at the pawn shop."

Hazel brightened. "Maybe not at the pawn shop, but it's a good idea." Lily did not know about opportunity shops. Hazel continued, "I will go to the seconds shop and buy some cheap clothes, after I have sold our things to the pawn broker this afternoon." This made Hazel feel better.

Kitty returned shortly with good news. She had a job at the grocer's a few streets over. She added, "I'll be able to get fruit and veggies real cheap."

Kitty planned to keep the job for the next few weeks, till the money from the Hadley's came through. Instead of working, she would prepare for the coming social season. She would need several ball gowns, shoes, hats, coats and very many things. The anticipation made her jittery. Of course, she would still keep up the pretence of working and give Hazel her 'wage' on a weekly basis from the bank account. All of Kitty's dreams were beginning to come true. It was now only a matter of time.

Kitty found another cart and horse on the streets. This time they only went on a ten minute's drive to a pawn shop in a better district. Hazel thought they would get a better price than in the desperate pawn shops near their flat.

Hazel spoke to the pawn broker, "Could you come out and have a look at the cart full. We wish to sell the lot."

The broker glanced in her direction, finished serving two customers and slowly made his way outdoors. He squinted in the sun light. The night was his lair. Like a spider from a web, he crawled out of his shop. He pawed his way through the clothes, paying particular interest to the green emerald dress. After banging the sides of the trunks to determine if they were solid, he licked his lips and squinted in the sun.

He grunted, "I'll give you half a crown for the lot."

Hazel huffed in disgust. "Not on your life. I know value, so save your breath." She wasn't even going to barter; it was a waste of her time. Hoisting herself up next to the driver, she made to leave.

Stepping in front of the horse the broker stopped the cart. "I'll give you one and a half guinea and no more."

Hazel made to think. The driver laughed to see such bartering. He said, 'Come on, you know that's a good offer."

Hazel stated, "One and eighteen."

"One and fourteen."

"One and sixteen."

"One and fifteen and that's it, Miss." The broker turned to walk away.

Hazel hopped down and said, "I'll take it, but you move the trunks in yourself."

"You have yourself a deal, Miss."

Hazel knew it was only a fraction of the

worth of such lovely clothes and trunks, but it was the best she'd get and it would make up one ticket to France.

Ω

After a few more days Celia told Beatrice, "I have some bad news."

Beatrice replied instantly, "It's the girls, isn't it? They should have been here yesterday."

"Yes, the letter we sent for them has been returned. So I sent Keith." Celia carefully neglected to say she had sent Keith a week ago. "I didn't want to alarm you before I had him check at the castle, but he has returned and said they left the castle a day after us." Celia glumly said, "I do not know what to make of it."

Beatrice sat up in alarm. "Have they run away?" Celia did not look well. She may have another turn.

Celia's voice shook, "It seems they have run away."

Beatrice's word tumbled out, "Where have they gone? Why would they run from us? We are not like Everett. Have we done something?"

Celia had considered the same thoughts all week. She replied, "I fear we have done nothing. That is what we did wrong. We did not listen to Hazel. She didn't really tell us what happened with James. I do not really remember once hearing her talk about him."

Beatrice contemplated Celia's insights. She thought Celia was handling everything very well. "Hazel said a tiny bit to me about him... Now you mention it, she was very disturbed by him... She seemed to think he would not agree to our idea, no matter what favour he owed me. Oh, we should have paid attention."

"They left this note." Celia passed the twin's

note to Beatrice.

As Beatrice read it, Celia insisted, "We must find them, Beatrice!"

Beatrice was at a loss. "Where would we start to look?"

"I am not sure. We must pray for guidance. There is nothing we can do. Now James has gone, we cannot even get his help. Though, he has been doing nothing but looking for Hazel. He seemed to have given up. Sailing off into the sunset, leaving us to search ourselves. They would have been gone before he had time to get to the castle."

"He most likely missed them by a few hours. He must have been so angry. No wonder he sailed away."

Beatrice added, "We need to find the girls quietly. We cannot have scandal after scandal follow them for the rest of their lives. Society is unforgiving when it comes to large scandals. The girls would never recover."

Celia agreed, 'You're right, but the middle class are reasonably easy to pay for their silence. We will cancel all our plans. They weren't public anyway. We hadn't even sent invites to their presentation ball." Celia had thought all of this through days ago. She continued, "The article was put in the newspaper last week, so we will have to continue telling our first story. We have been reunited with Hazel through James and Henry." Celia shut her eyes in relief and mentioned, "Thank goodness we never said they would be presented this year. I will write to Violet and have her kept at her ladies training. She was always so flighty, she could do with another year. Of course I expect she will be upset... We will have to defer visitors until we can sort out what to say. I do not want all the gossip coming this way."

"Yes, we will cancel our plans and lie low for a while. I will tell the butler, no visitors. People will probably assume we are sick." Beatrice thought a bit more. "I will get in touch with a few of my middle class contacts who served with Joseph all those years ago. They would keep a secret for his memory. He was good to his men and they will remember my kindness to them, especially at Christmas. They will search for us."

Celia was pleased. "That is the best idea I have heard. You are so clever, Beatrice." She should have told Beatrice earlier. The search could have started days ago. She wasn't very good at this sort of thing.

"When we do accept visitors we could allude to the girls going abroad. That will avoid difficult questions."

Celia agreed, "What a good plan. There is no shame in travelling. We can even tell the servants they are except the butler will be told we are expecting a messenger from the girls post haste. Then he will let the riff-raff in to speak with us. Of course Keith has been sworn to secrecy and will be paid out." There would be no use in telling Beatrice about Kitty's letters. Nothing could be done about them to find the girls faster and Celia nicely sidestepped conflict.

Ω

Charlie thanked Peter and Leah from the bottom of his heart. He promised to repay them someday soon. He still had some of his own money left and would use it to make a speedy journey to London.

Leah worried over him before he left. She gave him a bottle of silver water and various herbs. She repetitively told him the instructions. He was not completely better, but close to it.

Peter and Leah watched Charlie confidently walk toward the village to catch the coach. Though he still barely spoke to them, he now held his head high. His eyes sparkled. They hoped for his sake he would have a good and happy life somehow. Even if it wasn't with Lily. They prayed Lily and Hazel would be safe and well.

Barely past mid-day, Charlie's carriage rolled onto the London streets. He was amazed how quick and easy the journey was compared to when he had travelled from London to the castle, hitching a ride where ever he could.

Without hesitation, he went straight to the markets and bought some fresh, new clothes. Leah had cut his hair short and he had shaved properly. Once again he looked an entirely different man. A little thin maybe, but his physique was strong and firm. He was not the gangly youth he had been. Rather he had grown taller and wide set in the shoulders. His pale, clear face was offset by his black, brown hair. However, his stormy eyes stood out the most. Long, black eyelashes encircled dark blue eyes. He was noticed by all who saw him as a stunning male of a rare degree.

At Hadley House, he knocked on the door. The butler opened the door and enquired into his call. Charlie said, "I have a business with Mistress Beatrice. I must speak with her."

The butler cleared his throat and stared at the young man. "You can tell me with what it regards and I will pass it on." He was undecided if this young man should be knocking at the front, or the back door. He wore passable clothes. His accent was foreign, but pleasant. The butler had no real way to tell.

Charlie insisted, "No, I must speak with the Mistress."

The butler started to shut the door.

Charlie called in frustration. "I know of Lily. Let me speak to the Mistress."

The butler whipped open the door. "Come in, come in. Why didn't you say so." He led Charlie to the study. The butler was sure the parlour was too good for the likes of him.

Beatrice and Mrs. Clance came rushing into the study. Mistress Beatrice asked, "What do you know of Lily... of Hazel?"

Charlie was taken back. Somehow they knew 'Lily' was a false name. He wouldn't need to explain that to them then. He stated, "I have known Hazel all my life. We grew up in the same village in Canada. When Captain Everett took her aboard, I also started sailing with them. I know her... very well, but I have not seen her for a long time."

Celia was disappointed. So much so, she ran back out the door in tears. She thought the girls had been found by one of Mistress Beatrice's middle class contacts.

Concerned, Charlie said, "I am sorry I do not come with better news. I heard Hazel was with you, but had gone missing."

"Who did you hear that from?" Mistress Beatrice thought the news must have travelled far after all. So much for it remaining quiet.

Charlie revealed, "I am friends with a few of your... men. They knew of my connections with her, so saw it fit to tell me. I have told no one."

"Oh." Mistress Beatrice considered that fair. Charlie may have known where they were. The news was not to travel further. "We do not want their reputation marred in any way."

Charlie reassured, "No of course not. I will be very discreet."

"So you plan to search for them?" Mistress Beatrice was interested to know why.

"Yes." He didn't offer any more information.

Mistress Beatrice stared at him for some time. He may know something about Hazel. More than they did. He could potentially be a help. She decided to share all she knew. "The only lead we have is they stayed at Thomas Inn a week ago. I had a man tell me yesterday. I have a few other ears to the ground, but it has come to nothing as yet."

Charlie was encouraged. "The docks! Did you ask if they sailed with Captain James Everett? He was the one we came with."

Mistress Beatrice stood and paced to the other side of the room. She would have to be careful not to reveal their true connections. Charlie may not know Everett was Lily and Hazel's father and she was not going to tell. "No, I have already enquired. He left the day they came to London and they were definitely not with him. I have reliable witnesses who has already told me this much."

"Good. That saves me from having to ask around..." Charlie thought carefully. "If she was at the docks, I would presume she was catching a ship back to Canada. Probably under a false name, so it would be hard to detect."

"I didn't think of that. Hazel missed her family very much. She spoke of them lovingly. Yes, it seems logical she would return to Canada. Yet we were already planning to board for Canada on the ship two days ago. She knew we were all going to visit her Canadian family. But maybe she didn't want us to come. I haven't checked if any ships left the dock for Canada at that time."

"Well, that is where I will start. I will go to Canada myself, if necessary."

Mistress Beatrice took this possibility up. "I will fund you."

Instantly, Charlie refused. "No, I have plenty of money and besides I will probably become a sailor on a ship bound for Canada. That way I will get there for free."

"I insist. Here are twenty guinea. It would be faster it you cruised as a passenger. You may need to pay extra for a ticket at such short notice. You could bribe your way on board if you have to. A person usually needs to book weeks in advance. You will need extra money."

Mistress Beatrice saw him hesitate. She pleaded, "Please... Please."

Charlie took the bag of money, not wanting to see her beg. "My money is tied up in shares right now and would be difficult to access. I do need some ready funds, especially if I need to leave on the next passenger boat." He still had his pride. "I will borrow it and use it as a passenger. I will pay you back on my return."

Mistress Beatrice was a little confused. "How come you would be a sailor if you have means?" His accent was Canadian and so he was of indecipherable class to her ear.

Charlie said simply, "I was poor, then came into a substantial amount of money... reward money, for saving a life." He further explained, "I cannot purchase a farm right now, so I thought it best to leave the fortune in investments. My lawyer takes care of it."

Mistress Beatrice was satisfied with this answer. He had been poor, but now had stepped up to the high middle class. No doubt he deserved a chance in life.

As he was about to leave, she added, "Please tell them their Aunt and Mother love them very much and no matter that they have run away, we will welcome them home." Her eyes misted over.

Charlie's mind raced. Mistress Beatrice must

be Hazel's aunt, because now he thought of it, Hazel did look a lot like Mrs. Clance. She must be her birth mother and Everett her father. He questioned, "Is she with her brother, or sister?"

"Yes, her sister and a maid. They all ran together."

Charlie promised to write regular updates. He excused himself in haste. He had a lot to do and night was already falling.

Ω

Down at Thomas Inn, Charlie could find out no more. They were tight lipped. He was suspicious, but could not get anyone in the bar to talk. Information about Hazel and her sister must be valuable to someone. No matter how much he offered, no one would spill. Obviously they considered him a stranger, with a strange accent. Not one person did he recognise from his sailing days. A few sitting out on the streets said the sisters stayed at the Inn with a maid and a baby, but no one would say exactly where they went.

Charlie thought they may not know. Many persons of quality would stay at the docks for one night. Would the patrons pay much attention to two sisters? Especially considering they had kept to themselves in their room with the maid and child.

Mistress Beatrice had never mentioned a child. Hazel's sister must be married and travelling with her nanny and baby. Perhaps she was trying to escape her husband.

He should have asked Mistress Beatrice the sister's name. Not that it mattered, it was Hazel he searched for and it was likely they took false names. At last a drunk told him they had taken a cart, with their heavy trunks, in the direction of the Canadian port of call.

Charlie headed down toward the docks. Straight away he was told a Canadian boat did leave on the same day as the sisters. There were a great variety of passengers. Many women and children, so three woman and child could have easily slipped through the cracks under a false name. Hazel could be returning to Canada as she had always wanted. Charlie wished he was with her. Married to her and sailing her home to buy a property, but that was never to happen. She didn't want him.

Yet, he had to make sure she was safe. See her one last time. Then he promised himself he would move on for good. Not that he could imagine what he would do without her, but he would leave her be.

With a few extra coins slipped in the right direction, he purchased his ticket to sail to Canada in style. The ship was leaving on the morrow's tide and Mistress Beatrice was right, it would be much quicker. Within three weeks a ship could get to Canada. Alternatively, it could take him a month, or more to get a job aboard a cargo boat. Likely a cargo boat would stop multiple times along the way to drop off and pick up.

20.

Hazel held up a serviceable dress. "Look, Lily. I found the perfect dress and apron at the seconds store and it only cost me a few pennies. I am bound to find a job, now I look the part."

Lily raised one eyebrow. The dress was ugly and rough. However, it was what Hazel must do. She did not seem to be bothered by it. The working class dress reminded Lily of how different their lives had been. Hazel was a farmer's daughter, whereas she was bred a lady. Still, Lily was grateful for Hazel's resourcefulness. Never in a million years would Lily have been able to manage on her own.

Lily said, "It looks the part, all right."

Hazel laughed, "Yes, it's far from what you are used to, but I do not mind."

Harry had started to smile and for the first time he laughed along with Hazel. The twins looked at him in wonder and began to laugh to see such joy from a baby.

Lily sighed, "Well at least he doesn't noticed the direness of our situation."

"Babies settle after a few days and then they do not care as long as they are fed and dry. They're a world unto themselves."

Hazel had noticed the floor was swept and was well-pleased with Lily's effort. She was trying and that must be a good sign. They would only be staying a few months if she could find a job.

Yet, Hazel spent the whole week looking. She wore her serviceable dress, but it did not seem to help. The shop owners could tell by her voice she wouldn't fit. At home, she began to practice speaking working class English. Kitty helped her every night. Working class spoke quiet different from the Irish Hazel knew. In London, shop owners did not like to employ the Irish or people from the top shelf.

Ω

On Friday night Kitty bought home her wage that barely covered the rent. She pretended she didn't mind giving it all up. The grocer had given her the old produce as well. Carefully, she cut every bruise out and used the leftovers for the night's stew.

Kitty quietly worked in the kitchen area. She wanted to maintain the pretence as a maid even though she worked through the day. Besides, Miss Lily would not be able to do anything in the kitchen.

Kitty screwed her nose up as she looked around the tiny flat. Miss Lily had decorated it with silly lace curtains and a white sheet for a table cloth. She had dressed the bed up with other sheets and the new blankets. A tiny miniature of Mrs. Clance sat next to the bed. Kitty thought it frivolous They could have sold the sheets and had more money. Her Mother had sold all their sheets off and made a shilling. Kitty thought Miss Hazel indulged Miss Lily. She was spoilt enough as it was without adding to it.

Hazel could see they'd do all right if she could find a job. The following week, Hazel began her search again, but to no avail. Finally, on the third week, she ventured a little nearer the docks. She went into a bar. Not that she wished to be a waiter, but her choices were becoming less.

Hazel said, "Do ya have a job goin'."

The barmaid looked at her with a single glance. "No."

"All right then. Do ya know of a job?"

The barmaid looked at her again. She went to speak, then hesitated. Efficiently she served another customer and another. Then she nodded at the seats and said, "Take a seat. I'll be with you when I can." The barmaid thought this was a face she knew. Those green eyes. Her rich brown hair. The girl was just as James described. Wouldn't he be pleased to hear she had found the girl. She would send a boy for Captain Everett as soon as the rush was over.

Hazel waited patiently for the whole hour. She could very well get a job. The maid whipped outside and came back in shortly after, whipping her hands on a towel. She gave a wonky smile and said, "I'm Moira."

"Good to meet ya. I'm Hannah... Brown. I'd take any descent work." She pleaded with her eyes.

"Right. I may have something fa ya... Hannah."

"Oh, do ya." Hazel lent forward

"Only waitin' the tables."

"Anything."

"You'd get 6 pennies a week and a meal every day."

"Good. That'll ba fine. Thank ya."

"Will ya start now?"

"I can."

"You've got an apron. Good. I'll be behind the bar. Ya take orders from the tables and bring them to me."

"OK." Hazel eyed the other waitresses already working.

Moira saw Hannah walking away to start work, so she yelled, "Lucy, come over here." More quietly she continued, "Ya can have the day off ya wanted." She gave Lucy evil eyes as though to say 'don't say nothing'. Moria inclined her head to Hazel.

Lucy opened her mouth. Then shut it. Something funny was going on here. Minding her tongue, she replied, "Thank-ya, Mistress."

Moria and Lucy walked out the door together as Hazel started to take orders. Moria said, "That's the girl..."

Lucy squinted, "The girl?"

"James Everett's lost one. I bet on it. Look, come in tonight..." Lucy hesitated. Moria hurried on, slightly annoyed, "I'll pay you in full, still."

Lucy smiled and said, "Thank-ya, Madame."

"Well you've been a good worker and deserve a bit extra. Not a word to anyone though. About the extra, or ya won't get it."

"Not a word." Lucy left before Moria changed her mind.

For the next hour, Moria watched Hannah like a hawk. She was a good worker, that was something, considering she was James' rich daughter. Her movements were refined and her voice was not quite right. Captain Everett was rich, everyone knew. despite his rough talk. His daughter must have been bought up on some distant land. She was clearly a cut above. For some reason she was trying to talk like dock women, but not quite managing.

Moria wondered why she would want a job here. James would give his flesh and blood all the money in the world. Hannah would be a lady in his household. Yet she ran from him and the money. Moria was gagging to know, but the reward for finding Hannah prevented her from asking.

The boy came running in right up to the counter and said as clear as day, "He wasn't there, Madame."

Moria shot a look at Hannah who stood nearby taking an order. She didn't seem to notice a thing. Moria snapped at the boy. "Didn't I tell ya, quiet like! Come over here!" They went to the far edge of the counter, so Hannah wouldn't hear.

"Sorry, Madame."

"Just shut it. Did you say 'he wasn't there'?"

"He's gone off on his ship. Strange like. Not much cargo. Just left with the bare bones of a crew. No one seems to know why."

Moira cursed. *'Damn James', if only he was here.* She would have the reward. Leaning closer, she breathed her stale breath into the boys face. "Listen, let the word out. Whoever brings him to me on his return will be given a sovereign."

The boy's eyes lit up. A sovereign was more money than he had ever seen.

"Here's an extra two penny for your trouble. Listen, only give your street master one, he'll never know about the others the dirty, cheating sod. Take the others home to ya mother, she could do with them. Tell her they're from me."

The boy nodded and ran out the door. Moira could hear him yelling to others before the doors even closed. She glanced at Hannah, who was talking to a customer. Moria was relieved she didn't notice the boy.

Watching her for a bit, Moira noticed the men seemed to like talking to her. They treated her with a little more respect than the other girls. She was beautiful with soft, clear skin and stunning eyes. Her hair shined and bounced. Having her working in the bar could turn out quite good. The punters would come in droves. Some would recognise her as Everett's, without a doubt. The word would be spread to keep their traps shut, if they knew what was good for them. Captain Everett would kill them if harm came to his girl.

Moira would have to watch the naughty ones though. Not a hand was to be laid on her, even in cheek. She could set a few guards, a few pounds wouldn't be much. The night would be no good, it was too dangerous. Moria would set Hannah's hours during the day. Without letting her disappear to find another job, it was the best she could do.

Ω

Kitty resisted going back to the bank for a few weeks. She was tempted, but preferred to draw the matter out as long as she could.

By the beginning of the third week she could bear it no longer. Before the day began she went to her boss. "Could I have an hour for lunch? I have to go to the bank."

"The bank?"

"Yes... I have some savings I need to get."

"I am surprised you use the bank but, look, you're a nice girl. You can do my banking... I send the other shop girl every day to bank the takings, but let me warn you if any goes missing, I will have the law down on you so fast you won't be able to breathe. Still you are a good girl and it's quiet on a Monday. All the wives are doing their washing, not buying their veggies."

Kitty quickly agreed.

By lunch time the grocer had a few sales. He tallied up the money and wrote it in the book. He signed it and Kitty signed next to it. Before she left, she prudently counted it for herself.

As she walked, she ate an overripe apple. If all went right, she wouldn't be eating this crap for much longer.

With mounting excitement she went into the bank. Carefully she banked the grocer's takings. Then asked for her own account balance. Her heart soared when she was told her balance was over 500 crowns. She was rich and she would get more. Her withdrawal was only a few crowns, but in pennies. They were for her wage share to give to Hazel. Never would she work again. A few pennies a week were only a small sacrifice to pay.

Before she left the bank, she had another letter placed inside the safe box. The bank manager grunted when he took the letter. He was being paid well to hold this letter, but he still didn't show appreciation. He raised his eyebrow at Kitty. Still it was not his business to interfere.

Kitty nearly skipped down the road. She stopped in the bakers and bought a pink bun for her lunch. Then, she leisurely walked back to the grocer's.

The grocer glanced up at her return. "You took your time. I thought you had done a runner."

"Here is your receipt from the bank. I will be going now. I don't need the job."

The grocer started to complain. Damn that girl. She had left him in the lurch. But he paid her only a little attention as she left the shop. She wasn't that important.

Ω

After her first day working, Hazel flew home at four o'clock. She wasn't even at the pub till the six o'clock rush was over. Moira said she would be needed only from ten till four, with fifteen minutes for lunch. They were easy hours.

Bursting through the door, she told Lily the good news. The girls danced around the room as best they could and woke Harry. He was cuddled and kissed, but he didn't care for the excitement and proceeded to cry until he was fed.

Lily begged Hazel to tell all. She said, "Do you think it's all right working in a pub. What about the drunks?"

"I am only there till four and there are hardly ever drunks before four. I'll be home before five."

Lily was grateful Hazel would be home at nights. She felt like she had been stuck in the flat by herself for three weeks solid. She didn't think it safe to go out in this area. Especially not with baby Harry. Besides, there was nothing to go out for. Kitty and Hazel took care of everything they needed.

Ω

Over the next few weeks, Hazel worked every day. Moira seemed pleased with her and gave her a penny extra nearly every Friday. They saved four pennies a week. Hazel worked out it would take them another three and a half months to save enough for their passage to France.

Time seemed to speed by. Hazel and Kitty worked hard. But Lily was a concern. She seemed to become quieter, more sullen. Hazel always made an effort to be bright and chirpy when she came home. Occasionally, she would buy a little something for Lily. A chocolate, a ribbon, or flower. Lily always smiled, but it wasn't enough. Her days were long and lonely. The only way she kept on, was the hope they would be in France soon.

After a few months, Harry started to get sick. His temperature soared, he cried on and on through the night. Everyone was exhausted by day break. The doctor had been and gone. Harry would not take the foul liquid he left. To add, he had cost them a whole half a crown. The doctor would take no less. The cost would set them back a month, but Harry was by far more important.

Yet, Harry had not improved. Hazel left for work with a heavy heart and very tired. Lily might not manage by herself. She promised to send for Hazel if Harry got worse. Missing a day's pay would be for the best. If he did not improve Hazel would have to get Aunt Beatrice and Mother to help.

Lily could only settle irate Harry by pacing the room with him in her arms. By mid-day she was worn out and crying too. Her little boy was so sick and she didn't know what to do. She needed Hazel, she knew better. Rushing to the door, she ripped it open to find two women standing outside. Affronted, she opened her mouth in surprise.

One woman said, "We all can hears him."

The other added, "All night..."

Lily was flustered. She said in posh English, "Oh, I am so sorry. Did he keep you awake?"

"No, not really. We sleep through our lot often enough. I only woke now and then concerned it was mine sick in the night. I can't afford a doctor. The worry gets to ya. I have five to care for and Elma has seven."

Lily frowned as Harry started to hiccup staring at the strangers. "You fit all those children in the flat?"

"It's not so bad as Tilly, who has eleven."

Lily said, "Oh..."

Elma asked, "We were wanting to know if ya wanted help. All morning we've been wanting to knock on ya door."

Lily didn't know what to say. She tried, "I... I don't really know... He has a temperature... He won't stop crying."

"Well, I'm Rita and this is Elma like I said." Harry started wailing. "Here, let me have the bairn."

Lily handed him over, thankful for the rest. For a moment, they stood there in the hall staring at each other. Lily didn't know what to do.

Elma finally said, "Well, a cuppa tea would go down a treat."

Lily went brilliant red, "Of course, do come in. I am Lily."

The women looked at each other in amusement She was definitely a toff then. They weren't going to wait to be asked again. In they trotted.

Within minutes, Harry had his clothes off except for his nappy and Rita carefully offered him water from a cup. He seemed to calm instantly.

Rita informed, "Ya need to take the clothes off if he's too hot. Don't listen to the old sayings. Ya won't be burning out the illness, only making it worse if you bundle him up with clothes."

Lily struggled to make the tea. She burnt herself twice, but was proud when she had finished. As the women chatted, Harry started to chew on the handle of the cup. He bit it so hard, Lily started in a fright.

She said, "He's going to eat it."

The two women laughed. Rita said, "He is only teething. He needs a good bite. It will only be a few days and the tooth will pop through. Is he feeding all right?"

"Yes. Maybe a little short, but often."

"That's a relief then, it's by far worse if they won't feed."

By the end of the visit, Harry was on the floor sitting on his blanket for the first time. Lily was not going to admit to the women he had never been put on the floor in this building. Though, she had insisted on a rug. They gave her queer looks. After all he only sat there, not moving, chewing on the cup. His inflamed cheeks changed to a normal pink.

Elma said, "Ya need a few hard toys for him to chew on. I have a little wooden horse I can lend ya. I'll boil it and bring it by in the morning."

Rita was keen to return too. "I'll boil the wooden block I have and bring it round." They would have much to gossip about after this fine visit. Won't the neighbours be jealous?

Lily asked, "Why would you boil them?"

Rita laughed, "To clean them a bit. Boiling is the best way before handing on children's things."

Lily smiled abashed.

Elma patted her hand. "Well, ya wouldn't know, him being ya first." She didn't mention everyone else in her neighbourhood did know, from their younger years with all their brothers and sisters.

"Do you think toys will help?"

"Oh, for sure." Both women said at the same time. They all laughed at the coincidence

That night Hazel came home to find Harry grizzling some, but generally happy playing on the floor. Lily chatted about her visitors. Hazel groaned to think she had not thought of teething. She had been so busy, she had not thought. Besides, Mamai's babies didn't teeth with a temperature. They had wasted so much money on the doctor.

Hazel was glad to find Lily seemed better, but concerned she had told Elma and Rita her real name. Yet, she didn't have the heart to scold Lily. Harry's illness had been a great ordeal for her.

Ω

Lily made firm friendships with Elma and

Rita. Lily had never laughed so hard in all her life. The women were great friends. They still wondered why she was here, for Lily wouldn't say, but they were enjoying becoming acquainted with a lady.

They suspected it was to do with Harry. Never had they seen, or heard of a husband. Perhaps, she had been disowned by her family. Her snobbery wasn't as bad as they thought it would be. After all, she was a good laugh and lightened their day with her childish struggles to keep house. They taught her how to clean and cook properly for the shame of a grown woman not knowing. Secretly they enjoyed every minute with her.

By the time Harry was over seven months, he had teethed several times. He fevered each time and cried for long hours. The only thing soothing him was a good chew on the cool cup, or saucer. Lily had to watch him like a hawk, for fear he would break it and hurt himself. Elma reassured her the cheap cups were so thick it was very hard to break them. Always after only a few days, he came right. Lily worried less and less.

Hazel had become apt at her work. She knew the regulars and often found herself dancing around the floor through the day when someone played the piano. The bar was always busy despite the day time hours. Hazel thought the bar must be popular among the locals and never considered she may be the reason.

Moira didn't let on either. Hazel had bought in much more business than usual and was paid no more than Lucy. After James had taken her, Moria thought she would get a toff who could dance. Well, someone pretty with a few steps at least. She would keep the punters happy and they would keep coming.

Ω

Kitty did not send another note for a long while. She needed time to think about her next move. Kitty turned over in her mind a way of bribing for more money. Making the right move, at the right time would get her more money without actually letting the Hadley's catch up with the girls.

Instead of working on her feet all day, Kitty spent her time at the dressmakers, choosing shoes, hats and underwear. Everything had to be right. She sent back each dress at least twice. Nothing was good enough until every stitch was perfect. Empire was still most fashionable, with delicate lace film covering each piece. She would look beautiful in pinks, whites and light blue. She was presenting herself to society as a virginal maiden. Offering herself up to the marriage market like a lamb to slaughter. Men loved that sort of story. Damsel in distress

Everyone would know Kitty was an orphan, lonely, weak, and available. Of course assumptions would be made. Her fine dresses would speak of money, but really there would be nothing in the coffers. She would aim for a man with means. The larger means the better.

Always she had dreamed of her coming moment. Enjoying the shopping, the money and decent food. She had all that she had been deprived of most of her life. A decent high-class life, with plenty of food. Not a care in the world.

Kitty's father had destroyed her life and her mother had killed all hope. Kitty had been a pauper in an expensive house for too many years. Followed by working as a lowly scrub hand and then maid in waiting to Lily.

Yet, she wasn't really loving the rich life. No one was good enough. The dresses were not up to standard. Some colours were sold out. People were difficult and snobby. Others shut their door in her face. She spent days traipsing the shops and ended up with extremely sore feet. The pre-season was already well under way and the twins had not left. If they didn't soon, she would have to wait for next year. Still she could hardly complain for she had plenty of money to spare

Lily had run Kitty a hot bath one night in sympathy. She had dragged it all the way up from the fourth floor. Some neighbour had arranged it for Lily, so Kitty could soak her aching feet. They all had a good bath and returned it the next day. Kitty had resented having to get into someone's rickety old bath, but she had for the sake of pretence. Admittedly it had helped.

Finally Kitty thought of an idea to squeeze extra money from the Hadley's. She risked them actually finding their flat, but with the extra cash she wouldn't complain. So, she sent another letter to Mistress Beatrice.

Ω

The butler bought in a letter at lunch. Celia spotted the familiar cream envelop and quickly said, "Here I'll open it. It will be another invitation."

Beatrice did not intervene. Naturally Celia opened most of the invitations. Beatrice enjoyed balls, but did not love them with a passion as Celia did. Celia opened the invitation and glanced at it, then laid it by her cup.

Quite a number of weeks had passed since the girls had gone missing. They both worried to their wits' end. Once they had received a short note from Lily reassuring them they were safe. Receiving a message helped, but it wasn't enough.

As soon as she could get away, Celia went to read the note properly in private. She grated her teeth when she saw the perfect handwriting. Kitty had complete control over her.

Dear Mistress Beatrice Hadley,
For $250 crowns another letter awaits you at the bank.

Yours Faithfully
Kitty

Celia screwed up the note and threw it across the room. After huffing in frustration, she threw it into the fire. But still she was at the bank paying within the hour.

Dear Mistress Beatrice Hadley,
At nights Hazel works at Moria's bar, three streets back from the docks.

Yours Faithfully
Kitty

Celia felt so relieved. Something solid had been revealed.

So the girls were in London. Celia went red with shame. Why wouldn't they come to them? Celia promised herself she would listen to Hazel. The worst thought was Hazel working in a bar for a living. She wondered where Lily worked. Why were they still in England? Credit had to be given to Hazel for her determination to escape Everett. They must be so scared. Hazel had been right, Everett was never going to agree. He was one of a kind.

Celia waited for dusk to fall before she left. She said to Beatrice, "I have a headache, I think I might go to bed."

Beatrice was rather glum herself. "Yes, I know how you feel. I have had some on and off recently. I worry so for the girls."

"Yes, well goodnight."

Instead of going up the stairs, Celia slipped quietly out the door. The carriage she had arranged earlier was ready parked on the road. She stepped in and Keith got the horses moving toward the docks. Celia had to question Hazel's wisdom in working so close to Everett's lair. His influence was strong, especially at the docks. However, Hazel may not know about the picture and description circulated. Ironically, Everett had been gone all the time the girls had been in London.

Celia sat on the edge of the carriage seat. The anticipation made her hands shake. Finally, they pulled up outside an average English pub. Men hung out the doors. Beer was gulped and spilt. Loud laughter and hooting rang out into the night. Celia covered her mouth in disgust. Keith jumped down and spoke to Celia. "I don't think you should go in. It's not suitable for a woman. Let me go, Mrs. Clance."

Celia nodded. "Make sure you make her come." Keith turned, but Celia called him back. "It's for her own safety, Keith. Try to be nice about it, but do what you have to do."

"Right, Madame."

Celia hoped Hazel would come quietly.

After a few minutes, Keith returned, alone. He looked at Celia with sad eyes and shook his head. "The owner claims she has no Hazel working for her, but she looked out of sorts."

"A woman runs this horrid place! Bribe her."

"I tried. She walked away before I could offer a second bribe. I persisted but she wouldn't listen. The patrons did not dare to interfere and when I quietly spoke to a few, they did not know of a Hazel or where she lives. Madam, when they are tight lipped for no amount of money, then there is no budging them."

Her heart sank. The low class were a breed unto themselves. She knew there was no shifting them. Celia said, 'Take me home."

21.

Charlie's sail was smooth and pleasant. As he stepped onto Canadian soil he felt like he was home. He listened happily to the familiar sounds of people talking in French and Canadian-English. As he travel to his village, he found it even smelled like home. He looked around at the autumn trees with great maple leaves that were slowly turning brown. Then the green rolling hills with the wonderful variety of animals in the paddocks. Even the sun seemed to smile down on it all in a different way. Yes, to Charlie Canada really was the most beautiful place in the world.

Travelling by wagon, it took him a few days to get to Sussex. He was very keen on his return to see how it was and what things had changed since he left. First and most importantly, he hoped to find Hazel at the Donaldson's farm. Secondly, he wanted to see his family, especially little Annie. He had not felt so alive for such a long time. Surely, the cart could move faster.

As he came over the final rise, he caught his breath smiling for joy. There it was. His home! Nestled amongst hills, Sussex looked like it had a few new buildings. Beyond the village farmland spread far and wide.

Over to the left sat the formidable mansion of Mademoiselle Bella Fleur. Her husband had hoped many more mansions would follow. The area was one of the most beautiful he had ever seen, but alas there never had been any other mansions built.

The French revolution had put a halt on the French economy, with heads being cut off and all. Many French colonies had been affected. Charlie had not considered it before, but he wondered now if Mademoiselle had hidden in the mansion all these years to escape all the terrible deaths in France. She had lost nearly all of her wealth, he knew that much.

He had the driver take him straight to the Donaldson's' farm. Before they entered the gate, he asked the driver to stop. Looking over the tall grass he could see the smoke curling out of the chimney of the Donaldson's house. Their barn was still as it always was. A quaint new, little cottage had been built to one side. Charlie contemplated if he should watch them for a bit, or have the driver take him straight to the house before deciding he had left the life of spying behind in England. Anyway, night was not far off.

Charlie spoke to the driver, "Drive me up to the main house."

Until this moment Charlie had not considered what he would say to Hazel, or her family. Nervousness twisted through his belly. He would not think too closely on it. The words would come, as they had the day he met Hazel in the nut grove at Princes Risborough Castle.

Several dogs started to bark their announcement and the front door opened. Out came Sean senior. Charlie felt like running in the other direction, but he couldn't and he wouldn't. He was not a coward.

Charlie climbed down from the cart and went to shake Sean's hand. He realised this was the first time in all the years he had lived at the village that he had close contact with the Donaldsons. A little boy stood behind Sean holding his leg, peaking out to look at Charlie.

Sean politely said, "Have you come for the beef?"

"No, I came for a few more complicated reasons. My name is Charlie and I need to talk with you... about Hazel."

Sean hesitated a moment, "Hazel, Come in, come in." He led Charlie into the warm kitchen. He said as he walked, "Don't I know you from the village?"

Charlie replied "I lived in the village all my growing years. I have been away for some time, but it's a complicated story."

"Has it to do with our Hazel?" The whole kitchen was full of people. When they heard Sean ask about Hazel, they all stopped their chores. The kettle began to whistle, but no one moved.

"Yes it's..." Charlie could not hold back any more "Is she here?"

Sean's eyes flickered as pain moved across his face. Around the room there were a few sad faces. Charlie expected the worst, so Hazel must be dead.

Before Charlie could speak, Sean stated, "No. We have not seen her in years. We have only received a few letters... It's difficult for her... to write in her current circumstances. Besides Captain Everett has us watched. Her letters could be intercepted."

Charlie was greatly relieved she wasn't dead, but disappointed she wasn't there with the Donaldsons. He was feeling slightly awkward remembering how he used to spy on them with his Dad, but he wasn't going to admit that at the moment. He asked, "Has she written to you recently?"

Sean answered, "Not for weeks. We received a letter from her birth mother too. We are so relieved she has found somewhere to live that's away from that nasty Captain Everett. She seemed much happier."

Sally added, "But she suggested she would not be able to stay with Mrs Clance for much longer. She did not say why. It seems there are plenty of things she cannot say, for various reasons."

Sean said, "Before we go on we need to know how you are connected to her?"

Charlie leaned forward, placed his hands on knees and thought for a moment. Where would he start? "I was always drawn to Hazel when she lived here and I saw her leaving with Captain Everett that day. They drove through the village and stopped while Captain Everett went in for supplies. She was crying. The baker's wife asked what was wrong. I heard her say she had to go with Captain Everett. By the time Captain Everett had returned to the cart I had my few belongings and I hired an old nag with my last few coins. There is only one port nearby so I started to follow and eventually met up with Captain Everett at the port. He employed me as a deckhand."

They all listened to him intently.

Ben finally took the noisy kettle off the stove. No one else moved.

Charlie admitted, "I loved her from afar... for years when I lived in the village... I went to make sure she would be all right." Charlie put his hands together in a knot. "I had never even spoken to her in our younger years. I just kept an eye on her while we sailed. As time went on and Captain Everett became... worse, I grew really worried about her... Has she told you much about her escape?"

Sean said, "Not much. We know she can be resourceful and wild in her ways. I am sure she would go to great lengths to get away from Captain Everett. She has always hated him."

"She did go to lengths, that's for sure.

Somehow she stole some money from Captain Everett and I watched her... leave his London town house, dressed in finery. She ran to a ball and somehow met up with a friend of Celia Clance's, Henry Fletcher."

Charlie looked at the Donaldsons to see if they knew of him. "He sent her to Mrs Clance's sister, Beatrice Hadley, in Princes Risborough."

Ben butted in, "Did you follow her all that way?"

"No, I asked a few questions. I was very worried for her and kept a close eye on her, but lost her after the ball. Henry Fletcher's coachman told me he had dropped her at Princes Risborough Castle. I had to go to make sure she was safe. I did not know Beatrice Hadley was her aunt until later. She was even using a false name." Charlie went back to his story. "I introduced myself to her at the Castle. I had to... to see if anything could come of us. We spent the next few months getting to know each other. Then..." This was more than Charlie had expected to say. A tear slid down his cheek. "She simple stopped meeting with me... I am not sure why... "

Sean intervened, "Did she love you?"

"It seemed so, we walked, talked endlessly and she taught me how to ride. She showed me around the whole estate. We spoke of dreams... I am not sure what went wrong." The words came out from his hidden heart. "She cut me off. I didn't believe it at first... Then she left, with her sister and disappeared."

Sally enquired, "With her sister?"

"And a maid."

Sean stated "A maid... and her sister?"

"She has a few siblings from what I understand. I did not talk to many people about her, or the Clance's history. Hazel and I kept our meetings to ourselves... We didn't want interference."

Ben agreed, "I did that too, with Bessy,... We kept it to ourselves for a bit." Bessy smiled at Ben across the room. "We're married now, you may not have heard."

"No I hadn't. Hazel did not like pondering on her past much. I think it pained her too much to talk of you all."

Some nodded in agreement.

Sean grunted. Sally covered her mouth. They all missed her something terrible.

Charlie continued, "We expected them to be here. We found out they had stayed at an Inn on the London docks... as though to go aboard. Naturally Mistress Beatrice and I assumed she had returned to Canada. Perhaps with the others. I have been sent to find them."

Ben added, "We wish she had come here, but she can't."

Sally reprimanded Ben, "Shh, Ben. We are not to say... Wait for Dadai to speak."

Sean said, "No, it's fine, Sally. Charlie loves her and should know." He turned to Charlie. "She will never return here because Captain Everett has promised to destroy us if she does."

Charlie was shocked. Captain Everett could be moody and demanding at times, but he was usually fair. Though he may be overly obsessed with his daughter. No wonder she ran from him. She would hate him for holding her back from her family. He put his forehead to his hands and lend on his knee. This truly upset him.

Sean continued, "But, Charlie, we do have some good news."

Charlie looked up.

"She has somewhere to go that you do not know of, but we know because we helped organise another home for her. It's my opinion you need to find her to speak some sense in to her. She most likely did not want to get you tangled up in her mess. She must love you to spend all that time with you. I have never known Hazel to be close with any man, except for Ben and they were only brother and sister. She will be in France by now, Charlie."

Charlie was surprised, "In France?"

"Yes, with Mademoiselle Bella Fleur. Do you remember her?"

"From the mansion."

"She has shifted back to France, Trouville-sur-Mer and set up a ladies school. Hazel is to join her, live with her and help her train the ladies."

Charlie put his head back to his hands. He said in a muffled voice, "I am so relieved. She will be safe."

The Donaldsons watched as he struggled to control his feelings. Clearly, Charlie loved Hazel very much.

Charlie added, "I will return to England and go to Trouville to speak with her."

Ben stepped forward, "I will go with you."

The family gasped. Sean eyed his son. Ben did most of the farm work now, but Sean knew he would manage. He wasn't dead yet. "Ben, it would be good if you go."

Bessy said in a small voice, "I will go with you."

Ben turned to her. "I could not ask that of you, Bessy."

"I have always wanted to travel."

"We will talk about it back in our cottage."

Sean took a look at Sally to see what she would say. Little Sean piped up, "I go France, too." Everyone laughed. A little fun broke the tension. Sally turned back to the cooking and Bessy continued to set the table. Carrie made some tea and they all sat for a drink as they reminisced over story's from the village during the earlier years.

The most animated stories were of Hazel and her childhood. Charlie loved hearing about those stories. He had only watched her from great distances. He had not been able to get close to her until meeting her in England. The Donaldsons described Hazel's strength of character. Charlie knew of her stealth, but didn't mention anything along those lines. She was durable and quite tough despite her stunning delicate looks.

Charlie stayed with the Donaldson's for the duration of his visit. He was like family to them. Soon he would be gone they were sure. For Charlie it was like an answer to one of his dreams. He had always longed to be a part of the Donaldson family and now it seemed like finally he was. He wanted it to be like this forever. Charlie did not know, only Hazel would be able to say if she would have him. Time would tell.

He could not leave the village without catching up with other friends and family. His Father had disappeared. Charlie thought it was for the best. He had never been a kind man and he had treated his children badly. Still, Charlie enjoyed meeting with his sisters and brothers. Most of whom now were married. Some were happy, others were not. He was sad that he could not see Annie, she had moved far away. His sisters all told of Annie's love and marriage, and they had all promised to write and give her a message from Charlie.

Ω

At the end of autumn, Charlie left Sussex

with Ben and Bessy. They hoped to sail before the weather set in for the worst. It felt good to have travelling companions. Charlie was confident they would find Hazel at the other end of their journey. He felt good. He hoped Hazel was safe and she would see sense, that finally all would turn out right for him.

Ben and Bessy enjoyed every moment of their journey. Neither of them had travelled far before. Though Ben had often wished to go to Hazel, he always felt he couldn't while she was with Captain Everett. Then since she had escaped Captain Everett's clutches, she had been on the run and untraceable.

Now things had changed. She was in Trouville and he would see she was happy and comfortable. Otherwise he would not leave. He would buy a farm in France if necessary. His Father had already quietly agreed to fund him if it came to that. Hazel's welfare was on the forefront of their minds. Ben was young and had a whole lifetime ahead of him. Baby Sean would soon grow and take over the family farm in Canada so he felt no concerns there.

Bessy would support him he was sure, but he had not mentioned his plans to anyone else in the family. They would only worry and there was no need for that. Hazel may find happiness with Charlie, or working for Mademoiselle Fleur.

Ω

They had been sailing aboard Luxnon for a week when the pirates came. In his earlier travels Charlie had heard of pirates and their occasional plunder and destruction of other cargo ships. He had even seen a few at some of the ports Captain Everett had stopped at, but never had he seen any in action. Even more unusual was why they even bothered to overtake a ship with passengers. Usually they preferred to loot cargo ships, they would not get much on board a boat like this.

The large, quick pirate ship easily held Luxnon at cannon point. Being a passenger ship it was in no way geared for war, or protection against a proper fighting ship. To carry such weaponry on a passenger ship was just not profitable. The chances of being attacked were so low and weapons and ammunition take up space.

At first Charlie assumed there was some person aboard of importance. They rooted out every passenger and made them stand on deck. They were well armed with swords and muskets. Charlie wished he had his pistols, but they were packed away in his luggage. Another thought occurred to him. He hoped they would not find them for he would hate to lose them. They were a gift from Captain Everett and he had never seen a better pair.

Thinking further, he realised he had his bag of guineas hidden in his coat pocket. He depended on that money. He still had a substantial amount left.

Charlie carefully manoeuvred himself back behind the crowd as they jostled. Slipping his hand into his coat, he pulled out the bag of coins. Without moving his head much he scanned the area for a potential hiding place. He spotted a knot fallen out of one plank running across the deck. Holes would most likely be plugged at their next anchorage. By lucky chance it was open now. Gradually side stepping other passengers he positioned himself above it.

Looking from side to side he saw a pirate walking his way, talking to the crowd. He was just able to catch the words. They became clearer as the pirate moved closer.

The pirate yelled, "We are her' fa more sailors... We have had deaths. We'll take ya crew, unless there are others who can sail. Don't bother if ya have no skills. We will kill ya if you fail us... Be warned, if ya do not step forward, ya will be left with no crew to sail ya family home. We need eight sailors n'all so oo'll it be."

Charlie did not see anyone nearby step forward. He knew he would have to go with the pirates otherwise the ship would be left with just the passengers and himself. He was no good at sailing really, but he knew the basics. The pirate moved further down the crowd, repeating his message. Quietly, Charlie removed two guineas and slipped them in his mouth. He secured one in each cheek. At short notice, it was the best hiding place he could think of.

Scanning the crowd, he spotted Ben only a few people over. He hissed to get Ben's attention. A few others turned to look at Charlie, but not Ben. He pointed to Ben and indicated he needed to talk with him. One brave lad pulled on Ben's sleeve and pointed to Charlie.

Ben looked at Charlie and shook his head. He did not want to lose Charlie to pirates. No pirate was looking so Charlie nodded, to indicate he had to go with the pirates. He must go, for the sake of the passengers. They were already pulling out the crew ready to take them. Charlie would have stayed on the Luxnon if he had enough experience to Captain a ship, but he was far from that experienced, especially when it came to navigating.

Ben watched as Charlie lifted up the bag of money. Charlie pointed down at the hole. Ben scanned the area for any pirate who may be watching. None were too near. So he moved a few steps back to see Charlie drop the bag down the hole. Ben nodded to Charlie as he rose, to indicate he had seen the hiding place. Ben would fetch it later and hold it for Charlie should he make it to Trouville.

With that sorted, Charlie moved forward loudly stating, "I can sail." The two coins in his mouth made his voice sound hollow and lispy, but at least he could still be understood.

The pirate walked up to him and stood much too close. He breathed on Charlie's face. His breath could have killed a baby, but Charlie did not flinch The pirate growled, "So ya say ya can sail?"

"Yes."

"Doin' whot?"

Charlie lisped, "Started as a deckhand, then helped with rigging and other general tasks. I only crewed for a few years, but I'm all right. I know my place."

"Well, ya betta, or I'll enjoy killin' ya myself. Git on board wit ya then."

Charlie eyeballed the pirate right back. No good would come if they saw him weaken. He turned to leave the ship. He had nothing, but the clothes on his back and the two coins in his mouth. He would escape the pirates as soon as he could, but in the mean time he would play it smart.

In the end there was the Captain, four passengers and three crew who went with the pirates. The passenger ship was left short, but they would manage till they made it to Ireland and picked up a few more crew to help for the rest of the trip.

Ω

It was now the middle of winter, Hazel was

cleaning a table near the door during the quiet hour of her shift, when a boy came rushing in. Moria had popped out the back to fetch supplies.

The boy looked around for her. He said to Hazel, "Where's the bar, Mistress?"

Hazel eyed him. Was he going to cause trouble? The younger they were, the more trouble they seemed to cause. "Who's asking?"

"Me, Miss. I'm the one who's ganna get the sovereign."

Hazel was about the ask why, when three older boys ran in. The younger boy said, "I was here first!"

"No ya wasn't."

"The Miss saw me. I was too."

Hazel interrupted before they started brawling. "Tell me this minute, why are you fighting?"

An older boy sighed, "We wants the sovereign, Miss."

Hazel replied, "Well, he was here first. That is a lot of money. What is it you are telling?"

"That the Captain is here, Miss."

Hazel frowned. The Captain? "What Captain?", but the truth dawned on her before they replied.

"Captain Everett, Miss. He's in the harbour. Sailin' in."

She started to move in haste. Then she looked around her and noticed a few men watching her. Was she being watched? This whole time and she had never twigged Anger rose within her. How had they known? Not that she had time to think on it. She would have to give them all the slip somehow.

She went to clean another table, to make it seem like she was still working. Moria came in and she tried her best not to pay attention to the excited squeaks as the boys told the Moria of

Captain Everett's return. The youngest boy got the sovereign. They shot out the door in a race. Hazel knew they were going to wait for Captain Everett to anchor. Ships took a while to come in, giving her some time. At least two hours. The rigging and positioning took awhile. Captain Everett would wait for the best spot.

Eventually, Hazel went up to Moira who couldn't stop smiling. Hazel smiled at her, to keep her fooled. Hazel asked, "Could I go to the outhouse?"

Moria was surprised, this was a first. Hazel was usually good at going in her break.

Hazel quickly added in a whisper, "It's my time of the month. I have to go!"

Moira understood that all right. "Of course, love. Take your time. I know how it can be difficult."

Hazel walked out the back door. As usual, no one followed her. She went straight to the outhouse and opened and shut the door without going in. They could hear the door shut from in the pub at quiet times. Being winter was a blessing, for all the back doors of the shops stayed closed. She ran down through the open back yards till she got to the fence about ten buildings down. Quickly she untied her apron as she ran. She stood on a barrel, looked up and down the alley. Infested by night, yet empty in the daytime.

Quiet as a mouse she jumped over, making only a pat on the cobble stones beneath. She moved like lightening through the back streets. If she saw anyone she would go slow, so as not to warn anyone. She didn't know how many knew about her connection with Captain Everett. It was possible they could all know.

Hazel thought she might be able to get back to the flats in a good ten minutes. She walked smartly through the streets. Looking around to see if she had been noticed, she saw Kitty sitting on a bench. She rushed over. "Kitty come quickly!"

Kitty jumped a mile high. 'I have been caught out' she thought.

Hazel urgently whispered, "He's found me..." Of course Kitty did not know much about Hazel past, so she added, "The man who has been chasing me! We must leave right now!"

Kitty was still slightly confused about what was happening, "We do not have enough money. I left work early today. I may not get as much pay." She lied.

"We are not going by boat, but we have to leave London." Hazel started to hurry off.

Kitty's mind flew. She needed to write a letter before they left. There was more money to collect. She would not have time to go to the bank if they were on the run. How could she stop them?

Kitty scrambled after Hazel. "Where are we to go? Lily can't just up and leave with the baby!"

"She will have to. There is too much at stake."

Kitty could think of nothing else to say to swing Hazel's mind so she followed Hazel. They ran up all six flights of steps. They burst into their flat. Lily jumped in fright. Rita spilt her tea.

Hazel said sharply, "Rita, I am sorry, you have to go. It's urgent."

Rita scurried out the door, dying of curiosity.

Lily went pale as Hazel desperately told her the news. "Your right" she said, "We must go now!"

Hazel snapped at Kitty, "Go and organise a cart. We will pay double price. Hurry."

Kitty lost for words, ran out the door. Then stopped short. Creeping back she thought she should listen for a minute in case they spoke of her. Hazel could have been getting rid of her.

Lily spoke to Hazel, "Shall we take Kitty?"

Hazel replied, "No. We don't have enough money."

"We don't have enough for the boat anyway. We are short."

"Kitty should stay in London. She would be better to get another position in a house. I will write her the best reference. No one will question it."

Lily agreed, "Yes, it's for the best. We will tell her when she returns. We will have to ignore her pleas. We can promise to pay her back."

Fear ran through Kitty. If she could not stop them from leaving her, she would not be able to deliver them back to Mistress Beatrice and Mrs Clance. She would not get her final pay outs. Social seasons cost a lot of money to fund.

Without any useful idea's springing to mind, she ran to get a cart. She must keep up the act for now until she could think of some way of getting them to keep her with them.

Hazel and Lily ran around packing their carpet bags. Try as they might they could not make everything fit. They would have to leave the things they did not need and just take the necessities. Lily squeezed in the miniature of her mother. She could not leave it behind. They packed up within fifteen minutes. Kitty had not yet returned.

Lily said, 'I will pop next door and give Rita our keys. She will return them to the landlady. She has our rent in lieu so that will cover this week. It's not worth the while going to her for the few pennies in balance. The week is nearly up. I will tell Rita to come and get all we leave behind. She can share the things we can't take with Elma. I know she has always loved the sheet on the table." She hurried out leaving Harry to play with the block on his rug in the living room, Hazel could watch him.

Hazel went into the bedroom to fold the sheets for Rita. She wanted to keep busy while waiting for Kitty.

By the time Kitty had a cart out the front waiting, she still had not thought of any excuse convincing enough for them to take her with them. By the time she was on the sixth floor, she had slowed to snail pace tired from all the running about. Quietly she entered the flat. Harry sat on the floor by himself. She could hear someone in the bedroom.

That is what she would do, she would take Harry. Use him to barter for more money from the Hadley's Not that he looked like Lily. But he had the family baby clothes on, they wouldn't be able to deny that. The shawl was the Hadley's too. She tiptoed over. Harry smiled at her. Gently she picked him up. But as she tiptoed out of the room, Harry for some unknown reason started to grizzle.

Kitty glared at him. She hugged him closer and clamped a hand over his little soft mouth. That shut him up till she was down several flights of stairs. When she let go, he screamed, but it didn't matter they were too far for the twins to hear. No one else paid her mind.

She was not sure where the Hadley's lived. They were in a town house some where. No one around here was likely to know so she didn't bother to ask. She would head to the Square and ask around there. The rich were frequently in the Square. Someone there would know,

Ω

Lily spoke to Rita, "We have to go right now. I can't say anything so don't ask."

"But... yar my friend... whats goin on... why..."

"Don't ask. We have to run... It would help if you said nothing to anyone who may come asking after us."

"I never will... "

Hazel popped her head through the door. "Do you have Harry, Lily?"

A wave of fear washed over Lily. "No, where is he?"

"I went into the bedroom for a minute, came out and he was gone. I have looked down the halls. He wouldn't have gone far by himself."

"Did Kitty come back?"

"Maybe she did. She may have taken him down to the cart. You look around. I will go check."

Hazel dropped the bags on Rita's floor and ran down the stairs. The landlady had her door open and yelled out as Hazel ran past. "Two men from Moria's bar were here lookin' fa ya. They were an unlikely pair so I sent them packin'... You bedda not git involved with the likes of them - they're a bad lot."

Hazel ran on with barely a pause. She hoped Moria's men wouldn't come back.

Spotting a cart and driver out front, she ran over to them. "Did a pretty girl, with brown hair fetch you? Her name is Kitty."

"Yup. She just went past with a crying baby. I was just about to leave, givin' up. A sight it was..."

"Sorry, I can't talk. Please wait. We will pay you well. I must find her. Which way did she go?"

The driver pointed down the street, "That way."

"Please wait here." She called to the driver again.

Hazel thought quickly. Kitty worked at the grocer in this direction a few streets over. She must have gone to say goodbye. Kitty did not understand the importance of leaving quickly.

Hazel ran as fast as she could. Puffing she hurried into the grocer. He raised his eyebrows.

Hazel asked, "Have you seen Kitty?"

"No not for months. She only worked here for a few weeks."

Before the grocer finished talking, Hazel ran back out. She came to a sudden stop. Realisation dawned. For weeks, Kitty had given them money. Today Hazel found her sitting in the street, doing nothing. She had claimed the grocer had given her the day off...

Hazel shut her eyes. Damn Kitty, damn her. She had cheated them. But how, and with who. Kitty didn't know about Captain Everett's connection to Hazel, so it must be with Mother and Aunt Beatrice. She was taking Harry to them.

A stitch formed under her ribs, but despite the crushing pain, she forced herself to run all the way back up to the flat to floor six. She burst through Rita's door.

Lily was there waiting, twisting her hands.

Hazel gasped a few times. Then trying to speak she almost yelled, "Listen. I know where they are. Tell me quickly, where is the Hadley town house?"

"In St James Street, number 12."

"You get all the bags to the cart. Get him to go on Piccadilly to the end of St James. I will meet you there as soon as I can."

Lily called after her as she ran, "Where are you going?"

Hazel yelled back, "To get Harry from Kitty."

Hearing Hazel's answer, Lily realised for some reason Hazel thought Kitty had double crossed them. No, surely not.

Lily grabbed the bags ready on Rita's floor. She said, "If Kitty returns, please get Harry off her and don't let go. Do anything necessary"

Rita was concerned, "All right, love." as Lily ran, she added, "Write."

As she ran out the door, Lily called, 'I will."

Ω

Hazel once out of the flats, thought she would collapse She saw a neighbour who was about to unsaddle his horse. She said, "Please, let me take the horse. It's an emergency. Here take three pennies for a ten minute ride."

That was more than he usually got. As she mounted, she said, "Pick the horse up in ten minutes from the corner of St James and Piccadilly. I will leave it with a boy."

Before the man could respond, she took off at a gallop. Two mean looking men ran at her as she galloped around the bend. Hazel recognised them from the bar, but they didn't look so docile now. One of them swore as she rode off down the road.

The horse ran faster than Kitty could walk. Hazel had taken a direct route, whereas Kitty had to ask directions. Soon Hazel stood several doors down from the Hadley town house waiting, watching.

She saw Kitty carrying Harry, who had stopped crying and held on for dear life. He was in a fright. Kitty whipped him through the crowd.

Hazel ran up to Kitty and grabbed Harry. Kitty screamed. Hazel slapped Kitty hard over the mouth. Kitty lifted her hand in shock as

Hazel twirled and ran away. Not one person intervened. Both women were just working class. No one wanted to interfere in their business.

Ω

Hazel ran to the corner St James and Picadilly, holding Harry close to protect him. She veered through the traffic and ran through the edge of the park to the other side where Lily and the cart driver sat waiting.

Lily cried and wouldn't stop. Hazel squeezed into the seat next to Lily and they all hugged. Both were greatly relieved about getting Harry back safe.

The driver shuffled over as far as he could. He felt sorry to see the sisters, so distraught. The young maid who had fetched him must have stolen the baby.

At a good pace, the horse trotted out of the town. The twins continued to cry and hug. Struggling they tried to remain quiet, so as not to draw attention, but it was hard. No one could see their faces, so it could be a good thing they hid in each other's arms.

When he was some way from London the driver turned to them. The girls had quietened to a snivel. He asked, "Where are we going?"

Hazel and Lily looked at him, like he had asked them a stupid question. He waited patiently, for he was a kind man. He slowed the horses and gave them time to think. He could tell they were running. One was dressed in a maids outfit, while the other in a fancy dress.

They sat there dumbfounded for at least a few minutes. Lily asked, "Do we have anywhere to go?"

The driver suggested, "Far away if it's that

bad. Like Scotland. I can't take you, but I could drop you at the pub ten miles out. You could organise a ride from there."

Hazel slowly said, "Yes... We have an uncle there. Do we not?"

"Yes... but he is... a recluse."

"All the better."

After another short silence neither could think of any better option so Lily agreed.

In silence they trundled along the road in a two penny cart.